CHRONICLES OF THE HOST

Unholy Empire

D. Brian Shafer

Destiny Image Fiction

An Imprint of

Destiny Image₀ Publishers, Inc.
P.O. Box 310
Shippensburg, PA 17257-0310

ISBN 0-7684-2160-8

For Worldwide Distribution
Printed in the U.S.A.

This book and all other Destiny Image, Revival Press, MercyPlace, Fresh
Bread, Destiny Image Fiction, and Treasure House books are available at
Christian bookstores and distributors worldwide.

For a U.S. bookstore nearest you, call **1-800-722-6774**.
For more information on foreign distributors, call **717-532-3040**.
Or reach us on the Internet:
www.destinyimage.com

Dedication

To my beautiful wife, Lori, and my daughters Kiersten and Breelin—for allowing me the time to write this book. It's good to be back. Yes! I am ready to play Monopoly—finally!

"Some Thoughts About the Second Book From the Author"

I hope that you will enjoy the second book in the series *Chronicles of the Host*. As you read it you will see that just as the action has shifted from Heaven to earth, so the storyline has shifted as well. In *Exile of Lucifer*, I was writing from a heavenly viewpoint; consequently it was all angels, all the time.

The challenge in this book has been having the angels interact with the Bible story without simply retelling the Bible. I hope that I have achieved this. Obviously I have had to follow the biblical narrative; just as obviously I could not recast every detail. But I chose those parts of the story that I felt best carried the conflict being waged ultimately between God and Satan.

I hope you will have a great time reading. I have been gratified by the responses from readers of the first book. I welcome your comments and suggestions. Thank you and God bless you as you enjoy *Chronicles of the Host: Unholy Empire*.

Contents

Unholy Empire Cast of Characters:

Holy Angels

Darus	a gatekeeper in Heaven
Archias	an angel in training to Serus
Quinron and Tassius	angels assigned to Noah
Darus	an angel assigned to assist Noah as he gathers the animals
Romus	aide to Michael in Egypt
Joel	an angel who is a student of Crispin
Alyon	an aide to Serus in Egypt
Kreelor	former Temple Steward in Heaven, now sent to incite rebellion
Jakkar	a holy angel who guards Abraham's camp

Wicked Angels

Lucifer's Council of War

Condar	assistant to Kara in Egypt
Kara	a former wisdom angel and one of the Twenty-four Elders; now aids Lucifer
Pellecus	a former wisdom angel; a former teacher at the Academy
Rugio	a former warrior angel and Captain of the Fiery Host; now Supreme Commander in Lucifer's army
Prian	a former warrior angel and Chief Angel of the Watch; now aiding Lucifer
Lenaeus	a former wisdom angel; now an Angel of Light
Rega	a former member of the Twenty-four Elders
Belron	a former member of the Twenty-four Elders
Nan	one of Rugio's lieutenants
Errus and Jimerel	demons in Noah's time
Glacus	warrior assistant to Prian who attacks Job
Milicom	demon prince over Sodom
Darian	a spirit sent to deceive and/or murder Hagar
Sobek	demon prince of the Nile
Sar	demon prince over Goshen
Kanul	aide to Sar

Humans

A'dam	the first man
Eve	his wife
Cain and Abel	their sons
Noah	commissioned by God to build the ark before He destroys the world
Shem, Ham, and Japheth	Noah's sons

Kerz	leads the human opposition to Noah
Cyron	a wicked shaman in Noah's time
Abram/Abraham	a man called from Ur to Canaan
Sarai/Sarah	Abraham's wife
Lot	Abraham's nephew
Bera	king of Sodom
Kazak	Bera's high priest in Sodom
Hagar	handmaiden to Sarah
Ishmael	son to Abraham by Hagar
Isaac	son to Abraham by Sarah
Melchizedek	priest of Salem
Rebekah	wife of Isaac
Jacob and Esau	sons of Isaac
Rachel	wife of Isaac
Moses	son of Jochebed and future leader of the Hebrews
Aaron	Moses' brother
Seti	Pharaoh at the time Moses was born
Anipur	Seti's advisor
Rameses	son of Seti and later pharaoh of Egypt
Kephti	High priest of Amen-Ra, Chief deity of Egypt
Maret-men	a diviner and sorcerer for Kephti
Jannes and Jambres	court sorcerers for Rameses
General On	commander of Rameses' chariots
Korah and Dathan	rebel instigators who oppose Moses
Joshua	Moses' aide and successor
Caleb	friend of Joshua
Shammua	one of the 12 spies sent into Canaan by Moses
Balak	king of Moab
Zora	advisor to Balak
Balaam	a seer hired by Balak to curse Israel

I will put enmity
between you and the woman,
and between your seed and her seed;
He shall bruise your head,
and you shall bruise His heel.
(Genesis 3:15, RSV)

CHAPTER 1

"Guilt and shame
are wonderful weapons."

"A little dramatic perhaps, but I think it states our position quite well."

Lucifer handed the scroll to an aide, who bowed slightly and moved away from the council. All eyes were upon the supreme angel in whom they had vested their future. Lucifer looked down the gallery of faces that shared his lot. They had chosen to follow him in order to remain free. Now they were compelled to follow him to remain alive.

"You look at me as if I have all the answers," said Lucifer dryly. "But I'm afraid I don't. I can only assure you that ours will be a long struggle and its outcome will be decided by and in the minds of men." He looked keenly at the faces. "However, where the minds of men are concerned we have a decided advantage." He grinned. "I know the mind of man."

The scroll was making its way through the assembly, each angel reading it carefully. Lucifer carefully watched the attitudes reflected on faces as they read the covenant that tied them in allegiance to him completely. The assembled angels knew that their only chance of survival depended on the one who now commanded the attention of the room. He had been one of the greatest angels in

Heaven. And they had followed him in the greatest gamble ever. Now they were gambling on his ability to lead them further.

"Thank you all for your loyalty in these trying times," began Lucifer. "I assure you better days are ahead."

The earth rumbled a rolling sound that moved from deep beneath the cavern and disappeared somewhere within the depths below. Lucifer waited until the final echo and then continued. "Just as this rotten planet groans for relief, so does the justice of our cause. I know that from deep within you also desire to return to your rightful places in the Kingdom. Let me emphasize that all of you are instrumental in the conduct of this war. Without proper leadership and organization we don't stand a chance. The enemy is organizing—you can be sure. Michael and the traitorous angels are gathering their strategies and waiting upon the Lord for their next move." He smiled. "This is of course to our advantage—not to have to wait upon the Lord like an impotent and paralyzed army." The others snickered as Lucifer continued his summary.

"Since we lost our home in Heaven we have become an island of truth in exile. Hear me! Our movement represents the only hope of truth's progress. The Most High will never change and why should He? So long as He monopolizes and dictates truth on His own terms, there will never be hope for more sophisticated thought in the universe. I tried to introduce this to the Host, but they are so rotten with the old teachings that they are blind to anything refreshing. We tried to create within the Kingdom a wonderful opportunity for change, from which all angels would have benefited. I freely admit I underestimated the loyalty of the Host, but having taken a full third of the Host with us, I believe we made quite a good showing of it."

Pellecus stood to speak. "We struck a terrific blow in Eden by tying A'dam in with us very neatly. I'm sure it stung the Lord's pride to see His precious man betray Him openly."

"A'dam *did* have a little help," said Rugio, looking at Lucifer and grinning. Everyone laughed.

Lucifer held his hands up to stop the noise. "Nevertheless, A'dam made the choice of his own accord. I was astonished at how easily he gave in. Eve thought she was doing well by her husband. But A'dam—he disobeyed without cause."

"Yes, and the humans' disobedience was the key to everything— and still is," said Pellecus, who had debated this very point in Heaven with much vigor. "Now the Lord faces the unpleasant task of making the humans liable for the same basic crimes of which we are accused. Will He be just in punishing the one and not the other? Quite a gratifying dilemma!"

"But he *did* decree punishment upon the humans," chimed in Tinius, the former Keeper of the Holy Annals, whose position once gave him access to most of the recorded history in the Kingdom. "They were exiled from Eden just as we are exiled from the Kingdom. The ground is cursed because of them. And children, as we have seen recently, come only with great pain."

"And don't forget," chimed in Lenaes, an Angel of Light, "that the sentence of death rests upon them as well!"

"All of these things I am quite aware of," chided Lucifer, whose response silenced the council. He looked over the angels with disdain. "You are all quite eager in your counsel now that the judgment is pronounced. I was *there*, remember? I also received a judgment—a curse which all of you bear as well."

"The Seed of the woman," several of the group muttered quietly.

"Yes, the Seed. The Seed," repeated Lucifer, whose rage was apparent. "The accursed Seed of the woman prophesies our destruction." He was much louder now, almost screaming. "I have no care for A'dam and Eve leaving Eden! Nor do I care that A'dam must work the ground in sweaty frustration. Nor do I care that Eve has already born two sons in bloody pain. All that concerns me is the Seed and how to destroy it!"

Lucifer regained control of himself and spoke much more quietly. "And the Seed is why we are met today. Though a child of Eve portents our destruction, it is in the child's destruction that we may yet find our deliverance."

Lucifer continued the briefing. "I have worked alongside Rugio to divide our angels into principalities and powers, legions and troops. There can be no mistake as to our intentions, nor to our standing in this cursed world."

He gestured to their gloomy surroundings, a huge subterranean cavity deep below where Eden once commanded the attention of the universe. "It certainly lacks cheeriness, hmm? Nevertheless, though many of you hate it here, I prefer the seclusion of this cavern. The reason I called you here is to motivate you in your tasks. For unless we overcome the Most Holy One, ours is a dark, bleak future indeed! Much like this dreadful place."

As he finished these words a large drop of water fell to a dark pool, the sound echoing through the chamber. Lucifer snickered at the well-placed timing of the droplet. "This place reminds us that time is against us—drop by drop we inexorably await our doom."

"Pellecus will now summarize our situation both here and in Heaven. Following his report I will give instruction as to specifics in the strategy of this war. We will conclude with the adoption of this most holy covenant. You will treat Pellecus and Rugio as if they speak with my voice," said Lucifer, motioning to Pellecus to begin. "For indeed they do."

"Thank you, my lord," said Pellecus, taking his place in the center of the circle. "And might I add that if we do not speak with one voice in this undertaking, we shall not speak with any substance. We must remain united in this effort."

The demons nodded in agreement, looking to Pellecus, their supreme leader in matters of wisdom and philosophy. Pellecus had come to be Lucifer's chief spokesperson, passing down pertinent information through the levels of leadership that had recently been created. He also was considered the expert in all issues of doctrine and teaching, the caretaker of the True Teachings that had been compromised by those angels still occupying the Kingdom in the name of the Most High God.

Pellecus masterfully outlined the current position that the once holy angels now found themselves in. He fostered no lofty illusions, as their predicament was a precarious one that required utmost care and resolve. Step by step, he recounted how Lucifer had legitimately attempted to be named the steward of the now cursed planet; how the Council of Elders had put forth his name in nomination; how their efforts were subverted by a particular group of pandering angels; how the Host had been won to the other side; how they were subsequently betrayed, as were all angels, when the stewardship was handed over to A'dam; how they were unlawfully forced out of Heaven; how A'dam had proved unworthy and handed the authority of the planet over to them; and finally, how their greatest challenge lay not in battling angels for control of Heaven, but in compromising the woman's Seed and denying the fulfillment of the prophecy.

"Excellent summation," said Lucifer, as Pellecus took his seat once more in the council. "I am astonished that with such incredible talent on our side we are the ones who find ourselves convening in a dreary cave!"

The room exploded in laughter.

"Pellecus is quite right, however," continued Lucifer. "The Seed must never be allowed the chance to prosper. That point cannot be argued."

"So how do we stop it?" asked Tinius. "How do you stop something that the Lord Himself has prophesied? Why can't Rugio simply kill Eve and her brood and be done with it?"

A few of the angels affirmed the suggestion. Lucifer shot a knowing glance at Rugio, who stood to speak.

"As you are aware," began the warrior who had once commanded one of the most prominent legions in Heaven, "the thought of destroying the humans has already occurred to us. I sent my greatest angels—so that you might not soil your hands, Tinius." The assembly laughed at Tinius's expense. "But we cannot overcome them. We can only harass them—agitate them. Approach but not really touch them."

"Then what good are our warriors?" asked Tinius. "What good are principalities and powers that cannot exert force? Is there no way to defeat these creatures?" Tinius was beginning to make Rugio angry, but he maintained control. "Before Eden they were protected by God's presence. What protects them now that His presence has deserted them?" Rugio looked to Lucifer, who smiled and took over the conversation.

"We can overcome them, Tinius, provided they allow us entrance into or control of their minds," Lucifer said.

"That they allow entrance? You think they will ever trust us again?" asked an exasperated Tinius. He threw up his hands and shook his head in disbelief.

Lucifer looked directly at Tinius. "Trust is something you must win, Tinius—it is rarely offered. Will they ever trust a serpent again? I doubt it. They are acutely sensitive to their predicament right now. They still live in the shadow and sting of their disobedience. They have a very healthy fear of the Most High because they know they are guilty. That is why I said the battle is in the minds of men." He now addressed the group. "So long as the humans remain vigilant and closed to our purposes they are reasonably safe. We can only suggest, tempt, and compel. Even harass and frighten. But we cannot actually touch them without their consent—whether that consent is through ignorance or invitation."

"Then how can we possibly win?" Tinius blustered. "They are on their guard. If they know that we can be kept at a distance, then how can they be destroyed?"

"You just gave the answer, Tinius," said Lucifer. "*If* they know. They *don't* know. That is the key. Again I say that the only reason A'dam and Eve are resistant to our ability to completely destroy them is that they are still living in the wake of the catastrophe in Eden. They are guilt-ridden and ashamed. Guilt and shame are wonderful weapons. But while the wounds they inflict are fresh they can cause a human to remain alert, even remorseful. A'dam and Eve's wounds are fresh and so is their wariness of disregarding the Lord."

Lucifer rubbed his hands along the moist cavern wall. "You see the water dripping constantly along this wall? It will continue to be moist long after A'dam and Eve are dust." He smiled at the group. "Never fear. Time is on our side. And just as A'dam has already forgotten the covenant he made with the Lord and with his wife, so will the humans ultimately grow lax in their fear of God. And we'll settle the score with their children."

"What our prince is trying to tell you," continued Pellecus from the opposite side of the circle, "is that ignorance of the Most High is our greatest resource. As humans lose their interest in the living God, or seek to worship Him in misdirected ways, they can be managed and destroyed."

"So then our task is to keep their eyes off the Most High?" offered Tinius.

"No, my dear Tinius," responded Lucifer. "Our task is to keep their eyes on something else. The Most High will always be a presence in their hearts. He willed it so when He created them in His image. But that image has been tainted since Eden. Our task is to compromise the intuitive hunger for relationship with the Father through earthly, carnal, sensual means."

He walked around the circle, his eyes boring into each face. "A'dam and Eve are lost to us. The death sentence is already upon them—so be it. Let them return to the foul dust from which they were created. They pose no real threat to us themselves. It is the children who pose the threat. And their children afterwards. And on and on, until one day the Seed becomes a reality." A chill went through the room at the thought of the prophecy coming alive. "Pellecus?"

"And so brothers," continued Pellecus, "our task is to taint the Seed, just as everything else in this fallen world has been tainted. We will confuse the promise with carnal teachings and imaginations and fear. One thing about humans is very apparent. They have an insatiable need to make things right. To feel that all is not lost. They live on hope.

"Witness poor Eve in her guilt, which we are fanning most successfully with relentless accusation. But her grief teaches us a very important human attitude: the need for community—to be a part of something that makes sense, something greater than one-self; to be made whole again, as it were. And so we shall provide the means for humans to connect with something greater than them-selves." He grinned and made a sweeping gesture to all present. "We shall provide them something god-like." He glanced at Lucifer, who spoke up.

"Think of it," Lucifer said, purring his vision to the room. "All of you will become like gods to the humans! They will one day bow to you, sing praises to you, build temples to you. You will manipu-late simple elements like fire and create the illusion of power, mak-ing these beasts believe that the power resides from within. Vel, you always saw yourself as a warrior god! Tinius, imagine great images built in your honor! You will all speak through these human cattle as oracles and guide the destiny of nations through the prophets of the earthly gods that you shall become!"

The room filled with a charge of excitement as the disgraced angels saw themselves exalted to the rank of an earthly deity. Lucifer continued. "Why should generations of humans hence wor-ship an invisible God in the stars when the gods of earth are readi-ly accessible and responsive to their needs? When they ask, 'Where is God?' we shall provide the answer."

Lucifer took the scroll from one of the angels. "Mark me," he said, pointing the scroll at the angels. "The humans will need a God who has not turned His back on them. We will exploit that human need for the Most High. We shall supply to the humans ample gods who will fill that void." He looked up toward the cavernous ceiling, almost whispering now, "And we shall so thoroughly corrupt the children of A'dam and Eve that nothing holy will ever come of it."

He unrolled the scroll. "And the Seed of the woman will die in the unholy and unnatural ground in which it will find itself." Snickering at the delicious thought of it all, he said, "Can you imagine something holy being born in a world so profane?"

A rumbling from deep within the earth echoed again through the room, adding to the drama of the occasion. Lucifer lay the scroll in the center of the circle. A bright light emanated from his person, casting an incredible light in the room as he read:

Our place and position in the Kingdom has been subverted by those who would perpetuate an ancient and rotting system;

And we, who hold to the True Way, have been evacuated from the Kingdom unless or until the day of our restoration;

And we recognize that our Enemy is subtle and determined in His resolve to deny us our place in the universe;

And our Enemy is determined to destroy us by the Seed of His creation through prophetic appointment;

And we are likewise determined not to succumb to anything that smacks of humans and their Seed.

Be it resolved henceforth and forevermore

That we, the true loyalists and upholders of the Way, covenant together that we shall never cease from our labors in warring with the flesh, the Seed, and the spirit; the Flesh being all that is derived from A'dam and his kind; and the spirit being all that holds to Him to whom we once held allegiance.

We further agree together on this most holy occasion, that we shall henceforth and forevermore swear lawful obligation to Lucifer, the Morning Star, and his kingship and authority; and that in him we shall find our ultimate deliverance, or in lieu of, our ultimate damnation.

"All of you are in agreement with this covenant and its fundamental declarations. This text shall go down in our own earthly chronicles as witness to the justice of our cause. Tinius, I appoint you as the Chronicler of the Morning Star, with the duties of recording the teachings, my prophecies, inspirations, and history throughout the remainder of this great struggle. Since you raise so many questions, perhaps your talents will be better suited to answering them. We must preserve an accurate rendering of this conflict for posterity."

"Brothers! We shall shortly convene again as to the further conduct of the war. Until then—farewell."

"So be it," they said in unison.

Chronicles of the Host
Creation's Grief

The holy angels grieved with the Father as the children made in His image were cast into the darkness of a fallen world, never again to return to the near-perfection of Eden. Thus were the lines drawn quite neatly between the Kingdoms of Light and darkness. The battle, begun in Heaven, would be played out on earth, which seemed a grim place now, as creation itself reeled from the disaster that the sin of rebellion had brought to the universe.

For his part, Lucifer, despite all of his presumed powers, realized that his only ability to wage an effective war lay in the willingness of the humans to be deceived. Thus the war would be waged by both sides for the hearts and minds of future generations of humans. But the Father, in His grace and love, gave a measure of hope to the humans through the promise of a coming one, from the seed of the woman, who would crush Lucifer once and for all. The holy angels would aid men in the delivery of this Seed; the fallen rebels would seek to delay or destroy the Seed.

It was a great mystery to the angels of Heaven, as they watched Lucifer's rebels take authority on earth. Why didn't the Lord simply assume control? Why did He delay the end in favor of the Seed of the woman? What no creature, angel or human, anticipated was that the conflict would be fought not in the pride of war, but in the humility of love—not by the taking up of arms, but by the laying down of them.

Chapter 2

"How can these weak and disgraced creatures live like this?"

A'dam looked across the flatness that stretched before him, endless and uninviting. The sun, as always, bled through the heavenly canopy that was suspended between the greater heavens and the earth. Heavy with moisture, the air that once kept Eden vibrant now sustained life apart from Eden.

The man observed with a sigh that the bit of garden he tended was badly overrun with weeds—again. He cursed under his breath as a thorny plant scratched his leg. Bending down, he began tugging gingerly at the offensive plant, trying not to upset the melon sprig next to it. Other weeds flourished nearby. The man shook his head in disgust at the losing battle he waged as Eve walked up, their two sons behind her.

"The only thing this ground is good for is weeds and thorns," A'dam said, pulling violently now at the large thorny plant that had scratched him, not caring for the tender young shoots around it. "These thorns seem to grow overnight. And all these choking vines. And the mist doesn't nourish the earth as it once did." He finally pulled the thorny plant out of the ground and tossed it aside. "How I miss Eden," he said, wiping his dirty brow. "If only…"

He stopped and looked at Eve with the look of one who had blurted out an unmentionable. Since the catastrophe at Eden, the subject of their disobedience to God was a sore one—particularly since A'dam still held Eve largely responsible.

"I'm sorry, love," he said. "I only meant…"

"I know," Eve replied. She looked at the desolate wilderness that surrounded them, encompassing the whole of the land of Havilah. "I also long for Eden's comforts." Her gaze shifted to her sons, Cain and Abel, playing in the dirt. "How nice it would have been to raise our children in such a place."

Since being forced out of Eden, the two humans had wandered about in a strange state of exile; their once perfect home no longer welcomed them. The thought of the two very serious angels guarding the entrance into Eden was more than enough to overcome any delusions of a return. Eden was finished and that was that—and nothing caused greater heartache than living in one's loss, especially when the loss might have been avoided.

The lush forests of Eden with their gentle breezes and fragrances had given way to the ugliness brought on by sin. The earth, which one time yielded an abundance of fruit, now was stingy with its produce, cursed forever to all men. The joy that could have been childbirth had given way to a bloody and painful entrance of children into a fallen world. All of these realities were consequences of that dreadful day in the garden so long ago. But there was one consequence that far outweighed the loss of home in paradise—and that was the loss of heart with the Father.

A'dam longed for those days of fellowship and closeness with his Creator. He ached for them. Sometimes when the wind was just right and the wilderness quiet, or at night when the heavens blazed God's glory, A'dam remembered how things once were—how he had walked hand-in-hand with his Father; how he had shared great dreams of destiny; how he had ruled in his Father's authority. What sweet fellowship that was! Now A'dam's Father's ears seemed deaf and His Presence was as distant as the evening star.

It was in these moments of thought that A'dam most hurt. He would have given up everything now—all that God had given him—if only he could feel the love of God as he had once felt it. Sometimes his heart trembled with a violent pain as he contemplated his life. "If only" had become a pitiful lament that haunted him daily. And always the lament led to the same refrain: What if Eve had not disobeyed his instruction to her? What if he had been with

her that day before the serpent had sunk the venom of his persua-
sion deep into her heart? If only...

A'dam looked with gentle compassion at his wife, who was
tending Abel. He had long since healed of the anger he felt toward
Eve. For many months after the expulsion he had said scarcely a
word to her. He brooded. He seethed. He sulked. He put off her constant begging of forgiveness and let her stew in her guilt.

In time, however, he realized that whatever their plight, she
was still "bone of his bone and flesh of his flesh." The Father Himself had created her out of A'dam's very substance. They were forever united by that connection. More importantly, he had finally
given voice to the galling feeling that had plagued his mind since
that horrible day—the inescapable truth that ultimately the verdict
of guilt rested squarely upon him. It was easy to pass the guilt on to
Eve. Even now he felt the old anger stirring. After all, she was the
one who...

A'dam caught himself, the questions begging to be asked but
never voiced by Eve: What if he had held up *his* responsibility as
law-keeper in Eden? Should he not have rebuked the serpent and
with his obedience possibly atoned for the sin of his wife? Instead,
to his utter shame and the ruin of all humans, he had himself transgressed God's sacred law. Thus they both scratched about on an
unyielding, unfriendly, unholy world.

Eve noticed her husband's melancholy demeanor as he stood
over the thorny garden that helped feed their little family. She
watched A'dam, knowing that at times like this it was best to remain
quiet. The mood would pass; it always did. She understood that it
wasn't simply the thorns that were causing his current mood. He
was missing his Father.

Eve didn't really understand the depth of A'dam's loss. She
sometimes longed to know how he felt, but she could never get at
the heart of it. Perhaps if she understood his pain, she could somehow draw closer to him. The few times when she had tried to talk
to him about it, he was reluctant, distant, and sometimes angry.

But just how *did* she feel? She felt badly for her husband,
whose world forever changed in one decisive moment. She hurt for
her children, who would never know the beauty and security of
Eden. She missed the affection of the animals; the strolls with her
husband in the beauty of fellowship, the sound of A'dam calling for
her by the waterfall.

But above it all was the guilt. She would forever regret that she had given in to the serpent's subtle urgings. Now she was paying the price of a cursed world and a profound judgment. Eve accepted her punishment and could even live with it. But nothing seemed to appease the unshakable guilt that stalked her day and night. A'dam was hurting because he had lost relationship with the Father. Eve hurt because she had lost her relationship with A'dam.

Didn't she love God? Of course she did. She certainly missed the fellowship and protection that she once felt when the Father was present. She loved the Father. But she also loved her husband and her family. They were her world now. The intensity of the loss of God suffered by A'dam was very peculiar to her in light of the new world in which they lived.

"Ah well," said A'dam, breaking the silence. "See to the fire. I'm going to gather some more wood for the evening."

"Alright, my love," said Eve, as her husband walked away from her. She watched him disappear into the woods toward the river. She held her children close, tears welling up in her eyes, barely whispering the words, "My poor A'dam."

"My poor A'dam! My poor A'dam!"

The shrill voices were unheard by Eve as a raucous company of unholy angels fell over themselves with hysterical laughter. One who stood near her even imitated her crying in mock desperation, finally throwing himself down on the ground. The others howled in enjoyment.

"Poor A'dam indeed," said one of the angels. "Accuser! She's off again. Remind her once more whose fault it is that A'dam is now so poor!"

An angel known as Accuser followed after her. He streaked to her side and sidled up to her ear, whispering a droning, persistent message. Eve had recently become his charge, and his task was to hassle her, speaking death into her mind through accusation that it was all her fault…that her children would suffer…that her husband no longer cared for her. Eve began weeping bitterly. Abel and Cain looked at her with puzzled expressions. "Oh God, forgive me," she finally said. "Please…" She fell to her knees.

"Forgive me, Lord! Forgive me, Lord!" came the familiar mockery. Some of the rebel angels crowed from perches in the trees around them. Others watched from the trunk of a fallen tree to see what Accuser would leave of her. All eyes were on Eve—watchful, hateful, profane eyes. They watched as she stood to leave.

"Stay with her!" cried an unseen voice. "We must keep these creatures in constant touch with their failings."

Accuser took off again, waiting for Eve down the path. The others looked in the direction of the voice and became immediately silent. Many of the troop scattered as Lucifer emerged from the darkness of the woods; others snapped to nervous attention. Kara and Pellecus accompanied Lucifer into the clearing.

"What a pitiful life," said Kara, indicating the meager garden that sustained A'dam and Eve. "How can these weak and disgraced creatures live like this?"

"Because, Kara, like us they have a will to survive," said Lucifer. "That is the Creator's little gift, and His curse, to them—the will to survive. Their world has radically changed, but they cling to hope. Our task is to rob them of that hope and put an end to this war once and for all!"

"The war, the war. Always the war," snorted Kara, who had been absent from council meetings lately. "What can these pitiful human beasts possibly do to us? I think we overestimate them."

Pellecus could only shake his head in disbelief at Kara's colossal stupidity. "If you would attend council you would be briefed on the latest developments," he snarled.

"Don't presume to lecture me, teacher," returned Kara. "I am not one of your empty-headed angels. Besides I bring news from Heaven—that is why I have been absent!"

"What possible news could you bring to us?" asked Pellecus. "The holy angels are forbidden informal contact with any of us."

"True, the angels don't communicate with us anymore. But if one has a mind for gathering intelligence, one finds ways," Kara said, smug with his resourcefulness. "I thought that perhaps it would be prudent to send an embassy to the Kingdom from earth. To demonstrate our desire for some sort of understanding."

"I'm gratified to see that you haven't changed, Kara," said Lucifer sarcastically. "I would be disappointed if you weren't trying to cut your own deal."

"No, lord," said Kara. "As an elder I simply thought…"

"You are no longer an elder, Kara!" snapped Lucifer. "Neither on earth nor in Heaven. You are now one of us, the outlaws, remember? Whether that is helpful to us or to the holy angels I am not sure. I only know that you will never go near the Kingdom again."

"Of course, my prince," said Kara, glancing at a smirking Pellecus. "I never spoke to any angel. I merely was curious. And though the angels don't communicate with us, they do talk among themselves. I simple positioned myself on the outer edges of the Kingdom and picked up some information."

"In the future it will not be necessary for you to attend Heaven," said Lucifer. "As it turns out, since the humans fell from grace I have a legal right to accuse them before the Throne itself. Henceforth your intelligence gathering will take place on earth. I will represent us at court."

"As you wish," said Kara, shooting hate-filled eyes at Pellecus. "I must say that I am quite proud of the devils working under my authority. I will build for you the greatest intelligence-gathering network ever!"

Lucifer looked around at several of Kara's agents, who were listening from a distance to the conversation. "Very well, Kara. Our ability to ascertain the movement and thinking of humans will be a key to the war. Just keep your spies to the task at hand. I need information, not the ramblings of gossipy angels on the outer edges of Heaven."

"Of course," said Kara.

"You have piqued my curiosity, however," said Lucifer, motioning for Kara to follow him down the path used by A'dam and Eve. Pellecus followed behind. "And what do the angels say about it all? How do they feel about the anointed cherub who led them in glorious worship of the Most High God?" He smiled at the thought of the large administrative hole that the rebel vacancy had left."

"Of course they have aligned themselves with fierce showings of loyalty around the Great Throne," Kara began. "Hmph! Falling all over themselves to prove their loyalty for the Lord. Some of these very angels who now demonstrate their love for the Most High at one time considered throwing in with us! Hypocrites!"

"Yes, and chief among the hypocrites is Serus," said Lucifer, remembering how his steward in the end had betrayed him and remained loyal to the Lord. "There will be accounts to pay some day. This I vow!"

Kara continued. "The holy angels, as they now call themselves, have reorganized into new legions under new commanders. This of course was a necessity, since so many commanders came to our side. Nevertheless, they are equipped for war and only await the Lord's command to come against the demons."

"The demons?" asked Lucifer. "And who are they?"

Kara snickered. "*We* are the demons, my lord. And you are chief among us."

"Well, that is interesting," said Pellecus. "Often at the Academy we spoke of fallen angels, or demonized and devilish spirits. It was all conjecture of course, because nobody ever considered that an angel might actually...that is to say...at any rate, a demon was simply a spirit that turned evil. I suppose to them it makes sense to call us that. To the loyalists we *are* the evil ones."

"If one can be a demon and a liberator, then I shall enjoy the title of chief demon," Lucifer said, causing his two leaders to laugh aloud. "They are, however, quite brilliant in recasting us. To find themselves suddenly at war with former brothers is much more acceptable when your brothers have been demonized. Kills the sympathy, you know."

"Not unlike our recasting of our own legions," remarked Pellecus.

"Yes," agreed Lucifer. "Rugio actually devised the strategy. He reasoned that our angels would be better equipped for the war if their names reflected their particular...specialty. Make better fighters of them. So the legions, the warriors, those who have human assignment, shall be known by their influence: lust, anger, malice, lies, perversion, rebellion—whatever the assignment calls for."

"One of Rugio's more intelligent tactical decisions," admitted Kara. "Eve is already being hounded by spirits of accusation. Hopefully she'll succumb to their suggestions and destroy herself. A victory of sorts, hmm?"

"Possibly. But this war will not be won through the renaming of spirits. It will be won through subtlety and influence over humans," said Lucifer. "Let Heaven castigate us and call us all manner of names. It is the victor who writes the final chronicles. And the victor will be the one who controls the destiny of the Seed."

"Ah yes," said Kara. "The Seed. That is the other subject in Heaven. The Seed." He scoffed. "Stupid angels don't even know what they are so excited about. They only know that the Seed is what will ultimately destroy you..." Kara looked at Pellecus, who shifted his eyes downward upon Kara's remark. "Or so the prophecy goes..."

"You are quite correct, Kara, to be wary of the Seed," said Lucifer. "For in its fruition is my destruction—yours as well." Lucifer's sharp blue-grey eyes became dreamy and distant as he murmured the lines that he had rehearsed in his tortured mind ten thousand times since that day in Eden: "*I will put enmity between you and the woman, and between your seed and her seed; He shall bruise your head, and you shall bruise His heel*" (RSV).

He looked at Pellecus and Kara. "He will bruise my head. You see? I will bruise His heel. I may injure the Seed, but the Seed shall ultimately defeat me—bruise my head." He pointed toward Eve and the children. "You asked a moment ago what these beasts could possibly do to us. As for A'dam and Eve—they can do nothing to harm us. You see the children there? They are far more dangerous to us than A'dam and Eve."

"Those weak pups?" queried Kara, inviting some snickers from other of his agents, who were observing from the shadows.

"It is not the adult generation with which we must contend," remarked Lucifer, whose silent glare quickly stopped the snickering. "It is always the next generation of humans that poses the greatest threat to us. The children. The potential for the Seed to emerge." Lucifer looked intently at Abel and Cain as they followed their weeping mother down the path. "Always the next generation," he repeated, [**quelling**] the hatred he felt for all things human.

Crispin, the scholarly angel whose new appointment as head of the Academy of Hosts gave him an important voice in Heaven, sat across from Michael and Gabriel. They were discussing recent events and their impact on the Kingdom. Crispin was certainly correct in his assessment of the renewed fear of God among the loyal angels. All of Heaven was bathed with a refreshing sense of duty and obligation to the Most High. Since the horrible rebellion that saw Lucifer and many other highly placed angels expelled from the Kingdom, a newfound holiness had overcome the Host.

"The fear of the Almighty Lord is a quick counter to foolish notions of rebellion," continued Crispin, leaning back in his peculiar way. "It has a way of helping creatures keep a healthy perspective of their Creator. If Lucifer's crowd had respected that fear rather than tempted it, they might never have started this nonsense."

"I must say that the Academy is a different place," agreed Michael. "The vile attitude and poison of Lucifer's influence has vanished."

"Yes, the Academy is clean once more," said Crispin. "But all has changed, Michael. No longer simply a place for angels to grow in knowledge of the Most High, it has now has become a school of war—preparing the Host for the battle of the ages. Astonishing!"

"Perhaps this was the school's destiny," said Gabriel. "To train angels in warfare and carry out the will of the Most High in Heaven and on earth."

"They certainly are in readiness," agreed Michael. "The Host is eager to get into the fight. The only question is how to conduct a war that is so closely tied in with the hearts and minds of men. Our task is that of...what was it again, Gabriel?"

"Ministering spirits," reminded Gabriel. "We are to minister to the humans in the name and authority of the Most High on those occasions necessary when our intervention is necessary."

"Yes, and to keep Lucifer and his angels off their game," added Crispin. "Or should I say 'the fallen ones'?"

"Ah yes," mused Michael. "Demons, devils..."

"Fallen angels..." continued Gabriel.

"Evil spirits," threw in Serus, who had just arrived.

Everyone was amused at the new terminology that was creeping into the culture of Heaven. Crispin took exception to the attitude.

"It's not simply that the creatures fell and became demonized!" He stood up and gestured wildly. "There is more to it than that. Their new titles reflect the darkness of their hearts. They chose evil and therefore have become evil. I for one *prefer* the name 'demon,' or 'fallen' for these criminal angels, in order to distinguish them from the holy angels of the Most High! For the sake of the Chronicles and all that speaks true there must be a distinction."

"The Most High has declared them excommunicate and anathema to us—that is what really matters, Crispin," said Gabriel.

"Pardon us, teacher," said Michael, realizing that Crispin's academic sensibilities were upset. "We meant no offense. I realize for the sake of truth and teaching that such things are important. For me, whatever they are to be called, they are the enemies of the Most High and therefore my enemies."

"Amen," said Crispin. "I quite agree. Nevertheless I shall henceforth refer to them as 'demons' for that is what they have become."

The others smiled at Crispin's pure view of things. As they continued chatting, an angel came into the room and stood before

Michael. It was one of Michael's sentries, stationed on the outer edges of the Kingdom.

"What is it, Darus?" asked Michael.

"Lord Michael, the elder Kara…"

"Former elder, Darus," corrected Michael. "We must be precise about these things for the sake of the Chronicles."

Crispin shifted with a grunt in his chair.

"Yes, the former elder Kara," continued Darus, "was observed encroaching upon the Kingdom near the Lion's Gate."

"Are you certain it was he?" asked Michael.

"Yes, my lord," said Darus. "He had positioned himself at the gate with a couple of other angels…"

"Demons, Darus, demons," said Michael, looking at Crispin, amused at the scholar's countenance. "We must be accurate."

"Yes…um…demons were with him," said a puzzled Darus. "At any rate, they positioned themselves near a group of…angels…?"

"Quite right," said Michael. "Our side! Go on."

Darus was completely bemused but continued. "They were just inside the gate and when they were approached they vanished. We gave chase but to no avail."

"Thank you, Darus," said Michael. "Excellent work."

After Darus left Michael finally said, "Poor angel. I'll have to explain to him later." He then spoke to the group in a more serious tone. "That was certainly bold of Kara to eavesdrop on Heaven. Didn't even greet his old friends! That scoundrel!"

"They must be desperate for information," remarked Gabriel. "I would certainly like to know what Lucifer is thinking right about now."

"Well, it isn't as if we are not present on earth," said Crispin. "In fact, the humans have been assigned holy angels to comfort them and lend encouragement. We will carry the war back to Lucifer and keep his mongrel angels at bay through the authority given us by the Most High."

"Remarkable," said Serus. "What a ministry for an angel of the Lord—to protect His most precious creation! I suppose that in time, as more humans are present, our own influence on that planet might increase as well."

"Of course," said Crispin. "But the difference between our influence and Lucifer's is that we are under authority of the Lord, whereas the rebels are under no real authority except that which Lucifer can manage."

"Rebels managing rebels," mused Serus, who knew Lucifer better than any of them. "That could prove interesting."

"It certainly proved interesting once before," said Crispin, grinning.

"Cain!"

"Cain!"

"Yes, Father," came the response from the field of barley below.

A'dam watched his son bounding through the grain toward him. How his son loved the earth. He would make a great farmer. His eyes drifted to the side of the hill where Abel sat, watching over a group of sheep.

A'dam often wondered at the difference between his two sons. Cain was a natural fieldsman—he could grow wheat out of a rock, he and Eve would say. A bit of a temper, but that was to be expected from one who wrestled with the ground itself and won. Abel was much more at home among the flocks. The sheep came to him as if he were their parent. It was quite amusing.

Eve had recognized something else about Abel—he had a rather strange, melancholy attitude at times. He often preferred the solitude of the hills where he watched over the flocks or sometimes slept under the stars. A'dam thought that he was simply being obstinate. But Eve knew differently. She knew that Abel heard from God.

"What is it, Father?" said Cain, finally reaching A'dam.

"My son, it is time for eating," said A'dam. "Your mother has prepared the meal."

"What about Abel?" asked Cain, looking at his brother on the distant hill.

"He will be along shortly," said A'dam, also looking at Abel. "As soon as he finishes with the flocks."

The family sat down to eat. A'dam offered thanks to the Lord for the meal and Eve served some robust stew made from some of Cain's produce and one of Abel's lambs that had been trampled by its mother. The family enjoyed the food and fellowship at the entrance to the cave where they lived. A'dam had secured a natural opening in a cavern wall that also allowed smoke from a fire to be pulled up so they could have warmth inside the cave at night. It wasn't Eden, but it was home.

"Another lamb was born," said Abel, as he sat down to eat. Eve handed some of the rich stew to her son. "That makes five this month!"

"Wonderful, son," said A'dam. "The Lord is good to us."

"He's even better to Abel's sheep," said Cain, snickering. Abel laughed.

"God is very good to us," continued A'dam. "He has watched over us all these years, fed us, kept us, provided a place that is safe and warm..."

"Tell us about Eden again," said Cain. The boys loved to hear stories told and retold of life in Eden before the banishment. Abel settled himself next to Eve, his head in her lap as he slurped up the remainder of the stew.

A'dam looked at his little family, their faces dancing in the reflection of the evening fire. They all looked forward to these moments in the stillness of the night, with all the day's work done. Stories helped break up the long, hard day before another one just like it started. His sons each had their favorite stories about Eden— Eve and the monkey who would not leave her alone until she finally threw a melon at it; A'dam and the first time a hawk actually landed on his shoulder. Cain always enjoyed the humorous stories of life in Eden. Abel liked hearing about the Lord. Inevitably, though, the stories always ended up at their disobedience.

"It is very important that you know that we might still be in Eden today, had we honored God rather than ourselves. Always remember this. We were without excuse, and neither do you have an excuse to fail Him. In fact, it's time you began to worship Him."

A'dam looked tenderly at Eve, who took her cue and went inside the cave. The two boys looked at their father, not knowing exactly what he meant. A'dam seemed to be trying to find the words. His sons sat quietly before him, waiting on their father. Finally A'dam spoke.

"When I was in Eden, even before your mother was around, the Lord had fellowship with me, just as we are sitting by this fire together," he began. "It was a wonderful time when I walked with God." He looked at his boys. "I walked with God. You understand?" They nodded. "I sat next to Him, as we are seated. I knew Him...and I betrayed Him. I want you to understand this, because you must make your own way with the Lord. You must seek to please Him and obey Him always."

"Yes, Father," the boys said in unison.

"You don't understand, I know," said A'dam. "But your mother and I have brought you into a world that is not simply a place of shepherding and raising crops. It is a beautiful world but a dangerous one..."

A'dam looked around as if he were being watched by an unseen observer. He motioned to his sons, who leaned in to hear him whisper. "There is a promise. A promise that will avenge the damage your mother and I caused by our disobedience in Eden. One will be born who will overcome the evil that the serpent brings to this world."

The two boys looked at their father solemnly. They had never seen him in such a serious frame of mind before. "Your mother and I live for the day that you will undo the horrible damage we have done. The Lord told us and the serpent that one of our children would accomplish this." A'dam looked at Cain and put a hand on his shoulder. "You are our firstborn. We believe this to be your task." Cain swallowed hard, eyes wide. "And that is why you must both begin to worship the Lord in ways that demonstrate your loyalty to Him. To give back to Him of those things that you love most. To offer Him of your very best."

"You mean we are to bring an offering to the Lord?" asked Cain.

"Yes," said A'dam. "But you must not think you are offering to God from your own ability or strength. There is nothing worthwhile that we can present to Him. It must be done in simple belief and trust. That is how you worship God. That is how you overcome the evil in this world. And that is how the promise can be realized."

Abel looked at his father with a new understanding and compassion. The fire cast a glow on him that made him seem suddenly years older. In an instant, Abel's mind flashed back to glimpses of growing up and watching his father's passionate hope to recapture something he had thrown away. He remembered A'dam in worship, talking to God and offering Him the firstlings of the sheep. He also remembered the frustration and bitterness that sometimes rose up, as A'dam scorned the very earth he had himself brought a curse upon. Abel thought that he understood his father much better now.

"The next time the moon is complete in the sky," A'dam, continued, "it will be time for both of you to begin making your own offerings to the Lord. And remember, these gifts must be from your heart, complete acts of submission." He pointed his finger at both of his sons. "If you think for a moment that your offering is in and of itself worthy, you are in sin. You must offer something that does not smack of pride or self. It must be sincere and from your innermost being or it will not be accepted."

Abel turned to his brother after A'dam left them to join Eve. "Cain. We are going to begin offering to the Lord. Think of it!"

"And think of the promise!" said Cain excitedly. "But what am I to do about it? How am I supposed to make this happen?"

"You heard father," answered Abel. "By worshiping God and loving Him."

Cain had a concerned look upon his face. "Yes, that is wonderful. For you that will be easy. You already know the Lord, you talk to Him often."

"You know Him too," responded Abel. "You just have to listen to Him. Your problem is that you are always trying to please Him through what you do. I have learned that He is not interested in what we do, but who we are."

"Yes, but I sometimes feel that He loves you more than He loves me," said Cain. "And that is the truth of the matter. That is why he accepts you."

"Perhaps, brother," said Abel, "it isn't a matter of how much He loves you, but of how much you really love Him."

"So be it," sneered Cain. "I will make an offering to Him that is so worthy that yours will be like ashes in comparison." Cain stood up, holding a stick and pointing in the direction of the flocks. "All you do is raise the sheep and watch them. What kind of offering can come of that? I till the earth—a cursed earth at that—and force its harvest. I sweat, brother, and create from nothing! We'll see whose offering is acceptable and whose is not!"

Abel watched his brother storm off into the darkness. He had tried to better understand Cain, but the two had always been opposite sorts. "Someday, my brother," called out Abel, "your anger will destroy you!"

"I would say it is destroying him already," came a voice from the darkness.

Chapter 3

"Cain is a fool!"

Several of the fallen angels had assembled near Cain's field, awaiting the arrival of their commander, Kara. They spied Cain, who was working the earth and at times cursing it. Whenever he uttered an oath they laughed hysterically.

"Poor fellow," one of the angels, named Sellus, said. "Humans are so completely stupid. And so easily flustered."

"Particularly this one," agreed the other.

"Not so stupid that he doesn't understand the importance of bringing the Lord an offering," came Kara's voice.

The angels suddenly came to order and awaited Kara's appearance. He came gliding in and landed in their midst. He looked at Cain and smirked. "This one is a bit of a brute, to be sure," Kara said. "But he and his brother still pose a real threat."

"This temperamental beast?" said Sellus. "I can see the threat Abel poses simply because he seems sensitive to the Lord. But Cain?"

"Either of these humans could be the One who was foretold," said Kara. "Lucifer is quite clear on that point. I have my doubts about Cain, nevertheless we must beware. I have Abel watched as well, although we cannot get in as close to him." He scoffed. "The prophecy is quite clear that it will be an offspring of Eve." Cain uttered another oath. "I must admit that this one's unhealthy attitude of praise to the Most High provides a bit of comfort. Maybe even distances him some from the protection of Michael."

Sellus and the others shuddered at the mention of the archangel. Kara saw their fear and continued. "Ah, Michael. Of all the angels in Heaven, Michael is the most feared by us. And for good reason. His loyalty to the Most High can never be compromised. And for that I envy him and hate him all the more. "

"I dread the day of confrontation with him," said Sellus.

"As does every angel on earth," admitted Kara.

"Except for me," came a rough voice.

"Oh yes, Rugio," said Kara, not looking up. "I had forgotten how the sting of being bested by Michael has inflamed you." He smirked as Rugio appeared before them. "Given you a sense of motivation, hmm?"

"Don't test me, Kara," said Rugio, the chief of Lucifer's warrior angels. "I had Michael's sword once. I shall have it again."

"Perhaps this time you'll learn how to handle it," purred Kara. The other angels remained uncomfortably silent or slowly eased back into the darkness of cover. They all turned as Cain walked across the field, carrying a large stone to the side. Kara laughed as Cain threw the rock down on a pile of similar-sized stones.

"I honestly believe Cain is a bigger threat to the promise than we are," said Kara. "If *that* is the best the Most High can muster, we have little to fear."

"That is what brought me to you," said Rugio, as they watched Cain sit down on the side of the field on a fallen tree, wiping his brow. "Even beasts like Cain can change."

Kara looked at Rugio suspiciously. "What have you heard?" he asked.

Rugio smiled. "Apparently your teams are not as thorough as you believed," said Rugio with an acid tone, "or else you would know that both Cain and Abel will begin bringing offerings to the Lord very soon. Fortunately for our side we are not completely dependent upon your little spies for all of our intelligence. I have some 'ears' of my own, so to speak." Rugio enjoyed the effect of his words on Kara, who glared at Sellus and the others.

"Congratulations," said Kara. "Yes, my angels are still learning the craft of subtlety and spying," he said with forced good nature. "Just as your warriors are still learning the art of war." He looked at Sellus with icy eyes. "I see that I need to discipline my charges a bit more." Sellus slowly vanished into the darkness. Kara turned back to Rugio. "So, it's come to offerings to the Lord?"

"Yes," said Rugio. "That can only mean that they are growing closer to Him…"

"And the closer they grow to the Most High, the greater the chance for the Seed to emerge," Kara mused. "Interesting assumption, but it makes sense."

"Lucifer has assigned me personally to see that Cain doesn't become too close to the Lord," said Rugio. "I'll make sure his worship doesn't create any problems for us. He'll mourn the day he was born to Eve."

"Cain is a fool," said Kara. "All he needs is a little encouragement and he becomes enraged. A stone in a field can bring him down as easily as one of your warriors. I prefer the more subtle approach, something that requires thought and contests their minds—such as we are using with the parents. You know, ongoing accusations that keep them steeped in guilt and bitterness and consequently, alone."

"Do as you like with his parents," said Rugio. "And with Abel. But leave Cain to me. He'll be my first trophy of the war."

"And your last, I hope," said Kara. "Lucifer wants these passionate feelings for the Most High dampened before they become troublesome. Then we can be done with it once and for all. Offerings from the children of Eve are not a good sign." He glanced over at Sellus, barely perceptible to the side. "We are all depending upon you. It's your game now—to win or to lose."

"I will see to it," said Rugio.

He gave Kara a resolute look, then vanished. Sellus emerged from the darkness, with a curious expression on his face. Kara smirked at Sellus.

"Rugio will never be clever enough to handle this task," Kara finally said. "It requires subtlety, not brutality. This I know. And Lucifer will know this as well."

Chronicles of the Host

Cain

Thus it was that Cain, son of A'dam, became a source of effort on the part of those who had rebelled against the Most High.

Though all of Heaven wanted the honor of shepherding Cain through the conflict, the task fell to Serus, an angel who had proven his mettle in staying fast with the Lord during the critical time of darkness in Heaven. To Serus went the mission of watching the movements of Cain and reporting on his progress through life, which to a human was very long indeed, but to an angel seemed but an instant.

The Host anticipated many such assignments as the war carried on and more and more humans populated the earth. We continued to learn more and more of the unfolding plan of the Most High God, witnessing His marvelous and excellent wisdom in dealing with the rather inconsistent humans. Though the humans were separated from Him because of their disobedience, in the heart of every angel remained the hope of the coming one who would crush the head of the serpent.

All of us understood the significance of the offerings that the humans made to the Lord, though we never understood the Lord's pleasure in the offerings. Thus as the sons of A'dam prepared their offerings, all angels, both holy and fallen, took great interest in the proceedings. It seemed that something critical to the war hinged on the offering—something that would turn the war in a new direction...

"He rejected it," said Cain. "He accepted your offering and didn't even bother with mine." Cain kicked over the offering of grains and fruit that he had brought before the Lord, spilling it onto the grass. He then sat down and wept bitterly.

Abel walked over to his brother, trying to think of the right words, the right expression of feeling. The smoke was still rising from the offering he had presented; the aroma of fat still crackling over the smoldering fire hung in the air. He glanced at the remains of Cain's rejected offering, now scattered in the grass, and felt a deep compassion for his brother. Finally he spoke up. "I'm sorry, Cain," Abel said, placing his hand on Cain's shoulder. Cain pulled away from Abel's touch.

"I don't need your pity," he said, looking up with tear-filled eyes. "I have been rejected and you have been accepted. It has always been that way and it always shall."

"Cain, the Lord has no favorite between us," Abel assured him. "I simply brought an offering that pleased Him. You remember what Father said…"

"Father's offerings are accepted because he was the first," Cain replied bitterly. "But why are your offerings any different from mine?"

"Because mine was done in faith, from my heart—not by the sweat of my brow. The Lord requires faith, Cain. Father told us that."

"Father again?" Cain exploded. "Excellent advice, considering he is the one who disobeyed in the first place. If he had had faith in Eden none of this would be necessary."

Cain looked at his brother harshly. "And what do you know about anything that requires the sweat of your brow?" he demanded. "You have always tended the flocks while I have worked the fields. It is obvious that the Lord prefers shepherds to farmers." He scoffed. "From now on I'll be neither shepherd nor farmer."

"You can't simply give up everything because you suffered a loss," reasoned Abel. "Find out what pleases God and do that thing."

"How can you please a God who rejects your best effort?" came a voice. Nan, one of Rugio's lieutenants had finally crept into the conversation and was whispering into Cain's mind. *"You cannot please a God who plays favorites."*

Lucifer, Kara, and Rugio were watching the scene unfold from the side. Opposite them, and across the way, were Michael, Serus, and several holy angels. They had come down in response to Eve's praying for her two sons following the offerings. Kara was talking to Lucifer, in hushed conversation.

"Well, Kara," said Michael. "I see, as always, that you cannot let the humans play this out on their own."

"We're merely expediting the inevitable," said Kara. "Cain has complete control. We are only suggesting, not demanding. The choice, as always, is his to make."

"Nevertheless you are forbidden to touch him," said Michael, his belted sword beginning to glow. "Eve is praying for her sons and we are sent here in response."

"Things must be really extraordinary in Heaven these days," sneered Kara. "In response to the sniveling of a distraught mother, they send an archangel accompanied by…a traitor. To do what? Keep us from touching this human? We have no need to touch him, Michael. He is destroying himself."

Michael was disgusted with the scene as more and more demons flocked in to enjoy the spectacle. All the while Nan continued hammering away, whispering in Cain's ears how God had rejected him in favor of his brother.

"God does love you more, doesn't He?" said Cain, looking up at his younger brother. "Even though I am the firstborn, He loves you more."

"Cain, please," pleaded Abel. "That is not true. God loves you…"

"It is true!" said Cain, almost screaming. Cain stood up and leaned against a tree. "Your offering is still being accepted," he said, pointing to the smoldering remains of Abel's firstling. "I really think I hate you, my brother."

Abel was taken aback by Cain's words. Never had he seen Cain so vehement in his anger towards him. He had grown up with Cain and was used to his occasional bursts of anger. But this was something deeper—something that had to be dampened. Abel could only begin to pray to the Lord on behalf of his angry brother. He prayed silently:

"Most High God. You are the Lord who made Heaven and earth. You have accepted my offering and now I come to ask You to hear this plea. Lord, my God, help Cain to understand that You love him. Help him to grow in love of You. And whatever the enemy of my father might be attempting, I ask You to war for us, Lord, for we cannot fight him alone. War after my father's enemy and cause him to release Cain from his grip, for I see something unholy here."

Suddenly Michael's sword became a brilliant blue light. Lucifer watched intently as the others with him jumped back. The archangel lunged at Nan, sword drawn. Nan shrieked and disappeared into the sky, many of the demons scattering with him. Michael looked around with fierce eyes of protection. Rugio began stepping forward as if to fight but Lucifer stopped him.

"Interesting move, archangel," said Lucifer. "But not quite fair. None of us are to interfere with human choice, remember?"

"Unless a human chooses to pray a prayer of faith, Lucifer. I was compelled by the Most High to act—as is any assigned angel."

"But who prayed? Eve? She can hardly pray so bold a prayer as to release your authority here."

Michael smiled. "Abel prayed for his brother," he said. "You forget, Lucifer, that you can only try to *influence* the minds of men. You cannot know their minds—or know what they are thinking. Abel prayed to the Most High and I was instantly released to help him. Incidentally, it was a marvelous prayer."

Lucifer seethed as Cain began to recover from his anger. Cain stood up and began to talk calmly with Abel. Before long they embraced each other and left the place. "I'm sorry, Abel," said Cain. "I know the Lord loves me. And I don't hate you. I sometimes let my temper get the better of me."

"Next offering we'll do together," said Abel, as they walked off. The two groups of angels silently stared at one another for a moment. Finally Lucifer spoke up.

"Well done, Michael. It seems men *can* call on the Most High and cause you to act. It seems you have two masters now—God *and* the dirty humans." He walked over to Michael. "But you have taught me an important lesson today about this war. Next time I will be equally prepared."

Michael looked coldly into Lucifer's eyes for a few seconds and then disappeared. Kara turned to Lucifer with a look of concern. "I had rather hoped that Rugio would make a better effort of it," he said, watching Rugio speak with Nan over Lucifer's shoulder. "I suppose there will be other chances. Still, I might have tried something a bit more convincing."

"More convincing than your present approach, I hope," Lucifer said slyly.

Serus remained behind on Michael's orders to keep watch on the situation. He stood alone, looking at Lucifer, to whom he had once pledged loyalty. Snickering began to fill the air as Rugio and some of the other demons began harassing their former ally.

"Well, Serus," said Lucifer. "I have often wondered what my words would be to you when ever we met again."

Serus remained silent, ignoring Lucifer's comments.

"Tell me, Serus," said Kara. "How does it feel to be a traitor?"

Serus laughed. "You should know that, Kara. You betrayed so many."

"Well done, Serus," said Lucifer with an astonished tone. "You have become bold since we parted company. You would never have been so brash as to speak to one of my highest officers in such terms when you were in my service."

"That is because I am in the light now," said Serus. "I am free."

"No you're not, my misguided friend," said Lucifer. "You have exchanged one prison for another. You were worthless to me but I could have made you great. Now you are apprenticed to an archangel who will never share glory with you."

"Michael shares the glory with no angel," responded Serus. "He gives all of it to the Most High. So you see there is none to share."

"I will one day settle accounts with both of you," said Rugio, who was becoming increasingly angry. His reddish aura was beginning to manifest. "On my terms."

"That will be interesting," said Serus. "I'm sure Michael looks forward to that day." He then departed to keep watch over the human family.

"How I hate that angel," Rugio said, remembering bitterly the day that Serus had helped Michael escape Rugio's trap.

"Forget about Serus," said Lucifer. "We have a much more severe problem to deal with." He turned to Kara. "Call the council together immediately. We must take action." Kara nodded and was about to leave when Lucifer stopped him.

"Kara, despite your obvious appetite to become embroiled in this matter, I have a special assignment for you," Lucifer said, putting his hand on the former elder's shoulder. "I am removing Rugio from Cain. I know your ambition has made you eager to get into the game. Rugio is useful when force is necessary. But I need something..."

"Subtle?" offered Kara.

"Yes," said Lucifer. "And final."

"I am at your command," said Kara proudly.

The two walked on together as Lucifer continued. "Cain must be continually encouraged in his wreckless anger," he began. "It is our only hope in overcoming prayers such as Abel is capable of. In spite of this disappointing reconciliation between the two of them, you must compel him with everything in you to remain embittered toward Abel. I want a wedge driven between them so that Cain will become poisoned permanently."

Kara grinned. "I will not disappoint you."

"I am also sending along a very promising angel, who will become your assistant from this point on." Lucifer laughed. "You,

Kara, will plow the heart and mind of this tiller of the soil, and this angel I have in mind shall plant the seeds of his destruction."

"Who is this angel in whom you place such confidence?" asked Kara.

"You recall Berenius," said Lucifer. "He caused quite an uproar at the Academy of the Host—asked too many intelligent questions."

"Oh yes," said Kara. "He was one of Pellecus's favorites at the Academy. He specialized in teacher baiting as I remember."

"Yes, well, I'm leading him in a new specialty now," replied Lucifer.

"Really, and what is that?" asked Kara.

"Murder."

CHAPTER 4

"Let humans pray, so long as they are disobedient in their hearts."

Serus sat next to Eve as she stirred the evening fire. She and A'dam had discussed the events surrounding their sons' offerings and were trying to determine the best course to take. She felt badly for Cain, but was buoyed by Abel's report of the reconciliation that had occurred between the two brothers shortly afterwards.

Abel joined his mother near the fire and put his head on her shoulder, resting there. Eve looked at her husband, who smiled at her across the fire. She loved moments like this, when the family seemed together and safe—especially in the uncertain world they had made for themselves. Even Cain, who was bringing in more wood for the fire, seemed uncharacteristically good-humored. It would be a good night.

As Serus enjoyed the fellowship of the family, he thought about his own situation. How things had changed for him! While serving Lucifer in Heaven, he had been made to separate himself from the fellowship of the other angels. Now he knew of the power and importance of such community—especially when devoted to the will and purposes of the Most High God.

"Enjoying yourself?"

"Yes, Michael," said Serus, looking at the archangel who entered the camp. "I was thinking back to how I once was so lost in

Lucifer's world. I thank the Most High every day that I saw the true nature of things before it was too late."

"I only wish these poor creatures had," said Michael, indicating the family around the fire. "Things could have been so different for them." The two angels sat for a moment in silence.

"Michael, what will be Lucifer's next course?" Serus finally said, looking at the archangel to whom he was now apprenticed.

"Actually, Serus, I was going to ask that of you," answered Michael. "You knew Lucifer better than any of us. What would you suspect is going on in his mind?"

"To be sure the most significant thing that happened today was how you overcame Nan so strongly," said Serus. "I too felt Abel's prayer—but it wasn't directed at me. I mean, I wasn't compelled to act upon it for some reason."

"Serus, I can only say that as Abel prayed I sensed something building inside of me until suddenly I was released and knew exactly what must be done. It was as if the Most High Himself gave me an order upon the conclusion of that prayer. I was empowered from on high to act and I did."

"You certainly did," admitted Serus. "The look on Nan's face was unforgettable. And Lucifer didn't look too comfortable himself."

"I suspect that as this conflict goes on we will learn much as to the nature of the prayers of men and our part in them," said Michael. "But one thing must truly be unsettling for Lucifer: if humans can pray a prayer of faith that moves the heart of God and causes Him to act, or if they can pray and call angels down on their behalf…"

"Then Lucifer and his party have a whole new war on their hands," Serus said, finishing Michael's thought. "And THAT is what is on Lucifer's mind right now."

Lucifer quietly watched his leadership grasping for answers. He often wondered how he was to succeed in the war with such dissolution in the ranks. He counted on Pellecus to teach the new way of things, but even the new academy Pellecus was organizing could go only so far to indoctrinate these fallen angels. Somehow he had to clear Heaven out of their minds so they could see the potential in overcoming the enemy.

Tinius's voice finally rang above the chatter. "I don't understand this," he said. "Why was Michael able to rise up as he did on the strength of some ridiculous prayer?"

Pellecus could only grin at the idiotic question. "As usual, Tinius," said Pellecus, "you miss the point. And a very dangerous point, I might add."

The council that had convened upon Lucifer's orders was discussing a response to the earlier events. Lucifer continued to sit back and listen to his council as they discussed, deliberated, and sometimes wandered in an attempt to explain the challenge posed by Abel's prayer. Finally Lucifer stood to speak.

"One should never underestimate one's enemy," he began, "nor overestimate his own strength. It is apparent that the humans are allowed a very special grace: to call upon the Most High in their troubles. This could prove bothersome to us." He walked about the council place, this time in a deeply wooded area on a mountainside.

"Prayer is a privilege of spiritual creatures," snorted Tinius. "Why would the Most High pollute such an honor by allowing humans to pray?"

"Because, Tinius, humans *are* spiritual creatures," said Pellecus, assuming his teacher role for the council. "Oh, they have the curse of death upon them now, to be sure. But they are immortal. Their bodies will return to the stuff of earth one day, according to the judgment. But their spirits will live forever."

"In any case they can pray," said Lucifer. "And as we witnessed, when they do it effectively and in faith, however primitively, the Most High will respond. He always was one for sentiment with humans. The point is that we find ourselves contesting this disturbing weapon."

"And where do we begin?" asked Lenaes.

"The same place we always begin with humans," said Lucifer. "The mind. Let them pray. Let them pray all night if they want. Faith is the critical factor. Brothers, if we can rob the humans of their ability to pray with faith, then let them pray."

"But how can we do that?" asked Tinius.

"By cultivating another attitude that is devastating to faith," said Lucifer.

"Which is...?" queried Tinius.

"Disobedience. While it is true that the Lord honors prayers of faith, as we witnessed today, it is also true that the Lord does not honor disobedience, which we all witnessed in Eden. Humans, while spiritual creatures, have a tendency to stray."

"Disobedience certainly has its price," said Rugio. The others looked at him.

"What our chief is saying," said Pellecus, "is that God will not honor one who prays, if one is also disobedient. Let humans pray, so long as they are disobedient in their hearts. Prayer will become a meaningless expression—a pitiful call for help. They will get nowhere with the Lord; consequently Michael's efforts will be paralyzed."

"Yes, that is all well and good with people like Cain," said Rugio. "He is a brute. But what about Abel? He is a man of faith *and* obedience."

"Leave Abel to me," said Lucifer.

Cain sat on the ground to eat. He still had much to do to pre-pare for the harvest of grain that was growing bountifully in the field. He took a bite of the flat bread that his mother baked every day on the rocks by the fire. He could just make out an indentation on the bread from one of Eve's fingers. He smiled at the thought of her working the rough dough and working it into the little flat shapes that baked into this wonderful bread. He wished she were there so he could tell her that he loved her.

In the distance he heard the sound of Abel's horn, calling the flocks in. He was glad that he and Abel had come to terms and hoped that in the future they would become better brothers—even friends. Perhaps Abel really did mean well. Things were shaping up for a good future. Perhaps the next time he made an offering to God it would be acceptable.

"There he is, Berenius," said Kara.

"He doesn't look to be the brute that Lucifer made him out to be," said Berenius, looking at Cain. "He even appears quite content."

"He's a brute alright," said Kara. "As are all humans ultimate-ly. And we are to bring it out of him."

The two angels walked over toward Cain and began circling him. Kara kept a careful watch for any of Michael's angels as they steadily brought the circle in closer to Cain. Whispering as they walked, Kara began feeding thoughts into Cain's mind, hoping one would attach itself.

Cain caught himself thinking back to the previous day's events. Abel was very generous to offer that they build an altar together next time. He was fortunate to have so understanding a brother as not to shame him. Still Abel had been a bit smug the way he remarked that Cain was not a man of faith. "I am a man of faith," Cain reasoned. Just because he expressed it differently didn't mean he had no regard for the Lord.

After all, Cain was the firstborn —his rightful place of authority superceded Abel's and always would. Yet Abel found himself accepted and Cain the firstborn was rejected. Maybe Abel knew all along that the fruit of the ground would be rejected, and wanted to make the firstborn son look foolish. Abel always did have a smug attitude—especially in things regarding the Lord.

Kara smiled as he sensed Cain's anger beginning to well up. He continued to pummel Cain with accusations about his brother, whispering into his mind how Abel was secretly enjoying Cain's embarrassment. Berenius encouraged Kara in his relentless attack. Finally Cain stood up and cursed out loud.

"Excellent, my lord," said Berenius. "In a moment I'll begin to work on him."

"Abel has always been an obstacle to me," Cain said aloud. He threw a rock at one of his melons, breaking it open.

"Aha!" said Berenius. "There is the door for me, Kara. He said it himself—the obstacle must be removed! If this doesn't lead to murder I'll be a holy angel!"

Kara stepped back as Berenius moved in close to Cain, taking hold of his broad shoulders and whispering into his ear: "Abel will always be an obstacle. You will never be honored as long as he is permitted to run amuck and ruin your life. He tricked you, you know. He knew your offering would be rejected..."

Cain's face was growing reddish-purple as he thought about his brother allowing him to be made a fool of. "He knew," Cain muttered under his breath. Berenius looked at Kara and smirked, and continued the assault.

"You foul spirits," came a voice. "Is there no end to your deception?"

Kara turned to see Michael, with Serus and Gabriel standing behind him.

"No prayers this time, archangel?" Kara asked. "Pity. Berenius is doing a marvelous job inciting this creature to a rather poor decision."

Michael's instincts were to move in and crush this spectacle immediately. But, and Kara was correct, without the prayers that gave him consent to act, or without special instruction from the Most High, he could only watch. Kara found it delicious.

"And you, Serus, were given charge over this man?" Kara continued. "How dreadful that you will soon have blood on your hands."

Serus glared at Kara.

"I think we've made quite a bit of progress," said Berenius, backing away from Cain. "Just a little more and he will be choosing. These creatures can only take so much suggestion before their small minds are drowned in what appears to be the only choice available to them."

Cain's face was contorted and angry. He began walking away from the field. Berenius followed. As they neared the edge of the field Berenius suddenly lurched forward and fell to the ground as if pinned there. He was shrieking violently, and then suddenly still and quiet. The other angels watched in confused horror.

"*Cain,*" came a Voice.

Kara also fell to the ground, paralyzed with fear. Michael, Gabriel, and Serus, fearing the Voice in a different way, bowed in humble adoration of their God.

"*Cain.*"

Cain turned to see a bright light all around him. He could barely make out the figure of a man inside the intense brilliance. Berenius could only lie still, unable to make a sound even if he wanted to.

"*Why are you angry?*" said the Lord.

Cain was so frightened that he could not even speak. He stood in shock, shielding his eyes from the bright light.

"*Why is your face so downcast? Don't you see that if you do what is right and proper, you also will be accepted? But I must warn you, that if you do not do what is right, sin already is lying at your feet, ready to strike at you!*"

Upon these words Berenius was picked up by an overwhelming force and thrown down at Cain's feet. He struggled but again became immobile and speechless.

"The sin at your feet desires to have you—to deceive you and cause you to stumble. But you must master it."

Cain looked down, afraid to look further at the Lord's figure in the light. Had he been able, he would have seen a squirming Berenius directly in front of him. "You must master it, Cain, or it will master you."

Suddenly the light was gone and the voice disappeared. Berenius left with a shriek and disappeared into the earth. Kara protested, "Unfair! Unfair!" and quickly vanished. Michael, Gabriel, and Serus were alone with Cain, hoping that he would consider the Lord's words to Him.

"Will he relent?" asked Serus. "Or did Berenius plant the seed too deeply?"

"I hope for all humans that he will choose well," said Gabriel. "But we have seen in the past how well humans choose."

"I tell you it was the Lord Himself," said an exasperated Kara. "How long can we contend if He keeps interfering?"

Lucifer, Rugio, Pellecus, and Kara were gathered in another frustrating strategy session. All were silent except Kara, who recounted the events with Cain. "It was all going so well," he continued. "Berenius was doing a masterful job and Cain was seething. Michael and Gabriel were completely helpless. Nobody was praying, as I could tell. And then the Most High stepped in to interfere."

"Yes, how dare He?" asked Pellecus with mock outrage at Kara's babbling. He looked at Kara. "He is, after all, sovereign. Unpredictable, but sovereign."

"How like the Most High to interfere and counter our suggestions," Lucifer agreed. "We are fighting according to the rules. But as Pellecus points out, God is sovereign and can adjust the rules as He sees fit."

"But even God cannot interfere with Cain's ability to choose," said Pellecus hopefully. "That is our advantage. I believe that in the end Cain's low character will carry the day. We must remain vigilant."

"Agreed," said Lucifer. "The battle is in the choosing. Until the choice is made the outcome is still in doubt."

"So what do we do?" asked Kara. "If the Lord interferes every time we are suggesting to a human…"

"We must keep at it," said Lucifer. "Day and night we will hammer the humans. And should the Lord speak to their hearts we will seek to undo the damage He does by continuing a persistent, relentless attack. In short, we must wear the humans down."

"And they do wear down," said Pellecus. "As they proved in Eden."

Michael and Gabriel were in the Great City, walking down one of the many avenues that crisscrossed a wide boulevard in front of the Temple of the Most High. All of Heaven was thundering the news of God's intervention and hailing it a great victory for the Lord. Only Gabriel and a few others knew that the battle was far from over—or won.

"The Lord has called an assembly of all the elders and archangels," said Gabriel. "The Most High will deliver through the Chief Elder the new protocol in dealing with humans. It will then be disseminated throughout the Academy and become a part of the Host's new disposition in the war."

"The war," repeated Michael. "What odd words in Heaven. Who would ever have thought it would actually come to war?"

Gabriel looked at the Great Mountain of the North, the Most Holy Place where the Lord's Presence resided. "Who would have thought an angel capable of rebellion in this place? Yet it has happened. Who would have thought a human capable of rebelling in a place like Eden? Again, it happened. Short of God Himself, nothing is true, sure, or right." He smiled at his friend, Michael. "And that is why I am happy here in Heaven. In the end Lucifer must know that he cannot win. At least I believe that to be so."

They arrived at the Hall of Elders, where Michael and Gabriel seated themselves among the other high-ranking angels of Heaven. Many of these were recently appointed, having assumed the positions vacated by the angels who sided with Lucifer. Michael nodded at Crispin, who sat across the vast room with the other wisdom angels from the Academy of the Host. Crispin returned the nod cordially. Both Michael and Gabriel noted that the normally animated chatter among the angels was subdued.

The Chief Elder appeared on the dais with the full Council of Twenty-four and called the assembly to order. He then addressed the assembly.

"Most holy angels, greetings," the Chief Elder began. "I wish this were a different setting and that happy tidings brought us together here. But, as is evident by the new faces among you, there are some who have abandoned their sacred places in Heaven, thinking they might achieve some measure of glory on the earth. I assure you all that the only glory in Heaven and on earth is the that of the Lord Most High, holy be His name!"

"Most holy is His name," the angels said in unison.

"Nevertheless, the Lord Most High, in His infinite foresight and care for His creation, has instructed us as to our new disposition, and particularly how we are to respond to our former brothers, as well as to the fallen humans. I realize that there have been instances wherein some of those who have departed have actually approached the very gates of Heaven, some cajoling and mocking, others begging forgiveness and asking to return to their former duties. I must remind you that no unwarranted contact is to be made with any of these disgraced creatures."

He looked down among the crowd at a few angels in particular, who had had conversation with some of the outlaw angels across the gulf of the heavenlies. "I too am deeply moved by the loss of so many who once walked freely among us—who chose unwisely and profanely. Some of these very angels sat with me on the Council." He indicated the elders stationed behind him.

"They are no longer our brothers," he continued. "They are the enemies of our Lord, therefore the enemies of this Kingdom, and are to be despised."

The Chief Elder watched the effect of his words and then continued. "I shall now give instruction to the entire Host from the Most Holy Throne regarding these matters. It is our sworn and holy duty to disseminate this throughout the kingdom to our charges, so that all the Host will be in one voice and mind in the matter of how we are now disposed to our former brothers..."

Chronicles of the Host

A New Order in Heaven

A strange melancholy came over the hall as the Chief Elder spoke. It was a morose feeling, born of an understanding among the Host of how things had changed in Heaven. Indeed, those angels who remained loyal to the Most High now found themselves in a most unimaginable position—at war with a third of the Host!

The war was to be conducted on earth as well as in the heavenlies. On earth, the battle for the minds and hearts of men was to be waged through men's prayers and their willingness to call upon the Lord. In the heavenlies, a far more brual and violent conflict was in store as angel fought against angel in a grueling struggle that pitted the faith of men against the doctrines of demons.

And so it was that through the disgrace of A'dam, a second unholy age was unleashed upon creation. And for all the battles waged, and for all the angels cast down, and for all the power that Heaven could muster, the progress of the war was not to be determined by angels, but by men whose freedom to choose had already borne a horrible price...

CHAPTER 5

"How odd it is in Heaven these days."

Serus observed the Host as they left the assembly. Many of the angels who held positions of authority were grouped together in the hall, discussing the day's events and strategizing how best to deploy their legions when the war became more active. Others left the great hall, nodding encouragement to one another, speaking kind words that might deaden the sting of war.

"We need a recording of this for the Chronicles," came the familiar voice of Crispin from behind. Serus turned to see the scholarly angel, who had recently been appointed head of the Academy of the Host, giving orders to his new apprentices. "And please be careful with the text—I want this verbatim. This is war, after all!"

"Yes, my lord," said the exasperated angel whose duties to Crispin kept him busy indeed. "I have it all down in detail."

"Very good, Sarbus," said Crispin. "You are learning well!" Crispin smiled and looked over toward Serus. "Ah Serus," he said, waving. "Such extraordinary times, hmm? Sarbus, I'll see you at the Academy. Remember, one of these goes in the Hall of Records, one in the Great Library, and one in my study."

"Sarbus nodded in servile agreement and hurried away. Serus grinned at the angel's plight.

"Your apprentice reminds me of my time as Lucifer's apprentice," said Serus, baiting Crispin for one of his typically understated reactions.

"What? Are you comparing me to Lucifer?" blustered Crispin. "When I think of how shamelessly he ordered you about I am still appalled. That dark angel had you in chains that blinded you to his true nature. Besides all of that..." Crispin caught himself and smiled. "Don't you know it is improper to make a wisdom angel appear unwise?"

"You shall never appear unwise, Crispin," called out a voice from above.

Serus and Crispin looked up to see Sangius descending upon them. He embraced both of the angels, and they walked together through the magnificent doorway to the outside. They descended the stairs that opened onto the great square and then stopped suddenly as Crispin began talking.

"How odd it is in Heaven these days," he said as he surveyed the sea of angels pouring out of the hall. Serus understood exactly what Crispin was feeling at that precise moment. How very different this departure from the great hall was compared to that glorious day when the Creation was announced and the angels were dancing and singing throughout the Kingdom.

"It was certainly a different occasion when we met here last," agreed Sangius.

"I was at the Academy at the time," remembered Crispin. "I was talking to Michael." He smiled. "He was concerned that there was something afoot with Lucifer. How right he was." Serus and Sangius looked at Crispin in solemn agreement.

They continued through the square, down a wide pavilion that led through an ever-flowering garden and into a meadow where Crispin often found solitude from his duties at the Academy. They sat alongside a still pool of crystal water. After a few moments of silence, Sangius broke the reverie.

"Crispin," he began, "what does it all mean. I mean...what does this war mean to us angels?" Crispin thought about his answer for a bit and then looked at Sangius in a tender, almost fatherly way.

"What does it mean?" he repeated. "It means that our Lord shall lead us into a great conflict and will prevail. War means that you and I and every other angel loyal to the Most High will be engaged in some measure to ensure that His plans are carried out to the fullest extent. Every angel shall be called upon, to be sure. War means we have a responsibility unlike any other, all the time that angels have been in existence. It also means that we shall engage humans in a new responsibility as well."

As Crispin spoke, more and more angels gathered around him. Being one of the greatest teachers in the Kingdom, he was accustomed to this sort of behavior among the Host. Many of his students had become great teachers at the Academy in their own right, instructing the angels on the knowledge and ministry of the Most High. But Crispin was something extraordinary and whenever he spoke he drew attention to those wise enough to give a listen.

"I could not help but notice that as I spoke the word 'humans' many of you grimaced," he said, surveying the many faces surrounding him.

"Well, they did complicate things a bit," said an angel from the back of the crowd. Others joined in with affirming remarks.

"A'dam's transgression certainly did complicate things," agreed Crispin. "But that is not our concern. Our concern is the conveyance of this war to the enemy. Our foes are well organized and motivated. They are also cunning and ruthless and, as we all know too well, led by a very capable angel who has surrounded himself with strong leadership. Lucifer understands, as we do, that their only hope lies in destroying or deceiving the humans and preventing the Seed of the woman from ever bringing forth the One who will crush the serpent's head."

"But the humans know that God has promised their deliverance through Eve," said Kamas, an assistant to one of the Elders. "Why should they believe anything that Lucifer's angels would tell them?"

"Because humans are in essence spirits and therefore susceptible to spiritual persuasions," said Crispin. "Oh, I know they are cloaked in flesh and blood and that the judgment of death is upon them. But in the end, they are spirit."

"So we as angels must deal with them as spirits?" asked Sangius with a puzzled look upon his face. "How can that be? If they are judged and shall die, how can we help them? Can a spirit die?"

Crispin smiled. "If I understand correctly, they have doomed the physical natures that the Lord created. This is quite clear since the Lord said they should return to the dust from which they came."

The gentle teacher had a quizzical expression as if he was still sorting it out himself. He turned to Sangius with a hopeful look. "But somehow their spirits must survive. They are immortal. So what shall become of A'dam—the true A'dam, which is his spiritual nature made in God's image? This is something better left to the Lord's wisdom."

As the impromptu meeting continued, the subject changed to the more practical and yet tricky subject of the conduct of the war itself. All agreed that they would serve the Lord in whatever capacity they were called—even if it meant open strife with their fallen brothers. Word had spread throughout the Kingdom of the power of human prayer and how such prayer would be an important factor in angelic involvement. It was evident that when prayer was born out of a true acknowledgment of the Most High and belief in His ability and desire to provide such help, that the Lord responded.

But as to the nature of prayer, the angels wondered what limits the Lord might set upon human supplication. The humans had blatantly violated the trust of the Most High and willfully disobeyed Him. Were the angels now to help them out of the catastrophe they had created? Still, the mysterious connection between the Lord Most High and these creatures made in His image was astounding. It was not the duty of angels to question the Lord in such matters but to obey Him. And so spoke Crispin.

"From here on the concern of the Host is serving the Lord in this matter," he admonished. "If that means ministry to humans then that shall be our sacred calling. Our rather difficult challenge is that in their rebellion they have relinquished spiritual sensibilities to base and earthly impulses."

"Poor choices often lead to worse ones, hmm," came Michael's voice over the crowd. The angels dispersed and made a pathway for the archangel as he glided in to greet Crispin. Michael loved his former teacher and was not at all surprised to see him in the familiar role of interpreting events to others. He embraced Crispin warmly.

"To be sure, poor choices often escalate as we have seen here in the Kingdom," Crispin responded. "Lucifer might have stopped himself at any moment had he wanted to. A'dam might never have disobeyed had he truly not wanted to. In either case, both choices proved prideful and disastrous."

Just as he finished speaking the sound of trumpets blasted through Heaven, calling every angel to his designated commander.

Michael watched as the angels around Crispin dispersed, each to his
own legion in readiness for the same briefing that Crispin had been
alluding to all along: a call to war. It was with satisfaction that
Michael observed his angels in action—dedicated, loyal, and dutiful. Crispin caught the pleasure on Michael's countenance.

"You have trained them well, Michael," said Crispin. "They
are an efficient organization to wage war in the name of the Most
High."

"Perhaps," agreed Michael. "I am honored by their obedience.
But I wish that the need for such a mobilization had never
occurred."

"The war will be won by our Lord," said Crispin. "This we all
know."

"Yes," said Serus, who had been silently observing the dialogue between Michael and Crispin. "But when will Eve's child rise
up? At what point will the prophecy be fulfilled?"

"That is a puzzle, Serus," said Crispin, smiling at Serus's
recently discovered knack for asking pointed questions."Let's take
it up in my quarters."

They began walking toward the Academy. Since Serus was
attached to Michael personally, he did not need to attend a commander elsewhere as did the other angels. Sangius bade the group
farewell and departed for his duties at the Temple. The three angels
made their way down the now deserted pathway and into the
Academy. They didn't speak until they found themselves in
Crispin's study deep in the heart of the complex. This was always a
favorite spot for discussions and Crispin looked forward to such
moments.

"Now Serus, you had a question about the prophecy," said
Crispin. "But rather than give you my opinion I would like to hear
yours." He sat up in his chair and continued. "What do *you* think
will be the outcome of the prophecy? When will Eve's child 'rise
up,' as you put it earlier?" Crispin settled back in his chair and
awaited the response. He always enjoyed getting his students to
think through things for themselves. Michael smiled at Serus's
quandary.

"Well, obviously the Most High knows when and where the
Seed should come," Serus began. "And He is in control of the
prophecy. So at His time and choosing the one who shall crush the
serpent will arrive!"

"I could not have reasoned it out any better myself," applauded Crispin.

"But I didn't answer the question," said Serus with a bemused look.

"But you did," said Crispin. "The time and fulfillment of prophecy is a matter too lofty for mere angels. Ours is to help the humans expedite the prophecy in a way and manner of our Lord's choosing."

"Humans!" said an exasperated Serus. "That we should be allied with such capricious spirits! If we must depend upon the will of men to win this war we are defeated already—prophecy or not!"

Crispin smiled. "True, Serus. If we were to depend on men for *anything* as to the successful conclusion of this war we would be beaten already. Fortunately, we are dependent upon neither men *nor* angels."

"Either way, it seems quite obvious that of Eve's two children Abel shows some promise," interjected Michael. "Perhaps Abel will end this nonsense once and for all."

Before the others could respond, a figure appeared in the entryway. It was Gabriel. He stood there silently.

"Ah Gabriel, come in" said Crispin. "We were just discussing which of Eve's children might be the vanquisher of Lucifer."

"Abel seems a distinct possibility," said Michael. "At least he seems to have a true devotion to the Lord." He looked hopefully at Gabriel. "Don't you think Abel might be the one foretold?"

"I'm afraid not, my brother," said Gabriel sullenly. "Abel has been murdered."

Kara and some of his angels stood around Abel's cold body lying face down in the field. The back of Abel's head was encrusted with dirt, blood, brown straws of grass, and grains of wheat, evidence of the brutal attack he had suffered at the hands of Cain. Berenius congratulated Kara on the subtlety and success of the effort. Kara acknowledge the praise and remarked that with Abel out of the way, Cain should prove no hindrance to them.

"I would even say that the prophecy has been reduced to a shadow," Kara said smugly. "If the Seed must come through humans such as this, we have already won!"

More and more wicked angels gathered around the carnage. A few holy angels scouted out the situation, but they remained largely away from the area, sorrowful at man's ability to kill one of his own so readily. As the demons chattered among themselves, feeling better and better about their prospects now that Abel had been killed, Lucifer arrived with Pellecus to survey the scene.

"Well done, Cain," Lucifer finally said. "I knew that your brutal side could be exploited. It was only a matter of time."

"My lord," interrupted Kara. "I would like to add that Berenius and even I had a part to play in this victory. We were constantly speaking into Cain's mind thoughts of murder."

"Ah Kara," said Lucifer. "Ever desirous of glory. Yes, you and Berenius played a role in this matter. But it was Cain who chose. Remember that! If there is one thing we have learned in this war thus far, it is that humans ultimately will choose of their own free will. We can provide encouragement; we can inflame passions; but the choice to act is their own. We only have them when they surrender their complete will."

"The Lord made that quite clear when he tossed Berenius at Cain's feet like a pitiful newborn calf," said Pellecus, smirking. Berenius looked at Kara, who could manage only a scowl.

"Sin was indeed crouching at Cain's door...but the sin mastered him," Lucifer said, as everyone laughed aloud. He looked at Abel's remains. "And now Abel is dead."

Lucifer knelt down and touched Abel's cold face. He sat in this position for a moment and then looked up at the bewildered expressions around him. Finally he said, "You really should feel death. As I felt it in Eden when the serpent died. Death, brothers, is our ultimate weapon in this war. Death is what we are waging for. By defeating the Lord's plan at Eden we have become the caretakers of death. Each of you must learn of death...how it feels...how it comes. Whatever carnality we can evoke in men, it means nothing if it does not ultimately result in death."

He looked at one angel in particular. "Pellecus?" said Lucifer.

"Yes, lord," answered Pellecus, lulled out of an almost trance-like fixation on the body of Abel. "What is it?"

"You are always one to learn something new," continued Lucifer. "If you are going to administer the academy here on earth, you must acquaint yourself with death." He looked hard at Pellecus.

"For I assure you this is only the first of many crimes among men, and we must have a fellowship with death if we are to exploit it."

Pellecus hesitated for a bit, then walked over to Abel and bent down close to the body. After looking it over he knew what Lucifer wanted, and he suddenly entered into the corpse. Kara and the others stood back as if they were expecting something frightening to happen, but were unsure exactly what it might be. In a moment Pellecus emerged from Abel's body.

"Well?" purred Lucifer. "What did you learn, teacher?"

"Death is cold and dark," said Pellecus, a bit shaken but exhilarated at the same time. "It is void and empty. And it transforms quickly." He indicated Abel's body and assumed the role of a teacher giving a lesson in class. "Notice how quickly these humans begin returning to dust. Already Abel is changing in appearance. While inside his form, I could sense the decay already beginning. His physical makeup was breaking down rapidly. And there was nothing of the spirit in him at all. What inferior creatures are these humans!" Pellecus looked back at Lucifer and said in a matter-of-fact way, "Well, back to the dust with him!"

"And with all humans!" agreed Lucifer. "But let me demonstrate something even more remarkable—and useful to us in the future, I believe."

Lucifer vanished and left the others wondering at his behavior. They continued in quiet chatter, commenting upon Abel's murder and drawing a variety of conclusions as to its ultimate effect on the war. Kara was about to make further comment when an astonished look overcame him. He pointed across the field at a figure ambling toward them—the figure of Abel.

The angels looked at the body on the ground. It had not moved. The figure continued toward them and came to stop just at the edge of the meadow where they stood. The figure was semi-transparent, a spirit-like replica of the real Abel but with a bluish-white aura streaking about him. Pellecus smiled, realizing what was happening. The puzzled angels looked at each other in amazement as the pseudo-Abel transformed before their eyes back into Lucifer.

"Ah Kara," Lucifer said. "The look on your face betrayed your surprise."

"Naturally," admitted Kara. "I was not expecting to see Abel again—not alive anyway."

"And you didn't see him alive," said Lucifer. "You saw him dead...so to speak."

"I don't really understand," said Kara, feeling flustered for having been taken in by the specter of Abel. "Why should we encourage humans after such a loss by creating an illusion of a visitation from death?"

"Really Kara, you disappoint me," said Pellecus, exasperated. "We shall use anything to get the human mind off the Most High. That is the point!"

"Precisely," said Lucifer, who noticed the other angels listening to their conversation. He led Kara and Pellecus away from them and continued talking. "It occurs to me that despite the material nature of the battlefield, the war itself will be fought and won on a spiritual plane. Thus whatever spiritual deceptions we devise will ultimately be decisive."

"Why so?" asked Kara. "These creatures are incited through material passion. I should think that we would exploit their material tendencies."

"Humans are spiritual creatures, Kara," said Lucifer. He casually plucked a ripened piece of fruit that hung low on a branch. "They are spiritual creatures with a weakness for a good argument." He held the fruit in front of them and smiled. "Just as in Eden." He smirked and tossed it away.

"Remember that," he continued. "Of course we shall exploit every carnal desire that we can arouse in these filthy creatures. And though we can inflame human passion through physical senses, as you and Berenius did with Cain, nevertheless it is through the godlike freedom to choose that the battle shall be won. Choosing is a very spiritual discipline born out of the image of God given to men. A very tarnished image indeed."

Pellecus continued the dialogue. "Therefore, whatever we can do to distract humans from looking to the Most High will be useful. We shall have them looking everywhere but upward for their deliverance!" He laughed at the thought of it.

"Imagine," Pellecus continued, "the confusion we will be able to create by having humans believe they can be comforted from their fallen dead; or to have them make contact with benevolent spirits who appear to them in a friendly light of instruction, only to deceive them. Think of the potential in having humans worship our appearances because of a few simple manipulations of earthly elements."

"I promised all of you that you would be as gods on this world," said Lucifer. "The weakness of the human mind is ripe for deception!"

As they spoke, Rugio, the unquestioned commander of the warrior angels loyal to Lucifer, suddenly appeared before the group. Lucifer nodded at his commander as the group exchanged greetings.

"So Rugio, my valiant commander, how is the bloodstained brother?" Lucifer asked, placing a hand on Rugio's broad shoulder.

"He is in hiding, my lord," said Rugio. "Near the old encampment that he and his family once frequented."

"It seems that we can always count on humans trying to hide after they commit an indiscretion," mused Lucifer. "Of course he comes by it quite naturally, what with his parents trying to hide in Eden under the very face of God." The group burst out laughing. "I'm sure Eve will be quite astonished that it came to murder."

"She searches for him now," said Rugio. "Abel's flocks are scattered and she is afraid for her sons. A'dam too."

Lucifer looked solidly at the group. "She will fear much more than this in due course. There is far more at stake here than a dead son—and that is a dead dream. With Abel dies the only possible hope of this generation for the Seed to emerge."

"Until or unless Eve bears another child," agreed Pellecus. "They were commanded to fill the earth with their vermin, you know."

"Nevertheless Cain is useless to the prophecy," said Lucifer.

Before he could finish his thought, the very air around them became violent, and the earth itself seemed to wrench, throwing the group of rebel angels into confusion and forcing them to the ground. Lucifer tried to regain himself and determine what was happening. Rugio assumed they were under attack by Michael and his angels. Kara sat up stupefied. Pellecus simply waited until it was all over.

When the incident abated, Lucifer observed something very peculiar. He realized that though he and the others were greatly affected by the sudden outbreak of activity, the world around them was completely unscathed—even to the point that a fawn and her mother nearby continued nibbling on the same tender grass on which they had been nibbling immediately before the shakeup.

"Something extraordinary is happening," he finally said in a whispered tone.

As he began to make more comment, a long, low, horrible groaning sound pierced the air around them, paralyzing them with fear and wonder. The sound came from everywhere and yet from nowhere: a wailing, passionate sound as if the earth itself was groaning a horrible outcry heard only in the invisible, angelic world. Once more the physical world remained oblivious. When it was over Lucifer stood up in deep thought, attempting an understanding of what had just happened. Then he smiled at the others.

"Even the earth itself speaks to the crimes of men and angels," he said in a sullen tone. "Nature itself is a player in this little drama of ours."

"What was it?" asked Kara nervously.

"That was the blood of Abel," said Lucifer, "crying out for justice."

The sun wore on Cain as he walked through the land. He had long ago departed any familiar territory and had strayed deeply into lands that he and his family had never before traversed. He was hungry and very thirsty. But he continued eastward, away from his home, away from his parents. He was very alone.

The sound of a distant babbling creek buoyed his spirits, and with a newfound energy he bounded down a gently sloping hill to a small stream at the bottom. He half fell in, lapping the cool water greedily. After filling himself he sat up on the bank, reflecting on his prospects.

He was tired of running, to be sure. But he really had no place to go. He couldn't possibly return to his grieving parents. Neither did he wish to face the world alone. But he was a fugitive—running from God just like A'dam and Eve had done so many years before in Eden. How often he had heard the shameful story told by his parents when he was growing up. And just as often, he and Abel had agreed that they should never be in a position of running away from God.

He had traveled several days' journey from the place where he had killed his brother. The farther away he was from that horrible spot, the better he felt. But he knew in his heart that no matter how far he ran, the confrontation he had had with the Lord would forever be with him…

"Where is your brother Abel?"

Why must He play with me like that, Cain thought. *Why doesn't He simply kill me and be done with it?* Every night since the killing, Cain had not been able to sleep. He dreamed horrible dreams recounting the murder; he heard his brother's voice crying out to him. In a dreamy state he saw himself standing before the Lord, asking him, "How would I know that? Am I responsible for Abel?"

"What have you done?"

"Leave me alone!" Cain screamed.

In an instant his mind was flooded with the very words that his father said the Lord had spoken to him on that dark day in Eden, "A'dam, where are you? What have you done?" Now it was the son's turn to face a God whose will he had transgressed…

Cain looked at his reflection in the brook. He could not see the faces of Sangius, Serus, and Archias, a newly arrived angel from Heaven, looking down on him from the other side of the stream. What he did see was the mark of a fugitive, placed upon him by the Lord, that branded him a murderer and warned others not to kill him. Cain looked upon the mark and began to weep bitterly.

Serus looked at Archias, who had been sent to begin training in the ways of men on earth. Sangius shook his head in pity.

"One son murdered, one son branded a criminal," Sangius finally remarked as they watched Cain sobbing. "You are certainly getting an education in the manner of men, Archias."

"Yes," admitted Archias. "What an inglorious beginning."

Serus watched the sun disappearing over the high bluff to the west. "I just hope it isn't the end," he said somberly.

CHAPTER 6

"How disappointed Eve must be!"

Chronicles of the Host

Darkness and Light

True to the Lord's command, the children of A'dam and Eve multiplied into a very healthy human population. They grew remarkably in numbers, speaking the same language, forming one large, loosely-aligned society of tribes. Some founded cities or became herdsmen, while others reached inside themselves and became inventors or musicians. Thus did human culture wax stronger and stronger.

But as is the way with men, even as their culture flourished, so did their corruption. Even Seth's promising heritage was tainted over time. Men and women, who carried in them the image of God, who once called upon the name of the Lord, now cursed it. All of humanity had degraded itself to the point that day and night evil and vile thoughts were all that men contemplated.

For their part, Lucifer's angels had not been inactive all these years. They had sharpened their skills in tempting men, and in arousing unnatural passions within them. They had become experts in enticements that opened carnal possibilities among humans. Anger, lust, greed, idolatry, sorcery—all of these were encouraged among men, who then used their freedom to choose as a license to indulge their base natures.

So, a bloody trail marked the progress of humans, until now, as the council came together, it seemed that any chances of the Seed emerging in this sin-ravaged world was remote indeed. Some of those closest to Lucifer dared privately to believe that they would soon be positioned to force a compromise upon the Lord.

"How disappointed Eve must be that her hope in Seth was so wasted," Kara said, announcing his arrival at the council. He took his place around the large, black obsidian table that served as Lucifer's war room. "I hear that they are so compromised that one can hardly tell them from Cain's wretched line. Delightful!"

"Sons of God indeed," echoed Berenius.

"Truly it is remarkable how quickly these righteous ones have turned," agreed Pellecus, who continued his thought that had been interrupted by Kara's entrance. "As I was saying, these proud Sethites who presumed to call themselves the 'sons of God' failed to take into consideration the rather damaging qualities of the daughters of men. I'm afraid they have poisoned themselves utterly!" He smiled.

Kara sneered. "What Seed of prophecy could we possibly fear coming from these carnal freaks?" he asked, looking at the others in the room. "Surely the war is nearing an end. Man has failed the Lord dismally. He must be able to see it."

"It does appear that corruption begets only corruption where men are concerned," mused Pellecus.

"My agents have failed to find any sign of the coming one," Kara continued. "All they have witnessed is our seducing spirits at work among them. Sons of God indeed! I pity the deliverer who comes from this race. We need not fear any man!"

"Except one," said Lucifer, entering the cavern that served as his council place. The others rose to greet their leader and hail him as an impending conqueror.

"You are all fools to believe that this war is nearing an end," Lucifer said, as he seated himself at the rock table. "Mark me.

Somewhere among these perverse and fallen creatures the prophecy lives. We must remain alert."

"Perhaps," admitted Pellecus. "But you must admit, my lord,
that as humankind continues to be degraded the likelihood of something holy being born from something so rotten is diminished."

"Pellecus, you disappoint me," said Lucifer with a smug tone.
"Humans lost their holiness in Eden. Wherever and whenever the
Seed emerges, it shall come from something that is human and
therefore unholy." He looked squarely at the faces of the council.
"But I must admit that I am a bit puzzled. While it is true that
humanity is finished morally, it is also true that the Seed lives
somewhere among them."

"So you believe that God will choose among these men, in
spite of their rebellion?" asked Kara.

"No, Kara," replied Lucifer. "I believe He has already chosen."

"*Noah.*"

Noah looked up from mending the leg of one of his flock that
had been attacked by some wild dogs. There was nobody near. He
shook his head and went back to tending the lamb. He released it
with an "off you go now," and it took ginger steps toward the sound
of its mother's bleating. Noah smiled as he watched.

"*Noah.*"

This time the Voice came with more authority. Noah was certain that he heard it this time. He stood up and looked about.
Nobody.

"Hello?" he asked very softly, feeling a bit foolish. "Shem? Is
that you? Who is it?" He turned a circle as he spoke. "What do you
want?"

The angels watched in amazement as Creator and creature
spoke together about the grim reality of what God intended to do.
They watched as Noah's face, almost glowing in the light of the
Presence, belied his shock and fear. He was listening as one who
was trying to determine if it was all a dream, but coming to the
dreadful conclusion that it was all very real. Then as quickly as it
came, the light vanished and Noah was once more alone.

He looked around as if he was glad nobody else saw his encounter, and then hurried off to call his family together. Two angels immediately appeared at Noah's side—powerful looking warriors—who took up guardian stances around the man whose mission it was to save himself and his family from the coming judgment.

Serus and Archias were trying to determine who these new angels were. Their belts indicated that they were attached to Michael's command. Serus surmised that they had been assigned to Noah to protect him. The cold, steely eyes of these newly arrived sentinels spoke volumes to any who dared to interfere with Noah's mission.

They watched as Noah disappeared toward the bit of land he farmed, his angelic companions staying right with him. Serus was about to comment when Michael appeared next to them. Archias bowed his head in respect for the archangel. Serus nodded as well, but in a more familiar way.

"Well, it's begun," said Michael, hands on his hips, his brilliant sword sheathed in the golden belt about him. "It's begun."

"I noticed two of your angels are assigned to the man," said Serus. "Quinron, was one of them, I believe..."

"Yes," said Michael. "And Tassius. Those two are charged with keeping watch over Noah and protecting him."

"You think he is in danger?" asked Archias. Serus smirked, but Michael answered the rather naïve question with great tact.

"Archias, I set you with Serus so you might observe the ways of men," he began. "What have you learned about them?"

Archias thought about it for a few moments. He searched Serus's face for an answer. Serus simply looked back, stone-faced, and not a little relieved that Michael had not asked him the same question. Finally Archias spoke up.

"Well, I have learned that most men are driven by their passions. They seem insatiable and incredibly carnal. Yet I know they are made in the image of the Most High. So I have learned that men are unpredictable creatures, capricious and vain and..."

"And worthy to be spared?" asked Michael.

"Some of them, perhaps," Archias answered guardedly. "At least this one is deemed worthy enough by the Lord that you have set two warring angels over him."

"Exactly," said Michael. "The Lord has determined a great course that involves this man Noah. I suspect that the enemy will be aware of this very soon. He will seek to destroy or stop Noah in the task God has given him. It falls to the Host to protect him."

"Seems simple enough," piped in Serus.

At that moment a man stumbled nearby, very drunk. The man had matted hair and a vacant blackness in his eyes. Muttering to himself, he sat down on a large rock near where the angels stood. Behind him, two raucous devils appeared, laughing and sneering at the sight of Serus and Archias. When they saw Michael they sobered up for just a moment and became more cautious in their approach. They stood next to the drunken man, who was their assigned charge.

The man yawned a smelly, drunkish yawn, completely unaware that he was sitting among five invisible beings. The angels stared at each other. Suddenly the devils burst out in a shriek of laughter that would have unnerved Archias had not Michael been there.

"Well are you now called devils," said Michael. "For you are indeed slandering spirits who demean all that is created of the Most High God."

"What, *this* wonderful creature?" said Errus, one of the devils. He pointed to the man, who was leaning heavily to one side in the warmth of the sun. "Image of God, indeed! We are merely expediters of something already in the man's heart. Give way, archangel. You have no authority here!"

The other devil growled under his breath and looked at Archias. "What are you staring at?" he demanded. "Your God is responsible for this, not us. He made these detestable animals."

Archias didn't answer.

"True," admitted Michael. "Our authority is limited to the scope of the will of men for now. But that sword cuts both ways. And should this man ever call upon the Lord, we shall respond in his defense at your peril." Michael's sword began to shimmer slightly as he finished.

The devils glanced at the sword in Michael's belt, remembering his deft usage of it when they were forced from Heaven. He certainly had had authority *that* day!

"No doubt, no doubt," said Errus. "But on the day that this one calls upon the Lord I will carry your sword for you!" They burst out laughing again as the man slumped to the ground, very much passed out. "He doesn't even know his own name, much less the Lord's! Isn't that true, Jimerel?"

"When will you angels learn that the will of men is broken?" Jimerel demanded of Michael. "You are finished. Earth is ours and men are no longer interested in God."

"Yes, men's wills are weak," admitted Michael. "But there will come a day, and your master fears it, when a man shall be born whose will is not the will of men but of the Most High God."

"That myth?" came a voice.

Michael turned to see Lucifer and Kara making their way toward them. Errus and Jimerel almost leaped with joy at the sight of their leader. He would make short work of these arrogant angels!

"A myth. Is that what you call it now?" asked Michael. Archias noticed Serus turning away from his former master.

"No, Michael," said Lucifer. "That is what *they* are calling it"

"What a dreadful miscalculation on the part of the Most High," said Kara. "Within such a short period of time the hope of Seth has become a legend." He looked directly into Michael's eyes. "No human believes that prophecy anymore."

"This man, for example, is a direct descendant of Seth," said Lucifer. He began walking around the man, as if lecturing in a class-room. "At one time this man had a godly heritage, and he called upon the name of the Lord. Look at him, Michael. He's finished."

The drunken man suddenly stirred and stood up. Bleary eyed, he ambled off toward the settlement down the road. Lucifer looked at Errus and Jimerel and indicated that they should be off with him.

"Try to finish the job before the sun sets," said Lucifer. "The man is desperate. Perhaps he is ready to end it all—after he sobers up a bit I mean."

The pair of devils took off after their subject, steering him towards the town and the next drink. The man stumbled on, unaware of their presence.

"So you think that by preying on these wretches you will stop the prophecy?" asked Michael after they had gone.

"Well Michael, I don't like to take chances," reasoned Lucifer. "I have no idea where the Seed might try to emerge or through whom. So up until now my strategy has been the wholesale destruc-tion of humans." He smiled. "Of course, the humans are doing most of the destroying themselves!"

"You said 'up until now,' " replied Michael. "You have a new strategy? Perhaps you will start more in on the children of humans?"

"Actually, Michael, I am more interested in Noah," Lucifer said. "It seems the Lord has taken quite an interest in him."

Noah called his family together to tell them what God had spoken to him. Shem and Japheth sat next to their wives. Shem stirred the fire where large yams wrapped in leaves lay·cooking in the coals. Noah's wife looked at her husband with curiosity and a bit of nervousness—she had never before seen him so intense. Finally, Ham showed up with his wife and sat down. Noah was now ready to begin.

"Father, this isn't another one of your talks to encourage us to stay pure in this corrupt world, is it?" asked Shem woefully.

"You mean corrupt and *vile* world," corrected Ham. The young men laughed, but Noah spoke as if he didn't even hear them.

"For a long time I have told you how God has been patient with men," he began. "I know, I know. You have accused me of harping on the subject; maybe I have done that. I also realize that this idea has made us outcasts in our community. That is fine with me. At least those people know where we stand."

Noah stood up. "But something happened to me today that changes everything."

As he spoke, his words took on an authority that his family had never before witnessed. This wasn't just their father railing about the wickedness of the world; this was an oracle of God Almighty.

"Know this: the Lord will bring a flood upon this world that will destroy every living creature. He shall do this because He knows that men are continually plotting and doing evil. He is doing this because men no longer call on the name of the Lord but worship dark spirits in the guise of heavenly messengers. He will bring the flood because he made a promise that One would come to make all things right."

The family looked at each other, not knowing how to respond. Had he gone mad or had he truly heard from the Lord? God was going to destroy all living things in a flood? For a moment the group sat in silence, with the sound of the crackling fire the only noise. Finally Shem spoke up.

"You say that the Lord Himself told you these things?" he asked.

"Yes," said Noah. "Right over there." He pointed toward the meadow where the Lord had encountered him earlier.

"Well, if the Lord is going to destroy the earth, what is to become of us?" Shem asked."

"God has provided a way out for us," Noah said, scanning the horizon as if imagining in his mind where the best place might be to begin construction of the ark.

He explained to the family that they were to build a massive boat for themselves and two of every creature that lived on land. The boat would preserve them in the midst of the flood and would carry them until an appointed time when they would begin the world all over. "Once more men will call upon the name of God!" Noah exclaimed.

"And when do we begin the building of this boat on dry land?" asked Japheth. "The crops are just coming in. Are we to let them go in order to build this...this..."

"This ark," interrupted Noah. "This haven. This only hope!" He almost shouted it. Noah surmised the meaning of the looks he was getting from the bewildered family. "I know. It sounds insane," he admitted. "But one day—as death swirls around us—you will thank the Lord for the safety of this boat. The women will see to the crops. As for us, we begin work tomorrow!"

Unseen by anything human, two pairs of reddish eyes were watching the family from the side. Their owners had been listening to the conversation with great interest. The demons looked at the two large warrior angels at Noah's side with a bit of trepidation. They mocked and cursed the two holy angels, who ignored them and remained passive and dutiful.

"This will be interesting news for Kara," said one of the devils. "They begin work tomorrow."

"And so shall we," said the other, grinning.

Lucifer was scanning the group of assembled angels. He could read the anxiety in many of the faces. Some had been with him from the very beginning; others had thrown in with him at the very end—

but all were hoping that somehow he would have a plan…a direction…a newfound inspiration. Lucifer always seems to come up with something.

This particular group, which had become the core of Lucifer's leadership, had convened at his request in response to the Lord's recent visitation to earth. It included most of the members of the former Council of Worship who had assisted his efforts in Heaven. Stripped of their heavenly offices, they looked to Lucifer for earthly authority—the promised reward for their loyalty.

No longer the Council of Worship, they were now called the Council of War in the Heavenlies, or the War Council. The group was dedicated to forcing a peace that would leave them to conduct affairs on earth however they deemed proper, while recognizing the Most High's authority in Heaven. Lucifer thought it an "equitable and face-saving compromise," but he realized that it could only be achieved through a long and bitter contest.

"It will require much blood before this war is over," Lucifer had cautioned. He warned that the earth must be drenched with the blood of humans before the Most High would finally see the futility and waste of it all. "Blood will be the deciding factor in this war," he said. "Mark me!"

At this particular meeting, Kara began by reporting on the developments with Noah. Lucifer had issued a standing command that whenever and wherever the Most High made an appearance on earth it was to be investigated immediately. Kara delighted in the role of chief informant for the cause and related Noah's discussion with his family.

"Noah?" said Lucifer, pausing in thought.

"Yes, my lord," answered Kara with not a little pride in the efficiency of his network of spying angels. "That simpering vine grower who will have nothing to do with his fellow creatures." He made sure he had everyone's attention and then continued. "As you know I cast a rather wide net when it comes to gathering information." Looking about the room, he added with a hint of menace: "On everyone."

"Interesting," mused Lucifer, ignoring Kara's veiled threat to the others. "I sensed that the Most High was about to choose. He could so easily let it all go, what with the world so out of His control. How like Him to continue the game."

"So what does that mean, lord?" asked Tinius. "Would God truly destroy the work of His creation? The very men in whom He has vested so much love?"

"It is for love of men that His love is twisted all about," Pellecus offered. "Having made a commitment to bring about a resolution through Eve's seed, He now is faced with continuing even if it means destroying everything. He's trapped Himself!"

"This was the love we all trusted in," added Lucifer, "until it became destructive and wrathful. That is why we wage this war. The Most High is driven by love—it is an unhealthy obsession with Him. Now He finds that He can only express it in terms of wrath. What a perverse notion."

As the War Council meeting continued, Kara reported on the details he had learned of Noah's assignment, and how the Lord intended to re-populate the world with Noah's seed. He agreed with Pellecus's assessment that God had decided to preserve Eve's seed against a future date and thus carry forward the hope of *all* humanity in the coming one.

"So what now, Master?" asked Tinius with a twinge of sarcasm.

"Don't try me, Tinius," Lucifer responded, looking sharply at the angel who had offended him. Then he turned to the others with hopeful eyes. "Hear me all. I once said that our Lord always seems to leave an opening for us. He did so in Eden. He did so again with Cain. By naming Noah the Lord has exposed His plan."

As he spoke, Lucifer began to get caught up in the possibility of it all. "He has made it much easier for us. Until now we have had to be watchful of every family for signs of the coming one. Now we can concentrate our efforts on one man—Noah!"

"And what of the other humans?" asked Pellecus. "Shall we not continue to harass them? They are, after all, also made in God's image."

"If we destroy Noah they have no hope," said Lucifer. "We'll continue to foster the destructive habits of humans." He snickered. "They have become quite adept at bringing destruction upon themselves with our help!"

Rugio spoke up. "Where do we begin?"

Lucifer smiled at Rugio, supreme commander of all the warring angels under his control. Of all the angels he commanded, Rugio was the most blindly loyal. What the other angels found menacing in his attitude, Lucifer found quite useful. He turned to the warrior, and placing a hand on his shoulder, continued speaking. "Noah's name means 'comfort,' " he said, almost whispering. "I suggest we make things extremely uncomfortable for the man and his family."

Rugio nodded. "I'll see to it personally," he said, and vanished with his two aides.

CHAPTER 7

"Father, you really believe these people are worth saving?"

Chronicles of the Host

Noah's Progress

True to their plan, the angels under Lucifer's domination begin to attack Noah from every possible avenue. The holy angels guarding Noah and his family violently fought back the dark angels who tried with all their might to assault Noah's body or to bring about a mishap of some sort that might result in his death.

With the protection the Lord had placed over Noah being too strong to penetrate, attacks on his person were out of the question. Thereafter, Lucifer decided on another tactic—one that had proven very successful among humans thus far. He unleashed his angels among the populace, inflaming their base passions of mockery and discouragement, so that they daily hurled insults at Noah and his family, castigating them as freakish outsiders and fanatics.

As all of this continued, Kara worked hard among the members of Noah's own family, his sons and their wives, creating a subtle discord until they too began to murmur and grumble among themselves. Lucifer reasoned that whatever could be done to discourage progress on the ark must be attempted.

As for the Host of Heaven, ever watchful, they awaited instruction from the Most High as to how to contest the darkness opposing mankind. From time to time they were allowed to intervene when one of their fallen brothers transgressed his domain of influence. However, the greatest show of strength demonstrated by the holy angels occurred whenever Noah cried out to the Lord in faith-filled prayer. On those occasions, the Host appeared in greater numbers and, with effort, forced back the dark veil of evil spirits who were at the moment encroaching upon him...

"Noah! You crazy old man!"

"Better hurry—looks like a lot of water coming in!"

Noah ignored the laughter and jeering that had become routine after so many years. He didn't even look down from the scaffolding that hugged the huge ship. Instead he continued on, as he had been doing now for...could it be nearly one hundred years? He wiped his sweaty brow as he looked at Shem on the other end of the structure, squinting because of the distance.

Shem, however, did look down. He also had become used to the daily ridicule of the locals. But whereas Noah had hardened himself, Shem allowed the constant harassment to disturb him from time to time. He loved his father and would never speak a word against him. But this ceaseless work amidst unruly neighbors and the complaints of his wife sometimes drove Shem to the brink. All of his friends had deserted him years ago, and he was utterly committed to finishing the project out of respect for his father. But he had decided that when it was all over, he would settle a few scores.

Looking down this day, he noticed that one of the usual ringleaders, Kerz, was almost directly under him. Looking at the container of tar, Shem grinned a bit and then slowly eased the bucket to the side, spilling the black gooey substance out and over the scaffold. A large portion of the mess hit Kerz on the shoulder. Kerz yelped in surprise, then glared upward at Shem amidst the noise of the now laughing crowd.

"You! Shem!" he screamed. "You're just as crazy as your father!" He picked up a rock and threw it at Shem. It bounced off a massive beam and fell harmlessly to the earth. "You can't stay up there forever!" he yelled. "And I'll be waiting for you!"

Shem watched as Kerz walked away, most of the crowd following him. He heard the steps of Noah coming his way and prepared himself for his dad's disapproving lecture. Noah picked up the bucket that dangled halfway off the crude, wooden walkway encircling the final few feet of the ark to be completed.

"Shem," he began, looking at his son more with understanding than anger. "You mustn't fight with these people. We must be examples to them…"

"Father, you really believe that these people are worth saving?" demanded Shem. He stood up and faced Noah, a little taller than the old man. "You waste your breath preaching at them to return to the Lord. They curse you and the Lord every day. Why do you do it?"

"Because it is the Lord's will," said Noah. He patted the side of the ship. "Just like the building of this holy ark. It is God's will that I preach to these people. And it is God's will that we build—and so we build!"

"But how much longer?" wailed Shem. He looked down at his brothers.

"For one hundred years of this miserable planet's life Noah has labored on this ark, as he calls it. And in all of those years we have hardly been effective at all, much less impeded his work. Would someone care to explain to me why the greatest angels ever created cannot stop one old man and his family?"

Not one angel dared look at Lucifer straight on. Each deliberated in his own mind what answer he would frame should he be called upon—but nobody dared volunteer an answer. Lucifer, clearly disturbed, looked over his leadership. They were assembled upon a high spot that overlooked the meadow where the ark was being constructed.

"Look at it down there," he said. "For years we have had to watch this work take place. You hear that laughter down there? Those vile, harassing humans aren't laughing at Noah. It is we who are being laughed at! Rugio! What happened to your vaunted legions? I thought they were inciting people to torch this folly?"

Rugio looked at Lucifer. "My lord," he began, "as you well know I have several times assembled the humans in a riotous grouping with the intention of destroying the ark. But as they approach the site they begin to panic and break up." He shook with anger, his reddish aura beginning to manifest. "There is always a cordon of holy angels surrounding it."

"They are like an impenetrable wall," admitted Kara.

"There will always be opposition to our efforts," said Lucifer. "We have learned that. With most humans there is little or no covering. But those who are close to the Most High, such as Noah, or that tired old dog Methuselah who is finally dead, will always be strongly protected. If we are to win this war we must find a way in!"

They all heard the noise of construction resuming.

"Every spike driven...every plank put in place...every deck completed is another victory for the Lord," said Lucifer. "Kara! What of your efforts?"

Kara stood as if addressing the Council of Elders in Heaven once more. "My lord, I must admit that of all our efforts, short-failed as they might be, I believe mine have proven the most useful and effective."

"Naturally," said Pellecus sarcastically. "This is why the ship is almost completed."

"I only say this because we have learned the power of discouragement," Kara continued. "Noah is a man of faith. So be it. But I have seen his faith at times grow weary—even weak—through the persistence of a discouraging spirit working through those closest to him." Kara smiled. "It seems humans are hurt most by those who love them most!"

"Love is a powerful weapon when used correctly," mused Lucifer. "Go on."

"True, we have never stopped the ark's progress," Kara continued. "But those times that the work *did* slow down correspond with the times that Noah was discouraged. I believe that the ark is a schoolmaster for us—an academy of sorts—that is teaching us how to refine our tactics for future engagements."

Kara was quite animated now. "I tell you that more powerful than torches and curses by filthy outsiders are the wounds of one's own family! That, my lord, is a valuable weapon that makes the one hundred years' of human time and effort seem small in comparison."

Everyone remained silent for a few moments. A hawk circled overhead, lazily and elegantly riding the gentle breezes. Lucifer watched the graceful bird, now careening to one side, now to another, finally disappearing over the mountains to the west. Then he spoke up. "Just like that hawk, who seeks out his prey and strikes swiftly and unexpectedly, so must we engage our enemy in this war."

"Perhaps you are correct, Kara." He stood with the ark looming behind him, engulfing much of the horizon. "Perhaps we cannot stop the ark's construction. But what we *can* do is prepare for the next effort. You see, there will always be a next effort…the next battle…the next place where we can watch for the Seed to emerge so that when it finally comes out into the open it can be destroyed!"

He waved his hands in dismissal. "Let the ark be completed. If it is to carry the Seed, then we shall watch its progress. And like the hawk we shall be watching from afar…our prey's time of vulnerability…and then we shall strike hard and swiftly."

Behind him Lucifer could hear the sounds of rejoicing. The ark was finished! Turning to look at the family, he saw the raucous celebration turn into a time of prayer and thanksgiving led by Noah. Holy angels gathered over the family as they prayed, keeping a watchful eye on the dark spirits who were always nearby.

Lucifer looked at the angels gliding in from Heaven and positioning themselves around the family. "They too, like hawks, are patient and vigilant," he said, "swooping in on their prey, greedily holding it in their talons."

"I never thought that part of my duty to the Most High would include rounding up animals!" said Serus.

Serus and Archias walked alongside the pair of water buffalo, who suspiciously eyed the angels herding them toward the ark that loomed in the distance. A well-worn trail, fast becoming a path, indicated the way to the craft that would soon be the home of all sorts of creatures, human and beast.

"No, this way," yelled an exasperated Archias. He steered the brute back onto the trail, to the snickering of other angels who were engaged in similar tasks. All along the pathway leading to the ark were pairs of animals, some accompanied, but most being guided by holy angels sent to help Noah fulfill the Lord's command that animals be brought into the great boat.

As for Noah, he was amazed to see the animals coming to him, as if they had minds of their own. Of course he could not see the invisible herders, and he gave all of the glory to the Lord Most High.

"Look at it, my sons," he said with a feeling of pride in his God. "The Lord is so good. He sends us the animals so that our work is greatly lightened."

"Yes, Father," said a panting Ham, who was carrying a heavy bundle of straw up the gangplank leading inside the bowels of the ship. "But provisioning for these animals is quite another task!" Coming down the plank, Japheth met Ham and indicated that they were almost done with the straw.

"Father, I think we're nearly finished," Japheth said. "At least we're almost out of room for any more food."

Shem came running out of the entry, knocking a portion of the straw off Ham's shoulder.

"Hey! Careful there," yelled Ham, as he saw a portion of straw scatter at his feet. Shem ignored his brother and headed right to Noah, who stood at the end of the gangplank watching the animals pass by.

"Are the animals settling in?" Noah asked.

"Yes, Father," said Shem, "for now." He glanced nervously at a passing pair of brown bears, coached by the unseen guides who were shuttling them up the wooden walkway.

Noah smiled. He knew that Shem's fear of some of the animals was exaggerated. That was why he had put him in charge of caring for the larger ones, especially the cats. Noah placed his hand on Shem's shoulder.

"You have nothing to worry about," he said. "These animals will not harm us. They are special to the Lord. Look at them coming in…as far as you can see they come. And all on their own instinct!"

"Instinct, he says," remarked Darus, an angel who was at that moment wrestling a large boar up the path. The other angels laughed.

"They are under the Lord's care and complete control," Noah said. "Here now! This way, you old sow," he said, gently tugging on the great boar and pulling her back on the mark. Darus looked at Noah and said, "Thank you, sir."

"He can't hear you," said Archias, as he and Serus, having deposited their beast, moved out of the ark.

"Never hurts," said Darus, a little ruffled.

As he said these words a great noise came from somewhere down the path. Dust was being kicked up and the sound of branches crashing and trees being snapped could be heard, along with the sound of a trumpeting elephant gone mad.

"Japheth! Ham!" Noah screamed. "This way!"

Shem and Noah hurriedly made their way past the other animals toward the source of the disturbance. A mother elephant charged uncontrollably this way and that, scattering the animals into the bush.

"Again!" came the voice of Berenius, who, with the help of 20 or so devils, was tormenting the beast, causing it to react violently.

"Steer her to the village," he ordered. "The townspeople have had enough of Noah and his bloody animals!"

The devils were buzzing around the confused and angry animal like bees, swarming her ears and mind, and causing her to charge at anything and everything that moved. Suddenly the beast turned, crashed through some blackberry bushes, and charged toward the village.

"Stop that animal!" came the order from Michael, who had arrived on the scene with several others. Serus and Archias crashed into a group of devils riding the animal, scattering them. Michael drew his sword and swooped in, aided by other angels who were now showing up in strength.

The sight of Michael caused some of the devils to relent and shriek, disappearing into the woods. Berenius held tight, ordering his charges to continue the fight. Michael swung his sword at Berenius, narrowly missing the angel, who then gripped the elephant's mind in a tormenting lock that caused her to rear up madly.

Michael took another swing at Berenius, this time hitting him squarely on the shoulder. Berenius yelped and loosened his hold on the animal, looking about for any assistance that might be forthcoming. By the time Michael raised his sword for another blow, Berenius saw that he was being enveloped by heavenly angels and gave it up, cursing as he released the animal. He vanished into the air with what was left of his party.

Michael moved to the elephant and began speaking to her calmly and soothingly, finally causing her to stand motionless and dumb. Villagers came running out to meet the beast with clubs, spears, and torches. Kerz saw Noah arriving on the scene and pointed to him.

"There he is!" he said. "This man will destroy us all. The boat is one thing. But bringing dangerous animals near our homes is too much!"

The hostile crowd agreed, directing angry affirmations and oaths against Noah and his family. Noah's two angels, ever at his side, stayed near him as he walked to the elephant and began to pat her huge leg.

"There, there, old girl," he said, giving the beast a piece of cane to eat. "You see? She is alright. Just a little nervous."

"Hold her steady, "said Michael, as several angels ministered a calm over the animal, speaking softly and gently into her mind.

"What do you expect?" said Kerz. "Herding these animals into that stinking boat of yours—we will have no more of it!"

"Your gods are wicked," said Cyron, the local shaman. "You worship devil gods who have enchanted these animals. You are collecting them to use against us one day!" He threw some white powder into the air in an attempt to ward off the evil that Noah had brought into the village. "The ark must be destroyed!"

"No, hear me," said Noah, raising his hands. "Hear me, for this will be the last time I speak to you."

Noah motioned to his sons to help him climb onto the back of the elephant, who only a moment before had been charging wildly.

"You see? She is calm. At peace. Cyron, I serve no devil god. I serve the living God. You think that by sorcery I have brought these animals here to the ark? I don't pretend to understand any of this. I can only tell you that if you do not repent from your wickedness, you will all die."

The crowd murmured restlessly, their anger building.

"You threaten us?" asked Kerz, waving his weapon in the air.

"No," said Noah. "I invite you and as many as will accompany us. The Lord Most High is gracious. Anyone who will come with us and serve Him will be spared!"

The crowd burst out in laughter, jeering Noah. Shem was becoming angry and began looking for a weapon just in case.

"Just where are you going in that floating zoo?" asked Kerz. "The nearest river is miles from here, old man. You are in the hills, not on the sea. And you bring your shame to us all. All the villages around us are aware of your nonsense, and we are paying for it. The ark must be destroyed if you ever want to have fellowship with us again!"

The crowd again burst out in raucous agreement.

"Look out," said Serus, to Michael, who also had seen Lucifer, Kara, and a company of their demons coming in. "This is their chance."

"Well Lucifer, "said Michael. "Come for one last attempt?"

Lucifer landed near Kerz, ignoring the human who continued his carping at Noah. He walked among the mob toward Michael.

"No, archangel," said Lucifer. "We shall not attempt anything. Of course whatever these wretched humans want to muster is entirely up to them." He looked at Michael. "There might still be human blood on your hands before this is all over."

"I won't kill a human unless the Lord decrees it," said Michael. "Even one of these," he indicated the unruly mob. "But I am sworn to protect Noah and his family and no human *or* angel shall get through to them."

Kara sneered. "Never fear, archangel. We came to see the result of Berenius's plan to destroy the village. I see that he fell short."

"I told him the plan was useless," said Lucifer. "But he insisted on at least one more attempt. I never want to discourage an eager disciple. A pity really," he added, envisioning the elephant dashing through the village, destroying and killing as it went and inflaming the people to complete violence against Noah and the ark. "And where is Berenius?"

"The next time you see Berenius, my mark will be upon him," said Michael resolutely. "As it shall be on any angel who opposes the Lord's will."

"How dreadful that you are relegated to protecting these rebellious creatures," said Kara, amused at the scene. "How like the very animals coming into the ark are these humans. Horrible vermin!" As he said this he kicked at a man standing near him who was holding some of Cyron's emblems. Startled, the man winced in pain, gripping his gut and dropping the shaman's gear. Cyron scolded him loudly.

"Get them onto the ark," said Lucifer. "We are ready to continue this war on the other side of this." He looked over the crowd. The men were still clamoring for Noah's destruction. Women watched from a distance, carrying their babies. Children ran about carelessly.

"I am ready to see these people destroyed if that is the will of the Lord. Every dead human is another failure of the Most High! What a bloody god you serve!"

"Wrong, Lucifer," came Crispin's voice. He landed near Michael, nodding at the archangel. "Every human death is the result of human carnage and sin introduced so capably by you in Eden. It is not the Lord's fault but their own. Noah has told them the truth for one hundred years now. The choice, as always, is theirs."

"And the choice, as always, will be the wrong one," said Lucifer smugly. "It matters not to me how they choose. Death is death."

"Then we shall see you again, after the present judgment comes," said Michael, in a dismissing sort of voice.

"Of course, "said Lucifer. "And how prophetic, Michael. Judgment indeed is coming!"

He vanished in a violent, howling flurry that caused many of the villagers to scatter from the physical disturbance. The elephant, too, startled for a few seconds and then calmed down once more. Kara smirked at Michael and vanished with the others.

"What shall it be, Noah?" asked Kerz grimly. "Your family or the ark?"

Noah looked over the crowd for a few moments and then addressed them. "I go now. And I shall not see you again until perhaps one day when the Lord of Heaven and Earth judges all things."

A young boy of about four came running up to Noah and playfully handed him a half-eaten piece of fruit. The boy's mother hastily snatched the boy to keep him away from the "mad" Noah. The godly man wept as he saw the little boy being taken away with the other children of the village.

"Your blood be on your own heads! Your wives...your children...it is all on your own heads! The Lord have mercy on you all!" He tore at his clothes violently, ripping them midway down his body. The crowd watched curiously and was for the first time, quiet. There was not a sound in the village, except for some children splashing in a puddle nearby. Cyron looked around at the dumbfounded people, shrieked a curse against Noah, and rattled a talisman. He demanded that Noah leave and take whatever dark spirits accompanied him.

Noah sighed and turned away, motioning for his sons to leave with him. The villagers watched as Noah, Shem, Ham, and Japheth left for the last time, with the elephant lumbering behind, and did nothing to hinder their departure. Cyron continued his railing until Noah and his sons had disappeared down the pathway. Then the mob began breaking up.

Kerz remained where he stood, bitterly disappointed that Noah and his sons had come and gone without incident. His anger was so aroused that he picked up a stone and threw it at a dog strolling lazily nearby. The dog yelped and ran off. Kerz was so agitated that he almost growled under his breath.

Unseen by any of the others, one of Berenius's angels appeared next to Kerz. The devil, who was a spirit of anger, massaged Kerz's mind, speaking into it thoughts of destruction, of finishing this affair once and for all. Kerz looked at two or three rough-looking men in the crowd and motioned them over to him. The demon whispered the word *"tonight,"* into the heart of Kerz.

"Tonight," Kerz repeated the word to the men, patting his axe and looking around carefully. One of the men, whose front tooth was broken, grinned and nodded. Several devils who began appearing around the men also grinned.

"That's the last of them," said Serus, as Archias managed a female ostrich up the ramp and into the now noisy and foul smelling ark. "And I for one am glad of it."

"Tired of your duties there, Serus?"

Serus turned and saw Michael and Crispin standing on the first level of the ark high above him. He smiled and recovered himself. "Not at all," he answered. "I simply look forward to my next assignment."

"Well done, Serus," said Crispin. "You are learning not only how to handle animals but the art of diplomacy as well." Serus and Archias joined them on the deck.

The angels watched as Noah and his sons brought the remainder of the provisions aboard. Their wives were busy as well, preparing what might be their last meal before it all began. From time to time they looked up at their husbands but spoke very little. All felt like whatever was to happen was going to happen very soon.

Scanning the area around the ark, Michael could see thousands of the enemy, like a vast black cloud, encroaching but never daring to violate the protection of the great ship. He turned to the others and spoke.

"They are certainly biding their time," he said. "Waiting for another opportunity to strike."

"They have no other recourse," said Crispin matter-of-factly. "Their only hope is in the destruction of this family. This ship carries more than men and beasts. It carries the hope of the world!"

A brilliant light tore a hole in the cloud of devils, as Gabriel punched through the dark morass, scattering them like so many black birds. They regrouped just as fast, and the darkness enveloped the ark once more. Gabriel alighted at the spot where Michael and Crispin stood. They hailed him, and he embraced his friends.

"I have just received instruction from the Most High," Gabriel said grimly. "The wrath of God will no longer restrain itself. It is tonight."

"Noah shall awaken to a very different world," mused Crispin.

"And so shall they," said Serus, pointing at a group of men skulking about near the ark. It was a very drunk Kerz, followed by the men he had talked to in the village. They carried with them axes and torches in order to destroy the ark.

Cheers could be heard coming from the devils, many of whom swarmed the men and encouraged their behavior. Spirits of drunkenness and anger began taunting the holy angels who had begun gathering in defense of the ark.

Kerz looked stupidly at the great ship. He saw the wooden ramp leading into the ark and called the others to move in with their torches. He would take care of Noah personally, he said.

As the men walked toward the great ship, a sudden wind rose out of the heavens, scattering the demons, who shrieked as they fled. Michael and the others looked up to see a great hand coming out of a cloud. Kerz and his men saw nothing. He cursed the men for stopping and ordered them onto the ark.

They grabbed their axes and began running up the gangway, ready to kill whatever happened to come between them and their mission—be it animal or human. They stopped again, however, as the wood beneath them began to tremble. At the same time the heavens thundered fiercely, with great streaks of lightning casting a silvery, eerie phantom-like appearance on everything. Then the men watched the great door on the side of the ark lift by itself and shut with tremendous force.

Off to the side, Lucifer, who had just arrived, was observing the spectacle. The demon spectators had long since vanished, and only Lucifer and Kara remained to observe the Lord's handiwork. Lucifer looked across at Michael and the other angels who were bowing low, in anticipation of God's judgment upon the earth. Kara muttered gravely, "The very hand of the Most High has sealed the ark!"

"Nothing shall open that door now," said Lucifer, feeling a bit unsure at having watched the Lord's own hand seal the ark. "Away for now." He shot over to where Michael lay prostrate. "We leave you, Michael, until this wrath is done!" Michael looked up and caught a sneer from Kara before they vanished into the earth.

The men with Kerz fled in panic, leaving Him to face the ark alone. Fortified by his drunkenness, Kerz screamed an unholy oath and charged up the ramp. He was completely berserk in his hatred, having been whipped into a shameful frenzy by several demons who were determined to carry out Berenius's failed plan. Kerz began swinging his axe against the door, chipping away at the gopher wood. As he did this, the earth shook underneath him, and the gangplank teetered and fell on itself. Kerz was crushed between two large beams and died.

The earth continued to open in various places around the ark, and water came forth from the ground in a great torrent. In amazement, the angels watched the ground itself rage up in violent bursts, swallowing whole hills as great towers of water suddenly spewed forth from underneath. In the heavens, the sky had ripped open, and great blinding torrents of water began falling to the earth relentlessly.

In the nearby village, people ran in horrified panic. It had never before rained upon the earth! Some decided to make their way to Noah's ship and beg entrance. Others headed to higher ground—for the water was already rising to perilous depths. Cyron called upon his gods to help, but was drowned in a sudden flood that swept through his part of the village. Death was taking hold on earth as judgment fell.

Inside the ark, Noah and his family prayed to the Lord, thanking Him for their safety. Noah could only hope that very soon the screams of those trapped outside the ark would be stilled, for now he understood that every living person on earth was soon to perish...

But God remembered Noah
and all the beasts and all the cattle that were with him in the ark;
and God caused a wind to pass over the earth,
and the water subsided.
Also the fountains of the deep and the floodgates of the sky were closed,
and the rain from the sky was restrained;
and the water receded steadily from the earth,
and at the end of one hundred and fifty days
the water decreased.
(Genesis 8:1-3 NASB)

CHAPTER 8

"How much longer, Father?"

The huge wooden vessel plowed on through the darkness, creaking and moaning as it went. Apart from an occasional growl from some nocturnal prowler, or the grunt of some beast whose sleep was disturbed, or the chattering of monkeys disputing over a section of rafter, nighttime on the ark was peaceful. The animals had been fed, the families were asleep, and all was strangely quiet. Only the wind and the waves seemed to be active at night in a graceful symphony of motion—always motion.

Noah looked forward to these moments. This was his time alone with God—at least as alone as one can be with seven other adults and a boat full of screeching, growling, creeping animals. During the day there was so much activity aboard that time sped by in a blur of tasks: animals to feed, leaks to plug, straw to change, fresh water to distribute, sick animals to nurse. Then there was, of course, the smell.

Even the scarves Noah and his family wore over their mouths didn't keep out the pungent odor of very ripe animals quartered together a little too closely. A zoo is a zoo whether on land or afloat.

In all the activity of these daily tasks, amid the craziness of the situation and the confusion brought on by these very difficult circumstances, Noah and his sons did two things without fail at the twilight of a day. First, they gave thanks to the Lord for preserving them through another day's journey; and secondly, they encouraged each other that perhaps tomorrow would be the day they would finally see land. It usually went something like this:

"How much longer, Father?" asked Shem.

"That's for the Lord to decide," answered Noah, glancing again at the horizon through a slit in one of the upper decks of the ark. "When the time is right, we'll make land. In the meantime, be grateful that it stopped raining so many months ago."

"We can't go on like this," complained Ham. "This boat will not hold out. I've been plugging more and more leaks. And that split near the big cats' area seems to be getting longer. I don't think we did a good enough job with the tar."

"So why don't you repair it?" asked Japheth, who knew Ham's fear of the large felines.

"What—and get bitten? Not a chance. Father, I'm not going back near those cats. One of them snapped at me the other day, I'm sure of it!"

"They'll not eat you, Ham," Noah answered reassuringly. "The Lord has given them an appetite for grass, not people. Don't worry, I'll take a look at the crack." Noah paused for a few seconds and then continued, "My sons, you should realize something. If you've been counting on our skill to keep us afloat, know that we should have drowned a long time ago. It isn't the tar, nor the pitch, nor our workmanship that keeps us alive. It's not even your plugging up the leaks that allows us another day's journey, Ham. No, it's the Almighty who keeps us safe, and no other. Leaks and all."

The angels watching from a position in the rafters where the birds roosted smiled at Noah's faith. Here truly was a man who was well chosen of the Lord. Finally one of them spoke:

"Would that all men were like Noah in their faith," he said.

"Yes," agreed the other. "And as Crispin might say, would that all angels were also of such faith."

"Noah is a man of prayer, and that makes all the difference. And there he goes again!"

Noah turned and headed toward the one spot in the ark that was arguably the most private area available—the extreme front just under the upper deck. The three sons watched their father disappear into the darkness. Noah liked to usher in the nights alone from this haven. It seemed that from this place he could most clearly hear the voice of God. Noah could hear the animals settling in for the evening as the last glimmer of sunlight melted into the horizon.

A winsome sound echoed from below where water met wood and the stresses of the ship were most tense. Noah thought to himself how grateful he was that their lives were in the hands of God and not dependent upon their skill in building the ark. Even so, he could not help but echo the same concern that his sons had voiced: *When will this journey be over?*

His thoughts raced back over a hundred years in time. A hundred years? Had it been so long? It seemed like just the day before when God had appeared to him and told him to begin building the ark. A hundred years toiling. And now seven months on the ark. And no land. At times like this, the hundred years' construction seemed like an instant compared to the last few months on the water.

Surely, this will be over soon, thought Noah. But who could tell when the waters would finally abate? Sometimes while peering through a small hole that he had bored in the tar, Noah thought he saw the tip of a mountain, or an island, or even the outline of another ark on the horizon, only to discover that he was seeing only what his mind wanted desperately to see. He had long ago stopped alarming the family when he thought he saw land. Dashed hopes were not good for morale—especially on a crowded, stinking ship.

Noah prayed: "Oh Lord, God of all strength and mercy, I thank You that You in Your infinite grace have determined to allow us another day's journey in this, Your ark. Grant us the strength to continue. Keep us in Your eyes, O God, that we may be Your servants forever. Help me to lead my family in true recognition of Your purpose for us; to be an example unto them, and to be strong before them, for I am weak. And keep us, O God, until that day when You will deliver us onto dry land. Grant that our days upon this vessel may be shortened, and that Your answer might be forthcoming in Your own great wisdom and providence."

In the seventh month, on the seventeenth day of the month, the ark rested upon the mountains of Ararat.

The terrifying noise reverberated through the bowels of the ark, accompanied simultaneously by a tremendous lurching. Animals were jolted from their sleep, some floored by the impact. Feathers filled the air as birds, knocked off their perches, frantically struggled for a foothold. A crescendo of calls, screeches, howls, and just about every other sound imaginable came together in an ensemble of fear.

Then everything was still.

The angels assigned to Noah and the ark immediately redoubled their watch and formed a shield around the ark, now resting on top of a mountain. Within a short time all manner of devils began to encroach upon the atmosphere, but well outside the parameter set up by the holy angels.

Inside the ark, feathers and dust lingered in the air, and the noise of frightened animals subsided. Noah's family began emerging from what they had suspected was their last refuge. They gathered together, surveyed the situation, and wondered how long it would be before water began rushing in somewhere.

"I knew it, I knew it," Ham's wife cried out. "I told him to get in with those cats and fix that crack. Now we're done for!"

"No, I think we're resting on ground," Noah answered, tears in his eyes. "We have landed!"

Noah and his family gave thanks to the Lord for allowing them to feel earth for the first time in months—albeit through the bottom of the ark. As the first light of dawn began glimmering, Noah and his sons searched the horizon for the tops of mountains, trees, or any other sign of earth. They looked down below as far as they could see under the enormous wooden boat. Everywhere they looked they saw...

Water.

In fact, apart from the ark remaining stationary now, everything seemed quite as it had for the previous seven months. No apparent change! Still...at least they were on land.

Chronicles of the Host

Second Chance

True as always to His most holy word, the Lord brought forth a Great Flood upon all of the earth. Every living thing that inhabited land was destroyed, as the wrath of the Most High fell for 40 days and nights. But the Lord did not forget Noah and his family, nor the promise He had made to Eve, for the ark carried more than a man and his family; it carried the only hope that men might have to be free again.

But Noah and his family were fruitful, and did according to the word of the Lord, and the earth began to replenish itself. Thus did mankind start life anew on earth. We of the heavenly Host were hopeful that men would call upon the Lord once more, but it became apparent early on that our hopes were in vain. At Babel, human pride once more affronted the Lord by men's building a great tower, and making boasts of the accomplishments of mere men in comparison with the Almighty. And so the Lord destroyed the tower and confounded the language of men, so that from that day on, a great many languages were spoken on the earth.

Our fallen brethren continued their efforts against humanity. Not content with seeking out the promised one, they sought to imprison all of mankind in every manner of idolatry. Nations of people began to emerge, dedicating their newly founded cities and their prosperity to demon gods—fallen angels who took names such as Azazel and Belial, Shahar and Belphegor, Baal and Asmodeus. Encouraged by Lucifer, these vile spirits and many others began to incite men to worship them in great temples, sacrificing to their names in bloody spectacles, drenching their altars with innocent blood and their unholy names in disgraceful behavior. They perverted the idea of worship, performing deceptive tricks that made men think the gods were responsive to their wicked conjuring, only to find themselves dragged to perdition upon their deaths.

The holy angels could only watch as the world once more disintegrated into the rebellion that brought its previous destruction. How could the Seed come from this sinful people, bent on rebellion? But with confidence in the Holy One, and despite the haranguing of our enemy, we continued our vigilant watch—for we did not know that the Lord had already chosen, out of the land of the Chaldees, a man who would begin the greatest journey for the hope of all men that was ever to be taken.

> The Lord had said to Abram,
> "Leave your country, your people
> and your father's household and

go to the land I will show you.
"I will make you into a great nation and I will bless you;
I will make your name great, and you will be a blessing.
I will bless those who bless you,
and whoever curses you I will curse;
and all peoples on earth will be blessed through you."
(Genesis 12:1-3 NIV)

"Are you certain that we have not misunderstood the Lord's intentions regarding Abram?" asked Serus.

Gabriel and Michael looked at Serus and each other. The question was a good one, although there was clearly no misunderstanding. Abram was the man whom God had designated that they should keep. But because of the nature of men, the angels were a bit confused by what they considered Abram's often erratic behavior.

Here was a man—called by the Most High Himself into a wonderful relationship—who had panicked when a famine hit; lied about his wife to the ruler of Egypt, passing her off as his sister to protect his own life; and given his nephew Lot a portion of the land that God had given to him. This same nephew had caused quite an uproar when he had gotten himself caught up in a local war. Abram had rushed to his rescue, much to the dismay of his angel protectors, and was only now returning home.

Crispin remarked at the time on how foolish men were to always devise their own plans in light of God's unending ability to deliver from any circumstance. Still, Abram was something of a mystery.

The angels watched Abram leading his rescued nephew and all his servants with their war spoils. Abram was a vibrant-looking man, in spite of his age. His salt-and-pepper hair blew carelessly across his brow as he looked back at the column of men following him. Lot was close behind, walking next to a camel that was laden with silver taken from the camp of one of the kings they had defeated.

Lot called to Abram, "Uncle, who are they?"

Abram turned to greet the strangers who had caught up with his party. One he recognized immediately, much to his disappointment. But the other…the other was new to him and commanded an immediate respect that Abram didn't quite understand but knew was appropriate. Both these men were men of importance, and both had come to speak with Abram. But how different they were!

Bera, king of Sodom, was the first to greet Abram. Proud and petty, Bera all but drooled at the prospect of the spoils of conflict and of prisoners who would bring a good price at the market. Abram had never really trusted the king of Sodom, and the fact that a common enemy had thrust them together didn't set well with him. It was an alliance of circumstance.

Bera approached Abram's victorious returning party in the Valley of Shaveh. Stationing himself and some of his nobles at a point where he could see everybody pass, he scanned the faces of the captured, hoping to recognize important prisoners who would add to his prestige. Most of the people were familiar to him. Many of them were part of Lot's house, or were allies of Abram, such as Mamre the Amorite and his two brothers. Then came Abram.

"Your God has smiled upon us this day," said Bera as he surveyed several carts of plunder passing by. "When I return to Sodom I will make sacrifice to Him. You must be very great in His eyes."

"The Lord has delivered my enemies into my hands because He has willed it, not because of my greatness," replied Abram, "and because they were His enemies as well."

"How gratifying it must be to know that your enemies are His enemies," said Bera. "He has destroyed a great power in Kedorlaomer. The world will be grateful."

Abram couldn't help but feel a little uneasy in the presence of Sodom's king. It was as if he had befriended a wild animal who might turn on him at any time. The sooner they concluded their dealings the better!

"Now as far as settling the accounts of war," Bera continued, eyeing the spoils, "I have a proposition for you..."

Bera's voice faded as Abram focused on the other figure approaching them in the valley. As the stranger came closer, Abram studied the man. His appearance was kingly, but without the haughty demeanor of kings of this land. The stranger stopped about 20 yards from where Abram and Bera were conversing. He gave a command and the camel kneeled down. The man dressed in royal garments dismounted and, reaching into his pack, brought out a small bundle. He approached Abram.

"The blessings of the Lord be upon you," said the man, "for the marvelous victory He has wrought. You have defeated a scourge who has plagued this land for many years now. Please accept this humble offering of bread and wine for refreshment on your journey."

"Thank you, friend. I will," said Abram, taking the gift. "But whom do I have the pleasure of addressing?" Abram was still a little mystified by the stranger.

"I am Melchizedek, king of Salem and priest of the Most High God," he said. "Take also this blessing upon you, for this too is why I have come."

Melchizedek closed his eyes, stretched forth his hand toward Abram, and declared:

> "Blessed be Abram by God Most High,
> Creator of Heaven and earth.
> And blessed be God Most High,
> Who has delivered your enemies
> into your hand."

Abram fell to his knees, as did Lot and the rest of his people who were standing with him. Even Bera acknowledged the God of Abram and Melchizedek, albeit with a halfhearted bow of his head. Melchizedek took Abram by the hand and bade him stand. As Abram rose, he gestured to indicate all of the goods he had captured from Kedorlaomer.

"Please, take these things as my offering to the Lord for his continued deliverance of myself and my family," said Abram. Bera's eyes grew cold but he said nothing. "Truly all things belong to the Lord. Take them."

"The Lord of Heaven and earth does not require it of you. He has blessed you with these and many other things. He has preserved you and made you wealthy many times over," said Melchizedek. "But because your desire is to please the Lord and not to keep these things unto yourself, and because this expression is one of thanksgiving to God who has been with you, I will receive an offering up to the tenth."

Abram thanked Melchizedek and immediately gave the order to his servants for the transfer of one-tenth of all his goods to Melchizedek. He even provided the burden animals and servants to carry the goods back to Salem. While the spoils were being loaded on the animals, Bera's countenance was grim. He could not understand why Abram would so willingly give away so much to a stranger. *At least he didn't give away everything*, he thought to himself.

"The Lord bless you forever, Melchizedek, priest of the living God," said Abram. Melchizedek, heavily laden with Abram's offering, mounted his camel. He bowed a graceful nod of the head and departed. Abram and Bera watched him disappear on the horizon toward Salem. How humble was this king. Abram could not help but make a comparison between Melchizedek, alone on the desert, and Sodom's king with his retinue of servants.

Bera felt that it was now *his* turn to talk to Abram. He approached him, cleared his throat and began talking.

"As I was saying, in order to settle the accounts of war in an equitable manner, I propose the following division of the spoils. Let me have the prisoners, but you keep all the goods to yourself. After all, you were the one who defeated our enemies." Bera figured that he could make more of a profit selling live property at the slave market than by peddling merchandise. "I will take the people with me, but you keep all of the rest."

Abram turned to Bera and said, "I have raised my hand to the Lord, God Most High, Creator of Heaven and earth, and have taken an oath that I will accept nothing belonging to you, not even a thread or the thong of a sandal, so that you may never be able to say 'I made Abram rich.' "

"My friend, I intended no insult to you or your God," replied Bera. "I am merely proposing that I take the prisoners and you keep the goods. A very fair exchange, I feel."

"Fair indeed, Bera, considering that by right of conquest all of this is mine anyway—prisoners as well as goods. But I am interested in nothing except the rightful share that will go to the men who fought alongside me—Aner, Eshcol, and Mamre. They will each get a share. The rest you may keep. I will take with me only what I have eaten."

"Who am I to come between your conscience and your God? The bargain is made!" said Bera with a smug feeling of satisfaction that he had made a fool of Abram. Bera turned to some of his men. "You...and you there! Get these things back to Sodom. And be careful with the prisoners. They're very valuable to me."

With the goods divided between Bera and Abram's three allies, the two companies parted. How glad Abram was to be rid of Bera. He didn't particularly relish giving so much to him, but the thought of taking anything from Bera repulsed Abram completely. Abram looked down at the offerings of bread and wine that Melchizedek had presented to him. He pondered his dealings with the two kings as they set out for home.

Several evenings later, as Abram prepared for sleep, he began reflecting upon the recent events of his life. Who would ever have thought that Abram, an immigrant from Ur of the Chaldees, would consort with kings? Or become embroiled in local war? Or become so fabulously wealthy in such a relatively short time? If only his family in Ur could see what had become of him!

Many times he had discussed these things with his wife, Sarai. How fortunate they were to serve a living God, one who was concerned with them—not like the gods of his ancestors, who were deaf to the affairs of men and women. How blessed they were with cattle and goats, and silver and servants. There were very few estates comparable to his in all of Canaan, and Sarai was the envy of many ladies.

And yet, despite all the success and blessing, a larger question loomed in the back of his mind and seemed to make the significance of their prosperity pale in comparison: What did the Lord really intend? Why had God called Abram out of his homeland and away from his family? Surely He could have prospered him in Ur, if His intention were merely to prosper him. But there was more to it all: there was the promise.

Abram recalled the remarkable chain of events that led him from Ur to Canaan.

There was in those days an upheaval in the population of Mesopotamia: it seemed that everyone was moving somewhere! Abram's father, Terah, became caught up in this emigration fever and decided to move the family to Canaan. Despite the promises of opportunity that the new land might afford, Abram was hard-pressed to convince Sarai to leave her friends and family for this "land of purple"—as Canaan was called because of its purple dyes.

Ur was a magnificent city. The arts flourished; the culture was enviable; the library was magnificent; the palaces were beautiful; the commerce was tremendous. Ur represented a golden age of Sumerian culture. It seemed to Sarai that there was plenty of opportunity right there! But behind the facade of prosperity and perfection was a looming catastrophe. Ur was rotting from within. Idolatry, political corruption, moral degeneration, and finally war would take their tolls; the city of Ur was destined to become a casualty of time, a historical footnote. Terah's timing, it seemed, was impeccable.

Upon arriving in Haran, a stopping point on the trip to Canaan, Terah began to lose the urgency for travel and the family settled there. Abram recalled how his father decided that Haran, a sister-city of Ur with tremendous cultural and commercial ties, had "tremendous potential." In truth, he was simply ready to settle down again—and this they did for the next 20 years until Terah's death.

After his father's death in Haran, Abram heard from God. The Lord told Abram to leave his father's family there and move on to Canaan, where He would make Abram into a great nation! That meant an heir! What a promise—especially since Sarai was unable to have children. This time she didn't need as much convincing to move on—she just hoped Abram had heard correctly from God! They departed soon afterwards, and Lot, their nephew, came with them.

Many years passed and Abram grew prosperous. He found favor with the local inhabitants and soon separated from Lot because the sizes of their respective flocks were too large to inhabit such a small area. After Lot took his flocks east toward the Jordan, the Lord spoke again to Abram, promising that Abram's offspring would be so numerous that they would be like the dust of the earth!

Now the events of the last few weeks began playing themselves out in Abram's mind in a whirlwind of images: the messenger telling of Lot's capture; news of the defeat of the Canaanite coalition; organizing a pursuit with 318 men; Aner, Eshcol, and Mamre volunteering their aid; meeting the enemy at Dan and routing Kedorlaomer's forces all the way north of Damascus. Then the most recent encounter with the kings of Sodom and Salem. What eventful days!

You've certainly lived an interesting life, Abram told himself. But interesting as his life was, there was still the one missing piece of the puzzle that gnawed at him—which he thought about every day as he saw himself and Sarai getting older and older; which would make him feel complete; which would establish forever the integrity of the Creator's word—*they still had no heir*. And certain as he was that God was more than able to deliver on the promise, he could not help but be anxious as he saw the dream of a son and heir becoming more and more distant with each sunset.

CHAPTER 9

"How low the image of God has fallen among men."

The Council of War was waiting for Lucifer to determine their next move against Abram. Although there was no immediate sign that an heir would be born to Abram, the promise of a coming son hung over the rebels like a heavy fog—suffocating and dreary. Kara chattered on, insisting that his agents were on top of the situation and acting as if a positive breakthrough was imminent. Pellecus looked at Kara with his usual disdain.

For years now, the war against the Seed had been in a stalemate. Both the holy and the fallen angels had observed Abram's constant wavering back and forth. Often when it seemed that Abram might despair completely, he would recover his strength in the Most High. He always seemed to rediscover his faith—and that was the problem.

"Don't be so encouraged, Kara," said Pellecus. "How many times has human weakness and double-mindedness dashed our hopes?"

"Ah yes," said Kara, "but we must count on humans to win the war. And Abram is as foolish as any of them."

"The Most High's covenant with him is assured," Pellecus responded. "The Seed will come through him in spite of him. Our attempts to discourage him and bring him down through his wife's constant complaints or his own family's greed have thus far failed. I would declare the war a dismal failure."

"That is why you are not ruler here," said Lucifer, entering the clearing near Abram's settlement at Bethel, where they had assembled. All of the angels immediately came to order. Kara sat down, enjoying Pellecus's discomfort.

"I didn't mean to imply that the fault was yours, my lord," said Pellecus, trying to recover his indiscretion. "I merely am pointing out that the war goes without noticeable signs of progress."

"In other words, Pellecus, the war is a failure?" asked Kara, with relish. Others joined in Kara's effort, having various scores to settle with Pellecus, whom they considered the most arrogant among them.

"Enough of this!" snapped Lucifer. "The war is neither won nor lost. At this point I think it is fair to call it a draw."

Lucifer settled down among the others around the remains of a pagan altar, recently destroyed by Abram's men on his orders. Lucifer picked up an emblem of pagan worship, an amulet, that had been partially burned in the destruction.

"The war continues...as always," Lucifer said, focusing on the amulet as if he were speaking only to himself. "You see this relic? It was once a proud instrument of worship." He turned to Tinius. "As I recall, Tinius, this bit of ground was dedicated to you...one of your manifestations?"

"Yes, lord," said Tinius, a bit embarrassed. "I actively engaged many humans here in worship. I had assumed a local deity and was directing them in certain bits of sorcery. That is until the land became Abram's and he profaned this site."

"As I said, the war is neither won nor lost," repeated Lucifer. He cast the amulet to the ground. "Take heart, Tinius. Humans are incurably religious. I'm sure you will be able to raise another following elsewhere."

"In fact, lord, I already have," he admitted proudly. "Near Sodom the humans are begging to have the wisdom of...gods. I have begun to accommodate them."

"Excellent," said Lucifer. "Now if you might only achieve god-like wisdom!"

Everyone laughed.

"Many of you have achieved a following among the humans," continued Lucifer. "This is necessary and I encourage it. Some of the more vile among us, have even caused the humans to degrade themselves in the most debauched form of...of..."

"Worship, my lord," said Kara.

"Ah yes," Lucifer agreed, smiling. "Worship. How low the image of the Most High has fallen among men. I told you that human sensuality was a fine weapon. Now in the name of the Most High they behave in every animalistic way imaginable. So you see, the war is not entirely lost. Humans will always prostitute themselves for a price."

"Most humans, lord," said Pellecus, causing heads to turn his way.

"Yes, Pellecus," said Lucifer. "Abram has yet to fall to the sort of nonsense most humans are prey to. And it remains true that in spite of every setback, every attack, every weapon we have formed against him, his faith has survived intact." Lucifer threw up his arms in disbelief. "Do you realize that the Most High has not even spoken to him for 13 earth years and he *still* remains true?"

The group began muttering among themselves, speaking to the injustice of it all. Lucifer watched the effect of his words on the group and then spoke again.

"There are, of course, others who are true to the Lord," he said. "Others who have not bowed to the gods we create or given in to the usual human depravities. No, Abram is not alone. But he is the chosen one...God has made a covenant with him and the Seed will come through him."

Berenius stood, exasperated by it all. "This we know, lord," he said. "And if we could get to Abram all of the other faithful would become irrelevant to the outcome of the war. But we cannot get to Abram."

"Perhaps then, Berenius, we should not be going after Abram." Lucifer looked over the puzzled group with glowing confidence. "Perhaps we are trying to catch a leviathan when we should be fishing for smaller game."

He began pacing around the others, drumming his chin with his fingers as he spoke. "We need a new approach to the situation. Open force is useless right now—at least until Abram is in a position to compromise. What we need is something subtle...something indefensible...something that takes the battle out of the realm of combat and moves it into the realm of legality. And I believe I know how."

Michael and Gabriel were enjoying the worship and fellow-ship among the Host in the Great Hall. Duty to the Most High was the supreme honor, but basking in His Presence was a supreme joy. But by far the greatest and most glorious aspect of service to the Most High was when the highest-ranking angels were allowed to present themselves to Him in show of their unswerving and unend-ing loyalty.

This very special custom, known as the Day of Presentation of the Host, had taken on an even greater significance since the rebel-lion. Lucifer had taken with him upwards of one-third of the Host, including some of the most highly placed angels in the Kingdom. Their absence was noticeable and served as a constant reminder of the grim fate that awaited those who transgress.

The angels would approach the Most Holy Throne, and being careful not to look upon the Presence, would bow most humbly and speak a vow of loyalty to Him who was the giver of all life. Michael and Gabriel, as archangels, had already presented themselves. Now the teachers of the Academy of the Host were making their way to the Throne in solemn procession.

A hush that was uncharacteristic of the occasion swept the room, causing Michael to look up very discreetly in the direction of what appeared to be some sort of disturbance. *What could possibly be going on?* he thought to himself, as Gabriel too looked up. They both were amazed to see Academy teachers pulling away from a figure who made his way up the center of the Great Hall in measured steps. At the same instant, the name "Lucifer" was by now being echoed throughout the room.

Lucifer nodded at Michael, who barely restrained himself from personally removing him from so holy a proceeding. Gabriel looked on, astonished but not completely surprised at Lucifer's appear-ance. Such nerve! And yet, Lucifer carried on as if he belonged; as if this was something that was normal—almost expected of him. Lucifer continued up the aisle, by this time completely alone, robed in ceremonial garb that he no longer had authority to wear.

He bowed low before the Lord, unable, as any creature, to look directly upon the Presence. The Lord's voice boomed:

"Where have you come from?"

The Voice shook the room. Every eye hung low. Not one angel dared look up, although all were curious as to the outcome of what most expected to be Lucifer's last contemptible act.

"Roaming through the earth, mostly, Lord Most High," said Lucifer. "Back and forth, back and forth." He stole a glance at the angels about the room, silent and bowed low. "These no doubt are surprised to see me here, O Lord," he continued. "Perhaps some don't realize that I have been granted a right of protest here…a right to bring just and true accusation before Your Presence."

Lucifer enjoyed having such an audience again.

"I must admit, Most High, that Your angels have been quite up to the task of protecting Your covenant relationship with Abram, as well as the few other humans who have not bowed to me. The very few." He motioned to those angels around him. "They are to be commended."

Michael seethed as Lucifer continued his showy monologue. *Why doesn't the Most High simply deal with him and be done with it?* he wondered to himself. Many in the room wondered the same thing. Lucifer continued.

"This, I am afraid, is what brings me here," he said, enjoying himself and wishing his fallen colleagues could witness his performance. "I come to bring accusation to You, as is my right. But what good is an accusation when there is no possibility for moral indiscretion? By this I mean, Most High, how can Your creatures possibly choose fairly when they are so covered by Your concern; so blessed in their lives; so protected by Your Host; so…managed?

"In short, Most High, given such privileged circumstances, Your chosen ones would never curse You. There is no choice! Why should Abram or one of Your other servants choose a more independent course when their destiny is already decided? Now admittedly, Lord, there are very few on earth who truly serve You…"

"Have you considered My servant Job?"

"Yes, Most High," responded Lucifer, grateful that the Lord was taking the bait. "It is in fact Job of whom I speak. Abram I have seen as flawed but faithful. But Job…he is of a very different character indeed."

"Job is blameless and upright. He is a man who fears God and shuns evil. He chooses to do so freely. There is no other man like him upon earth."

"But that is my point, Most High," said Lucifer, still mindful enough of his position to keep his head low as he spoke. "Does Job fear God for nothing? Have You not placed around him and his household a hedge of protection? Of course he fears You. Why shouldn't he? This is not like Eden where I dare say the game was much more fairly played out. A'dam chose poorly—but of his own freedom. But, my accusation is not of A'dam nor of Job, Most High. Job is innocently and ignorantly protected of You. But I confess that it is Your will in this matter that I accuse."

A hushed but very real gasp filled the room as angels heard the Most High accused by Lucifer. Lucifer enjoyed the effect and went on.

"Consider, Most High—You have blessed the work of Job's hands, so that his flocks are everywhere on his land…of course he serves You. I maintain, Most High, that the only reason that Job or any human will serve You is because of those things You provide—nothing else. It is not because of Your image that they bear, great as Your image is, or out of truly free choice that they serve You. It is out of fear that You will…forgive me, Most High, no longer deliver those material things of which they have need. Thus they are compelled in secret to choose You openly.

"But hear me, Most High: If You will only stay Your hand and allow me to strike everything that Job owns—all of his possessions—he will surely curse Your face as would any human. And then You shall see that Your covenant with Abram is useless and wasted among such capricious spirits!"

"Everything Job has is now in your hands. But on the man Job himself, you shall not lay even a finger."

Lucifer nodded in agreement. "As you wish, Most High."

"What's his game, Crispin?" asked Michael. "How dare he come into the Great Throne room and profane such a sacred convocation?"

Michael, Serus, Gabriel, and Crispin had grouped up following Lucifer's spectacle in the Great Hall. All over Heaven the angels were talking about Lucifer's return. Some wondered if he might be allowed to return permanently? Others were stunned that he actually had access to the Throne at all.

Crispin looked at Michael as a teacher looks fondly at his student. "We have learned a great deal today, Michael. Something of which all the Host must become aware." Crispin settled into the soft grass and continued as the others closed in.

"First of all, Lucifer's appearance is apparently authorized by the Most High. He obviously could not gain entrance without the Lord's permission. And he stated in his brash way the reason for his coming. Lucifer is apparently granted a right of accusation—to bring before the Lord Most High the names of individuals with whom he has particular grievance."

"But why should the Lord allow a criminal the right of accusation?" asked Serus. "It seems most unfair."

"On the contrary, it is out of fairness that the Lord allows such behavior," said Crispin. "It's also a brilliant move on Lucifer's part. Think of it! If Lucifer is not allowed accusation before the Lord, then he can argue that the Most High fears the freedom of men and therefore must interfere with that freedom by creating in certain instances, situations in which men might not choose freely. Interfering with their destiny, as Lucifer put it. And if that be the case, then the Lord becomes unjust in the eyes of His creation if He holds as criminal those who exercised their freedom to choose evil in light of those whom the Lord compels to choose good. It's quite a clever move, really."

"Then Job is merely a legal ploy?" asked Michael. "I still don't understand the Lord taking the bait from Lucifer."

"Really, is that how you saw it?" asked Crispin.

"What do you mean, teacher?" asked Gabriel.

"It was not the Lord who took the bait," he said, smiling a sly smile.

Rugio's legion circled Job's estate, looking over the vast herds that dotted the landscape—in some cases blotting out the very grass by their numbers. Job was at one of his wells, watering some of the sheep. Rugio's anger burned within him as he watched Job tenderly stroking a newborn lamb near the well.

Job was a man of about 80. He has a very large family whom he enjoyed more than anything else in the world. They lived in Uz, which was to the east of Jordan, and where he was considered the greatest man among all the people of the East. His wife was good to him, and he had been blessed by the living God with seven sons, three daughters, and thousands of animals.

Job looked at the late afternoon sun and wiped his sweaty brow. He took a drink of the cool water from the well. Tonight he would build an altar of thanksgiving and with his family celebrate God's goodness and provision. He always spoke of the Lord, and hoped with all that was in him that perhaps his children would one day serve the living God as he did. Even though they were at this very moment indulging in a feast that Job considered unrighteous, Job would sacrifice an offering to the Lord on their behalf, as he often did, perhaps atoning for his children's sins.

Rugio and his troop alighted near Job, on the side of a hill overlooking his house. As they landed the sheep scattered, prompting Job to look up. Perhaps a wild animal had startled the animals. Seeing nothing alarming, he went back to his work, instructing his servants on the construction of a new wall next to the well. Kara and Lucifer joined Rugio.

"Poor Job," sneered Kara. "Pathetically ignorant of what is to befall him."

"I can hardly wait," admitted Rugio. "I have been hard-pressed to keep my warriors from tearing him apart."

"Remember this," said Lucifer, addressing the warriors who stood at attention before their unquestioned leader. "You may destroy all of his livestock, every herd, every living beast on this wretched piece of Uz. But you may *not* touch his person. This we will respect—we will win this war justly."

"As you command," they asserted. Rugio smiled proudly at his troops.

"They are ready to work your will, my lord," said Rugio. "These are my proud destroyers!"

"Destroyers of cattle, Rugio!"

Lucifer and the others looked up to see Michael with a troop of holy angels arriving on the scene. The devils growled and cursed as the holy angels descended around them like a thousand snowflakes. Rugio shook his head in disgust. Kara moved in closer to Rugio's warriors. Lucifer greeted Michael as if greeting an old friend.

"Welcome to Uz," he said. "Michael, I haven't seen you since last we met...in Heaven, I believe. Ah yes, in the very Presence of the Most High! Although I didn't see too much of you. As I remember your head was bowed too low."

Lucifer's angels snickered.

"I remember that shameful time," said Michael, who commanded his angels to surround Job and his family. The angels immediately set to the task, and created a blazing shield between the humans and the devils. "We knew of your legal right to attend the Lord. We simply didn't believe you had the arrogance to actually do it."

"Ah Michael, bitter as always," Lucifer said. He walked over to Michael, whose arms were folded in an impassive stance. "War does away with humility. This is a contest to the death. Death is a great motivator."

"You would know, Lucifer. You traffic in death," came a voice from behind Michael.

"Crispin? Dear teacher?" said a bemused Lucifer. "Aren't you a bit out of your academic fortress? This is a battlefield, not a classroom."

"You are mistaken, Lucifer," said Crispin dryly. "I'm here to see a lesson taught, not to teach."

Michael's angels laughed at Crispin's retort.

"And it is I who shall be doing the teaching," said Rugio, inflamed at Michael's appearance and giving off a reddish hue that also manifested a grotesque transformation of his countenance into an ape-like angry visage. Lucifer looked at him sternly and he calmed down, the horrible face returning to normal.

"Remember, Lucifer," said Michael. "You will not harm Job. Not even touch him."

"Is that why you are here?" asked Lucifer in mock surprise. "To protect Job as if I would go back on my word to the Most High? Really, Michael, has it come to that? I promise we will not touch Job. Only Job." He smiled.

Before Michael could respond, Rugio ordered his angels into action. Like a dark cloud, the devils fanned out, shrieking in delight at the prospect of injuring someone so near to the Lord's heart. This would be a good day!

As the day's events progressed, different servants came to Job with fantastic stories of disaster after disaster. First, a company of Sabeans incited by some of Rugio's angels had taken the oxen and donkeys and put all of the herdsmen to the sword. Lucifer loved the look on Michael and Crispin's horrified faces as the servant reported on the Sabean raid.

"Easy to manipulate, those crude Sabeans," said Lucifer matter-of-factly. Michael glared at Lucifer, frustrated that he could not make a move against him. He looked to make sure that Job was secure.

"But elements of nature," continued Lucifer. "Now those are something a little more spectacular. At least to ignorant humans. Is it any wonder that humans worship us as gods in their ridiculous ceremonies? Just look at Rugio's skill in creating lightning that can kill whole herds of sheep as well as their herdsmen!"

The angels watched as devils filled the air over the sheep on the far western part of the estate and began to manufacture great bolts of lightning that shot down, burned the sheep, and killed the men with them. Crispin turned away, ashamed that angels—former angels, that is—might be able to perform so hideous a task. Even as the smoke and smell of burning flesh filled the air, yet another servant came running to Job, bloody and out of breath.

"Master, Master! The Chaldeans have taken the camels and killed the servants with them. We lost every man and animal from your stables!" he screamed. He then dropped at Job's feet in exhaustion. Job could only look around incredulously. He called upon the Lord to take whatever He wanted but to spare Job's children.

"Job does have an incredible weakness for his children, doesn't he?" said Lucifer. He looked slyly at Michael, who understood what was happening.

"Surely you would not take this man's family!?" pleaded Michael. "They are innocent in this!"

"Innocent?" responded Lucifer. "They are away at a drunken party. This man, their father, atones for their sins every day with a burnt sacrifice. No, Michael, they are not innocent."

Rugio appeared suddenly from the south and gave Lucifer an indication of victory. His troops swooped in behind him, chattering about the destruction excitedly.

"We destroyed them in the house," he reported. "We collapsed the walls by a great wind. Every one of his children died!" He looked Michael squarely in the eyes. "All of them, Michael!"

Just as Rugio said this, a servant came galloping up on a camel and fell to Job's feet sobbing. The man reported that all of Job's children had died in a tragic accident. The house had collapsed on them, he said. They hadn't a chance.

The angels watched as Job fell to his knees for a few moments in total disbelief. His wife was shrieking hysterically in the background, somewhere near their house. Lucifer and Kara watched for Job's reaction with great anticipation.

When he stood up Lucifer said to Michael, "Now watch the reaction of one who knew the Lord but lost all. This is the nature of humans whom you defend!"

Job ripped his clothes and went into his house. When he emerged he was completely naked and his head was shaved. His wife continued sobbing in the doorway, watching to see what he was going to do. The angels watched as well. Job fell to the ground and began...to worship.

"What?" said Lucifer, exasperated and growing more angry. "Is he actually worshiping the Most High?"

No demon around Lucifer dared say anything.

Finally Crispin spoke up. "As I said, Lucifer, a lesson about humans and faith is being taught to us—all of us."

Lucifer screamed a horrible oath and disappeared into the sky over Uz. A great cheer went up among the holy angels as Job continued lifting praise to the Most High. Rugio, Kara, and the rest of their murderous troop dissipated in astonishment.

"Naked I came from my mother's womb," called out Job, loud enough for his wife to hear. "And naked I will depart! The Lord has given and the Lord has taken away!" He looked up into the sky, tears still streaming from his eyes. "And I say blessed be the name of the Most High God!"

"What, again?" whispered Michael to Gabriel.

Gabriel lifted his eyes in surprise at Michael's words and glanced in the direction he was looking. Making his way once more through the sacred assembly was Lucifer, bold as ever. He made his way up to the foot of the Throne and bowed a sweeping bow. How many times would the Lord endure Lucifer's rude interruption of the gathering? Every eye was upon the fallen angel, who had once graced this room with marvelous praise. Now he brought only disgrace.

"Where have you come from?"

"Ah, great Lord," Lucifer began. "Once more I come from roaming through the earth and going back and forth in it. Most recently from Uz, Most High."

"Have you indeed considered My servant Job? There is no one on earth like him; he is blameless and shuns evil; he fears God and

is upright. What's more, he maintains his integrity, though you incited Me against him to ruin him for no reason!"

The very room trembled upon the Lord's last few words, as every angel felt the Most High's apparent disgust with Lucifer. Lucifer weathered the rebuke and continued on sharply.

"Skin for skin, Most High!" he responded. "Even a man like Job would give all he has for his very life. As long as you allow Michael's legions to hedge him in, he will remain loyal to You. But stretch out your hands against his body, O Lord; strike his flesh and bones and he will surely curse You to Your very face—or I know nothing of humans!"

Michael could not believe Lucifer's extraordinary brashness. Inwardly he seethed at his enemy's casual manner and unwanted presence. Still, as Lucifer had pointed out, he had a legal right to bring charges against humans to the Lord.

"Very well. Job is in your hands. Do as you will to his person, but you must spare his life."

"As you wish," said Lucifer, bowing as he left.

Job's wife had hardly spoken since they had lost their children. She and her husband had tried their best to continue on, but it was very difficult to start over at their age, with no family or servants to help. She looked at the countryside of Uz, once one of her great pleasures, now a painful reminder of the tragedy that had overtaken her. As she kneaded the bread and prepared to bake it for the day's meal, she heard her husband coming in from the field.

"I think I made some progress today," Job called out as he drew a long drink from the well near the house. "Those fields will yield crops once more, I swear!" Job emptied the dipper and wiped his sweaty brow. He then made his way around the house to the oven in the back where he knew his wife was working. "We must have hope."

Unseen to both of them, a number of evil angels were watching. Awaiting the signal, they snickered among themselves. They were a brutal-looking lot, who had given over completely to their base character and were now permanently and horribly disfigured—an appearance that many of the once beautiful angels had become accustomed to.

The leader of this crew, Glacus, a warrior of Prian's legion, lunged out at Job, glancing his body, and then swirled back around quickly to sink his teeth into Job's shoulder. Job didn't seem to feel the attack. Other devils joined in the assault and soon, like a pack of wolves on an unfortunate animal, they covered Job's body, biting, clawing, and shrieking with delight at the havoc they were causing.

Job's wife turned to greet her husband. She looked at him, at first thinking the sun was playing with her eyes. She rubbed them and looked again at Job.

"Woman, what is the matter with you?" asked Job.

His wife suddenly began to scream hysterically, while the devils rolled with laughter. Job looked at his arms and noticed boils beginning to fester up right in front of his eyes. He felt them coming up everywhere from his face down to his ankles. His wife wouldn't even look at him.

By now Lucifer had arrived with Kara and a few other higher-ranking demons. They watched the progress with great interest—and with great hope. Lucifer had staked a good measure of his pride on the collapse of Job's integrity. He ordered the noisy devils away from the house and concentrated on the final assault on Job.

"I think now, Kara," said Lucifer.

Kara nodded, walked over to Job, and began to speak into his mind that God had truly abandoned him. Whispering directly into Job's ears, Kara told Job what a fool he had been for trusting in a God who had thrown him over, destroyed his family, ruined his commerce, and now attacked his body. Kara was better at the art of accusation than any other angel—apart from Lucifer, naturally.

Job moved to an old fire pit, which only a week earlier he had used as a place of sacrifice to the Lord in the presence of his now dead children. Lucifer watched at first with curiosity, and then with growing trepidation as Job gathered some ashes and began throwing them all over his body. He covered himself from head to toe with the sooty remains, and then sat down and began to scrape the boils with pieces of broken pottery. Kara and some of the others began to laugh at the sight of dirty Job scraping his wounds.

By now Michael had arrived with several angels, all of whom watched the scene in shame. Lucifer looked at Michael with a smirk.

"Well, archangel, I always did say that humans were a dirty lot."

Several of Lucifer's angels started laughing.

Before Michael could answer, Job's wife came out in a sobbing rage, one of Kara's devils neatly grasping her head in a tight, wrench-like grip. She was through with it. She had given up. The devil, a spirit of discouragement, had done his job well, and she had succumbed. She was amazed and further enraged at the spectacle of Job sitting in ashes and scraping the boils with shards of pottery.

"Are you still holding on to your integrity?" she said angrily. "Sitting here in ashes and mourning? Your God has abandoned you! Can't you see that?"

The devil grasping her head whispered into her mind the words, "Curse God!"

She immediately blurted out hysterically, "Why don't you curse God and die?"

Job looked up at her for a moment as all of the angels awaited his reply. Lucifer's gamble depended on the next few words. Job lifted his eyes and said, "You are talking like a foolish woman! Shall we accept only the good things from God and not the bad? Blessed be the name of the Lord!"

<hr />

Chronicles of the Host

Failed Gambit

Much to Lucifer's surprise, as well as his rage, Job proved on that day that humans are indeed quite capable of maintaining a faithful choice even in the most pressing of circumstances. Job maintained his integrity, even though a great debate with his friends, who, though well-intentioned, misunderstood completely the nature of Job's condition.

Our enemy, though discouraged in his failed attempt at disgracing the Lord through Job, continued as before, wreaking havoc upon mankind in general, and on Abram's family in particular. But the Lord reaffirmed His covenant with Abram, and because of Abram's belief, the Most High accredited him with righteousness, something that we angels thought impossible for any man. Our enemies attempted to spoil the sacrifices at this solemn occasion, but the Spirit of the Lord made a covenant with Himself and affirmed Abram's destiny as a father of multitudes. And with the covenant came a dreadful prophecy:

"Know for certain that your descendants will be strangers in a country not their own, and they will be enslaved and mistreated four hundred years. But I will punish the nation they serve as slaves, and afterward they will come out with great possessions"

What this meant for the humans seemed painfully clear... what it meant for our wicked enemy was something altogether unfathomable...

CHAPTER 10

"This is dangerous faith, my brethren

"Abram grows older," said Pellecus. "Look at him."

"Pitiful wretch," agreed Kara. "How can he possibly hope to have a child at his age? The promise of the Most High grows as old as he!"

Several of the angels in the group laughed at Kara's remark. They watched as Abram opened a flap on his tent. He stood gazing on the horizon where his men tended the flocks, which were being moved to water. Even though Abram was an old man now, he still loved the nomadic life of a herdsman. He would never admit that to Sarai, however; she preferred a more settled lifestyle. From within the tent he could hear her snapping at one of the servants.

"What a delight marriage must be," said Kara. "Especially when one is married to so vocal a woman as Sarai."

The others laughed.

Several holy angels encamped about the area stood silent sentry. Jeering devils tried to provoke them but to no avail.

"Come now, that was humorous," said Kara to one of the angels who stood beside Sarai's tent. He looked back at Kara but made no voice. "War certainly brings the worst out of the Host, doesn't it? I recall in Heaven you had a marvelous sense of humor, Jakkar."

The angel remained silent and resolute.

"I should think that he would move if one of us attempted to enter the tent," said Rugio, who was inspecting his ever-present legion that dogged Abram night and day. Jakkar eyed Rugio and made a slight movement toward the sword in his belt.

"There, you see," Rugio laughed loudly. "It *does* move!"

Another harsh word from within the tent pierced the air—this time directed at Abram, who had gone in to speak to his wife. The devils were howling with laughter at Abram's predicament.

"We may not have to defeat Abram," said Pellecus. "Perhaps his woman shall destroy him for us!"

"Perhaps she will," said Lucifer, who had appeared suddenly in the camp.

Upon his appearance the holy angels heightened their alert. Within seconds several more angels swept in from Heaven and surrounded the tent of Abram and Sarai. Lucifer watched the commotion caused by his arrival.

"You know, the more I am around the angels of the Most High the more important I feel!" he said.

His angels laughed loudly.

"Too bad Michael isn't here to witness such tactical efficiency. I'm sure he would be proud!"

The sound of a piece of pottery crashing inside the tent was followed by Abram's frustrated exit. Sarai stuck her head out of the tent and screamed after him.

"I tell you I cannot live like this anymore," she said. "I am too old to have a child." She dropped her head and began sobbing. "The Lord has kept me from having children! But without a child we will have nothing. Nothing!" She disappeared back into the tent, weeping.

Sarai was an attractive woman, even though she was approaching 80 years of age. True, she had lost the youthful beauty of earlier years, but she was still quite desirable. Several times in their married life other men had looked at her with eager eyes, and Abram was aware of their attention toward her. She disappeared back into the tent and wept.

Lucifer turned to greet his demons and thanked them for assembling as he had requested. When they had vacated the area for a more secluded place of meeting, he called them to order and began speaking.

"It is, I am discovering, the nature of warfare to try different tactics, different strategies, until a proper and successful ploy can be realized," he said. "The reason I had you assemble in Abram's camp was to make observation. When faced with a formidable enemy, it is wise to make note of him." He turned to various members of the War Council and asked them," What did you observe this day?"

The Council looked around at each other for a moment. Some offered hopeful comments about the fact that no heir had been born to Abram. Others mentioned that the pair of humans were becoming older and would soon be altogether too old to have children. One remarked on Abram's unsettled nature.

"I see a different picture than my colleagues," said Pellecus, who stood to speak. "I see Abram, recently visited by the Lord in dramatic covenant. I see a man, who though discouraged at times, is propelled by an inner hope that remains steadfast—Abram is a man of faith!"

"Precisely," said Lucifer. "Abram is a man of faith. I suspect there isn't much that we can do to shake that hope. It has become a part of him. The Lord has even declared him righteous because of his belief!"

Lucifer looked forlornly at the group.

"This is dangerous faith, my brethren. Faith such as this cannot be discouraged...but it can be distracted!"

"Distracted?" asked Kara. "In what way?"

"Kara, you should know as well as any about distracting humans," said Lucifer. "You have done a remarkable job in Egypt setting up a complete cosmology of gods and goddesses for those deluded people to waste their faith upon."

Kara beamed with pride.

"So it is with Abram," continued Lucifer. "If we learned anything in Eden it was that women have a definite need for security...for family. Eve wanted wisdom for A'dam and herself and went to the greatest lengths to obtain it. Her simple-minded husband went right along with it in order to appease her."

He laughed aloud, remembering the looks on A'dam's and Eve's faces after they realized what had happened.

"Do you remember how A'dam walked into that meadow where the trees stood and, rather than rebuke his wife for breaking the law, broke it with her?"

"Yes, lord," said Pellecus. "That was a great day!"

"I suspect," said Lucifer, "that in Sarai's distress is great potential as well.

"Yes," admitted Pellecus. "Unfortunately we have no serpent here."

"Haven't we?" asked Lucifer slyly.

Sarai stirred the pot that bubbled with the savory mutton Abram loved so well. As she hummed to herself, she thought about how far she had come in her life. Ur seemed like another world now. Her husband was a good man, but was lost in his devotion to a God who seemed at times distant to Sarai—especially in this matter of a son.

There it was again. She couldn't make it more than a few minutes in any day without thinking of the promised son. How cruel was a God who made a promise so long ago and never made good on it. She watched her body getting older—sometimes she thought she was seeing herself age before her very eyes! It wasn't that she blamed Abram—but what god or devil had enticed him to believe that he would have a child in his old age? She even would have settled for Eliezer, their chief servant, to become their heir. But Abram said the Lord had promised that they would indeed have a son of their own. And so they waited.

The voices of some of the women servants in the camp came to Sarai's ears from the brook where they were washing. If only she were young again—like one of them. Like Hagar, her favorite. Yes, if she were young again, like Hagar, she would surely bear a son to Abram. She stared longingly in the direction of the women.

"If only you had a second chance," came a voice into her mind. *"Look at all of those wonderful young women. Perhaps Abram no longer finds you desirable..."*

Sarai shook off the thought and tried to get back to her preparation of Abram's dinner. She stirred the meat, then cast a glance once more in the direction of the chattering younger women.

Kara stood next to her, demonstrating to a group of demons the technique for suggesting to humans in order to elicit some sort of choice. Lucifer watched from a distance as well.

"Notice that the holy angels cannot interfere when a human is open to suggestion. Rules of the game," he smirked.

Kara indicated several holy angels who stood by witnessing the spectacle, unable to intervene unless Sarai's life was threatened. They would move in an instant should Sarai call upon the Lord in any way.

"As you said to Abram, the Lord has abandoned your womb. If a son is not born to Abram there will be no heir...no heritage."

Sarai wiped away a tear from her eye. She stood up as the women came by on their way around the camp. One by one they filed by. Only Hagar came to her and bowed to her mistress.

Sarai looked at Hagar, who noticed her stares.

"Is something the matter, lady?" asked Hagar.

"No," said Sarai, "It is nothing. I was only noticing how beautiful you are. Egyptian women certainly are lovely."

"Thank you, lady," said Hagar, a bit perplexed. She then continued on her way and entered Sarai's tent to make it ready for the evening.

Of course! Hagar! Kara shot a glance at Lucifer, who nodded in agreement.

Sarai watched as Hagar disappeared in the tent.

"Hagar would make a lovely mother," Kara began, speaking into Sarai's mind. *"If only you were young again like she is. But you will never be young again. And the Lord has abandoned your dreams for a son of your own."*

Sarai began to weep again as Kara continued. *"Why should your dreams be shattered by a God who plays games with your life? He may not give you a child, but does that mean one cannot be born to Abram? If you cannot have a child, why not let your favorite servant bear a child for you?"*

What was she thinking? Sarai shook herself and tried to imagine her husband and Hagar having a child together. Of course it would be of Abram's house and therefore could become his legitimate heir. But Abram would never go for such an idea. He still was holding on to the promise of his God. She shook herself.

"I must give up such foolishness," she said aloud, and tried to get back to the business of preparing food. But Kara was unrelenting.

"And give up what might be your last hope to have a son?" he purred.

She stared ahead in fixed thought, with a blank look on her face. Kara weighed in on her, steadily pouring forth words of desperation.

She suddenly dropped the utensil in her hand and called out, "Abram! Abram!"

Crispin had just completed a lecture at the Academy. How he loved his role as a teacher to the Host. He watched as the final student left the large hall where he held sway as one of the greatest instructors in Heaven. As he made his way back through the room he noticed a group of angels just outside, chattering animatedly about something.

"What's this?" asked Crispin. "What is all the jabbering about?"

"The woman is with child," said one of the angels. "Sarai has finally conceived!"

"No, no, you have it wrong," said another. "It is not Sarai who carries the child of Abram. It is her handmaid, Hagar."

"Hagar?" repeated an astonished Crispin. "Incredible!"

"Even more than incredible, Crispin," said Gabriel, whose entrance into the conversation broke up the little impromptu meeting in the hallway. The angels quickly dispersed. Gabriel watched as they headed off in different directions and then continued.

"To produce the child of promise," said Gabriel, with an exasperated look. "When will these humans ever learn to trust in the Lord?"

"When will we ever learn not to underestimate the cleverness of our opponent?" said Crispin. "A very subtle ploy on the part of Lucifer. I must admit it makes sense—at least from his vantage."

"How so, teacher?" asked Gabriel.

Crispin motioned Gabriel to follow him. They continued down the hallway toward Crispin's office, speaking as they walked through the many passages that made up the bowels of the Academy. Arriving in Crispin's quarters, they sat down together.

"What is it that Lucifer fears more than anything else?" Crispin began.

"Michael perhaps," Gabriel smiled. "His own angels turning on him…"

"You miss the point, archangel," Crispin responded. "More than Michael, more than his own wretched devils, Lucifer fears the fulfillment of the prophecy pronounced at Eden. He fears the one who will avenge the Most High for A'dam's transgression." He leaned back in his large chair. "And he will do anything to prevent it from happening."

"So how does Abram's having a child by Hagar prevent this?" Gabriel asked. "Is it not an issue of Abram and therefore a legitimate contender for the prophecy?"

"An issue of Abram, yes," agreed Crispin. "A legitimate heir, no. Like I said, it is a masterful stroke on Lucifer's part."

"So what is his game?" asked Gabriel.

"I'm not altogether sure," said Crispin. "But something tells me he is playing it quite well."

Hagar had never been happier. Not only was she the favorite female servant in the great house of Abram, but she was carrying the future heir of Abram's possessions. She felt her importance for the first time in her life. Many of the other servants related differently to her, addressing her now in terms more appropriate for a mistress of a household rather than a handmaiden. Not that it bothered Hagar. She had never been respected as a person of any worth. Now she was second only to Sarai—and in some ways she felt even more significant.

Several devils who had been assigned to Hagar watched as she walked through the camp near Hebron. Amused at her newfound pride, they enjoyed watching the sniping and gossip that was beginning to tear apart the community underneath the surface. She had even begun ordering some of the other servants about as if she were a great lady herself.

"What a pitiful display of human pride," said one of the devils, a spirit of discord, whose specialty was inciting bitter feelings among humans. "She actually thinks that she has a reason to be haughty among her peers."

"It amazes me how quickly humans, given the proper motivation, will turn on each other" agreed the other, who was a gossipy spirit. They had been working to divide the camp and cause a rift in fellowship between Sarai and Hagar. Their poison had in fact been working, and Sarai had begun recently to develop hard feelings toward Hagar. As they spoke Kara and Tinius came into the camp, gliding in from the east.

"All these holy angels," Tinius said with disdain. "Have they nothing better to do than stand about all grim-faced and serious?"

"Well, there *is* a war, Tinius," said Kara. "Hadn't you heard? And these stalwart holy angels of the Lord are preventing you and me from..." He turned and addressed the angels of God who remained stationed at the main tent entrance. "Exactly what *are* you preventing us from? Killing Abram? I promise you that won't happen. That would spoil everything." He walked over to the sentries. "You see, I want to see the finish of this little drama when Hagar gives birth to the creature who will become heir. That will be delicious, won't it?"

The angels didn't even flinch, but remained silently at their posts.

"Bah! Is it any wonder that we sought refuge from the Host? Heaven is filled with such dull spirits!"

He walked back to Tinius, who was quite amused at Kara's taunting of the angels. Kara ordered the spirits of discord and gossip to continue their work, and promised that he was sending more devils to create tension within the community. He and Tinius then continued on to their pre-arranged meeting with Lucifer's recently established inner circle of leadership.

"I think we will be able to report something quite satisfactory," said Tinius, as they reached the edge of the camp. "Lucifer should be pleased with the progress here."

Kara smiled at Tinius's naïve take on things. "Lucifer will never be satisfied until he can rest." He looked back and saw Sarai speaking to Abram and Hagar. "And he shall never rest as long as the prophecy hangs over him."

The seven demons who made up Lucifer's Supreme Council had convened in an abandoned temple complex outside Ur-Nammu, the place of Abram's birth. Ur was a flourishing city-state and, along with Isin and Lasra in Sumeria, had become religious centers well exploited by some of Lucifer's more capable agents. Of all the people in the region, however, the Amorites showed the greatest promise. They were in the midst of a great cultural and spiritual revival, and the Amorite nations of Mari and Assyria showed promise—as did an emerging city called Babylon.

Lucifer's Supreme Council was made up of seven demons, each given authority over a different region of the world, and each with great numbers of fallen angels under their control to engage in the political and religious affairs of nations. Though the central battle remained as always in the region of Hebron in Canaan with Abram, Lucifer realized that he must think globally as well.

They had divided the world into regions, with the area that had formerly been Eden at its center. Lucifer had vowed to one day make his throne there—at the heart of the garden where the two trees once stood. After the dispersion at Babel, the world was sectioned by Lucifer into seven geographical regions. Within each region were large numbers of nation groups, with the principal devil being the regional prince, aided by a hierarchy of other demons who helped govern the affairs of men from the greatest to the least. Each of the seven rulers on the Supreme Council was given authority over one of the seven great regions that comprised the fallen earth.

"No nation on this cursed planet must be given an opportunity to discover the true Creator," Lucifer had said when he established this advisory group. Lucifer had come to view these seven primary rulers as the cornerstone in his strategy to deal with the world at large. He had taken his cues from Heaven, and entitled these seven lieutenants "elders."

With the help of the seven elders of the Supreme Council, he had devised great systems of philosophy and religious fervor that fed the minds and hearts of men the world over with empty nonsense. He spawned scores of religious expressions the world over, inspiring priests and shamans, prophets and oracles, sorcerers and charlatans, who oversaw ritualistic and often carnal acts of devotion—to everything from simple woodland gods of the forest villages, to the great gods of Memphis and Luxor in Egypt.

"Religion is our greatest weapon," Lucifer had said. "It is the stuff of deception and war—of devotion to things invisible—and a leash on the feeble minds of men who desperately need to be loved by something greater than themselves. It is something that arouses passion among men so that in an effort to become one with the divine they will sink even to killing one another! Let men be religious—zealous even—so long as they remain blinded!"

"Reports," said Lucifer gruffly.

The members of the Supreme Council began recounting the situations within their areas of global influence. Apart from the activity centered around Abram and his progress, where a tighter control and a more watchful presence were warranted, the world was largely quiet—and deceived. The council had divided the earth thus:

Kara—whose influence was centered around and in the great Nile region and the peoples of Egypt—proudly spoke of the great temples being erected to the pantheon of gods that the Egyptians found irresistible. He believed that Egypt would be a key to the war and was encouraged by the advances that its people seemed to be making. The great religious center at Luxor, also called Thebes, was where he ruled.

Pellecus was governor over a vast area that stretched from Assyria westward all the way to the great ocean and across to the coast of Tarshish, to the great northern seas where very few men had explored. He sensed however, in the Macedonian plains and the Greek islands, a people who were given to debate and the pursuit of knowledge. He believed that from his region he could launch many pet philosophies. There was something almost noble in these people's desire for human truth. Mycenea was his seat of power until the city of Athens became the dominant site of culture and influence in the Greek world.

Rugio was given all of the lands of the Indo-Aryan peoples east of Jordan and into Cush. He also maintained a hold over sparsely populated Arabia. He was rallying the warlike attitudes of the many nomadic and mountainous people in his domain, and hoped to create in them a great world power built upon the might of arms and violent conflict. He chose Babylon as his seat of power.

Prian, former Angel of the Watch, was given authority over the great peoples of the east—vast stretches of land that encompassed the nations of the Orient. He too was very encouraged by the established families of Xia and Shang, who were driving the nation toward world empire. Prian and his many charges had introduced the worship of ancestors into the hearts and minds of the people, and his demons often appeared as recently departed relatives to give counsel and comfort to the living. He preferred the Henan Valley as his stronghold.

Lenaes, an Angel of Light, was given the vast tropical and subtropical regions, from the great nation of Ethiopia and all the nations that lived in the great jungles south of the great desert, to the west

of Egypt. Lenaes created among the great peoples of Africa a network of forest gods and animistic spirits that he used to keep them
under fearful and superstitious control. He preferred Ethiopia as his
center of authority.

Rega, who had formerly served with Kara as one of the Twenty-
four Elders, had been authorized to rule over the vast numbers of
native peoples that populated the great northern and southern con-
tinents across the great ocean. He saw much promise and great
intelligence among the peoples there. Envious of the great pyramids
of Egypt, which by earth standards were already ancient, Rega
dreamed of establishing cultic centers of worship dedicated to a sun
god with great pyramids as well. He also intended to create bloody
spectacles of human sacrifice to further demonstrate his complete
control over the hearts of the people. He looked to build his seat of
authority in due course.

Belron, an ambitious angel who had been promised a place of
authority by Kara during the attempted rebellion in Heaven, was
given domain over the peoples scattered among the great islands of
the seas. Though not as prestigious as his brother demons, he
enjoyed the simple, nature-worshiping peoples of these islands.
They were easily deceived and quite fearful of the gods of the many
volcanoes that dotted the ocean.

So far as those lands that God had now promised to Abram
and his son, should he ever have a son, the council had determined
that each one of them would have a hand in the areas in and around
Canaan. This would be the center of the conflict until the end of the
age, or until they had wrested the prophecy from Abram's hands...

"And how does one wrest a prophecy, if I may ask, dear
prince?" asked Belron. He had become bold of voice since being
named to the council and was determined to cast as great a shadow
as any of these rebel angels. Lucifer glared at him.

"You must forgive Belron, my lord," said Kara. "He is new to
positions of importance and is therefore given to foolishness."

"I intended nothing foolish, my lord," said Belron, feeling the
iced looks of the other elders on the council. He looked across the
cracked altar that once served as a sacred place for the people of Ur.
"I am merely asking what our next move should be."

"Well done, Belron," said Kara with delight. "After all, one must learn to crawl before one learns to walk. At least on this council!"

"Enough!" said Lucifer. "His question is incisive."

Lucifer stood at the head of a dais where once stood the priest of this fallen temple, recently destroyed by an earthquake. He indicated the carved reliefs on the walls, marvelously stylized bulls and lions and serpents. Many of them showed the cracks of the recent disturbance, and some of them had all but been destroyed.

"At one time in this temple, great words were spoken through some of our most creative demons. They were worshiped by men and depicted by them as the creatures you see around you on these walls. Men like to see what they are worshiping. That gives us an enormous advantage over the Most High. While those like Abram, who are in covenant with the Most High, strain to even hear his voice, we as gods of this world can appear readily before the eyes of men. Thus we are more believable."

He picked up a broken piece of the altar that had fallen to the temple floor and threw it onto the top of the altar that was serving as their meeting place. Dust from the rock's forceful landing flew into the air and created a haze above the altar. As it settled Lucifer spoke.

"But like this crumbling center, which once held great promise for us and now is abandoned and disgraced, so too does the prophecy spoken in Eden and again to Abram speak of a dismal future for all of us."

He looked at the crew of elders, his eyes glowing a slightly reddish tinge through the cloud of dust and repeated the words, "All of us."

Lucifer continued talking, taking his place once more at the head of the altar. The seven demons, fully aware that they were tied together in an uncomfortable but unalterable destiny, hung on every word he spoke.

"You asked about the prophecy delivered to Abram, dear Belron. There is much to be said about that particular word. Most of it is dreadful news for us, to be sure."

"All the nations in the world are to be blessed by this man's descendants," said Pellecus. "All of them."

"It isn't all of the nations that concern me," said Lucifer. "It is one descendant in particular—foretold in Eden. He is the one with whom we ultimately contend."

"Arrgh! The Seed! The Seed," growled Rugio. "Ten thousand blasphemies upon that accursed Seed! Are we to sit and plan and play gods in our temples while the day of this avenger draws near?"

Rugio's eyes burned fiercely blue as his aura manifested itself in an intense burst of anger. Those seated next to him moved away during the demonstration. Lucifer gave him a quick look, and Rugio slowly calmed down.

"And what would you have us do, Rugio?" asked Kara snidely. "You showed us once how well your warriors could hold an archangel—do you really think you can prevent a prophecy?"

Rugio leaped across the altar and barreled into Kara, who shrieked in fear at the sight of the charging warrior. Kara didn't even have time to draw his sword before Rugio had him pinned in his massive arms. Rugio picked Kara up and flew to the ceiling of the temple. Kara was screaming for Lucifer to force Rugio to stop the attack. Pellecus looked at the two and shook his head in disgust. Others were howling in laughter. Lucifer watched for a moment and then ordered the scuffle to stop.

"Is it any wonder that we have been ineffective until now?" Lucifer finally asked, as Kara seated himself once more at the altar, albeit a bit more humble than he left it. Rugio also sat down, and gave one of his warrior aides a nod of satisfaction. "If my leaders cannot maintain order, how can we expect the rest of the legions to stay intact? I forbid you to fight among yourselves anymore. If you must war, use the humans, fight each other on earth's bloody fields—but NEVER again in my presence."

Kara and Rugio both nodded in agreement as Lucifer continued.

"Now as I was saying, we have been ineffective up to this point. Oh, we have learned a great deal about warring with humans—how they succumb to temptation, sin, and disease; how to deceive them and lead them through dreams and visions. But in regards to our goal of winning this war, brothers, we are at a loss.

"We have tried outright conflict, and have been stopped by Michael's angels. We have attempted discouragement but have been overcome by simple faith. We tried with Job to run a case against the true nature of men, and found that Job proved faithful. All of these and many more weapons we have found to be effective among humans in general." He was almost growling in frustration as he went on. "But these...these covenant leeches have proven most resilient to our every tactic."

"You paint a most encouraging picture, my lord," said Belron gloomily. "Shall we surrender *now* or *later*?"

"But I believe in Hagar we have a new opportunity—and a deadly one," Lucifer said, ignoring the comment of Belron. "As you all know, the woman Hagar, the servant of Sarai, has conceived Abram's child. It will be a son undoubtedly. And I have assigned Berenius to the coming child to give it the proper guidance it will need."

Pellecus smiled as he watched the downcast faces around the table slowly begin to perk up. Another plan! Lucifer always had another plan. Even Belron's countenance lifted. Only Pellecus and Kara knew what Lucifer was about to divulge and they were enjoying the effect of the revelation on the group.

"The child presents an interesting dilemma for our enemies. In Abram we have a rather peculiar faith—a flawed faith if you will. He has hoped for the promise of the Most High; waited for years. Then in his own wisdom, and encouraged by Sarai's desperate pleadings, he has now thwarted the plan of God. Rather than have the legitimate heir as promised through Sarai, Abram will spawn a pseudo-heir from Hagar."

"And she is an Egyptian, no less," offered Kara. "That is delicious!"

"More importantly, she is a fool," said Pellecus. "From the moment she conceived she has become proud. Even now we are hammering Sarai with a spirit of jealousy, in order to drive a wedge between them."

"To what end?" asked Belron.

"Don't you see?" Pellecus asked in an astonished tone. "Once the child is born, he becomes the heir-apparent. He becomes the caretaker of all that is Abram's. The prophecy will travel through him—and instead of all the nations of the world being blessed, they will be abandoned. Abram will have settled for an inferior heir and the world will find itself seeded by a very different family indeed!"

"And the bloodline of Seth will be finished!" added Kara. "It will disappear within the dregs of these human creatures."

Belron nodded silently as if finally understanding. "This child becomes the seed...a new seed...a false seed," he said.

"More important that that," added Lucifer. "He becomes *our* seed! This is why Berenius is assigned to him. To nurture him—to bring him up in the proper respect of the gods of this world and to lead the world in a glorious revival. I tell you this child and *his* seed shall one day rule this planet! The world shall finally become that for which we have fought so hard and we will finally have the freedom for which we long."

"What about the mother?" asked Belron.

"Once the child is delivered the woman becomes immaterial to us," said Lucifer. "Besides, from what I understand, Sarai will handle Hagar for us."

Lucifer nodded to an aide, who brought out a large book. *The Prophecies of the Morning Star* was a collection of Lucifer's inspired words that he was keeping as a testimony to his role as spiritual authority on earth. He opened the book, which was fast becoming sacred among the angels who had vacated Heaven.

"I wish to share with you a word of hope for us all," he began. "The Most High is not the only voice in the cosmos. When once before we met and I opened this book, these sacred writings became the impetus of our movement. They have survived our expulsion from Heaven, and they shall bear witness of our triumphant return!"

He began speaking loudly now, his purplish aura casting an eerie light on the temple walls. "I promise you, brothers, that one day our voices shall be heard over the pretenders in Heaven! Let these words stir your hearts to courage and the continuance of this struggle." He then began to read:

Rise up, O seed of Morning Star
Rise as a dawning day over Eden bright and glorious before
its shame;
With all creation, host and human, trembling at thy name.
Rise up, O seed of Morning Star
And take thy place among the earth, among the nations of men,
Remaking in their hearts and minds an image born of sin.
Rise up, O seed of Morning Star
The Host of earth and Heaven watch thy destiny unfold
Until that grand and glorious day,
When Heaven sees the shame of its way
And we, the true Host, will increase the glory of our fold.

CHAPTER 11

"The plan is truly inspired."

Chronicles of the Host

Ishmael

Lucifer and his council awaited the delivery of the child whom they hoped would confound the plans of God, and Hagar, encouraged by her status of mother-to-the-heir, began to despise her mistress Sarai, causing bitter feelings between the two women and much grief for Abram. We angels observed such behavior and put it down as the folly of human nature. But neither the Host of Heaven nor the rebel angels could have anticipated what would follow with Sarai and Hagar...

Abram sighed a deep sigh. He had grown weary of the constant complaining of his wife. How could he express to Sarai that she would always be the love of his life; that even though Hagar carried their future child, he and Sarai would raise him together as his mother and father; that she mustn't allow Hagar's proud demeanor to get to her?

It had gotten to the point that he hated going back into the camp, preferring the company of livestock to that of squabbling females. Abram looked at the camp in the distance, the sun hanging low in the western sky near Hebron. He could almost hear Sarai's voice now, starting in the moment he returned to their tent. Sometimes he wondered if they had made a mistake in bringing Hagar into this situation. Had they done the right thing?

"O Lord Creator," Abram said aloud. "You promised us a son and we have a child coming. Yet I have not heard or felt Your voice since Hagar conceived. I did this for my wife, O Lord, as she was so very distraught. If we acted in haste, forgive us. But don't abandon us; don't abandon Your promise…"

The noise of the wind blowing through the grass and the sounds of animals nearby were all that he received in answer. He ordered Eliezer to call the servants in to camp. It was time to return…again.

Berenius had made quite a study of human conflict. His observations led him to believe that Sarai would eventually have her fill of Hagar and would demote her to one of the lesser servants—after the child was born, of course. So his current assignment was to continue fanning the flames of jealousy and to keep a tense situation on edge. Ultimately it was necessary to remove Hagar from the situation completely to ensure that Sarai alone would raise the child.

"Well Berenius," came a voice, "is Hagar as forward as ever?"

"Ah Kara," responded Berenius, as he watched Kara gliding in from the east. "Yes, of course. She only now ordered that from now on she should be served in Abram's tent. That was a little suggestion of mine," he added with a smile.

"Very good, Berenius," said Kara. "You are certainly headed for greatness. But remember that the key is to keep the flame burning at a steadily increasing rate. She must have the child first—then what happens to her is of no consequence."

They watched as Sarai carried a bundle of material into her tent. Within seconds, she came storming out of the tent, calling for Hagar. From tent to tent she went, finally looking in Abram's own tent. Her voice could be heard all over the camp.

"How dare you take my rings?" she demanded. "And what are you doing in my husband's tent? Get out of here at once! And never get into my things again!"

Hagar came out of the tent, looking very upset, but taking her time about it. She glanced at some of the other women in the camp, who were snickering at the tongue-lashing she had just received. As she walked, Hagar passed Abram coming from the fields. She smiled and greeted him, then began to weep. He looked at her quizzically, then with growing understanding when he heard Sarai's angry voice from within the tent. Abram stopped, and looking a bit embarrassed, walked into the tent to try to soothe his wife.

"Another little suggestion," Berenius said. "I proposed to Hagar that she begin to wear some of Sarai's jewelry—you know—befitting the second most important woman in Abram's household. She went for it completely and the results have been most gratifying!"

"Yes," agreed Kara. "But as I was saying, a slow and steady antagonism is called for here. Hagar must have the child while still a part of this household. Afterwards she can be driven off...or even murdered..."

"Murdered?" said Berenius with interest. "Now that is news. By whose hand?"

"Daron specializes in presenting humans with a choice of self-destruction that is very attractive," said Kara. "Hopefully she will die by her own hand."

"I understand," said Berenius. "But why must she die? I enjoy playing my little game with her."

"Because, Berenius, we want this child to be completely freed from his birth mother," explained Kara. "This is why it is of utmost importance that she remain with Abram until the child is born. He must be born in the house of Abram."

They walked through the camp as Kara spoke. At one point a large dog, sensing their presence, began barking and growling in their direction. A servant kicked the dog, which yelped and looked at the demons once more before lying down.

"The plan is truly inspired," said Kara. "And an honor for you that you are a part of it. Once the child is born, Hagar is in some way removed to ensure that Sarai never feels threatened by the real mother's presence. This will help Sarai's long-suppressed nurturing feelings for the child to take over completely. She will raise the child as her very own—with no threat from Hagar. This also will legally bar the claims of any other child of Abram—even if it should come from Sarai's tired womb."

"Brilliant," said Berenius, imagining the plan's progression.

"You see? Even if Abram and Sarai *do* manage to create a child of their own, Sarai can never let the second child replace the one who came to her in her grief. Hagar's child will always remain the firstborn and legitimate heir." Kara snorted and added, "Even if the Lord Himself were to conceive a child in her womb, the legal right would belong to the issue of Hagar!"

"But will Abram honor that?" asked Berenius. "I mean, the promised child must obviously come from Sarai's womb."

"The promised child will be the firstborn of the house of Abram," said Kara. "It is the custom of these people that the first-born is the heir. This is irrevocable."

He smiled. "No, dear Berenius, I don't see how it can be over-turned. Do you see the brilliance of the plan?"

"Very subtle indeed," came the voice of Michael.

The archangel stood nearby with Serus. They walked over to Kara and Berenius, who smugly greeted them.

"So that's the game," said Michael. "Rather than stop the prophecy you'll simply provide a poor substitute...a fraud."

Kara gave a mock look of concern.

"Is that any way to talk about a baby?" he asked sarcastically. He then added, "Besides, the decision belongs to the humans. It always is their choice!"

"And should they choose to create a surrogate through Hagar, so be it," added Berenius. "After all, a child has been prophesied. What matter who the parents are?"

"Yes," said Kara in a surly tone. "And with a simple-minded father who waits for an empty promise, and an insanely jealous wife whose ability to bear children slipped away years ago, we are doing them a favor." He gave Michael a puzzled expression. "You should be thanking us, Michael, rather than opposing us."

Michael looked at Kara with searing eyes. Serus moved for-ward as if to take some sort of action against Kara and Berenius. They burst out laughing at him.

"Come now, Serus," said Kara. "I have never seen the warrior side of you. Is this what comes of angels who associate with archangels?"

"Better than what becomes of angels who associate with trai-tors," said Serus.

Kara smirked.

"Still bitter after all this time, I see," Kara said.

As they spoke, several fallen angels began closing in on the area, chattering like crows in trees. They were hoping for a contest between Michael and Kara, looking for an opportunity to avenge their defeat at Michael's hands during the ill-fated rebellion. Michael noticed the demons closing in but never flinched. Serus looked about and prepared himself for a possible fight.

"You can't possibly thwart the plans of the Most High, Kara," said Michael calmly. "The prophecy will hold in spite of what you do."

"Mark me, archangel," said Kara, his anger rising a bit. "You forget you are dealing with humans. Humans! The very creatures who overthrew the Most High in the garden! One can never predict human behavior—you would do well to remember that."

He laughed aloud, joined in by catcalls and jeering of the now several hundred devils who had joined the mob. Some of them taunted Serus, calling him a traitor for having abandoned Lucifer, and daring him to try something bold with them. Berenius joined in at Serus's expense. He hated Serus with a passion. Serus—his one-time co-conspirator—now apprenticed to Michael, the greatest angel in Heaven.

"You're right, Kara," said Michael. "If we must depend on humans to win this war, we have lost already."

Before Kara could answer, a great disturbance broke out in the camp. All of the angels turned to see what was the matter. Kara broke off from Michael and hurried to the scene where Hagar, with a small bundle of clothing in her arms, was being run out of the camp by the women. Sarai was standing at her tent looking defiant and egging the hostile women on. They had endured all of Hagar that they could, and Sarai had insisted that Abram put her out.

Hagar was weeping bitterly, crying that she carried Abram's child, but it was to no avail. The many devils that had gathered were swooping in and out of the crowd, agitating them even further in an attempt to have them kill the woman rather than let her get away. Some of the women even stooped to pick up stones but were stopped by the men. Kara was stupefied as Hagar brushed past him.

"What is the meaning of this?" Kara demanded to nobody in particular. "They cannot force her out...not yet!"

Berenius scurried about trying to redeem the situation, but it was out of the control of the angels: human will had forced a decision that was unstoppable by mere angelic suggestion. He was completely bewildered. He even tried to approach Abram, who was already in prayer for Hagar and therefore untouchable by the rebels. A large contingent of warrior angels had surrounded Abram, and

Berenius had to content himself with watching Lucifer's thoughtful plan unravel.

As the noise of the camp subsided and the women danced and laughed in a victory celebration, Michael strolled over to where a shocked Kara stood, incredulous as to what had just occurred.

"How could this have happened?" Kara said, mumbling to himself as he rehearsed in his mind his report to Lucifer on the turn of events. "Only moments ago we had control of this situation. How could..."

Only now did Kara see Michael standing nearby. Quickly regaining his composure, he ordered the demons who were still flying about to come to order. He then looked at Michael smugly.

"Like you said, Kara," beamed Michael, "one can never predict human behavior." With that, he vanished.

Serus looked at Berenius and repeated Kara's previous rejoinder: "You would do well to remember that!"

Following the archangel's lead, he vanished also.

Hagar had wandered several miles from Abram's community. She could neither return to his camp nor go into Hebron even to beg for help, as she was marked for disgrace. The only hope for her lay in Egypt, and so she made for the road to Shur. The darkness of the night made travel difficult, and, finding herself by a spring, she settled there until morning began to break.

Daron, the angel of whom Kara had spoken, had been stalking her along the way. His ability to seduce desperate humans into self-destruction was renowned in the invisible world of spirits. He tracked the poor woman like a predator after wounded prey.

Tonight, however, he was on a very different mission—a mission not to destroy life but to preserve it—by encouraging Hagar's return to the camp so that the hope of a false heir might be realized. As he looked upon the exhausted woman, the words of Kara rang sharply in his mind. "Find her, Daron, find Hagar and bring her back to the camp. She must not return to Egypt."

A quickly convened council of the seven had reasoned that should Hagar manage to escape and live, the child would grow up with a vengeful heart, seeking to bring honor to his disgraced mother and claim the heritage of his father. And while the future civil conflict within Abram's house would be amusing, it could also prove unpredictable as to its outcome. Such strife might prove even a greater disaster than if the child were raised in Abram's tents. At least with Abram the child could be managed properly, and the prophecy might diminish in significance with each passing generation.

How to do it? That was the issue at hand. Daron decided that perhaps if he appeared to her as an angel of light—one who was very friendly—he could persuade her to return. Humans were always looking for signs. Such a visitation would surely get her back.

Or perhaps he should appear as Hagar's own mother, who had died in Egypt. That would do nicely—a mother pleading in anguish for the safe delivery of her daughter's child. Yes, that would do.

Suddenly a light shone all around the rocky area, creating a bluish-white world in which Hagar's silhouette was barely discernible in the intense brightness. Daron had felt this Presence before and immediately fell to the ground prostrate. It was the Lord Most High in the guise of the Angel of the Lord.

"Hagar!"

Hagar could only make out a figure standing in the core of a brilliant light. At first she thought it might be one of the demons who had plagued her sleep recently. But there was something different about this Person—and she was not afraid.

"Hagar, servant of Sarai. What are you doing out here? Where are you going?"

At first Hagar could not speak. But something within told her that this was a good presence, and she felt strangely at peace. She answered.

"I...I am running away from my mistress, Sarai."

"You must return to her," said the Person. *"You must go back and submit to her."*

"But she hates me," said Hagar. "And she hates the child within me. She said that she would never accept my child as her heir even though it was all her idea! I will have nothing for me *or* my son!"

"But you shall, Hagar," came the Voice. *"You shall have a son and I will increase your descendants so that they shall be too numerous to even count. I will give you a great inheritance of your own! Hear me:*

You are now with child and you will have a son,
You shall name him Ishmael, for the Lord has heard your misery.
He will be a wild donkey of a man; his hand will be against everyone
and everyone's hand against him,
and he will live in hostility toward all his brothers!"

She bowed down and began to worship the Lord, realizing at last with whom she was speaking. "You are the Most High God, who sees me in my grief, who saves me in my distress. Blessed be the name of the Lord God—the God of my master Abram and my mistress Sarai!"

As quickly as it appeared, the light disappeared. Hagar rubbed her eyes, which were burning from looking into the brightness of just a few seconds ago. She looked back toward Abram's camp—the way she must now go. But she went with a new sense of purpose. She now understood that she didn't have to prove her son to anyone. Whether or not she would ever be esteemed in Sarai's eyes, she now knew that she was esteemed in the eyes of the Lord—and that was all that mattered.

Daron recovered from the Lord's visit, completely amazed at the turn of events. The Lord Himself had actually done what Daron had set out to do. But why? It made no sense. Hagar was returning to the camp to have her child! Yet the prophecy given to Hagar made it clear that this son—Ishmael—though he would become a great nation in his own right, would not be the son of promise.

Hagar would no longer feel the need to advance her son in Abram's eyes. Why? Because, the Lord, it seems, had bought Hagar and Ishmael off by giving them an inheritance of their own. Daron left immediately to report to the council, wondering why the Most High allowed Hagar to return to Abram.

"Because the Most High has a sentimental weakness for human folly," said Kara. "That is why Hagar has returned to Abram."

Kara's pride had been stung by Hagar's abrupt decision to bolt. It showed a critical flaw in his thinking about human behavior—the very thing he had admonished to Michael. He had vowed he would never again be caught by surprise. And so he spoke before the council, defending his plan and blaming the primitive natures of humans for his inability to anticipate what had happened.

"I sometimes think the Lord is just as capricious as the humans He made in His image," said Lenaes, who had risen to Kara's defense. "Both God and man can be wildly unpredictable."

"Yes," said Pellecus. "But by now you should realize that the Lord is fully committed to these creatures. He didn't have to send Hagar back. He could have allowed her to die in the wilderness. After all, she does not carry the child of promise." He looked sternly at Kara. "Not anymore, at any rate."

"Don't lay the blame at my feet, my learned friend," Kara shot back. "You and the wisdom of this council saw the possibility of substituting a fraudulent heir in the hope of capturing the prophecy."

"Enough of this," said Lucifer, who seemed bored at the council. "It's clear that we were mistaken. However, there is one bright spot to Abram's folly. The Most High will create a nation out of Ishmael that will prove bothersome to his brothers. We can look forward to exploiting the bad blood that will exist between Ishmael and the true child of promise for years to come!"

"So what do we do now, my prince?" asked Rugio.

Lucifer smiled at his favorite warrior.

"We wait, Rugio, we wait. Abram has proven that, though he is a man of faith he is also a man of folly," said Lucifer. "He has been tested many times by the Lord and failed. Recall that when he was called out of Ur, he delayed arriving in Canaan for years."

"Yes, but ultimately he arrived and in so doing was obedient to the Lord," said Pellecus. "And God blessed him mightily."

"And when the famine hit Canaan he fled into Egypt rather than trust in the Lord," Lucifer continued. "As a result of that little episode he almost lost his wife Sarai out of fear of the king, and he picked up the troublesome Hagar!"

"Still the Lord has seen his heart and declared him righteous," said Pellecus.

"Most recently he listened to the desperate pleadings of his wife and conceived through Hagar a false heir, and we were all hopeful. Nevertheless, he has created a nation that will one day plague him!"

"And still the Lord allowed Hagar back into the camp," said Pellecus. "And still, and still, and still! My lord, I admit that the pattern of failure we see in Abram is encouraging. But the prophecy is alive and well. It seems pointless to continue!"

For a moment, Lucifer looked at the members of the council, who were completely silent.

"And still we must," he said, almost whispering.

"What are we to do, lord?" asked Rugio. "We are your servants."

"We wait for another test, Rugio...and another. If we can depend on one thing about humans, my brothers, it is that they have a propensity for failure. I predict that someday Abram will face a test that will strike at his very core—and *then* we shall see how righteous this man really is."

Chronicles of the Host

Abraham

Hagar indeed returned to Sarai and humbled herself, and in due time gave birth to a son, whom she named Ishmael, as the Lord had instructed her. The boy grew up, and Abram was very fond of him; but there remained the vacancy of an unfulfilled promise, as he and Sarai did not hear from the Lord for many years. The promise, it seemed, had been silenced.

None of the Host knew when or if the Lord would deliver the promise. Some speculated that perhaps the Most High was punishing Abram for his rashness in the incident with Hagar; others thought that Ishmael might turn out to be the one foretold.

Crispin often said that the foolishness of angels in speculation is almost as foolish as the speculations of men, and so he was proven correct. For when Abram was 99 years old, the Lord appeared to him, encouraging him that the promise was indeed alive—and that Sarai would give birth to a son!

The Lord also established a covenant of circumcision, by which all the future male children were set apart to the Lord in a symbolic act of the sacred and the profane. Most significant of all, as far as the prophecy was concerned, was that the Lord changed Abram's name to Abraham, meaning "father of nations"; He also changed the name of Sarai to Sarah, meaning "princess of nations."

At Mamre, the Lord appeared again to Abraham, in the company of two angels. They prophesied not only the birth of Isaac, but also the destruction of Sodom and Gomorrah, two cities whose wickedness cried out to the Lord in Heaven. A promise of life and a promise of death were thus spoken by the Lord. Now this was a terrifying prospect for Abraham, whose nephew had taken residence in those vile cities.

Abraham pleaded, for the sake of those few righteous who might live within the cities, for the Lord to stay his wrath. And so it was that God Most High, out of love for Abraham, sent the two angels who had accompanied him at Mamre, to warn Abraham's nephew Lot of the soon-coming judgment upon Sodom and Gomorrah...

CHAPTER 12

"This is the freedom Lucifer promised."

Michael and Gabriel resolutely made their way toward the great plateau on which the cities of Sodom and Gomorrah were situated. They took no pleasure in carrying out the Lord's judgment. Still in the guise of the men who had met with Abraham earlier, they walked the dusty road eastward down the plain that began sloping lazily toward Jordan. Word of their approach had already preceded them; jeering devils reproached them nearly every step of the way.

"Who is the principal of this city?" Michael demanded of one of the demons who harassed him from the roadside. "Who is the strongman in Sodom?"

"Ah, Lord Michael," came a hissing voice. "You shall see when you are overcome. Two great princes of the Canaanites rule these cities."

"Not Bera and Birsha, the earthly kings of Sodom and Gomorrah," retorted Gabriel. "What dark spirit holds sway here?"

"Know that the god Milicom rules these cities," came the hissing voice, barely audible among so many spirits. "He is very powerful and is worshiped by these and many others who live in and around the two great cities."

"Milicom!" said Michael in disgust to Gabriel. "Just another lust-filled devil who incites depravity and bloody appetites among the humans. Playing at God! If only humans would see through the nonsense that these hateful creatures conjure up."

"Milicom is a great god," said another voice from the roadside. "And he will destroy you, archangel—you and any other creature who profanes his cities with its presence!" The devils broke out in laughter all around.

The number of fallen angels was increasing as they neared the wicked cities, creating a veil of sorts that Michael and Gabriel had to wade through, like a dank fog that was becoming darker and darker. Michael wondered if he should not call in some more angels to scatter these harassing spirits, but decided to wait until they reached the city gates, which were now in their sight. Gabriel also kept a weary eye on the spirits, who were closing in but not really touching them.

The cities of Sodom and Gomorrah were situated a few miles apart in a great plain to the east of Beersheba. Bera, king of Sodom, and Birsha, king of Gomorrah, ruled the wicked cities in vile contempt of all that was righteous. The people of those cities had given themselves over completely to their passions, and in doing so, had so far removed themselves from the Most High's holiness that He had decided to destroy them before their wickedness became like a plague unchecked.

"Make way for the archangels!" a voice cried out.

Unseen to the humans who were passing through the city gate, devils created a pathway for Michael and Gabriel, jeering them but never daring to touch them. This was easily one of the most vile spots on earth. Everywhere the carnage of sin was evident. Humans engaging in every aspect of unchecked passion filled the streets. Laughter, screaming, and cursing filled the air. Sometimes it was difficult for the archangels to distinguish between the voices of humans and those of the fallen angels—both chattered and carried on in the most disgraceful manner.

"This is the freedom Lucifer promised," said Michael with disgust.

"He certainly delivered," Gabriel responded, looking at the grim consequences of rebellion all around him. "The angels who went with him are no better. Sin is sin in the eyes of the Most High—whether of men or of angels."

"Michael! Gabriel! Welcome!"

The two angels looked up in the direction of the voice.

"Welcome to my little principality!"

Up on a balcony the once-holy angel who was now worshiped as Milicom, the Devourer, smirked at the two angels. He was surrounded by large warriors who took on his own appearance, that of a human body with the head resembling a locust. Michael was repulsed by the hideous creature.

"Come now, Michael," said Milicom. "I know that my form has changed. But it is a small price to pay for being a god. In Heaven I was merely one of millions who served in the Temple sanctuary, bowing and scraping to a God who never listened." He indicated the recently constructed temple that had been dedicated to him. "Now it is I who am listened to...worshiped by men! Just listen to them."

"Worshiped? You have merely captured the hearts of men already deceived, Milicom," said Gabriel. "Nothing more. You are no god, but a disgraced angel who, like thousands of your brothers, has established himself as a local god to harass and deceive. Nothing more."

"Enough!" Milicom roared, startling some of his guard. "I have sworn to serve my master, and he has established me as prince here!" He looked at Michael with suspicion. "Why do you disturb the peace of this city? We have done nothing to you."

Michael indicated to Gabriel that enough discussion with the proud Milicom had occurred, and they continued on their way. Milicom's threats continued roaring in the background, even over the din of the city. "These come to bring dishonor to this place. Watch them!" he said.

Michael and Gabriel stopped for a moment and then turned away from the would-be god. They ignored the chatter of other demons, who demanded respect and warned of the danger that would befall Michael and Gabriel should they cross Lucifer in any matter. The angels were amazed at the sheer number of fallen spirits who roamed these streets at will, inciting men and women to every sordid behavior imaginable.

The presence of the two strangers in Sodom drew many stares, as men and women looked upon them with growing curiosity. Aroused by the swirling dark spirits around them, and emboldened by the increasing cover of darkness as the sun set, many of the men, both young and old, began calling after the pair with lewd and suggestive remarks. Michael and Gabriel ignored the debauched comments and continued toward the place where Lot lived. Hopefully they could remove Lot before the judgment began.

"There he is. Sitting in the gate we passed earlier."

Michael and Gabriel came upon Lot, seated at the entrance to the city. They looked upon his countenance, which suggested a weary and divided heart. Lot's decision to settle in Sodom had become more and more burdensome, and he knew in his heart that he did not belong with these people. But where was he to go? Though vile by any standard, Sodom afforded Lot the commerce for his livestock that he needed to support his family's expensive tastes. And so he sat at the gate—neither in nor out, neither hot nor cold.

"Lot!"

Lot looked up vacantly at the two strangers. Suddenly he gathered his robes and, getting on his knees, bowed low before the angels, recognizing them as an embassy from the Lord. He lay with his face to the ground until Michael urged him onto his feet. The few people who had stopped to watch the spectacle of Lot throwing himself on the ground continued on their way.

Many of the dark spirits of the city had begun to envelop the area, and with their arrival a crowd of the men of Sodom began to gather. The jeering devils defiled the name of the Lord and demanded that Michael and Gabriel leave the city at once.

"They all favor their prince in this city, don't they?" mused Michael, looking upon the locust-headed spirit creatures that were swarming them.

"They have taken on the appearance of that which moves them," agreed Gabriel in a grim tone. "And so have the men! "

He indicated the men of Sodom, who were beginning to close in around them. As more and more of the devils arrived, the crowd of men grew and became more and more emboldened in their lewdness. Lot became increasingly nervous and urged that they come to his house at once.

"Lot, we are afraid of nothing in this city," said Michael. "We are here in the name of the Lord Most High. We shall spend the night here, in the square of this town."

"The town square," mused Gabriel, looking about. "Perfect, Michael...the seat of Milicom's authority in Sodom. What better place to rest?" Michael smiled at his brother's ingenuity.

Lot responded nervously, "Nevertheless I beg you to enjoy the hospitality of my home. In the morning you may leave as early as you wish. Only, for my sake, do not stay in the city tonight."

Milicom had just arrived on the scene, stirring up his charges, who in turn were inflaming the people through their debased minds. The men began to shout loudly now, demanding that Lot mind his own business. Michael looked up at Milicom, whose smirk belied his enjoyment of the disturbance. It wasn't often that he could demonstrate his authority over men and spirits in the presence of an archangel!

"Very well, Lot," said Michael. "We shall come to your house. But I think you are inviting trouble upon yourself in your eagerness to serve us."

The group hurried down a narrow street just off the square, where Lot lived. The men in the town followed from a distance, egged on by Milicom's lust-filled devils. Milicom smiled and said aloud, "Yes, Michael. Lot is inviting much more trouble than your realize."

Throughout the meal that was set before them Michael and Gabriel remained aloof from Lot's inquiries. He understood them to be somehow connected to the Lord, perhaps through his uncle Abraham. He tried in subtle ways to coax information out of the mysterious strangers who shared his food. But they remained silent.

"Lot!" came a drunken voice from outside.

"Let us in!" came another.

"We will have those two men who are in with you," said yet another man. "You have shown them your hospitality. Now let us show them ours!"

A roar of approving laughter followed the last words, as a crowd pressed in on Lot's house. Lot looked up at his guests, who seemed indifferent to the disturbance and continued eating. He went outside, quickly shutting the door to his house, to talk to the men in hopes of turning them away from their carnal intent.

"Please don't do these things. These men are my guests," he pleaded.

"Out of our way, Lot," said an old man with wine on his breath. "We will have those men. And if you don't step back we'll have you, too!"

"Look," said Lot. "I have two daughters that you may use for your purposes. Only don't touch these men."

The crowd growled in anger, demanding that Lot move out of the way or suffer the consequences. Someone through a stone, which glanced off Lot's shoulder. Another grabbed Lot and began to pull him out of the way. Others reached up to pull Lot into the street, despite his protests.

Milicom was watching from the rooftop across the street. He ordered the spirits under his command to cause the men of Sodom to charge the house and tear Lot apart in the process. Hysterical, shrieking spirits moved in and out of the crowd, attaching themselves to the minds of men and fueling a lust and anger that could only be satisfied in the most foul ways.

The commotion was attracting other Sodomites, including some of the king's soldiers, who joined in the effort to bring Lot down and break in the door. *If only Lucifer were here to see this,* Milicom thought to himself proudly. *He would give me even greater territory!*

Lot suddenly felt a strong arm pulling him back into the house. He was thrown onto the floor in the middle of the room and looked up to see the two men standing in the open doorway!

From his perch, Milicom saw Michael and Gabriel in the doorway. "There they are!" he shrieked. "Take those two now!" The demon-inspired men of the town charged Michael and Gabriel.

"There they are!" said a man, who led the charge to Lot's door. Others followed him as they rushed Lot's house.

The men stopped for a second as Michael suddenly swung his arm out in a cutting motion. The humans saw only his hand coming down—the demons saw in his hand a great sword. Then a brilliant flash of light pulsed from Lot's front door, blinding the men of Sodom and sending them scurrying about in a hopeless rage. They staggered in confusion as they left Lot's house. The sword of the archangel sent the demons scattering, too. Even Milicom was knocked off balance for a moment as Michael cut a mighty, gaping hole in the air.

In the meantime, Gabriel was inside the house talking to Lot. "Gather your family and whoever else is with you and take them out of this city. For we have been sent to destroy it and all who live here."

Lot quickly rallied his family. His sons-in-law thought he was joking. But the angels seized the family and led them out of the city personally, for they understood that Lot had the compassion of the Lord upon him.

Milicom, however, watched helplessly as Lot and his family made their way through the city, easily avoiding the many blinded men who staggered about. He quickly went to his temple and entered into the heart of Kazak, the high priest whose cult worshiped the demon. Taking control of this man, who had given himself completely to darkness, Milicom caused him to speed to the home of Bera, king of Sodom.

The priest stirred up in Bera's heart murderous thoughts against Lot.

"How dare Lot invite strange men into his house?" raged Kazak. "These men were undoubtedly spies sent by Abraham to scout out Sodom for conquest on behalf of his nephew. They have defiled the gods of Sodom, and Milicom, our great god, has been profaned! His wrath will be upon you, O king, if it is not appeased."

"I should have killed Lot when he first came," said Bera, barely containing his hatred. "Abraham, he now calls himself. The father of nations! Bah! His ambition has become a threat to us all in this valley!"

He quickly arose, with great anger, and ordered the captain of his personal troop to assemble a squad of men to find Lot at any cost. As he put on his garments of war he spoke to the captain of the troop.

"Kill them on sight, do you understand?" said Bera. "All of them!"

Kazak smiled as the soldiers left. So did Milicom.

When the fugitive party reached the gate of Sodom the angels stopped. They ordered Lot and his family into the mountains for their own protection. Lot looked at the distant mountains.

"Please, sirs," he begged. "We will never make it to the mountains in time. Let me take my family to a nearby town called Zoar."

"Very well," said Michael. "We will spare Zoar, though the rest of this valley will perish. Only go—and do not look back, lest evil befall you!"

Lot and his family scurried away, hurrying up from the valley toward the little city of Zoar. Michael and Gabriel turned to see the high priest, Kazak, sword in hand, leading a mob of citizens. With them were the soldiers sent by Bera.

"There are the profaners!" shouted Kazak. "Destroy them! Soldiers—hunt down Lot and his family who have escaped the city!" The soldiers ran through the gate and gave chase.

The crowd suddenly stopped and got quiet as Michael and Gabriel began to transform before their very eyes. The human disguises gave way to their angelic appearance! Seeing the archangels in all their authority, Milicom's devils scattered. The men of Sodom were awestruck. Even Kazak was taken aback for a moment.

"The judgment of the Lord is upon this place!" Michael shouted. The archangels held their swords toward the heavens.

By this time Bera drew up on horseback, amazed at what he was seeing. Kazak recovered and, inspired by Milicom, who was still in control of his mind, began shouting that these were demon gods sent by Abraham, and that they must invoke the gods of Sodom to war against them.

A flash of light streaked out of the swords of the archangels into the sky and burst like thousands of particles, which began to rain down on Sodom and the other wicked cities in the valley judged by the Most High. Large stones of fire fell on the city, as the people shrieked and scattered, running for cover. Fire and fallen animals added to the chaos. The wardens of the gates thought the city to be under attack and ordered the gates sealed, trapping the people inside.

Kazak rushed back to the temple and was killed when a stone hit him as he prayed to Milicom. He died at the bloody altar as he invoked the name of the god who by now had deserted him, for Milicom had fled when the wrath began to fall. Bera took cover in his palace, hoping to escape through a tunnel that led outside of the city. But the house was quickly consumed by fire, and the king died as it collapsed upon him.

Within minutes the entire valley was consumed by this fire from Heaven. Even the soldiers in pursuit of Lot were killed by crushing, flaming stones that fell outside the city. Lot's own wife perished horribly when she looked back, against the archangel's command. Then the fire stopped falling.

Miles away, Abraham could see a great plume of smoke rising in the east. He made his way toward the smoke with Ishmael, and the two of them looked into the valley, foul with the smell of sulfur, where the cities had been overthrown. He thought of those he knew in that city, and wondered if perhaps his nephew had escaped. The servant with Abraham remarked about the great column of billowy, white smoke that rose high into the air.

But Abraham saw something else—perhaps for the first time. Looking upon the smoldering city of Sodom, and hearing the faint screams of the dying, he sensed the significance of the promise of God that Abraham should bear a Seed to His name. It was no longer about Abraham's longing for a son, but God's promise of a savior...

Abraham began to weep. He now understood in his heart that, unless God acted to reconcile humans to Himself, as grim a fate as had befallen Sodom awaited all of mankind.

Chronicles of the Host

Isaac's Birth, Ishmael's Scorn

What a day of rejoicing when Isaac was born! The Host of Heaven celebrated noisily along with the house of Abraham. This was also a very important time for Serus, Michael's apprenticed angel, who was given the important assignment of watching over the boy's progress.

As the child grew, we witnessed with some amazement how deeply humans could love. Abraham was devoted to the son of his old age. He instructed Isaac in the ways of the Lord. Though he loved Ishmael, and was comforted by the Lord Himself that Ishmael would become a mighty nation, it was Isaac, the child of Sarah's womb—the child they had waited so long for—who was the object of Abraham's greater love.

It so happened that over time Ishmael, true to the prophecy spoken over his life, began to mock Isaac, and once more Sarah demanded of her husband that Hagar and her child be sent away. Encouraged by the Lord, Abraham sent Hagar and Ishmael away. The Angel of the Lord appeared to Hagar again and guided her and Ishmael to a new life away from Abraham.

As we watched the boy grow in strength and stature, we understood that nothing could separate Abraham from his son...nothing, that is, except the Lord Himself...

"Serus!"

"Well, Gabriel," said Serus. "Welcome to Hebron!"

Gabriel walked over to where Serus stood, watching Abraham and Isaac in conversation. The old man looked somehow younger now, as if Isaac had invigorated him. Serus enjoyed watching the two of them together, and indeed was finding his current assignment as guardian of Isaac quite fulfilling.

"Abraham loves his son so," said Serus. "Just look at the two of them! There rests great hope in that boy for all humans. A fine lad!"

"Yes, Serus," said Gabriel. "A fine lad."

Serus noticed that Gabriel seemed quite sullen. The archangel kept his eyes on the two humans—father and son—enjoying the day together as they worked with a new bow that Isaac was making.

"Gabriel, what is the matter?" asked Serus.

Gabriel looked at Serus and smiled a rather weak smile.

"Serus, you understand that as a servant of God you are called upon to execute very difficult tasks at times?" asked Gabriel.

"Yes, of course," said Serus guardedly. "Am I being relieved of this assignment?"

"No, Serus," said Gabriel. "In fact you are to carry through to the very end of this task. You have been given a very special season in the life of the promise. It is a great honor for you."

"Yes, Gabriel, a great honor," agreed Serus, still uncertain where Gabriel was taking the conversation.

"As I said, we are not always to understand the things of the Lord," Gabriel continued. "Our honor is in serving God without question as to His motives…"

"Excuse me, Gabriel," interrupted Serus. "But what is going to happen?"

Gabriel watched as Isaac walked off to try out the new bow that he had made with his father. He then looked at Serus and answered.

"A test. Abraham is going to be tested by the Lord."

"Tested?" repeated Serus. "What sort of test?"

"A sacrifice."

"Oh," said Serus, relaxing a bit. "What is to be sacrificed?"

"Isaac."

Abraham was hoping that Isaac would get a kill his first time out with the fine bow he had made. It was a sturdy weapon, and should bring down a deer or wild pig if his aim was good. The camp seemed empty whenever Isaac was gone—even for short ventures like this.

As for Ishmael, the last report Abraham had received was that he and Hagar had settled in the wilderness of Paran toward Arabia. He had taken an Egyptian wife and was raising his family in the desert. It warmed Abraham's heart to know that God was taking care of both of his children.

"Abraham!"

Abraham by now recognized the voice of the Lord as one would recognize the voice of a friend. He immediately responded.

"I am here, Lord," answered Abraham, squinting in the sun as he looked around.

"Hear Me, Abraham. You must take your son, your only son Isaac, whom you love so very much, and you must go to Moriah with him."

"Yes, Lord," said Abraham, a bit confused. *"And then what?"*

Serus and Gabriel stood and watched from a distance as Abraham received instruction from the Lord. Though Serus knew in his heart that whatever the Most High did, He did with great wisdom and forethought, it perplexed him to watch this scene unfold. Here was the son of promise—the child in whom both men and angels had been hoping—about to be delivered unto death.

He looked to Gabriel for answers, but Gabriel could offer none that would satisfy Serus's queries. Is the Lord going to bring back Ishmael after all? Is this not the son of promise? Surely the Lord is not going to have Sarah bear yet another child. All of these questions rang through Serus's mind as he watched God and man in dialogue. He felt pity for Abraham. And he was very sad himself.

"When you get to the mountains of Moriah, you are to sacrifice your son as a burnt offering," the Lord said.

"A burnt offering?" Abraham repeated the words. "My son?"

"*Yes,*" said the Lord. "*At a place that I shall disclose once you are in the region of Moriah.*"

"My Lord and God," said Abraham. "For some 50 years I have walked with You. Always You have shown Yourself a true and faithful Lord. During times of great stress You were my relief; whenever I strayed from Your trust You brought me back; when You promised me a son, You delivered a son—even in my old age and even when my wife's womb was barren.

"And now, O Lord, You ask me to give back to You in sacrifice the greatest love of my life—the very son You promised me years ago. You ask me to offer in sacrifice the person I cherish most on earth along with my wife. Lord I know that the vile nations around us offer their children to the devil god Molech. You are a righteous God and yet You ask for the life of my son. I don't understand…"

Abraham looked down at the bits of sinew and shavings clinging to his feet—evidence of the bow he had just made with Isaac. Even now the boy was out hunting, totally unaware that his life had been claimed by the Most High. Abraham swallowed hard, looking now at Sarah's tent. How could he explain this to her? She had finally come to the point of trusting the God who had called her from her family in Ur. Was she now to trust that the same God had called for her son's death?

"Lord Most High, I don't understand," Abraham said, strangely feeling a surge of peace beginning to overtake his anxiety. "But this I know. If Isaac is indeed the son of promise, and if indeed You are calling me to do this, then I believe that Isaac's destiny is assured."

He pulled his knife out of his belt and held it high to the Lord, the flint blade shimmering toward the heavens. "And should it come to the killing of Isaac, if that is Your will, then I believe that the promise is assured—even should You raise the boy from the dead! Blessed be the name of the Lord!"

CHAPTER 13

"As Isaac goes, so goes the promise."

Serus trailed a short distance behind Abraham's party, which was making its way toward Moriah. Along with the father and son were two servants, and a donkey on which was the kindling for the burnt offering. Abraham and Isaac had gathered the wood themselves the day before. Abraham's mind drifted behind to Sarah. He had told her he was taking Isaac on a three-day journey to sacrifice to the Lord. She had cautioned him to be very careful of Isaac. Abraham looked at his son, who was enjoying the adventure of exploring a region he had never before visited.

Serus had gone on alone—Gabriel said that he must make this journey on his own. But other angels had picked up on the news and were beginning to show up at various points along the way. Many of the devils watched in disbelief as the boy of promise walked by on his way to execution. They mocked Serus as well.

"Some guardian!" shouted one. "Save him, if you are a true angel of God."

"Perhaps the test is yours, Serus," suggested another. "To see if you will be bold enough to rescue Isaac from his father's blade!"

Serus ignored the jeering rebels and kept a watchful eye on Isaac. For three days they continued up the sloping hills toward Moriah. When they finally arrived in the region, Abraham ordered the men to make a camp. He then told them that he and the boy would go and sacrifice to the Lord, and that they would both be back.

"Both of them?" asked a puzzled Kara, who arrived at the last moment with Pellecus in order to watch the spectacle. "Abraham and Sarah will be sending for Ishmael within a week! You see, my plan worked after all!"

"It's truly an amazing thing," said Pellecus, very puzzled by it all. "I still wonder about this whole thing. I am suspicious of the Most High."

"Such delicious irony," noted Kara. "The poor boy is carrying the very wood on which he is to be sacrificed!"

"Seems a cruel joke, I must admit," said Pellecus. "Carrying the instrument of his own execution."

A crowd of devils jeered Isaac as he walked by them, carrying the bundle of wood on his shoulders. "Kill him!" they shouted, calling him all sorts of vile names.

"I believe the Most High can share the stage for only so long," said Kara. "And then He must act to recapture it!"

Pellecus could only muster a "Kara, you're a fool" look of disdain.

"It's true. It happened in Heaven, too. I always knew that the Lord could not stand to lose face," Kara continued. "Obviously, the fact that all eyes were upon Isaac got the better of Him. I tell you, the Lord is no more righteous than Lucifer. They both enjoy adoration and will go to any lengths to justify it. Once Isaac is dead Lucifer can press his case and end this war on those grounds alone!"

"Quiet," said Pellecus. "They are beginning!"

Isaac dropped the bundle of wood that he was carrying exactly where his father instructed him to. Abraham then put down the knife and the firepot that he was carrying and looked at his son, tears in his eyes.

"Father, what is the matter?" asked Isaac.

"It is time to make sacrifice, my son," Abraham responded.

Isaac looked about but didn't see the usual animal.

"The Lord Himself shall provide the sacrifice, my son," said Abraham. He then motioned Isaac over to him and hugged him for a long time. Isaac wasn't sure why his father was acting like this, but he remained in the embrace. At length Abraham released him.

They began to build an altar and arrange the wood on it. Isaac was still looking about for the animal that was to be sacrificed. Abraham took a cord and began to tie up his son.

"Father, what does this mean? You're not going to kill me?"

"The Lord has commanded it so," said Abraham, beginning to weep.

Isaac also began to weep.

"But Father, I don't understand!"

"It is not ours to understand, my son," said Abraham. He picked up the boy and lay him on top of the wood. "I love you, my son."

He picked the knife up and held it in his hand.

Serus could not bear to watch what was about to happen. He turned his face from the altar. He could see the leering faces of dark spirits who had come in to watch the killing of Isaac and, hopefully, the death of a promise.

"As Isaac goes, so goes the promise," Kara said haughtily. "And then the prophecy will be nullified!"

Pellecus nodded in polite agreement, but secretly wondered if that was really true.

"There he goes!" said Kara, as Abraham raised the knife.

"Abraham! Abraham!"

All of the angels looked up and saw the Angel of the Lord streaking out of Heaven in a blazing light. It was the same angel who had appeared with the other two at Mamre. Abraham dropped the knife and fell to his knees. The Angel came and stood at the altar. Isaac was still trembling and wondering whom his father was talking to, since he could see and hear nobody else.

"Do not touch the boy," said the Angel. *"For you have truly shown Me that you are a righteous man who loves Me. You did not withhold from Me your very own son!"*

Kara and Pellecus had vanished immediately upon the Angel's arrival. Once more they were incredulous at the turn of events in this war. The other fallen angels likewise dispersed at the Angel's presence. All who remained were Serus, Abraham, and Isaac. The two men were now weeping tears of relief. Then the Angel disappeared as well.

"Look, Father—over there!"

In a thicket was a fine ram, caught by its horns. Abraham untied Isaac, and together they sacrificed the ram in the name of the Lord on the very altar that had been intended for Isaac. Serus watched proudly as father and son worshiped together. He was also proud that his Lord had spared the boy of whom he had grown so fond.

A Voice called out from Heaven, *"I swear by Myself that because you have not withheld your own son, I will bless you with an uncountable heritage. You will possess great cities and all nations on earth will be blessed because you obeyed Me!"*

Serus followed the two back to the base of the hill where the servants had set up camp. He had seen a great thing today—how obedience proved greater than a sacrifice. He had seen how a man could please God by trusting Him enough to give up everything. And he had seen that the promise was alive and well—that all the world would be blessed through the seed of Abraham because he had obeyed at Moriah.

Chronicles of the Host

Sarah

It is a bittersweet thing to watch the life and death of a human. Like a soft flower that springs forth in its glory and then disappears all too rapidly, so it is with humans, who never realize how quickly life passes until death is upon them. So it was with Sarah, who died and was buried by Abraham in a cave purchased from a local prince.

One of Abraham's last actions before his death was to send for a wife for Isaac from his own people in Ur. He would not have Isaac marry one of the Canaanite women. Afterwards Abraham was buried next to Sarah, and we angels remembered him as a most faithful man.

With the birth of twins to Isaac and his wife, Rebekah, it was evident that a new phase in the building of the great nation was underway. For the word of prophecy spoken over these two brothers was that the elder brother would serve the younger. And so it was that when the children were delivered, the younger son, Jacob, grabbed the heel of his elder brother, Esau—an action that seemed to portray their relationship from that point on.

Jacob and Esau

Jacob was a rascal of a boy and man. With the encouragement of his mother, Rebekah, he managed to take both the birthright and the blessing of his older brother, Esau. This was puzzling to the angels, who deliberated as to how such unruly creatures carried within them the seeds of Lucifer's destruction.

From that very day Esau swore murderous revenge upon his brother Jacob. It would, we thought, be our mission to protect Jacob from Esau's murderous threats. The Lord, as it turned out, had a different plan for Jacob...one which we foolish angels did not contemplate...one in which a future nation was to be born out of a great struggle with the Lord's Angel at Mahanaim...

Jacob watched as Laban said a tender farewell to his daughters. Leah and Rachel presented their children one by one, and Laban invoked a blessing over them. Tearfully, his eyes met the eyes of his beloved daughters, whom he would most likely never see again.

Leah, the eldest, who had become a pawn in a treacherous bid to keep Jacob within Laban's hire, hugged her father and wept. Memories flooded Laban's mind: how Jacob had agreed to work seven long and difficult years for Laban in exchange for Rachel's hand in marriage; how Laban had substituted Leah for Rachel in the wedding chamber; how Jacob then agreed to work seven more years in order to also marry Rachel; and how God had blessed Leah's womb to bear many sons to Jacob.

Rachel, the more beautiful of the two girls, next stood in front of her father. Having been barren for years, she had recently given birth to Joseph, who was instantly Jacob's favorite child. Rachel was the woman Jacob had wanted all along. She too had become a tool in Laban's hands to keep Jacob at work. Now both of his daughters were leaving for good. It was time to let them go. Laban tenderly kissed his daughter, Rachel, and blessed little Joseph.

Laban said his final farewells and blessed Jacob as he went, "May your God be with you always, Jacob, as He has proven Himself strong all these years. And may He ever be witness to the covenant made between us that we shall never harm each other again!" With that, Laban and his party headed back home to Haran.

The daughters watched their father disappear into the wilderness. Then, as if stirred out of a dream, they began preparing their children for the day's journey. The activity of a camp on the move was comforting to Jacob. It seemed to him that he was always on the move. Always in search of the next well...or the next pasture...or the next dream. Always pursuing or being pursued—

—by an outraged brother from whom he had stolen a birthright and a blessing
—by an unreasonable father-in-law who had been tricked out of his flocks and did not want to allow his daughters to leave
—by a faithful God, who had made a promise to Abraham and his descendants that they should be blessed and was closing the ring on Jacob even now...

The company of animals, family, and servants made its way west. Jacob couldn't help but feel a sense of foreboding as the land began to take on familiar features—they were getting closer to home...closer to Isaac...closer to Esau.

They were coming into the land...the very land that had been promised to his grandfather Abraham so many years before. His father, Isaac, had often told Jacob the stories of Abraham's early wanderings in Canaan: how he met with God as one would meet with a friend; how he was willing to give up his son Isaac on the altar of sacrifice if that was what the Lord required; how Abraham was faithful in so much. Isaac had faithfully burdened the responsibility of leading the family in Canaan; of raising his sons Esau and Jacob and maintaining their closeness with God. Soon it would be Jacob's turn to lead the family of promise in the Promised Land. His father had always led a simple life of faith in the Lord. Jacob felt so distant from the Lord these days.

He surveyed the arid land around him, peering into the vastness of the open terrain. The sun was beginning to descend into the western horizon, though it was still light enough to see. But it was getting colder as the day gave way to darkness. Jacob searched the twilight sky with his heart and mind.

He could almost feel Abraham looking down upon him from the heavens as he retraced the steps that the patriarch had made so many years earlier. *Are you disappointed in me, Father Abraham?* Jacob thought in a half-serious-half-cynical frame of mind. *I'm sure my father, Isaac, is wondering what ever happened to the family of great promise*, Jacob continued in his thoughts. *Such promise...two great sons to carry on the heritage!*

Jacob chuckled to himself. "What sons of promise! One marries out of the nation—what a scandal *that* was. The other son is a schemer returning to a land promised to him, but that he hardly even knows!"

Jacob shook his head and laughed a little...then he sighed. And yet, he couldn't help but feel a sense of destiny in all of this...as if events that had great purpose were overtaking his life in a way that he could not understand. Had not the God of Abraham and Isaac prospered him even while he had been under Laban's bondage?

God had remained faithful all the time he was away from his father and mother, hiding from the wrath of his brother Esau. The reality of the living God began to encompass Jacob in a way that he had never before realized. His heart was pricked a little as he wondered whether somehow he could know the Lord as his grandfather had...as a friend.

He shook himself from such a foolish notion. How could one whose name meant "deceiver" be a friend to the God of his fathers? Perhaps Esau should have received the birthright after all. Just maybe God would choose another family...another Abraham. Then Jacob could live out his days a wealthy shepherd with family and privilege.

But he knew too much about the promises of God from his fathers. That God would make good on His word to the family...that there was much more at stake than Jacob's little concerns...that somehow the world was to be blessed through the holy covenant that God had made with Abraham.

*If only there **was** a way to be a part of all this,* Jacob thought. He then did something he hadn't done with real intensity in a very long time.

He prayed.

"God of my father, Isaac, and grandfather, Abraham. If You are truly wanting my family to be blessed, and to be a blessing, I pray You would give me a sign that You are leading me..."

"There he is," a voice said from the darkness. "There is Jacob."

"And what are we to tell him?" asked another.

"*We* are not to say a word," came the answer.

Before he could even finish his prayer, Jacob saw several figures appear before him on either side of the roadway. Expecting his mount to become frightened, he gripped the rein a little tighter. The animal passed on, totally unaware of the angelic presences. Jacob rubbed his eyes, blaming the sighting on the twilight dimness that was closing in. He passed one of the figures on his right and looked around to see if anyone else could see them. He then turned to see if the apparitions were still there—expecting them to be gone. But there they stood!

"This is where we will camp tonight!" Jacob shouted to the caravan. "This is the camp of God!"

He turned again to see the angels, but they were no longer there. He squinted his eyes to make sure and looked one more time. Only darkness.

"My lord, there is water nearby," said a servant. "We will go and fill the jars and water the animals."

"Good," said Jacob. "Tell me. Did you see anything a few minutes ago?"

"Not that I know of, my lord," said the servant. "Should I have?"

"Apparently not," mused Jacob. "Thank you."

The servant turned to leave, puzzled by his master's question. The noise of the camp being set up brought Jacob out of his reverie. He found his wives and began telling them everything that had happened. He called the place "Mahanaim" or "double camp," because, in addition to his own camp, it was quite obvious that there was an unseen camp nearby—of the Host of Heaven. They were indeed a "double camp"!

The fact that he had seen angels gave Jacob a greater confidence that whatever happened to him and his family, the Lord was watching over the situation. He surveyed the camp as it settled down into the evening's routine. How fortunate he was to possess such capable and loyal servants. He watched as the men divided up the night's routine of watching, waiting, and securing the animals.

Later that evening, the smell of a meaty stew served by Leah jolted Jacob's memory. He looked at the thick red mixture of meat and herbs and, as the steam entered his nostrils, his mind took him instantly to another time...another place...another stew...a very costly stew...

The shout of triumph from the field told the tale: Esau had hunted successfully again. This time it was an old boar which had been rooting around the camp for some time but had proven itself illusive. Esau was determined to hunt down this wild pig and kill it. Today he had succeeded.

Jacob and his mother, Rebekah, watched Esau's athletic figure romping towards them through the fields around Beer Lahai Roi. Rebekah held Jacob closely at her side as Isaac (her husband and the father of the two boys) ran out to greet Esau. Esau's front was covered with the blood of the great beast and in his hands were the large tusks—a trophy of his greatest kill to date.

"I did it, Father, I did it!" shouted Esau. "I killed that wild pig! You should have seen him go down. He never even knew that I was on his heels, tracking him like a lion..."

Isaac listened with great enthusiasm to Esau's adventure. He beamed with pride as Esau described the final moments of the pig's life and how he delivered the mortal wound by cutting the animal's throat—he even made a slitting motion with his finger underneath his own throat. Jacob saw Isaac look at Rebekah with pride. At times Isaac would glance at Jacob as if to say, "Are you getting any of this?"

"I suppose you had to fight the pig for the knife," Jacob finally blurted out sarcastically. He felt Rebekah tighten her grip upon him. "Was that the blind old boar that has lived around here since Grandfather Abraham was herding?"

"Poor Jacob. You'll never make a hunter, will you? I don't know if you'll even make a man," returned Esau. "Did we truly come from the same womb?"

"That's enough, Esau," Isaac interrupted. "You and your brother must stop this constant fighting about your life's paths. God has chosen a different part for Jacob. Not everyone can be a man of the fields like you. Some are assigned...well...other roles in life. By that I mean..." Isaac was getting uncomfortable in his monologue. "Well anyway, it was a fine hunt, Esau. Where is the animal?"

"Just on the other side of the black rock, near the big cedar tree," answered Esau, pointing.

"Take me to him, my son," said Isaac. "I would like to see your kill!"

The two walked off together in the direction from which Esau had come. Jacob held back bitter tears.

"Why doesn't Father love me as he does Esau? he asked.

"Do not worry, my son. Esau is the comfort of Isaac. You are my comfort. Esau is a hunter and a lover of the outdoors, much like his father. God has made you a man of the tents. But remember, yours is the greater destiny!"

The destiny business again, Jacob thought. How many times had his mother told of the circumstances of the twins' birth. Of how the prophecy described two nations within her; how the older brother would serve the younger; how Esau had been born first, and how Jacob came out with his hand around Esau's heel, thus earning the name "Jacob" or "one who would be a supplanter." Destiny is a wonderful thing if it is practical. But Jacob simply couldn't see how Esau would ever serve *anyone*—much less the brother he despised...

Blurred images began racing through Jacob's mind—bits and pieces that vividly recalled the shame of his name: a savory stew...Esau's appetite...Jacob's plan...a bargain made...right of first-born for the price of the stew...Esau swears to this...he eats and drinks...the deal is done...

More images: A dying old man...another plan...Jacob deceives his father, Isaac...lies...Jacob steals Esau's blessing...Esau's return...a mournful weeping from the tent...rage..."Run away, Jacob, run away!"...hasty departure...guilt...despair...fugitive...

"Master! Master!"

"Yes...what is it?" answered Jacob vacantly. He had been lost in thought ever since the red stew was set before him.

"We met with your brother, Esau, as you commanded," said Jacob's servant. Jacob saw the company of men whom he had earlier sent out standing before him. The fact that they had already returned indicated that Esau must not be very far.

"Good. And what does my brother mean to do?" asked Jacob.

"He is coming to meet you—and in force," the servant answered. He described Esau's band of about four hundred men who were even now making their way toward Jacob.

"Esau will settle this his way," Jacob surmised. "Here is what you are to do. Divide the camp into two groups so that at least part of us will survive an attack.

"It will be done according to your word," replied the servant. "And may the God of your fathers go with us."

Jacob prayed to God. He reminded the Lord that he was returning to Canaan as He had instructed; he prayed for deliverance from the hand of Esau; and he reaffirmed the promise made to his family that they would become a great nation. *You can't make a nation out of a dead man*, Jacob thought to himself as he prayed.

Having sought God for protection, Jacob now developed a plan of his own. Perhaps if he could not defeat his brother outright, he could buy him off. He instructed the servants to begin taking parts of the herd out towards Esau, leaving at different intervals so that there would be spaces of time between groups. As they approached Esau, the servants would explain that these were gifts from his brother Jacob, who was returning in peace. Jacob watched as the peace offerings went out of the camp in separate groups: goats, rams, ewes, cows, donkeys, and bulls.

Maybe now when Esau sees my face I will find acceptance, Jacob hoped.

As he watched the last group of animals and servants cross the Jabbok, Jacob prepared his own family for the crossing. Leah, Rachel, the two handmaidens and the 11 children said their goodbyes and went on ahead, taking most of Jacob's personal effects. He watched them cross the little stream. He was quite alone...or was he?

"Who's out there?"

Jacob could see a figure in the starlit night standing on the outskirts of the abandoned camp. The stranger stood motionless. He called out again.

Perhaps it is another angel, he thought to himself. Jacob decided to investigate. Slowly, crawling through the brush, he crept up on the figure. By now he could see that it was clearly a man. *Could Esau's party already be upon me?* he wondered.

When he was only a few feet away from the man, who remained motionless, Jacob sprang into action. He jumped upon the intruder and grabbed him, throwing him to the ground. The two men began wrestling with each other, a tremendous contest of wills and strength. Dust flew in the air as they rolled on the ground, each unwilling to let up his grip on the other.

"Why doesn't he simply defeat the human?" asked one of the angels watching the battle. "Jacob could be beaten easily."

"Because Jacob is learning a valuable lesson from the Most High," said the familiar voice of Crispin.

He was leading an excursion of some of his students from the Academy, instructing them in the ways of men. He had come to teach how angels can be instrumental in human history in very positive ways when they act in the authority of the Lord.

"Teacher, what is the lesson here?"

"What would you surmise is the lesson being taught here to the man Jacob?"

Crispin looked at his students, proud as a father of his newborn child, as they watched intently the conflict between the angel and the man. He loved to see his students thinking so keenly. So refreshing from the days when the Academy was being infected with Lucifer's proud doctrines.

"I believe Jacob is being taught to persist in things that matter to humans," offered a student.

"Indeed?" responded Crispin. "Such as…"

"Well…security, material possessions which seem to hold men's hearts so easily. I believe Jacob is learning to fight for what he has!"

"Hmm. Interesting," mused Crispin. "But I would suspect that part of the problem that humans have is fighting for those things they have…or wish to have. It's called war, and it results in many deaths on this bloodstained planet."

"I think he is learning that he must face his fears," said another. "The angel is here as a symbol of all that Jacob fears!"

"Very good!" said Crispin. "And what is it that Jacob fears?"

"Well…"

The conversation stopped for a few seconds as the pair of wrestlers tumbled right in front of the group of angels. Jacob had just about pinned the angel when he was thrown off in another direction, groaning in his fatigue. The angels continued their discussion.

"I believe Jacob fears Esau," said the angel, with just a hint of pride.

"True, true," agreed Crispin. "He does indeed fear Esau. Yet he intends to face him tomorrow."

Finally an angel stepped to the front. This was a student named Joel, whose name meant "The Lord is God." He was a worship angel who was receiving instruction from Crispin in order to begin teaching at the Academy of the Host.

"Teacher, Jacob fears that which is most fearful among men. He fears himself."

Crispin turned to the student, who was fast becoming one of his favorites. He gave him a proud smile.

"Just so," Crispin responded. "And well put, Joel." He pointed to the man who was breathing heavily from the exertion with the angel.

"Jacob is not fighting an angel. Jacob is fighting Jacob."

"What do you mean, teacher?" one of the students asked.

"Jacob has been at war with himself since he was a child. Humans have a distinct need to know something about themselves. I know it sounds bizarre. But humans are born into this world without a knowledge of who they really are. Their heritage was damaged in Eden. Thus, they look for themselves in everything but their own hearts.

"The many temples dedicated to gods, which are either born in the minds of men or encouraged by our fallen brothers, are merely the human attempt to know who they really are—ultimately they are searching for the Most High with whom they were once connected."

"But they have broken fellowship with the Lord," said another. "How can they possibly know that they have need of Him—unless He tells them?"

"He does tell them," said Crispin. "Or how often has the Lord spoken to humans in their dreams? Remember Jacob's dream at Haran? Or how often did the Lord speak to Abraham as he looked at the starry night sky? Recall that the Most High told Abraham his heritage would be as many as the stars in the evening sky.

"Mostly, however, the Lord speaks to the spirit of man—his very heart. And though fellowship is broken, as some of you have pointed out, humans still maintain enough of the image of God to realize that He is indeed real, and that the most important mission in life is to discover Him. Thus we have the fraudulent temples set up in the names of demon gods who seek to deceive until the man's last breath; and thus we have our Lord, who has promised that one day through the Seed of Eve would come a hero to vanquish this darkness once and for all."

He looked over his students with compassion. "And thus, my dear ones. We have Jacob, who will find himself when he discovers the Lord in a marvelous new way. This is why I said he wrestles with himself. For until a human finds his way back to the Most High, he never truly knows who he is."

"Let me go," shouted the stranger. "It is daybreak!"

"No. Not until you bless me!" replied Jacob, who by now understood that this was no ordinary man but an angel from God—maybe even God himself! Jacob had fought too far and too long to quit without some sort of spoil. Though exhausted, he tightened his grip upon the stranger in a renewed vigor.

Suddenly, a sharp pain shot down Jacob's leg. His hip felt as if it were on fire. Jacob yelped in pain and let the man go. They stopped the struggle and looked at each other intently.

"What is your name?" the angel of the Lord asked, looking Jacob squarely in the eyes.

Jacob stood to his feet and tried to walk a few steps away from the man. He limped from the encounter—his hip throbbed with pain with every step he took. Jacob's eyes met the eyes of the man who had injured him. Those eyes seemed to bore directly into his soul. Jacob felt his heart sinking within him as he considered his options at this point. What was he to make of this bizarre event? Those eyes! And that question...that name...

Suddenly all the shame of a lifetime of deception began to fill Jacob's heart as he realized the significance of this meeting with the Lord. So that was it! This was God's way of rendering a just verdict before Esau's impending slaughter.

Deceiver! Trickster! This is who I am, Jacob thought to himself. He just wants to hear me say it!

He also had the realization that this spirit or angel also knew Jacob for what he had become, as if he could see all of Jacob's life in one moment of time and knew everything about him.

You know who I am, Jacob surmised in his mind, as he struggled to answer this mysterious man. I am Jacob: deceiver of my brother, liar to my father, swindler of the father of my wives. Is that what you want to hear?

For the first time in his life Jacob felt humbled and ashamed. Maybe God's justice was timely. Perhaps the day of settling accounts had arrived. A tear hung in the corner of his eye. He looked up at the figure and spoke.

"I am...Jacob," he answered.

The stranger continued to look at him, though Jacob could no longer look him in the eyes. "The deceiver."

As he spoke the words, Jacob felt a sense of shame. He awaited the response of the stranger with whom he had wrestled all night long. The man looked at him with great compassion. Jacob watched the other become brighter and brighter. Other angels began to appear all around them, until soon the very place was brilliantly lit up as if in daytime.

"You are no longer Jacob, the deceiver. Your name will be forever changed to Israel, 'one who struggled with God and has overcome.' "

Jacob was caught off guard. He was not expecting this. "But tell me your name, " Jacob demanded.

"Why do you ask me?" the angel replied. He then lifted his hands over Jacob's head and blessed him. "My name is not important."

Jacob dropped to his knees and knelt in front of the man as he spoke. While he was being blessed, Jacob, now Israel, recalled the blessing his father Isaac had bestowed upon him, thinking he was Esau. But the sense of guilt was no longer present—his past was finally being put to rest. When the man was finished, Jacob looked up to thank him.

He had vanished. From that day forward, Jacob called that place "Peniel," meaning, "I saw God face-to-face and was spared." He hurried to join his family, ready to face Esau whatever the outcome. But it really didn't matter what happened to him now—he had faced the Lord's angel at Peniel—and had become Israel.

Chapter 14

"The time for the prophecy is at hand."

Chronicles of the Host

Israel

It was much to our enemy's discomfort that Israel became one of the greatest families in that whole part of the earth. His twelve sons were sure to continue the proud heritage, and the future of the Seed seemed secure against the day that the Lord would choose to reveal the one to come. Settling finally in Goshen, In Egypt, the generations of Israel prospered.

But darkness was awaiting a day in which it might strike a blow against the Lord's people. The threat to our enemies of one man in covenant with the Lord was terrifying; but a whole nation in covenant with the Lord was intolerable. And Israel was truly becoming a nation. Lucifer, now known by us as the Adversary, and his leadership, saw in the greatness of Israel the seed of their destruction.

By the grace of God working in the life of Joseph, Israel prospered in the land of Egypt while the rest of the world endured famine. Yet we knew that Abraham had been told of a period of

*bondage in a foreign land, and we wondered if this would ulti-
mately be a place of plenty or imprisonment So long as the
king of the land was favorably disposed to the Israelites, they
prospered and grew mightily in Goshen.*

*Ever watchful, Lucifer and the council reasoned that if in fact
Israel had become a nation, it would take another nation…a
mighty nation…to bring great Israel to its knees and crush the
Seed forever in one humbling blow. Thus did our adversary
seize an opportunity when a new king came to power in the
land of Egypt—a powerful king who had sworn to elevate the
gods of Egypt to a new glory, by humbling the shepherd God
of the Hebrews…*

"Of all the nations we have managed to hold in our authority,
I must admit that Egypt is our most gratifying achievement!"

The others agreed heartily as Lucifer outlined the brilliant way
in which his greatest demons had become the pantheon of Egyptian
deities. He looked around the sanctuary of the marvelous temple
complex at Thebes, called Ipet-isut, one of many temples that
housed the greatest of Egyptian gods, Amen-Ra.

Amen-Ra was to the Egyptians a most powerful divinity,
whose favor enabled great powers of magic and sorcery among his
priests. The personal god of the pharaoh, Amen-Ra was the divine
source from which the rulers of Egypt maintained their throne.
Lucifer indicated the great stone rendering of the god.

"These humans have become quite adept in their abilities to
create such magnificent buildings and statuary," Lucifer said. "Of
course it is nothing in comparison to Heaven…but then what is?"

The others looked at one another in bitter agreement.

"Still, we have done well for ourselves these past few years,"
he continued. He looked at the team of leading devils who depended upon him in the great struggle. "Brothers, in a comparatively
short time we have managed to wrest the minds of men away from
the Most High and turned their attention on such nonsense as these
gods of Egypt!" He looked up at the image of Amen-Ra. "Sorry old
fellow!"

The others laughed.

"And where is *our* Amen-Ra?" asked Lucifer.

"Kara? Playing at god, my lord," said Tinius, who was jealous
of Kara's assumption of the most powerful deity in the world.

Tinius had his own ambitions to regain the p
since he lost his holy place in Sodom at God's co.

"The priests are performing a particularly sac.
today, and it was an occasion for a bit of…theatrics. They an
old temple at Memphis. But of course you know Kara prefers it he.
at Thebes."

"Ah yes," mused Pellecus sarcastically. "So Kara is entertain-
ing the priests?" He laughed at the thought of what was transpiring
in Memphis, upward from Thebes at the base of the delta near
Goshen. "The human priest mumbles a bit of foolishness and
throws some incense into a fire and the image, by Kara's influence,
speaks or some such thing."

"Worshiping a piece of stone carved in the image of a god! I
don't know which is more amusing to me. The fact that these
humans bedeck themselves in ridiculous garb and actually speak to
these granite visages, or that they take them off their shrines every
day to give them food and water!"

"What a pitiful disposition for the image of God," said Pellecus.

"Pitiful, yes," agreed Lucifer. "But it is with such foolishness
that the world is lost to the Most High. Humans have a tendency to
wander from the truth. Thus we have the great gods of Egypt—our
brethren in disguise—being attended upon by humans small or great
in places from mud houses to palaces. The world crawls to us!"

"Not completely," said Pellecus, with a bit of reservation.

The little bit of light that shone from the sanctuary door fell
upon the face of the image of Amen-Ra as a priest came in and
offered before the statue gifts received from a sacred assembly. The
priest was in a white robe, his head shaved completely. He bowed
as he came, lit a small golden censer, said a few words in deference
to the idol, and prostrated himself. Lucifer and the others watched,
amused at the scene.

"You were saying, Pellecus?" Lucifer went on.

"I was simply pointing out that not all of the world crawls to
us as this eager priest, my prince."

"You mean the Hebrews, of course," fumed Lucifer, watching
the priest as his chanting became more vocal. "This poor human is
deluded. He comes to us because he believes we have something to
offer. He is blinded to the Most High, Pellecus."

"Yet he cries out to a god," remarked Tinius.

Lucifer pointed at the man. "The image of God that is in him cries out for some sort of meaning, Tinius. This world cries out for meaning. It is a cruel God who places within men a hunger for the divine yet bars the way to its Presence! The gods of Egypt and other nations are responsive to their patrons—that is the way we have created them. It also helps us to play on the fears and foolishness of men." He sighed. "But that is the way the Most High wishes to play the game. So, we will fill the void that burdens all humans, be it in the gods we create or in wanton pleasure. It makes no difference which."

"And the Hebrews—the children of Israel?" asked Pellecus meekly.

"They will never crawl to us, Pellecus. I don't consider the Hebrews to be of the world. They are a different people altogether. They have a capacity, through God's covenant with Abraham, to have meaningful relationship with the Most High—more so than any other people on earth. This makes them deadly to us. They carry within their vermin the Seed of our destruction and the hope of the world."

"Ah yes," said Pellecus. "All the world shall be blessed by the seed of Abraham. And if I recall correctly, whoever curses his seed will be cursed, and whoever blesses his seed will be blessed!"

"I only hope that the Hebrews find the mud pits at Pithom and the royal city of Raamses a marvelous blessing," Lucifer responded.

"There has been talk of a coming one who will lead these people out of Egypt," commented Berenius. "My ears in Goshen have been reporting to me of such talk."

Lucifer looked at Berenius with a baneful look. He then looked at the priest who continued in his mantra to Amen-Ra. "If only the world were made of such as this deluded, but enthusiastic, priest," Lucifer said.

He walked over to the censer that the priest had lit. Waving his hand in the fire, Lucifer caused the censer to light up brilliantly, casting a strange shadow of the god on the wall. The priest looked up from his prayers and, wide-eyed, called upon the Amen-Ra in greater fervor, thanking him for the visitation and for granting him greater powers. He then left the room.

"Well, well, another miracle," said Lucifer.

Even Pellecus laughed. Lucifer stood silent for a moment.

"What disturbs you, my lord?" asked Berenius.

Lucifer looked up. "As long as the Hebrews believe in this one who will set them free from their slavery, they will never crawl to anyone except the Most High."

"But it has been over four hundred years since the family of Israel moved into Goshen and settled there," griped Tinius. "How long will they believe in this cause?"

"Adversity works in strange ways, Tinius," said Lucifer. "We have learned that among the humans. For some it causes hopelessness to set in; for others it strengthens resolve. I thought that perhaps when the most recent Pharaoh came to power and enslaved these wretched Hebrews, they might finally succumb to human cruelty."

"Whether they are kept under heel by the taskmaster's whip or by our own interference is of no importance," said Pellecus, "so long as another four hundred years passes...then another...then.."

"Except for the words spoken to Abraham," interrupted Lucifer. "The Most High prophesied that for four hundred years the people would be in Egypt and then they would return to Canaan. We are at that point in human history."

He walked over to the statue of Amen-Ra, tucked away in the holy shrine, and prayed a mocking prayer like the priest had just done. "Grant me your powers, O Amen-Ra, that I may overcome my enemies!"

All of the angels laughed. Lucifer turned to them.

"You asked me, Berenius, what was disturbing me. It is the idea of these Hebrew mongrels having such hope."

Berenius looked to the others to see if they understood whatever it was that Lucifer had said.

"Don't you see?" Lucifer said in exasperation. "The time for the prophecy is at hand. The Lord always makes good on his word. At least up until now. It has been over four hundred years, and everything within me tells me that the one who will lead them out of Egypt will soon be born...perhaps he is already born."

The room fell silent for a few moments as each demon imagined an uncomfortable destiny closing in just a little bit more.

"Well, what's done cannot be undone," said Pellecus, breaking the spell. "If he is to be born, he shall be born. If he lives now, he lives."

"Of course it can be undone," said Lucifer, almost with contempt. "Anything humans do can be undone. It's just a matter of how. Look at this great temple and this statue. How long will it stand before another king who worships another god comes and destroys it; or a great earthquake devours it; or time destroys it as it does all things on earth? If I have learned anything on this miserable planet, it is that things can be undone!"

"Then let us deal with these creatures quickly!" a new voice sounded within the chamber.

"Ah, Kara," said Lucifer. "Welcome to your temple."

"As Amen-Ra I am served by many, but as Kara I serve only you, my lord," said Kara with a slight bow of the head.

"Well put," said Pellecus. "From exalted god to servile lackey in so short a time."

Kara scowled at Pellecus but was too concerned with other matters to respond.

"My lord, I have just returned from the temple at Memphis. The talk among the priests is of nothing but the Hebrew deliverer. Even Seti is disturbed by the evil portents."

"Of course, Pharaoh Seti is disturbed," said Lucifer. "He is surrounded by fools. What with all the talk of a deliverer in Goshen and his wise men in a panic every time they see a falling star! I wonder that Egypt has risen to such greatness in the world."

"Then it's true," said Kara, with a nervous expression. "The time of the deliverer *is* approaching." Kara suddenly burst out in anguish. "My lord! I am the prince of this great land. If the gods of Egypt lose face they shall be overturned...these creatures might even find solace in the God of Heaven! Even Seti..."

"Never fear, Kara," said Lucifer soothingly. "Your gods will be preserved. Seti shall maintain order And we will deal with the deliverer."

"Then you have a plan?" asked one of the angels with a mixture of hope and dread. "You know how to deal with this coming one?"

Lucifer smiled and looked at Kara. "Amen-Ra, I believe is a bringer of dreams, is he not? Does he not speak to the pharaoh and the high priest of Egypt in dreams and visions?"

"Yes, of course," said Kara, beginning to understand. "He does indeed."

Kara stepped away from the group and stood in front of the statue of Amen-Ra. Before their eyes, Kara transformed himself into the form of the god, Amen-Ra, complete with the same headdress and shape as the image. Pellecus nodded as if he agreed with the plan, not having even heard it. The others watched in astonishment.

"No, my brother, in answer to your question, I don't have a plan to deal with the deliverer," Lucifer said.

As he finished speaking, Kara waved his hand before the face of the stone idol. The eyes of the image of Amen-Ra flared up in a fiery dance. Kara grinned in delight.

"But I believe Amen-Ra has!"

"Where are you taking us?" asked Serus.

Serus and several other angels stood among the many mud huts outside the new treasure city of Raamses in Goshen. They watched the people moving about, many scarred and disfigured from the whips and abuse of the foremen at the brick pits. Serus found himself becoming incensed at what he saw.

"I don't understand why the Most High permits his people to remain in such bondage," he finally spoke up.

"I didn't bring you here to voice your opinion on the condition of the Hebrews," said Romus, one of Michael's chief aides. "I have brought you here to watch a particular family among these poor humans."

As they continued through the dirty street, Romus stopped. He indicated a woman who looked like most of the other women in the small community. She was careworn, and looked older than she really was. The recent years of slavery had taken a heavy toll on the men and women of Goshen. How far they had fallen from the favor they had found with the pharaohs of Joseph's days!

"That is Jochebed, the Levite," said Romus. "I want you to watch over her, but not to go near her." He looked around as if making sure there were no unfriendly ears about.

"Not go near her?" asked a puzzled Serus. "How are we to..."

"Because the enemy would like to destroy her," continued Romus. He pulled the angels in and spoke discreetly. "In just a few days she will give birth to the one whom the Lord will use to take his people out of Egypt. She is the mother of the deliverer of Israel! Therefore I wish you to protect her from a distance and not draw attention to her until the child is born."

"So the time of the deliverance of these people is at hand!" said Serus excitedly. The other angels in the group began chattering excitedly. Romus hushed them.

"But the deliverance is at hand," continued Serus in a more subdued tone. "So then my task is to watch over this family and keep them from mortal harm. And should anyone, be that person Hebrew or Egyptian, attempt to harm her before her time, am I authorized to remove that threat?"

The angels looked at each other. They knew, of course, that Serus was clarifying whether or not they might take a human life— something that a holy angel could never do without proper sanction.

"Yes," said Romus. "All of you are so authorized."

They watched as the woman Jochebed disappeared down the street, carrying a small basket with a meager supply of bread and vegetables of some sort. Romus watched her until she was out of sight and then looked at the group.

"But it is not a human threat that concerns me," he said somberly.

＋══════════════════════════════╍╇

"O gods of Egypt, look down with favor upon thy servant, Seti, son of the morning and evening stars, guardian of the sanctuary of Amen-Ra, and of upper and lower Egypt, great and unconquerable king!"

Seti looked down from his great throne as the last of the petitioners filed out of his presence. Upon their leaving, he took off the heavily bejeweled headdress that he wore when he received nobles and made judgments on behalf of matters personal to the royal household.

He stood up and was immediately attended by several royal pages. He brushed them away.

"Leave me," he said. Seti walked off the polished stone dais on which stood his throne and to the royal chamber, the king's private suite of rooms. Before he entered, he said to one of the omnipresent palace pageboys, "Summon Anipur to my chambers."

Seti looked about his rooms, recently installed and built onto the great house begun by previous pharaohs. The palace at Malkata in Thebes was one of the many royal residences that the pharaoh lived in throughout the year, but it was his favorite of all. He could feel the presence of the great kings who came before him in this place and it gave him comfort. He gazed at a relief that depicted a map of the great Nile River, and began to think of the heritage and the responsibility that had befallen him.

Seti's predecessors had precariously maintained Egypt's great world empire, which at one time stretched from Nubia in the south to portions of the Euphrates River north of Syria. The pharaohs had consolidated their political influence by increasing the power of the priests in Egypt and had erected great cultic centers of worship, chiefly at Thebes. These kings also re-established the prestige of the traditional gods of Egypt, who had fallen under difficult times under the nomadic Hyksos invaders.

The Hyksos had finally been expelled from their northern capitol of Avaris by Amosis some 250 years before Seti, and his successors immediately began not only the traditional gods of Egypt—headed by Osiris, Horus, and Isis, with temples built in their honor—but also the relatively newer gods of Amen-Ra at Karnak in Thebes, Ptah of Memphis, and Harkhti of Heliopolis.

With so great a heritage, Seti had much to live up to. Someday he would have a son and heir who would carry on the glorious tradition of this great dynasty. It was the thought of passing on a great legacy that made him think once more on that which had been plaguing his mind lately—the talk of rebellion in Goshen.

"Yes, great one, bid may I enter," came a voice in the antechamber.

"Yes, yes, come in, come in," said Seti, who was pouring himself some wine. "Have some of this Minoan wine. Delicious really."

"Thank you, great one," said Anipur. As you wish."

Pharaoh handed a cup to his chief aide and watched him drink. He then drank some from his own goblet. Seti indicated that they should both be seated.

"How is your wine?" Seti asked.

"Splendid, divinity," said Anipur, who had never been comfortable with the casual relationship that Seti often brought him into. After all, Seti was a god incarnate!

"Yes, those Cretans certainly know their wines," commented Seti. "Undisciplined lot, though. And quite licentious. What they need is a bit of Egyptian virtue!"

Anipur nodded in agreement.

"Alright, alright, I'll out with it," said Seti. The pharaoh set his glass down and went over to a cupboard that contained all of his maps. He selected a scroll and brought it over to the low table at which they were seated. It was a map of the delta region of the Nile, principally of Goshen and the way to Canaan along the King's Highway, which ran through Canaan to points north and east.

He began with a recounting of the events leading to the current situation in Goshen with the Hebrew slaves. Anipur, of course, had heard all this before, and was quite knowledgeable in Egyptian history, but he listened with rapt attention. He hated the Hebrews with a passion and was jealous of the land that they occupied. Anything he could do to cause Seti to deal swiftly and brutally with Israel advanced his personal goal of becoming a governor over the rich province of Goshen.

Seti continued painting an increasingly menacing picture: how the Hyksos had come in as part of a general migration and ultimately became an invasion by foreign peoples; how they had driven the legitimate pharaoh south and established a new dynasty that was sympathetic to the Israelites; how under Joseph's rule and subsequent Hyksos pharaohs the Hebrews prospered; how eventually the great leader Amosis had overthrown the Hyksos and established a new dynasty in Egypt; how succeeding pharaohs were weary of the threat of open borders peopled by foreigners; and how Amenophis I enslaved the Hebrews and set them to work rebuilding the glory Egypt had once known.

Anipur listened as Seti concluded his retelling of recent events in Egyptian history. Seti looked at his most trusted advisor, cupping the wine goblet in his hands.

"And now, the Hebrews talk of a delivering spirit—one who will lead them out of Egypt! They have hope in such a man. A man who would destroy the hopes for my yet-to-be-born son to have a glorious reign. I am already getting older. Soon it will be my successor's time. I want him to inherit a glorious Egypt—not one emptied of its commerce. Who will build the cities of my son if the Hebrew slaves ever rebel?"

Anipur averted his eyes from the pharaoh and began talking. "Great one, there has always been talk of a deliverer. Every pharaoh since Ahmose has dealt with this legend. Have no fear, son of Amen-Ra. The Hebrews cling to the hope of a god who has deserted them. Perhaps in Canaan their god has power. But in Egypt, Amen-Ra has stilled the voice of the god of Joseph."

Seti shook his head.

"No, Anipur," said Seti, who was trembling. He looked around as if embarrassed at what he was about to disclose. He then lowered his voice and continued.

"I grew up with those same tales of a deliverer," Seti continued. "I used to think it was a tale concocted by my father to discipline me—you know—'if you misbehave the deliverer will come!' " He smiled at his servant. "But I speak of something else—something dark, and not of a child's tale. I speak of something that the gods themselves visited and warned me about. Something told me by Amen-Ra himself last night as I dreamed!"

"Tell me the dream, great one, and I will try to divine its meaning."

Two figures, unseen, stood next to the men.

"Yes, great one," said Lucifer. "Tell the fool your dream."

"It's very simple to work in a human mind, isn't it?" said Kara smugly. He was satisfied with his visit to Seti the previous night. "His mind was completely open to my suggestions."

"Of course," said Lucifer. "He is deluded, like all humans." He shook his head in disbelief. "The pharaoh hears what is in his heart to hear. But I am interested in hearing his recounting of your visit. It should prove interesting."

He looked at the proud Kara and added, "It will also demonstrate how effectively you rule as prince over this nation."

"Meaning what?" said Kara suspiciously.

"Meaning that we rule a nation only when we rule its leaders. We must effectively become the mover behind the man—a strongman of sorts. As the leaders go, so goes the destiny of nations. Egypt is the greatest nation on earth. The gods of Egypt are feared. It would be a pity to waste such strength at such a critical time in the war."

"I dreamed that I was at the Temple of Amen-Ra in Thebes. As I made my way into the sanctuary, I saw all of the former pharaohs—all of my predecessors—mourning over the land of Egypt. Even my father was weeping. I went to my father and asked him, 'Father, why do you weep?' He answered me, 'I weep because the greatness of Egypt is no more! The gods of Egypt have been profaned!' He continued his weeping, and I walked on. I came to a room that contained images of all the great gods of Egypt. One by one down the line I saw their terrifying visages:

The Crocodile-headed Nile god, Sobek

The Frog-headed fertility goddess, Heka

The Earth god, Geb

The sacred Scarab god, Khepara

The Bull god, Apis

The Ibis-headed Thoth, god of sacred knowledge

The goddess of the sky, Nut

The god of harvest, Hapy

"As I continued, I noticed that images of many of the less powerful gods stood behind these great gods. Looking upon the images, I saw that they bled from the corners of their mouths and from their eyes and ears. I was terrified!"

Seti held his cup out for more wine, and Anipur obliged him. "I tell you, Anipur, never have I had such a dream!"

"Continue, great Seti, that we might divine the meaning of this foreboding dream," said Anipur, handing him his cup.

"I ran from the room and entered the next room, the antechamber before the sacred shrine of Amen-Ra, I saw the high priest of Amen-Ra, making oblation to the great god. He was chanting sacred texts and burning magic scrolls, but the god was not responding. He wailed aloud, and I went to him and asked him what this meant. He told me that Amen-Ra was in darkness, because a darkness was coming on the land. He said the gods of Egypt bled from their eyes and mouths and ears because they no longer respond to men.

"I then determined to approach Amen-Ra myself, and went to the shrine. When I opened the door, the shrine was empty! I began to weep. After a while a light appeared in the room—it was Amen-Ra himself—and he told me that the Hebrew foreigners had profaned the gods of Egypt. He said that they must be dealt with before the one who was foretold came and set them free. I asked him what must be done..."

"Yes, great one," said Anipur. "What did the great Amen-Ra tell your majesty?"

"That the time was at hand for the rebel deliverer to be born— that the only way to save the honor of the gods of Egypt and retain the glory of the pharaohs, who were crying out from their tombs, was to destroy the Hebrew children as they are born!"

"What?!" asked Anipur. "Destroy the newborns?"

"Only the males," Seti said, trembling. "Amen-Ra commanded that the newborn males be killed by the Hebrew midwives, but that the females be spared."

"Amen-Ra is a merciful god," mused Anipur. "And wise, great pharaoh. For in killing the male children we will steal the hope of this foretold deliverer once and forever! We shall be rid of the threat they pose to us—and their shepherd god!"

"It is our only hope," agreed Seti grimly. "It is the will of Amen-Ra and therefore the will of Seti!"

"Thus shall it be done," said Anipur. "And the gods of Egypt will forever honor your name, great one. I shall assemble the Hebrew midwives and give the order. And I shall have the priests of Amen-Ra offer sacrifices to the god for three days!"

"Yes, yes," said Seti. "See to it!"

Anipur bowed his head low, arms out front as Seti left the room.

When he was sure he was quite alone, Anipur smiled and picked up the pharaoh's wine cup. He held it up in the air and said, "I honor you, Amen-Ra, for your wisdom in dealing with these rebellious Hebrew slaves."

"Thank you, thank you," said Kara, mocking Anipur's toast.

"Well done, Kara," said Lucifer, watching Anipur drink from the pharaoh's cup. "I would say Amen-Ra's message to the pharaoh last night was quite clearly heard."

"Yes, and Anipur's message was just as clear," said Kara. "His hatred for the Hebrews will prove useful in the coming struggle. I believe he will make a marvelous governor in Goshen. He knows how to handle...obstacles."

"Agreed," said Lucifer, watching Anipur. "Just don't let him get too used to drinking from the pharaoh's cup. If we have learned anything since our great struggle began, it is that ambition can be deadly." He looked at Kara accusingly

Kara nodded his head and looked at Lucifer. "For men *and* angels," he said.

CHAPTER 15

"Go after the child!"

Chronicles of the Host

Seti's Fury

Just as Seti had commanded, Anipur told the Hebrew mid-wives the pharaoh had decreed that all male children born to Israel must be killed on the spot. It was a grand strategy that our enemy had concocted, aimed not at Israel, but at the Seed he so dreadfully feared.

But the midwives feared God rather than man. Encouraged by the Spirit of God and ministering angels, they took care to hide the children rather than murder them. This only incited Lucifer's rage further and, acting through Anipur, agents of Pharaoh began combing Goshen in the search for children.

When they found a newborn male, they tossed the poor child into the river. Sobek, the demon crocodile god of the Nile, was drunk with the blood of the innocents, and saw the carnage as a sacrifice to himself. But what of the deliverer? Surely the time for the prophecy was up. Surely the words spoken to Abraham that his children should leave Egypt, and with plunder, were about to come true!

Berenius, still bitter from the inability to contain Hagar years earlier, had been given the task of rooting out the child. He sent his demons throughout Goshen, and wherever a newborn male was discovered, they would get the word to Anipur by speaking through one of his priests.

Unknown to much of the Host however, and to all the enemy, there was born to Amram and Jochebed, of the tribe of Levi, a male child whom God had selected to lead the people out of Egypt. Serus and the others watched for the agents of Berenius and knew that it was only a matter of time until the child was discovered. Jochebed knew, too, that she had only a short time with the child before she must do something desperate...and piercing to a mother's heart. She kept him as long as she could. Then, setting him forth in a small ark of reeds onto the great river, she entrusted the child to the Most High God—never dreaming that she was not losing her son, but launching her deliverance...

"There he goes," said an angel.

"Mind that ark!" came a command from Serus.

"He's alright," said Alyon, one of many new arrivals sent to aid Serus in the protection of the child. Alyon had gone into the water to inspect the ark. "The ark is fine. No leaks at all!"

Serus looked about at the swarm of holy angels.

"Where are all these coming from?" he asked. "They are sure to draw attention to the child!"

"Jochebed is praying to the Most High," answered another of the new arrivals. "The archangel Michael has dispatched us to watch over the child. And Michael will be here soon himself."

"Keep a watch for the enemy, then," said Serus. "And watch that child! The current is picking him up now!"

The little ark began moving into the main portion of the river now, steadily increasing in speed as it drifted downstream. The angels wondered how long they were to follow it and what their mission was to be once the ark landed. Was there someone to take the child on the other end?

Sobek, the Nile god, stood at his temple beside the river, watching his priests perform their customary act of worship to him:

sprinkling the sacred water of the Nile over one of his images. Formerly an angel of worship, Sobek much preferred the adoration of these silly humans to his own humbling of himself before a God who seemed indifferent to his worship.

The priests also cared for the live crocodiles kept in the temple pools. Sobek thought of how foolish men were to keep such creatures and call them sacred. But he was a god who was feared, and the crocodile struck terror into the hearts of the men and women who depended on the Nile to survive.

Now the crocodiles in the great river were getting their fill of Hebrew blood in this most recent aggression on the part of Lucifer. Sobek was proud that, of all the gods in Egypt, he was the one who should be responsible for the death of the Seed.

Lucifer came into Sobek's temple and greeted him. Sobek bowed to his lord and welcomed him. They stood at one of the images of Sobek and looked over the river at the great structures flanking the other side.

"Yours is a great divinity in a country that is so dependent upon this river," said Lucifer. "You are certainly a god to be esteemed."

"You humble me, my lord," said Sobek, his crocodile teeth showing in a crooked and bizarre smile.

"I am grateful for the fact that so many of our brethren have found themselves as gods of this world," said Lucifer. "From Egypt to the farthest span of this planet, we have set ourselves up as local deities, controlling the hearts and minds of men given to such nonsense." He looked at Sobek. "I only wish that the gods were more attractive!"

"Ah, my lord," said Sobek. "One does what one must when one is a god!"

"Yes," agreed Lucifer, "which is why I am here. You cannot help, but know that the search for the deliverer is in full detail right now. We have killed hundreds of newborn males."

"That is most gratifying," said Sobek.

"Yes, but not reassuring. The Lord is not a fool. He will surely make an attempt to rescue the child. However, he is bound to the rules of the game and subject to the whims of human choice—just as we are. Therefore we must be vigilant in watching for subtle human plans to get the child out of Egypt."

"Berenius has not uncovered the child yet?" asked Sobek.

"No," said Lucifer. "And I suspect that he will not until a move is made to actually take the child out. And that is where the Host will make their mistake."

He laughed as if imagining the scene.

"They will cover the child with great numbers of angels, and in an attempt to save the poor lad will only end up exposing him. Then we can kill him at our leisure."

Sobek nodded in understanding.

"But there are only a few ways to conceal a child and take him out of the country. They cannot take him west into the desert. They could possibly take ship into the Great Sea, at which point the child will be trapped onboard an isolated vessel. He might be smuggled across land, but I have seen to it that Anipur has doubled the border patrols."

Lucifer walked over and placed his hand on the head of one of Sobek's images that lined the several steps into the small temple.

"So my dear Sobek, god of the Nile, it is quite possible that the child shall be smuggled down this great river." He looked at him. "And should he get by, it will mean destruction for us all—do you understand?"

"My lord, I can assure you that if the child is on my river, he and the mother shall never leave it alive!"

"That's well and good," said Lucifer. "I believe you are a capable angel." He indicated the priests who were finishing up their river blessing ceremony, chanting the name of Sobek. "But never make the mistake of believing you are as great as these priests believe you to be!"

"My lord," said Sobek, showing his ugly lizard teeth. "I am Sobek, the terrifying god of the great sacred river Nile! I serve only you! Have no fear about the child. All that I do is in your service. And I promise you, by the name of this sacred site, that this river shall one day turn to blood!"

By the time Michael arrived, the angels under Serus's command had created a parameter around the little reed vessel making its way slowly down the Nile. As far as he knew, the enemy had not yet been alerted—but it was only a matter of time. He immediately ordered the angels who had accompanied him to scout ahead farther down the river.

Serus was glad to see his mentor and hoped that the defensive measures he had taken were adequate in the archangel's eyes. Michael flew over to Serus, who had stationed himself just above the ark. Michael inspected the setup.

"Excellent work, Serus," he said. "As long as Jochebed continues in prayer we can maintain quite a force here."

"Yes," said Serus, "her prayers have increased our strength considerably. If only humans realized the value of calling on the Most High."

"How is the child?" asked Michael.

"Quite safe," said Serus. "There are angels below him as well as above."

"Good," said Michael, looking about. "Then we'll just have to see how long before the enemy gets here."

"You won't be waiting very long, archangel," came a voice above them.

Michael and Serus looked up to see Berenius, with a large number of angels, looming above them. He was smiling at Michael.

"Still guarding the Lord's precious plan," said Berenius. "I am touched by your loyalty, Michael."

"Stay away, Berenius," said Michael, who pulled his great sword out. The sword gave off a magnificent blue aura that backed off some of the devils. Berenius only smirked.

"You're wasting your time with that," Berenius said. "The woman Jochebed is even now despairing of praying. I suspect it won't be long before she gives up altogether."

Michael could sense that the strength from the woman's prayers was not what it had been only moments before. He noticed that a few of the angels that had made up the defensive line had already been called back to Heaven.

"Sobek will be glad to host the child," said Berenius. The angels with him howled with laughter. "He is lord of this river, you know."

"He is lord of the deluded minds of men," said Michael. "He has no real power here!"

"Then you had better tell them that," said Berenius. "I believe Sobek would argue otherwise."

Michael turned to see three of the largest Nile crocodiles he had ever seen swimming rapidly toward the ark. Above them with a troop of reptilian-looking devils was Sobek, who had come to finish the fight. At the same time, Berenius and his troops swooped in and began clashing with the holy angels who surrounded the ark.

"Tighten it up!" shouted Michael. "Come in close to the ark. Mind those crocodiles before they get to the child!"

Michael himself dived into the water and killed the first crocodile with one swing of his sword. The creature sank deep into the Nile mud. The other two were already opening their ugly jaws in anticipation of crushing the little ark. Serus grabbed the ark and pulled it out of the water just as the mighty jaws snapped together in a loud crash. Serus set the baby down in the reeds and stood watch.

Sobek faced Michael and came down hard with his sword across Michael's shoulder. Michael winced and swung back, just clipping the Nile god. He gave orders for an attack, and the others joined in and began hitting the archangel from all sides. Some holy angels managed to jump into the fray, and within seconds swords were flying and bright streaks of light were breaking in every direction.

"Go after the child!" Sobek screamed, as he ducked another parry by Michael. "Kill it now!"

Berenius immediately broke off the fight and pursued the ark, intending to drown the child. Several of his attending warriors followed.

From the shore, a little girl watched the progress of the ark, unaware of the great battle that was occurring over the river. Her eyes remained fixed on the ark, which now rested in the reeds near some steps leading up to a pavilion. The child crept over toward the walkway, careful not to be seen. The ark was safe, it seemed. She was about to come into the open and check on her little brother when she heard voices coming toward her. She ducked down to watch what would happen.

"A child, my lady!"

The angels and demons immediately stopped fighting, when they realized the child had been discovered by another human. Sobek cursed Michael and flew over to the bathing pavilion where the child had settled. Serus continued to watch over the child, even as a woman gently took the baby from the ark.

"Bring the child to me," came a voice.

As if in a gallery or arena, the angels now watched, all of them eager to see what would be the fate of the child. The woman handed the child to a very regally dressed lady, a princess from the house of Pharaoh. She held the child curiously at first, and then looking at the ark, realized it had been placed there for safety.

"Destroy that vessel," she commanded. She looked at the little three-month-old boy and had compassion for him. "I will keep this child. He shall be my son! He shall be a prince in Pharaoh's house."

"My lady?" said one of the handmaidens.

"Yes," the princess repeated. "It shall be just as I say. Have an offering of thanksgiving made for me in honor of the god Sobek, for bringing me a child in my loneliness!"

"Yes, lady."

"And since I drew my son out of the water, I shall name him Moses."

"Well, Michael," said Sobek. "This is a very interesting development. It looks as if the deliverer of the Hebrews shall be raised as one of the oppressors in the pharaoh's own household!"

All of the devils standing near Sobek burst out in mockery and laughter. Some of them even spoke the name 'Moses' over and over.

Michael looked about but did not respond. Serus also kept a weary eye watching the baby as the princess wrapped him in soft Egyptian linens.

"Not only that, I get a thanksgiving in my honor," said Sobek. "I think this is even better than delivering the child to one of my crocodiles."

"Indeed," agreed Berenius. "Instead of being a Hebrew devoured, Moses shall become a devourer of Hebrews!"

"And the people will remain in bondage," added Sobek, looking hatefully at Michael. "You hear Michael? It's over! The deliverer has become the oppressor!"

"And the Seed shall consume itself," added Berenius, smiling.

Chronicles of the Host

House of Pharaoh

And so it was that the child Moses was indeed raised in the house of the god-king Seti. Raised alongside the prince and heir Rameses, Moses learned all of the wisdom that Egypt offered: military tactics, diplomacy, history—the greatest places of learning that existed on earth at that time were open to his young mind.

Holy and wicked angels alike watched him grow from boy to man. We clung to the hope that he was the deliverer, while the enemy sought to keep him enamored with his life as a prince. And as for Israel—the nation toiled in backbreaking slavery for another 40 years, waiting for their deliverance, hoping that someday their God would return to them.

But Moses knew that he was a cast-off Hebrew, and it was in his heart to feel compassion for his people and to be moved by their affliction. Indeed the day came when he rose up and killed an Egyptian who was beating a Hebrew. When the crime was discovered, Moses fled Egypt into the wastes of the desert in Midian. He believed that his life in Egypt and his part in the nation of Israel were finished. We the Host also wondered if indeed he was correct. Perhaps deliverance should come from another. In fact, Moses' part in the nation of Israel was only just beginning...

"So Moses has just crossed the frontier into Egypt," said Kara. "I wondered if he would return. I knew we should have killed him in the desert."

The council had just received word that Moses, former prince of the household of Seti, was returning to Egypt in order to confront Pharaoh and demand the release of his people. The messenger stood by to answer any questions the council might have. They looked at each other.

"Triumphant return, hmm?" mused Pellecus. "Or complete madness!"

"How many troops has he with him?" asked Rugio.

"None, my lord," said the messenger. "He travels alone."

Kara sprang to his feet.

"Alone?" he asked. He began to laugh. "Moses intends to release from captivity a nation held by the most powerful country on earth by himself?"

"He brings with him the assurance of God, excellency," said the messenger. "He met with the Most High on a mountain and was ordered to go and speak with the pharaoh. From what I understand it was in rather spectacular fashion—the Lord spoke to him from a burning bush."

"A burning bush? The Most High always did have a dramatic bent," said Kara.

All eyes looked to Lucifer, who stood amidst the statuary in Seti's recently completed tomb. Rather than following the conversation, he seemed mesmerized by the splendid treasure that was heaped around the room: gold cups, ornate furniture, beautifully carved figurines, jewelry of all sorts. They were meeting in the antechamber next to the large stone sarcophagus which held the recently entombed Seti.

"I am always amazed by how much the Egyptians want to live forever," he finally said. "I mean, it is in the nature of humans to desire to live beyond this present world—it is also their curse. But these Egyptians have taken it to a greater sophistication. The City of the Dead that lies about us—an entire complex of tombs and temples dedicated to the idea of achieving immortality!"

He indicated the burial chamber they were in. "Look at all the meaningless trinkets that they have buried with this man." He smirked. "The great Seti! Every man on earth once trembled at his scowl, and now his body rots away in a splendid tomb, surrounded by dazzling treasure."

Lucifer vacantly picked up the pharaoh's cup.

"We were discussing Moses, my lord," said Pellecus, interrupting Lucifer's rather philosophical interlude.

Lucifer turned to the group.

"Yes, well?" he said.

"Well, my lord, we have watched this man Moses since he was saved by Pharaoh's daughter. For 40 years he grew up in the greatest house of Egypt, but fled as a fugitive after he committed murder. We then followed him for another 40 years and hoped he would die an uneventful and unremembered death in Midian. Now he comes as one called by the Lord to release His people. If Moses is in fact the deliverer sent by the Most High, then perhaps we should take measures," said Pellecus.

"And what measures do you suggest?" asked Lucifer. "Shall I appear to him in a burning bush and send him back to the desert? Perhaps Kara should speak to him through an image of Amen-Ra? But I agree that whoever the deliverer is, the people of God must remain captive. It would be a critical error on our part for them ever to leave Egypt."

"Yes indeed," spouted Kara. "The building projects of Rameses must continue if Egypt is to remain at the forefront of the nations."

"Your petty pride in Egypt is misplaced, Kara," said Pellecus. "There is much more at stake here than your precious temples. If Israel leaves Egypt we shall never again have such an ability to control their destiny."

"Yes," added Lucifer. "Better that we fight the Seed on our own ground, where we can use the power of the greatest nation on earth to grind these people into the dust from which they came."

"And Moses?" asked Pellecus.

"If Moses has met with the Lord on a mountain, and the Lord has sent him to the pharaoh, then we should accommodate him," said Lucifer. "Let him see Rameses."

"But he will demand that Rameses let the people leave Egypt," said Kara.

"And what do you think Rameses will do, Kara?" chided Lucifer. "Rameses is far more capable than his father, whose glory rots next to us. He is much more cunning than that servile opportunist, Anipur, who served his father and now serves Rameses as governor in Goshen. And he is much more dedicated to the gods of Egypt than any priest in the land."

The council looked at him, not completely understanding his point.

"And as Kara has already said, Rameses is engaged in the greatest building projects ever seen in the history of Egypt! Do you think he is going to allow his labor to be freed on the words of a desert prophet? And a fugitive at that?"

"I see," said Pellecus. "So you are suggesting that a confrontation might be just what is needed? Interesting."

"What a better display of our might against theirs. Think of it! The gods of Egypt against the desert God who appears in...what was it? A bush?"

"A burning bush, my lord," corrected Pellecus.

"Ah yes, a burning bush. The God of Moses is a theatrical genius, but in comparison with the might and power of the gods we pose in Egypt He is nothing!"

"But we are talking about the Most High God!" said Kara. "How can you say He is nothing? The gods of Egypt are, after all, only we your servants."

"Yes, God Most High is still the greatest living Person in Heaven. I will not deny that. He is a most capable adversary."

He set the cup of the pharaoh down. "But He is also a God who is limited by human frailty. Mark me, brothers. This time no mother's prayers will be lifted for Moses. No angels will be able to contest for him. He will be in this alone—him against us. The Hebrew God, hindered by a failure of a man, a fugitive murderer, a man who is slow of speech—against Rameses, Amen-Ra, and the might of all the gods of Egypt. It will be a marvelous stage on which to demonstrate our power to the world!"

The gold and jewels in the room began to glow in the light of Lucifer's aura that was manifesting as he spoke: "Moses will be humbled, the slave rebellion crushed, and like this great pharaoh who lies forever buried, the Seed will be lost to history, forgotten in the dust of Egypt!"

The city of Thebes was bustling with activity. Its new building projects rivaled any in the world. Rameses had set forth an intense campaign to make Thebes the greatest cultural and religious center in Egypt and, therefore, in the world. He loved inspecting the latest progress of his planned cities. Thebes would be the envy of all!

The pharaoh surveyed the final stages of the temple of the spirit of Menmare Seti, a mortuary temple begun by his father, Seti. Rameses also planned a new southern section dedicated to himself, one on which his own throne name, Usermaatre Setepenre, would be inscribed.

He was proud of the heritage that he carried, and felt the great responsibility to hand down an even greater Egypt to his own successor. His god-like authority was unquestioned; his great army was undefeated in battle; his priests were servile and supportive; and the people were happy. All was well in Thebes. All except...

"What?!" said Rameses. "The deliverer again?"

"Yes, great one," said Kephti. "It has been told to us in a vision."

"Yes, yes," said Rameses. "Another vision. Who was it this time?"

"The great Anubis, dread god of the underworld, saw fit to visit Maret-men, one of my greatest wise men."

"Yes I know all about Maret-men," said Rameses. He's all full of tricks, that one! Dabbling in all sorts of black and mystical arts. Plus I don't like my excursions into the projects interrupted by the visions of dubious magicians."

"Maret-men is indeed mysterious," said Kephti. "Great in the art of sorcery and magic. The gods of Egypt speak to him because they know that he is jealous for the welfare of your kingdom, majesty."

"The man is possessed by a spirit," said Rameses. "If he weren't of such value to me, I would have him impaled for blasphemy—and for interrupting my view of the work on my father's temple!"

"Majesty?"

"Very well, send for him!" Rameses said, as he took a seat on his council chair of state that always traveled with him for impromptu meetings. "And send for my wine!"

"I have sent for him already, divinity," said Kephti. "I shall summon him."

"You are quite confident, aren't you?" asked Rameses, as he received his cup.

Kephti bowed low and excused himself from Rameses' presence. They were meeting in an uncompleted portion of a wing dedicated to Seti's victory over the Ethiopians. Huge reliefs on the wall depicted Seti charging ahead of his troops on his royal chariot, running over scores of the enemy. Rameses would some day commemorate his own recent victory against the Hittites at Kadesh.

Maret-men entered Rameses' presence, head bowed low, with Kephti behind him. He waited until Rameses acknowledged him and then he spoke.

"Great Pharaoh, lord of Egypt, sacred of Amen-Ra..."

"Yes, yes, go on," said Rameses. "I understand you had a visitation by one of the greater gods."

"Yes, divine one," said Maret-men. "The god Anubis journeyed from his great underworld domain to speak to me in the night. He told me that the deliverer has already crossed your borders."

"Crossed my borders undetected?" asked Rameses, glancing at his military aide-de-camp and grinning an incredulous grin. "Is his army invisible?"

"He travels alone, majesty."

"Alone?"

"Under the protection of his God, great one."

Rameses sipped his cup and held it in both his hands for a moment.

"Ah yes, the Hebrew God," he said. "Governor Anipur reports to me that these Hebrews in Goshen cry out to this God."

"Not only that, but they believe that they will soon be set free, great lord," added Rash-eman, Rameses' military attaché. "I was recently in Goshen and heard precious little else."

"Real or not, even a perceived deliverer could be trouble-some," said Rameses. "Tell me, Maret-men, did the great Anubis tell you when we shall encounter this man?"

"No, Majesty," said Maret-men. "But very soon."

Rameses considered the discussion for several minutes, con-ferring with his chief aides. Finally he spoke:

"Send for Anipur, my governor of Goshen. I want a report from him on what is happening in Goshen. And as for you, Maret-men, you will remain at Thebes in the company of Kephti until the deliverer presents himself. I suggest you speak further with the gods and determine how best to handle our enemy."

"As you wish, divinity," said Maret-men, bowing.

"There he is," said Sar. "That is the deliverer!"

The raucous demons who ruled with Sar in Goshen laughed and jeered wildly. They had been spoiling for a showdown ever since learning that the deliverer had crossed the frontier into Egypt. Now they were at Goshen, watching Moses meet with the elders of the people to tell them that God had sent him to bring them out of Egypt.

Kara had given orders to Sar to discover whatever he could about this man and report immediately to the council. But Sar had decided that rather than take the subtle approach, he would decide the contest here in Goshen and receive the greater glory. He and his strongest warriors loomed over the meeting in Goshen as Moses spoke with the elders of Israel.

"Kanil!" called Sar. "Move in closer. But beware the Host. There are many angels acquainted with this man."

Indeed, thousands of angels had gathered over and in Goshen since Moses' arrival the day before. Since being named governor over the region, Sar had never seen such a large assembly of holy angels in Goshen. He understood that this man had the prayers of his people with him, and *that* would be troublesome.

"Whoever this deliverer is certainly inspires the people in prayer," said Sar, looking at the ever-increasing numbers of angels.

"Kara will be interested in that," agreed Sar's scribe.

"Kara will even be more interested after we destroy the pestilence right here in Goshen. He'll never make it to Thebes!" said Sar confidently.

"But Kara ordered only that we gather information," said another aide.

"Kara wants information so that when the deliverer arrives in Thebes, he can destroy him there," sneered Sar. "Why should he receive the glory for our work? Why must Thebes be the center of all we do? No! I will destroy the man here in Goshen—in the very midst of his people!"

"Lord Sar!"

It was Kanil—looking quite harried.

"What is it?" said Sar. "What have you learned?"

"I have learned that we cannot get anywhere near the elders," said Kanil, whose aura was just now beginning to abate. "Excellency, he is well protected. I had only just made it near Moses when I was cast out."

Sar had already ordered one pullback from the parameter they had established around Goshen. He intended to hold his position for now. But how could he defeat this man, much less get the information Kara wanted? He looked at the thickening canopy of angels around Goshen—turning the very atmosphere a milky white with their radiance.

"These angels are stifling," Sar admitted. "Lucifer's assumption about the amount of support here is incorrect."

"Excellency, are we not going to wait until more reserves come and destroy the enemy here in Goshen?" asked Lek, a former wisdom angel, who had taught at the Academy of the Host and now served as Sar's liaison to the council.

"Idiot!" snapped Sar. "There will be no reserves. Kara does not see Goshen as important enough to warrant more legions…not yet, anyway. All he is concerned about is losing face in Thebes. That is where he is holding the bulk of his legions."

Sar looked down upon the massing angels doubtfully. "Kanil and Lek, come with me!" he said. "We must get that information for Kara!"

The three demons got as close as they could before they were resisted by the Host, whose cordon held tightly. The holy angels would not give way, and even the slightest penetration of their lines was quickly resisted. Sar regrouped with his aides.

"It is useless to try this," said Sar. "We will never break through."

As they spoke, directly below them was a child of perhaps seven, carrying a cat in his arms. The boy was stroking the cat and talking to it. He had just walked out of the defensive parameter that closely hugged the area around Moses. All three demons realized their opportunity.

"Now is your chance," said Sar. "He is outside the angelic net."

"I'll have your information directly," said Kanil, who slipped away.

Chapter 16

"The gods of Egypt shall not fail you!"

Kanil stalked the child, who was nearing his house in Goshen. The demon had decided to enter the cat before the boy had a chance to take it into the house. Just in case this one got away, Kanil was also scouting other animals but he preferred a cat.

Sitting down in front of his house, the boy let the cat go. It purred and rubbed up against the boy, making him smile and speak sweetly to the animal. From inside the house the boy's mother called him, and he stood up. Before he could pick up the cat, Kanil made his move and entered the feline.

The cat convulsed wildly, spitting and raising its back. The boy jumped back, and the mother appeared at the door. When she saw the cat's behavior, she chased it off and scolded her child for bringing home a stray animal again.

Now firmly in control of the cat, whose heart was racing, Kanil quickly guided it through the crowded streets of Goshen to the place where the elders were meeting with Moses. Taking the animal through the layer of angels, he was surprised at the ease with which he passed through. Apparently the Host did not detect his presence in the cat; or perhaps they did but could not attack him inside the animal. Either way, Kanil took the cat right into the house where

Moses sat with the elders. He perched himself in a window seat and listened.

Moses had just recounted his story to the people: how he had indeed been raised in the pharaoh's house; how he had fled Egypt, intending never to return; how God Himself had spoken to him through a burning bush; how he had returned to Egypt, and intended to go to the court of Rameses in Thebes.

"But you are old," said one of the elders. "And God has called you to deliver us?"

"Do not be taken in by outward appearances," said Moses. "I admit that I have nothing to offer you in myself. But God has spoken and will do mighty wonders for Pharaoh, who will drive us out of the land."

"What sort of wonders will you perform?" asked another.

Moses demonstrated for the people the signs that God had given him. First his staff turned into a serpent. Then he placed his hand inside his cloak. When he pulled his hand out, it was leprous. Next he stuck his leprous hand inside his cloak and pulled it out again—this time it was back to normal! The elders were astonished at the displays and began to worship the Lord.

"I will go to Pharaoh," said Moses finally. "And we shall see that Rameses and the gods of Egypt will fear the living God!"

It will take more than magician's tricks to secure the release of these people, thought Kanil, who immediately left with the cat to report to Sar.

"Serpents out of sticks," said Lucifer. "Interesting approach."

Sar had just made a report to Lucifer and the others in the Council. He told them that Moses had the support and confidence of the elders. He also said that he needed more forces to deal with Goshen.

"Never mind Goshen," said Kara. "After we deal with Moses at Thebes, Goshen will fall into place."

"For the moment hold Goshen with what you have," suggested Lucifer. "Should the battle warrant it, we will send you whatever is needed. I suspect that we will need greater forces here in Thebes."

"As far as Moses is concerned, we need to deal with him in a way that impresses Rameses," said Pellecus.

"Moses comes with a bag of tricks," said Lucifer. "I suggest that we prepare our magicians to duplicate whatever Moses manufactures. Rameses will be less impressed with Moses if he sees that his own wise men are able to do whatever Moses does. We have learned in our dealings with humans that they are hungry for visible signs, for outward demonstrations of power."

"True, my lord," said Pellecus. "But we can never match the Most High for demonstrations of power."

"Except in the minds of men, Pellecus," countered Lucifer. "Men are driven to discover the divine—some spark of God. But in their corrupted state they are limited to searching for it by any means they deem possible or we deem prudent. And so we offer up these nonsense gods, visitations in dreams, appearances from the dead—anything that will keep the minds of men distracted from the mind of God!"

"Very well," agreed Kara, who felt the urgency of concluding the discussion. "Amen-Ra shall speak to Maret-men and have him prepare the court sorcerers for a confrontation!"

"Rally all of the greater gods in Egypt," said Lucifer. "This is a time for great religious expression. Get the priests engaged in much activity. I want the gods of Egypt to shine during this season of conflict with Moses, so that when Moses is finally defeated, it shall ever be remembered as a victory by the Egyptian gods!"

"It shall be done," said Kara. "The gods of Egypt shall not fail you!"

Maret-men and Kephti had left the pharaoh at Seti's temple and walked down some stone steps leading to a favorite walkway for the privileged of Thebes. They passed through the river gates and crossed the river by the special ferry reserved for the priests. They were headed to the eastern bank of the Nile—to the old city of Luxor and the great temple at Karnak.

Rameses wanted further consultation from the gods, and Maret-men was pleased to oblige his pharaoh. Ever since he was a child, Maret-men had been able to communicate with the other side—the world of the dead and the place of the gods. It was something that had been a part of his family history and he felt it was a special gift given to him by the gods. He would thus use the gift for the glory of Egypt.

Of course such men were of great use to Kara and the other demons, who were in a position to exploit such dedication. What Maret-men believed to be the favor of the gods was merely a deception that was multiplied the world over in the form of holy men, sages, oracles—all of whom thought they were creating magic but did not realize they were being used by it.

Maret-men washed himself in the ceremonial manner and then put on the special robes that he used when calling upon the gods. He sat in front of a great bronze bowl that contained a mysterious black-colored water—from here he could see the future and communicate with the dead. Lighting a small oil lamp, Maret-men sat in front of the bowl and began chanting the mantra that he believed conjured gods and spirits to his side.

Kara stood by, waiting for the appropriate moment to speak to Maret-men. Once the customary ceremonies had occurred, Kara appeared to him as Amen-Ra, chief of the gods of Egypt. He explained to Maret-men that the deliverer was soon to arrive. Amen-Ra said that the gods of Egypt were rising up in anger against the Hebrews, and that all of the temples were to begin an intense time of oblation. He also told Maret-men how to deal with Moses at Rameses' court—and suggested that the sorcerers be present.

"The gods of Egypt will stand with Rameses, for he has done well in honoring the gods," he concluded. "Moses and the Hebrews will become disgraced in the land. And the gods of Egypt will be forever exalted as the Hebrew god is humbled. Thus speaks Amen-Ra!"

"Your majesty, Moses is here in Thebes!"

The royal chamberlain bowed low as he made the announcement to Rameses, who was taking a light meal in a garden with his wife, Neferteri. He looked up from his plate, acknowledged the message with a slight nod of his head, and sat back, enjoying the light music that was being played nearby.

Neferteri was a beautiful woman who was revered by her people. Known affectionately as "The Mistress of the Two Lands," Neferteri was active in religious and state affairs. Rameses often deferred to her and even allowed her to meet delegates of foreign nations and conduct other matters of state in his name. A most capable woman, she had stepped out of the traditionally invisible role played by most pharaohs' wives, whose chief duty was to produce an heir to the throne.

"My lord, does this deliverer worry you?" asked Neferteri.

"Inasmuch as I can finally deal with him—no, my queen," said Rameses. "The fact that I once shared my father's love with this man is what disturbs me. He was once Egyptian. I looked up to this man, who was taken from the Nile god and given an Egyptian name and heritage. Yet he was ungrateful. He might have been great in Egypt. He chose rather to become a rebel and fugitive. And now he returns to vex me."

He poured his cup of dark red wine out on the ground.

"Would that the crocodiles had finished with him! But the gods have left it for me to complete the work. I should have him arrested and executed on the spot for the murder of that Egyptian in my father's time."

He stroked Neferteri's cheek softly.

"But rest assured, my pet. We will deal with this man Moses, my one-time brother, and his god quickly. Maret-men has assured me that the gods of Egypt shall prevail over the Hebrew god of the desert."

"You have certainly become religious of late, my king," said Neferteri coyly.

"Not religious, my queen," said Rameses. "Merely prudent."

Michael, Crispin, and several other powerful angels walked alongside Moses as he traveled the long corridor toward the official reception room in Rameses' palace in Thebes. They carried a special anointing of protection, from the Lord Himself, that would protect Moses from any harm. As they approached the great bronze doors that were intended to impress foreign heads of state, diplomats, nobles, and priests, Michael also noticed the great numbers of fallen angels who were watching his every move.

"This is reminiscent of the visit that Lucifer made to the Throne during the trouble with Job," he commented. "Only this time it is we who are entering the enemy's camp!"

"Yes, Michael," said Crispin. "This is indeed a vile and wicked place. The heart of the enemy. Lucifer has staked a great deal personally in Egypt. A model of his ability as ruler over this world, so to speak."

Moses looked at Aaron as the bronze doors swung slowly open, with the words bidding their entrance: "Enter ye into the dread presence of the great Ra! Beloved incarnate of Amen; servant of Isis and Osiris; protector of the holy places; and of upper and lower Egypt, Pharaoh! May he live forever!"

Moses and Aaron entered the vast reception room. It was decorated in motifs celebrating the various victories and accomplishments of the great dynasty to which Rameses belonged. The pharaoh sat on his receiving throne of state, his wife next to him on a lesser throne. His greatest political advisors and military commanders stood at one side. To the right of the throne were the priests of Amen-Ra, god over Egypt and ruler over Thebes in particular—the chosen deity of Rameses' dynasty.

All eyes were upon the desert prophet and his troublemaking brother. The court had heard much in advance of Moses' mission and were interested to see how Rameses would deal with this insolence.

Unseen by the humans were Lucifer, Kara, Rugio, and Pellecus, along with the other principle rulers over Thebes. Some of them appeared in the guise of the gods they represented, including Sobek, the Nile god who had missed his chance with Moses years earlier.

Kara was proud of the way he had managed Egypt and was anticipating a great victory that would forever place him at Lucifer's right hand. He addressed Michael as the archangel entered behind Moses.

"Welcome to Thebes, archangel!" said Kara. "Welcome to my little domain!"

Michael ignored Kara and maintained a strict watch of the situation. Crispin, however, felt compelled to answer Kara.

"Thank you, Kara," said the scholarly angel. "You have done well in Egypt. The Hebrew slaves have built for you an incredible empire. It's unfortunate for your king that the Most High God has other plans for his source of labor."

"We shall see who is king and who is slave soon enough," Kara snapped.

"Moses," said Rameses. "I never thought to see you again—alive."

Some of the men in the room snickered.

"Rameses, you know why I have come," said Moses, looking at his brother Aaron. "You know why we are here."

"Yes, I understand there was quite a stirring in Goshen when you arrived there a few days ago. News travels fast in Egypt. Perhaps too fast!"

The court again laughed. Aaron began to speak.

"The Lord God, the great I AM, says to Pharaoh, 'Let My people go that they may worship Me freely in the desert.'"

Rameses sneered at Aaron.

"Why must you speak for Moses?" he asked. "As I recall, Moses, when you were in my father's house you were quite an orator. Has service to your god also caused you to be slow of speech?"

Again the room filled with muffled laughter.

"Hear me, Rameses," said Moses. "The Lord demands of you that you let His people go."

"Great priest of Amen-Ra!" called Rameses.

Kephti came forward, bowing low.

"What is it, great one?" he asked.

"I am familiar with the great gods of Egypt," Rameses began with mock seriousness. "I am intimate with the living gods of my fathers, the pharaohs. But I am not familiar with this god of whom Moses speaks. Are you?"

"Great Pharaoh, the god of the Hebrews is a simple god of the desert, quite unlike the great gods of Egypt. He prefers to be worshiped as one god. He is a Canaanite deity, therefore far inferior to the gods of Egypt, who are great in power. He truly fell to disgrace when your great fathers expelled the foreign invaders who occupied the kingdom during the time of the Israelite migration into Goshen. It seems that when the Hyksos invaders were defeated, the Hebrew god also fell into impotency."

"Well said, Kephti," said Rameses, as the priest bowed and returned to his place among the other priests. "Moses, I see no need to either fear your god or heed his command—if it be His command. I believe that you are a troublemaker with a score to settle. I believe that you have concocted this whole affair for personal favor among the people you abandoned years ago. Go away, Moses. And tell your people that the only place they shall go is back to the brick pits to build cities for my son!"

Michael placed his hand upon Moses to encourage him in his confrontation with Rameses. The devils who filled the room were enjoying the contest; Kara in particular was smiling at being able to host such a spectacle.

"Well, Michael," Kara finally said. "It looks as if Moses' message is not getting through to the pharaoh!"

"I thoroughly enjoyed Rameses' charges against Moses that he is nothing but a pretender. Excellent!" added Pellecus.

"This contest is just begun," said Crispin. "You, of all angels, should realize how foolish it is to presume upon the Lord—or his messenger!"

"Don't lecture us here, teacher," said Kara. "This is not one of your classrooms and we are not your students!"

"Perhaps this is not my classroom," said Crispin. "But I believe a great lesson is about to be learned here!"

"Rameses, the God of the Hebrews has met with us," Moses continued. "He demands that you let us worship Him in the desert. He also promises great judgments to befall Egypt should Pharaoh not heed His word."

A rumbling of whispered conversation broke out in the room.

"Judgment upon Egypt?" asked Rameses. "I alone judge Egypt! I see no need to allow you or your people any such freedoms. In fact I have a report from Anipur, governor of Goshen. Anipur!"

Anipur, Seti's former advisor and now Rameses' governor in Goshen, stepped up to the throne and bowed. The old man, still quite adept at statesmanship, was a valuable advisor to Rameses.

"Yes, great king?" Anipur said.

"Tell Moses and the rest of this court the report you gave me of Goshen," Rameses began. "Tell them of the great disruption that has occurred since Moses' arrival in Egypt."

"It's true, great one," said Anipur. "The Hebrews are simple people and easily distracted. When Moses arrived with news of a deliverer, the production of these people fell dramatically. Indeed, the taskmasters and foreman report increased instances of outright insolence, as these people talk more and more of their freedom."

"You see, Moses?" said Rameses. "You and Aaron are causing nothing but trouble. You are filling their heads with nonsense and their work is suffering. Now get back to Goshen. And remove the hope that these people carry in their hearts—for I shall never let your people go."

Kara moved over to Kephti and spoke into the priest's mind. Kephti looked at Pharaoh and asked if he might approach. He then whispered into Pharaoh's ears and returned to his place in the court.

"My high priest has come up with an excellent idea," said Rameses. "Since the people are so distracted, it is obvious that they need something else to occupy their minds. Therefore I issue this decree: Let it be set down that the Hebrew children will continue to make bricks in Goshen—but they will not be provided straw. They can find it themselves. And to make sure that they are not idle, high priest, I also believe that they will maintain their daily quota of bricks."

He stood up and walked to Moses.

"Not one brick less per day, Moses" he said. "Perhaps a bit more labor is what is needed. I have been too soft with these Hebrews and they have become lazy. Now go! Tell your people that there will be no freedom for them—now or ever!"

Lucifer turned to Kara as Moses and Aaron left.

"A very gratifying meeting," he said. "I commend your suggestion about the bricks. That should put Moses in well with the people!"

"He'll be back," said Pellecus. "As Crispin said, this contest has just begun."

"Yes, he'll be back," agreed Kara. "Provided his people don't tear him to pieces!"

Chronicles of the Host

First Blood

And so Moses returned to Goshen not with a promise of deliverance but with the burden of harsher labor. We moved in as a caution, to protect him not from Lucifer but from his own people. For Israel was enraged that Moses had caused such hardship to come upon them, and they complained bitterly.

But Moses, encouraged by the Lord, promised the people that he would go back to Pharaoh, and that the Lord God would bring the people out of Egypt in great power. Thus Moses did indeed return to Pharaoh, this time in Luxor at the great temple of Amen-Ra at Karnak. There Rameses was being attended by the priests in an annual ceremony reaffirming Pharaoh's position as god-king...

Chapter 17

"It will take more than tricks to release your people."

"Moses? Again?" asked Rameses.

"Yes, divinity," said Kephti. "Maret-men foretold that he would return. I believe he will continue until he is destroyed."

Rameses looked at the great temple around him, then stepped off the ceremonial dais and took off the robes he had worn for the occasion. He looked at Kephti.

"I understand a man's devotion to his god," said Rameses. "It can be intoxicating. But it can also be a snare. I believe Moses has become devoted to a god who will in the end abandon him as He has done to the rest of the Hebrews. Send for Moses. I'll see him in the temple garden. And send for Maret-men and his magicians!"

"Yes, my king," said Kephti, who was incensed at the thought of Moses profaning the great temple of Amen-Ra. "I will see him to the garden."

Kara had assembled the council in order to display the might of Egypt that was under his control. Knowing that Rugio was quite jealous of his position in Egypt, Kara wanted to make sure that Rugio and any others who had doubted his abilities, would be stifled once and for all.

Lucifer arrived with an angry look upon his face.

"What is the meaning of this, Kara?" Lucifer demanded. "You have no authority to call the council together. Only I have that privilege!"

"My prince, it is out of respect for your authority that I assemble the council," Kara answered. "Together they will see how your authority is exercised through me to oppose the Most High in this rather intricate game."

"Then I suggest that you play the game well, Kara," said Lucifer. "I cannot afford to have my authority look foolish."

"Trust me, my prince," said Kara, as he escorted Lucifer to the garden complex.

Moses waited nearly two hours before Rameses finally appeared. The pharaoh came in with several of his aides, as well as Kephti, a few priests of the temple, and Maret-men and his two sorcerers. They assembled themselves around Pharaoh in their usual positions.

"Moses, you have returned," said Rameses. "Forgive my lateness; I was in the midst of a dedication to the great god whose house you are in. Perhaps if your god lived in a temple so marvelous, I might be willing to take you a bit more seriously!"

His attendants laughed.

"The Lord God has no need for houses made by men," said Moses, who was once more accompanied by Michael and Crispin. This time Serus and several warrior angels had also come. "For He is not merely an image carved by men that frowns upon worshipers. He is the great I AM, the living God of Abraham and Israel. He demands once more that you let His people go!"

"Moses, twice now you have come to see me," said Rameses. "And I have been in a generous mood. But you are beginning to wear on me—you and your desert god. For the last time I shall not free your people. Why should I? Who is your god that I should listen to him?"

Moses looked at Aaron and nodded.

"Behold, Pharaoh, the power of the Lord!" Moses said.

Aaron threw down his staff. The crowd laughed at first and Rameses could only manage a quizzical look upon his face. But then the staff began to move and quickly transformed itself into a cobra.

Rameses stepped back in astonishment and the others gasped at the sight.

"You dare try to frighten me with magician's tricks?" asked Rameses. "Really, Moses, you disappoint me. Bring two staffs here at once!"

Two servants came back with rods. Rameses ordered them given to Maret-men and his sorcerers. They understood at once what he wanted.

"Highness, my greatest sorcerers, Jannes and Jambres, stand ready."

"Bid them commence," said Rameses.

"Time to get in the game," said Kara, who moved in near Jannes and Jambres.

"It is only by such subtle deception that you rule here," said Michael. "These men think they are calling upon the gods for great powers!"

"And so they are," said Kara, smiling.

Jannes and Jambres began reciting a series of incantations summoning the great god Thoth, who was lord over the secret arts practiced by the magicians of Egypt. They continued calling upon the god, begging his intercession.

"I believe Thoth has arrived," said Kara, as a wisdom angel called Condar who had thrown in with the rebellion arrived.

"Condar, be so good as to accommodate these two servants of yours," said Kara.

Condar looked at the angels around him—both holy and profane—and realized that this was no ordinary display of power. He nodded at Lucifer but was quite surprised to see Michael.

"Even the archangel is present," said Condar. "I shall try to do something truly spectacular for you, Michael."

"Your manipulation of earthly elements is hardly spectacular," said Michael.

"Ah, but we must play by the rules that the Most High has set up," said Kara. "Now, Condar!"

Condar walked over to Jannes and in an instant entered his mind, so that Jannes convulsed for a second or two and then was completely under the control of Condar. Jannes took the two sticks as Jambres continued praying to Thoth, and tossed them down on the floor.

The rods lay still at first, but within seconds they began to quiver and move. They suddenly became cobras as well so that three snakes slithered along the floor of the garden. Rameses looked up at Moses with a smirk.

"Your magician's tricks mean nothing, Moses," said Rameses. "It does not surprise me that you would retain some of the knowledge from the fine education my father gave you when you were in his house!"

"My king, look!" said one of his aides.

All eyes were upon the snakes. The one that had come from Aaron's rod quickly consumed the other two snakes so that they completely disappeared. It then became a staff once more. Aaron bent down and picked it up. Thoth was furious and, throwing Jannes down in a rage, came out of him.

"Let the people go, Rameses," said Moses. "Or a far greater and more terrible demonstration of the Lord will occur that will humble the very gods of Egypt!"

"Leave me, Moses," said Pharaoh. "It will take more than tricks to secure the release of your people!"

Sobek was enjoying the visit of Pharaoh at one of the river temples along the Nile. Rameses' presence was an indication of the importance of the Nile river god, and Sobek enjoyed the esteem of his brother gods.

Pharaoh had finished dedicating the season to Sobek and was preparing to perform the rite of deluge, that is, the pouring forth of Nile water from a sacred pitcher to ensure the seasonal flood that was the lifeblood of Egypt. He held the pitcher in his hands and began to recite the customary words.

"Rameses!" came a now familiar voice. "You have not heeded the words of the Lord God Almighty to let His people go!"

Rameses, visibly annoyed, set the pitcher down and looked at Kephti, who immediately went to fetch Maret-men. Moses and Aaron moved to the little pavilion that served as the small place of ceremony.

"Moses," said Rameses. "You are really trying my patience. I thought you had left Thebes for good."

"I will not leave until you have met the demands of the Lord of Heaven and earth," said Moses.

"Rameses is the lord of Heaven and earth," said one of the attending priests. "He is the god incarnate, Amen-Ra!"

"You are disturbing a ceremony dedicated to the god Sobek," said Rameses. "You are tempting the anger of the Nile god!"

"And you are tempting the anger of the living God," replied Moses.

Sobek was in fact very angry. He ordered his agents to find Kara and bring him at once. Sobek wasn't sure how to handle Moses. He had tried to kill him once before, but the child had been well protected. True, this time there weren't as many angels around. Still, the ever-present Michael again stood beside Moses in Pharaoh's presence.

"Michael, you are certainly persistent," said Sobek. "Don't you know that you are opposing the power of the Nile god?"

"Moses opposes you in the name of the Most High, Sobek," said Michael. "And your powers are meaningless."

Sobek saw Jannes and Jambres returning with Maret-men. He also saw that Kara had arrived with sufficient forces to make him feel more comfortable. He smiled at Michael.

"We shall see how meaningless my powers are," he said.

"This what the Lord says," began Moses. "Egypt's pride is this great river which the Lord Creator blessed upon this land. Yet you have profaned that which was given by the living God and made it into a thing to be worshiped—an abomination in the sight of God! Therefore, the Lord God shall turn this 'sacred' river Nile into blood so that every living thing within it shall die. Thus shall your god Sobek be humbled; thus, perhaps, you shall see that the power of God is greater than that of the gods of Egypt!"

"Then it is here on the river that we shall make our stand!" said Sobek. He quickly ordered the legions under his command to create a wall between the sacred river and Moses. They stood shoulder to shoulder, massing until the river itself was blotted out by their presence. Sobek himself stood in front of the massed legions.

"I defy the living God of Moses," he said.

By this time Pellecus had arrived with Lucifer and was waiting at a distance to see the outcome of the contest. He whispered to Lucifer:

"Does he know what he is doing, defying the Most High?" Pellecus asked.

"He is not speaking to the Most High as much as he is speaking to the human sorcerers," Lucifer said, indicating Jannes and Jambres, who in turn boasted aloud that Sobek cried out in defiance of the Hebrew god.

Moses raised his staff and pointed it toward the river—directly where Sobek stood defiantly in front of the massed devils. The power of the Lord shot forth, throwing Sobek to the ground and scattering the wall of demons like so many hornets whose nest has been disturbed. Sobek was paralyzed and in a panic.

Lucifer and Pellecus both moved back as the brilliant light, unseen by the humans, streamed out of Moses' staff and into the middle of the river. Moses then walked to the bank of the river, treading directly over Sobek, and dipped his staff into the Nile. Suddenly from the middle of the river a thin reddish streak could be seen, which became more and more pronounced.

Fishermen and barges stopped whatever they were doing and looked in wonder as the Nile turned red with blood! The red ribbon continued expanding until it reached both banks of the Nile, creating a stream of bloody red water. Sobek's own image began bleeding from the eyes and teeth. The crocodiles in the river, the very image of Sobek, began thrashing about, dying or moving out of the poisonous water.

Rameses looked in disbelief at the scene. He looked to the priests, who only offered prayers to Sobek, to overcome the Hebrew god's visitation upon the river. But Maret-men spoke soothingly to the pharaoh.

"Majesty, this is only another trick of a prophet without a god," said Maret-men. "The Nile does indeed flow red, but not because of the power of a god, but the tricks of a magician! Behold!"

Upon his cue Jannes and Jambres took the pitcher that Pharaoh had been holding and with Kara's involvement, turned the water into blood. Pharaoh's fear turned into anger as he looked upon

Moses. Rameses took the pitcher, smashed it at Moses' feet, and turned away in anger.

Lucifer, Kara, and Pellecus moved over to Sobek, who was still cringing in fear at the bank of the now red river of which he was lord. He looked up, still reeling from the power that had shot forth from Moses' staff.

"You have failed, Sobek," said Lucifer. "If Kara had not duplicated this with the sorcerers, Rameses might even now be freeing the Hebrews. And the Seed would flourish at another time and place."

"My lord," said Sobek. "It was not a trick. It was the power of Almighty God!"

"Enough!" screamed Lucifer. "You are not worthy of a great god in Egypt. Be gone! I'll deal with you at another time!"

Sobek looked at Kara, who was muttering curses at him, and Pellecus, who smirked at his plight. Sobek then spoke one more time.

"I leave humbled. The great god of the Nile has been vanquished. But mark this, Kara! You who sit at the seat of Amen-Ra. All the gods of Egypt will be called upon to face the God if Israel. And if I can be so easily overcome, so shall all the gods of Egypt be...including Amen-Ra!"

He then vanished with an angry shriek.

"He's right about one thing," mused Lucifer, looking over the red river, where dead fish were already piling up on the shore. "The gods of Egypt will have to face Moses. How long you can keep up the farce through Maret-men is questionable."

"I suspect that the judgments will come in ever-increasing complexity," said Pellecus. "This seems to be the pattern of the Most High. Sobek proved quite disappointing in his collapse."

"Sobek was a fool," said Kara. "I will see to Moses' defeat personally."

"Yes, Sobek was a fool," admitted Lucifer. "Nevertheless, I agree with Pellecus. The Most High will increase the pressure upon Rameses and his priests. We need more power here to deal with Moses. If he should prove successful in gaining access to Pharaoh's heart, we are finished!"

"Moses will never get Pharaoh to change his mind," said Kara.

"See that he doesn't," said Lucifer threateningly. He then vanished.

Pellecus smiled at Kara.

"How convenient that we are in a temple setting," he said with a bit of menace. "You had better pray to Amen-Ra for wisdom!"

He then vanished also.

Chronicles of the Host

Judgment

Just as Pellecus had surmised, the plagues against Egypt intensified, each event aimed at a particular god of Egypt. For the Host, it was a wonderful time of watching the Lord dismantle the proud gods of Egypt in great terror and judgment.

Judgment Two: Heka, fertility goddess
Following the humbling of Sobek, god of the Nile, the Lord caused a great multitude of frogs to come upon the land. Since these were sacred to the fertility goddess Heka, the Egyptians would not touch them. But Jannes and Jambres duplicated this judgment as well; thus Pharaoh was not impressed, although he later begged Moses to pray to God and get rid of the frogs.

Judgment Three: Geb, god of the earth
Moses then stretched out his staff and struck the ground. Millions and millions of gnats came from the dust of the earth. Geb, maddened by his inability to counter Moses, begged Kara for assistance. This time the magicians Jannes and Jambres could not duplicate the miracle; they called upon Pharaoh to make peace with Moses.

Judgment Four: Khepara, the scarab
Next Moses commanded that great swarms of flies, sacred to Khepara, the scarab-headed god, to swarm the Egyptians. They poured into all the houses of the Egyptians, including the palaces and temples of Rameses and the priests of Thebes. And to demonstrate that God was indeed in control, no flies

plagued Goshen, where the Hebrews lived. Still Rameses would not relent. He refused to let the people go.

Judgment Five: Apis, the sacred bull

The Lord then caused a pestilence to sweep the land so that the livestock of the Egyptians began to die—cows, horses, goats, sheep. Even the sacred bulls of Apis at Heliopolis died in the plague. Pharaoh sent to Anipur in Goshen, who confirmed that indeed not one Hebrew animal had died in the plague. All of Egypt cried for relief. But still Rameses remained hard to Moses' demands. But at the insistence of the priests, he convened a meeting to discuss further the strategy against Moses...

CHAPTER 18

"Is there nothing the gods can do to help us?"

"Great one, every district is reporting that their animals are either dead or near death," said On, governor-general of Egypt. "The army stands ready to move into Goshen and crush this rebellion in a final bloody battle!"

"That would be utter folly," countered Kephti. "It would be exactly what Moses wants us to do. If we go in forcibly against the Hebrews they will certainly defeat us with their sorcery."

"Lord Pharaoh," insisted On. "I command the greatest and best trained army in the world. Give me the word and I will take the great divisions, including the veterans of Kadesh, and the chariots, and destroy every Hebrew in Egypt!"

"That would be defeating the purpose of keeping them," said Anipur. "We need the slaves to build our cities!"

"*You* need them, you mean," said On. "If you had a better handle on the situation in Goshen, we would not be facing such a catastrophe."

"Enough of this nonsense," said Rameses. "If my own council fights itself, how can we possibly overcome the Hebrews?"

Rameses stood up from his place at the council of war in his palace at Thebes. As he walked the sound of dead flies crunching under his feet could be heard throughout the room. Most of the live flies had dissipated, but the millions of dead ones created a horrible stench throughout Egypt. Pharaoh looked down at his feet.

"Look at my beautiful palace," he said. "And the sacred sites. They are covered with dead frogs and gnats and flies. The country reeks of dead animals. The river is still rotten, so that we dig for water like desert scoundrels. And Moses demands that we release the people. But how can we? If we give up the Hebrews, we will lose the ability to recover from the disasters that have befallen us"

He looked the council over.

"I am open to suggestions as to how to deal with Moses," he said. "I cannot, as much as I would like to, resort to the military option just yet, Commander On. But be patient, for I promise that one day you will be in hot pursuit of Hebrew blood."

The council was silent for a moment.

"Majesty, may I speak?"

It was Maret-men.

"Of course Maret-men," said Rameses. "I have hardly heard from you since you last were able to duplicate Moses' crimes against us—some three plagues ago."

"Great one, it is true that the arts of Egypt have fallen short in duplicating the works of the demon god of the Hebrews," said Maret-men. "But I propose something new. Rather than duplicate a work against us, pray allow me, majesty, to create a work of evil against Moses. I shall use all of my powers to conjure up an evil spirit that shall harass Moses, so that he will beg to work in the brick pits of Goshen!"

"Interesting," said Rameses. "The black arts of Egypt, the secret knowledge and dark wisdom of centuries against a simple desert spirit—a demon, as you have proposed. What do you think, Kephti?"

"I believe the gods of Egypt are crying out for revenge, majesty," said Kephti. "What better way to destroy the wisdom of Moses' god than with the wisdom of our own gods? It seems quite fitting."

"Agreed," said Rameses. "See to it!"

Kephti, Maret-men, Jannes, and Jambres met together to discuss the strategy against Moses. It was decided that all the priests in the land must enter into a time of ceremonial cleansing and fasting in preparation for the great that would be raised from Thebes. Once the period of cleansing was complete, they would bring upon the Hebrews and upon their prophet a plague worse than any in Egypt's history.

"Then it is settled," said Kephti. "I shall proclaim a time of cleansing and fasting among the priests throughout the land, and then we shall conjure up such a fierce wrath against Israel that they will kill Moses because of their affliction!"

"But Lord Kephti, you cannot enter into a temple for the cleansing," said his aide, pointing to a reddish outbreak on his arm. "Sir, forgive me, but you are unclean!"

"What?" said Kephti, looking at the spot. "When did this happen?"

"And there! And there, another one!" said another priest, pointing to Kephti's neck. The high priest recoiled. "Bring me a mirror at once!"

In the meantime the others began noticing similar outbreaks upon their own skins. Jannes and Jambres lifted each other's tunics and found spots all over each other's backs. Maret-men also was breaking out with unclean, festering boils.

"This is another offense by Moses' god!" said Maret-men.

"We must leave this place before we offend the gods!" said Jambres, who left the room in the temple of Seti where they had met.

Jannes was soon behind Jambres, declaring before he left," This is the work of God! We have offended Him! My lords, we cannot fight against this!"

Kephti looked at Maret-men, who had developed an ugly boil on his right cheek. They could hear the voices of other priests and temple workers discovering the boils upon their bodies and vacating the building.

"My lord," said Maret-men finally, "we also risk offending the gods if we stay any longer in the temple."

"Is there nothing the gods can do to help us?" Kephti pleaded in a whisper.

"Moses!"

"Yes, Aaron," said Moses.

"The plague on the priests has shut them out of their own shrines," said Aaron. "They can't approach their temples or perform their duties."

"I only wonder how much longer Rameses will persist in his stubbornness," said Moses. "He is destroying his people because of his pride."

"When are we to confront him next?" asked Aaron.

"Today, Aaron," said Moses, looking at the sky. "Today."

Chronicles of the Host

Pharaoh's Hardness

Boils—a judgment against Thoth, god of sacred and mystical knowledge and the priesthood of Amen-Ra;

Hail—a judgment on the goddess of the sky, Nut

Locusts—humbling of the harvest god, Hapy

Three more terrible judgments fell upon Egypt and her gods, but Rameses refused to hear even his advisors, who begged that he send the people away before there was nothing left of the nation.

Kara was steadily losing face with Lucifer, as he saw his vaunted gods being cast down one by one in succession. He vowed to make his stand with Amen-Ra, where he himself would lead the fight against Moses. He vowed that the light of Amen-Ra, god of the sun, would shine upon the deeds of the evildoer Moses, and would destroy him. The Lord God answered Amen-Ra, god of the sun, with...

"Darkness...three days now, mighty Pharaoh!"

Rameses arose from his bed and went to a window, where his body servant stood with the linen drapes drawn. For the third day Thebes woke up to a world as black as the previous two days. Darkness had fallen upon Thebes, the great city of Amen-Ra!

"Where is my council?"

"They are awaiting your decision, Majesty," said the chamberlain.

"Very well," said Rameses grimly. "Send for Moses."

"Finally we will get some satisfaction," said Kara. "Rameses has sent for Moses."

Kara and Pellecus were walking the darkened hallway of Rameses' palace. The country had crawled to a virtual standstill, except in Goshen, where the light of God miraculously shined. The distinction between Egypt and Goshen had never before been so obvious. Kara was infuriated—and embarrassed.

"I certainly hope we have some satisfaction," said Pellecus. "We have paid a terrible price for this contest. Egypt is already hard-pressed to recover."

"Amen-Ra shall avenge this day," muttered Kara.

"Amen-Ra?" said a voice in the darkness. "The temple of the great sun god has never been so dark!"

It was Lucifer.

"My lord," said Kara. "Rameses has sent for Moses. Perhaps there shall now be an accounting!"

"Or a release," said Lucifer gloomily. "Rameses' council has grown weak of late. He is liable to begin listening to them and their demands that the Hebrews be driven out."

"Not all of the council is vacillating," said Kara. "Despite it all, the army is still intact. I feel that it will still come to blood!"

"Perhaps," said Lucifer. "I only wish we could get to Moses himself. I sent several of Rugio's greatest warriors to destroy him. One of them even assumed control of an asp and struck at his heel but the venom was useless."

"So how can we defeat Moses?" asked Pellecus. "He is too well protected."

"Yes, Moses is too well protected," said Lucifer. "The only way to get to Moses is through the people. The very people he seeks to deliver will ultimately be the weapon we shall use against him!"

"But what about now?" said Kara.

"Egypt is your charge," said Lucifer. "I suggest that you make things very uncomfortable for Moses this time!"

Moses stood before Pharaoh, accompanied by Michael and several other angels. The council was silent, watching Rameses as he paced back and forth in front of the prophet. Michael glanced at Lucifer and Kara and the crowd of fallen angels that were attached to Amen-Ra and his priesthood.

"A bit dark in here…again," said Michael. The angels with him smiled.

"Not as black as the end of this little episode shall be for Israel," retorted Kara.

"Ah, Kara," said Michael. "You who took the name and guise of Amen-Ra, greatest god of Egypt, whose glory is the sun! How difficult it must be for such a god to be imprisoned in darkness!"

"Gloating is not becoming to an archangel," said Lucifer. "Besides, Michael, the game is not yet over."

"I am not gloating, Lucifer," said Michael. "I am feeling compassion for the people of this land who are deceived by fallen gods and led by prideful humans. I even feel compassion for these who advise Rameses."

"Humans are naturally contrary," said Pellecus. "The fact that they have fallen into rebellion and are susceptible to other voices besides the Most High is their own choice—not ours."

"Yes, but you compel them," said Michael.

"Ah, but they choose, Michael," said Pellecus. "And that is all the difference. I suspect that, should Rameses allow the Hebrews their freedom to return to the land of their fathers, they will eventually fall into the same pattern of rebellion. If we don't catch them on this side of the Red Sea, we shall catch them on the next!"

"The Most High shall decide that," said Michael.

"Why don't we let Pharaoh decide?" said Lucifer.

"Moses. You have been a vexation to me ever since you returned to my country," Rameses began. "You have been an offense to me since you threw away the generosity of my father and fled to the desert. And now you and your witchcraft have devastated my country. I must admit that your magic is greater than ours. You have not been idle these years in the desert. You truly must have studied under a master of the black arts."

"It is not by magic that you are vexed," said Moses. "It is not witchcraft that blots out the sun. It is not black arts that disgraced your priests. It will not be something devilish that will secure the release of my people." Moses held out his staff, causing several of Pharaoh's entourage to jump back in fear lest something terrible come forth. "It is by the mighty hand of the living God that these things happen!"

Rameses was burning with anger. Kara sidled up to him as he paced. Rameses pointed to his council.

"These my royal council have urged me to give in to your demands," said Rameses. "It is not for love of your people, nor is it with my consent that we do what we are about to do. Nevertheless, I am compelled by the wisdom of this council to agree to your demands."

"What?!" said Lucifer. "Is he releasing the people?"

Kara smiled at Lucifer and said. "Have no fear, my lord. There is more."

"But you must make a concession to me," continued Rameses. "You have destroyed my land. You have ruined my crops. We are laid waste. I will let your people go, but they must leave behind the livestock of Goshen in payment for the damage you have done to my country. That is my demand!"

"Rameses, not one hoof is to be left behind in Egypt," said Moses. "Every animal is to leave with us. We shall need them to worship our God."

Rameses could not believe his ears. He looked at his council with complete shock. He threw down the wine cup he was holding.

"Not one hoof?" he said.

"Great king," said Kephti, "let us consider our position..."

"Pharaoh, let me kill this devil here and now," said General On.

Michael quickly became alert to the situation, and the angels protecting Moses closed in around him. Rameses turned and looked at the prophet.

"*He should not leave here alive,*" Kara spoke into Rameses' mind. "*He has already robbed your children of their heritage. Shall he also...*"

"Moses! Get out of my sight. Your people shall rot in Egypt. They shall never leave here! You understand?!"

Moses turned to leave.

"One more thing, my one time brother," Rameses continued. "Never come before me again! If I ever see your face again, you shall die!"

Michael could just make out the pleased look upon the faces of Lucifer, Pellecus, and Kara. *So that's their game,* he thought. *Rameses has finally threatened Moses personally.*

"You think in threatening Moses personally you can stop him?" said Michael as he watched Moses leave with his angels.

"We decided to make things a bit more dramatic," said Kara. "We've decided it is time to unleash death in the house of Pharaoh!"

Michael paused for a moment.

"Never fear, Kara. Things shall become more dramatic," said Michael grimly. "And indeed death is about to enter the house of Pharaoh."

+≈━━━━━━━━━≈+

Every firstborn son in Egypt will die,
from the firstborn son of Pharaoh,
who sits on the throne,
to the firstborn son of the slave girl,
who is at her hand mill.
There will be loud wailing throughout Egypt—
worse than there has ever been
or ever will be again."
(Exodus 11:5-6, NIV)

Chronicles of the Host

The Death Angel

A terrible punishment, unimaginable among the Host, was to be the final judgment rendered against the pride of Egypt. The Death Angel, a being we had never before seen or contemplated in Heaven, went through the land and visited every house in Egypt. Death came to all the firstborn sons in the land, and indeed a great wailing went up into the night.

But in Goshen, the children of Israel had been instructed to paint the blood of a lamb on the sides and tops of the doorframes. When the Death Angel saw this act of obedience on their part, he passed over that house, for the blood of the lamb meant safety for all who dwelt within that house.

Pharaoh's own son was killed that night. Kephti, high priest of Amen-Ra, a firstborn himself, also died, pleading with Pharaoh to set the Hebrews free. Finally humbled, Rameses, the god-king, summoned Moses in the middle of the night. Bereaved of his own son, and at the insistence of his council, he ordered Moses out of the land with all his people and their livestock.

Thus did Moses lead Israel out of bondage, just as had been foretold to Abraham some 430 years earlier. With great celebration did the people leave Goshen, taking with them the spoils of Egypt and all of their possessions.

Ahead of them was a bright future in a land long promised to them.

Behind them a dark cloud was gathering...

CHAPTER 19

"How quickly these people disintegrate into madness."

Rameses looked over his balcony at the reflection staring back at him in the garden pool below. He could only stand to look at himself for a second, because of the shame he felt since the Hebrews had left several days earlier. His firstborn son, the heir to the crown, was dead; the land had been ravaged; the priesthood had been profaned; and the gods of Egypt had been humbled. He had lost face with his wife, his council, his people, and himself.

Unseen by him was another figure on the balcony—another who had lost face. It was Lucifer. He stood over Rameses, looking at the once proud king. He knew what must be going on inside the broken man's mind—because the same things were going on inside of his own mind—anger for having underestimated the enemy.

How could the situation have changed so quickly? Kara was a fool, but who could have withstood so powerful a combination of Michael's angels in such great numbers? Who could have anticipated the Lord's powerful intervention? Still, had they made a mistake in how they had waged the war? Should they have been more subtle?

Perhaps they had been too subtle. Perhaps they should have taken an aggressive stand from the beginning and waged war with chariots and not with words. Perhaps it was not too late to execute vengeance upon the Hebrews, who were nearing the frontiers of Egypt. As Kara had pointed out, the one great Egyptian institution that remained intact and at full strength was the army—the envy of the world.

Yes! That was it! The Hebrews would never expect an attack now. They thought Egypt was finished. One more strike. One more blow for Egypt. One more chance to draw the blood of Moses on the end of a charioteer's pike!

Lucifer liked the idea. It would take a powerful voice to convince Pharaoh to pursue the Hebrews, a voice that would fan the flames of his anger into a white-hot rage that could only be cooled by the blood of Israelites—and one Israelite in particular. They were only a few days' march out. That many people could be overtaken in a matter of hours! But it would not be Neferteri or Maret-men who would convince Rameses. Not even General On, who had been urging military action all along, could convince Rameses to overtake the Hebrews.

No, this would take the voice of a god...the voice of Amen-Ra himself!

"Rameses!"

Rameses turned to see who was calling him.

"Rameses!"

"Amen-Ra!" said the pharaoh, who dropped to his knees and began weeping. "Why did you abandon your people?"

"Why do you sit here while the Hebrews escape?"

"Great Amen-Ra, I was compelled to let them go. You saw what they did to the land. It is ruined!"

"I did not raise you to be Pharaoh over Egypt to witness its destruction. Egypt shall enter a new golden age...but not until the Hebrews have been destroyed and the gods of Egypt avenged for the wrongs done to them."

"But what can I do?" asked the pharaoh. "They have left the country by now!"

"The Hebrews are reaching the sea and will soon be strewn along the beach with the water at their backs and the desert in front of them."

"But their God goes with them, and he is a desert god!" pleaded Rameses. "How can I face them in the desert?"

"The Hebrew god is a trick of Moses. He is a sorcerer and must die for profaning the gods. His magic and tricks cannot stand in the face of the might of Egypt."

"The army?" said Rameses.

"You will cut them down in the desert and their bones shall be bleached there and will serve as a reminder to all who would defy the gods of Egypt and the pharaoh of that land. They have yet to face a trained army—especially one that has never tasted defeat!"

"But it is all I have left," said Rameses.

"Do you realize that the Israelites are at this moment going through the plunder they have taken from the homes of Egyptians? That they are sharing food in their families and that their firstborn sons are with them? That the noise of livestock goes with them? That they speak of humbling the great pharaoh and his gods?"

Rameses could feel the anger welling up inside of him.

"The firstborn Hebrews," he muttered under his breath.

"How is it that the firstborn of Pharaoh should die, while the firstborn of slaves are still alive?"

"Great Amen-Ra—are you sure that I shall be victorious?"

"I promise you that if you pursue the Hebrews, you shall overtake them. It will be as a day never before in the history of Egypt—and the world shall speak of the terrible day forever!"

"So be it!" said Rameses.

"Your majesty, we have deployed the men into four great chariot divisions: Amon, Ptah, Ra, and Sutekh. We also have deployed the royal guard of Pharaoh. We have amassed six hundred chariots besides cavalry! My king, we shall overtake the Hebrews and cut them to pieces."

Rameses was looking at a map with General On and other military leaders. They were in a camp that overlooked the last few miles between them and the Israelites. Following the Hebrews had been easy, as evidence of their trek was strewn throughout the desert. But as Amen-Ra had promised, they had placed themselves between the Egyptians and the sea. It boded well.

"They have left quite a trail leading to their destruction," Rameses noted.

"Majesty, the cloud!" came a cry from the camp. A messenger had just received news from a scouting party. "The cloud that guides the Hebrews!"

"What a foolish display of their god," said Rameses, looking at the smoky white billows in the sky. "The very cloud he uses to guide them through the desert is a beacon for us! Finally the gods are with us! General On! Prepare to overtake the Hebrews. Kill them all if necessary. But I want Moses and Aaron alive."

"So be it, great one," said General On.

Rameses looked at Maret-men, who was easing himself out of Pharaoh's presence. He had fallen into royal disfavor ever since the contest with Moses had gone poorly. Rameses called aloud, "And just to ensure that the gods remain with us, Maret-men will ride with you."

"But great one," pleaded Maret-men. "I am a seer, a holy man. I am not worthy of so bloody a sport. I beg you to let me stay with you, great one, and call upon the gods to give us a tremendous victory!"

"No, I want you with the troops," said Rameses. "To assure them that the gods are with them…as they have been with you."

"Yes, my pharaoh," Maret-men said reluctantly.

"Call assembly!" Rameses commanded. "I will address the army. And remember, General—bring me Moses and Aaron alive!"

"It shall be done as you speak," said General On. He looked at Maret-men, who was visibly shaken by Rameses' order. "Come, Maret-men, be of good courage! Call upon the gods for us. Call on them for a great victory!"

"I shall, General On," said Maret-men, climbing into the war chariot and putting a helmet on his head resignedly. "Though as for calling upon the gods, General, I think we shall all be speaking with them soon enough."

Lucifer stood next to Rameses in his war chariot. The driver was at attention, awaiting his sovereign's next command. For the first time in days, the pharaoh was feeling like a king. His troops looked splendid and would soon avenge the honor of his gods and the death of his son. He would return to Egypt a different king!

"There they go, Kara," said Lucifer.

Kara had just arrived with the rest of the more important angels who helped him administer Egypt. All of them wanted to be in on the finish of Moses, and were encouraging the troops. Many devils swooped in and out of the chariots, shrieking wildly and screaming bloody oaths against the Hebrews.

"They are magnificent, are they not?" said Lucifer proudly. "The Israelites have never faced such a formidable enemy!"

"But what if the Most High fights for them? Will they be willing to engage?" asked Kara hesitatingly. "They saw the judgments in Egypt."

"You forget, Kara, that many of these men have lost a firstborn son," Lucifer answered. "They would war against Sheol itself, if needs be. Nothing will stop them from pursuing the Israelites, even should it cost them all their lives!"

Rameses stood proudly on his chariot, inspecting the divisions that had assembled in colorful array. The proudest and most powerful divisions of Egypt, Amon, Ptah, Ra, and Sutekh, veterans of the Battle of Kadesh, hailed Rameses as their lord. Pharaoh's personal guard, the Rameses Division, stood nearest the king. Jannes and Jambres had been made honorary commanders of the Horus Division, and nervously took their places at the head of their troops. All eyes were on Rameses.

"Sons of Egypt! Today you shall avenge the blood that has been shed throughout our land. Many of you have lost sons, brothers, and friends because of the sorcery of Moses and these wicked slaves. As you kill today, remember your dead. As you butcher today, recall the tears of your wives and mothers. As you destroy the enemy on the shore, you shall avenge the honor of the gods who go with you! Hail Amen-Ra!"

"Hail Amen-Ra!" returned the soldiers enthusiastically.

"And hail Rameses!" said another whose words were taken up by all.

Rameses lifted his hands to silence the army.

"Go now. And may the gods of Egypt smile on you today as you are drenched with the blood of Hebrews!"

One by one the divisions pulled out in succession as a trumpet sounded each division's signal. Rameses watched as the dust cloud rose high into the sky—a sign that was sure to strike terror into the hearts of the Israelites. Under his breath Rameses said, "Let not one of you come back alive if you do not bring back Moses!"

Michael was standing with Serus as Moses stood on some rocks near the sea. The people were pressing in, wondering where they were to go from here. Some of them even began complaining that perhaps this was a trap set by Rameses to have them backed up against the sea. The people, young and old, male and female, the heritage of Abraham, clinging to all of their belongings, looked to Moses for answers. And he had none to give.

"Michael, where shall the Lord take them?" asked Serus. "His cloud that separated them from the Egyptians is gone. They'll be here soon."

Michael looked to the west. A black cloud, thick with dust and demons, was beginning to bleed into the desert horizon.

"They are already here," Michael said. The noise of raucous, hate-filled devils could be heard over the dull roar of horses and chariots. "I had better stand near Moses," said Michael. "These people might turn on him."

Michael moved down near Moses just as the Hebrews spotted the first elements of Pharaoh's army. The women began screaming and rushing to the shore with their children. Panic began to fill the camp as Rugio and a troop of his commanders swept in and out of the crowd, spreading fear. Just as Michael had anticipated, many people began cursing Moses for his betrayal of them. Some were even organizing themselves as an embassy to beg Rameses' forgiveness.

The divisions could be seen in a line all along the top of the slope that looked down upon the Israelites. Above them, swirling about in delight, were thousands of devils urging the slaughter on. The divisions stopped and looked down upon their prey, awaiting the trumpet for the final charge.

Suddenly, out of the midst of the raucous darkness, Lucifer and Kara flew out and appeared in front of Michael. With relish, they surveyed the panic and growing disorder within the Israelite camp. Lucifer looked at Michael and smiled an unkind smile at him.

"How quickly these people disintegrate into madness, Michael," said Lucifer, as a woman screamed at Moses for endangering her child. "There will be much blood on the sand today!"

"Yes," agreed Kara. "Beginning with Moses, if these people have their way!"

"You proud spirit!" replied Michael. "Do you believe that the Most High has delivered these people to die in the desert?"

"It is of no consequence what I believe about these creatures," said Lucifer. "It is what he believes that matters!" He pointed toward Rameses' chariot just arriving on the hillside overlooking the Israelites. "He believes that Moses killed his son. And now he will avenge himself upon Moses."

Serus arrived and stood near Michael, eyeing Lucifer, Kara, and their aides with contempt. They returned his contempt with icy stares of their own. Serus told Michael that the buildup of enemy angels over the Egyptians was considerably larger than their own numbers.

"There is nothing more we can do here, Serus," said Michael, watching the encroaching devils. "Our forces are hampered by the fear of these people. If only they would pray in faith!"

"Ah, faith," sneered Lucifer. "Such a dilemma that you must play by such rules." He glared at Michael. "This is why you shall ultimately lose this war, Michael. You are dependent upon the prayers and faith of people whose very nature is neither prayerful nor faithful!"

"First they cried for Moses' help," said Kara. "Now they call for his head!"

Michael ignored Kara and moved in support of Moses, who was making his way to a large rock. He intended to say something to the people. Michael deflected a rock thrown at Moses by an angry father who wanted to return to Egypt with his family. The rock fell harmlessly to the ground—much to the surprise of the man who threw it.

"One last speech by the deliverer," said Kara. "This should be amusing."

"Perhaps," said Lucifer, who noticed the wind picking up. "Perhaps..."

Moses stood upon the rock, Michael on one side of him and Serus on the other. He raised his hands to get the people to be quiet. Aaron swallowed hard and prayed to the Lord that Moses would be able to get through to them—and that he had an answer as to what they were to do.

"Rugio!" cried Lucifer. "Get some legions in here at once!"

"Yes, my lord," said Rugio, who immediately organized some warriors to agitate the people further.

Lucifer had decided to continue enraging the people so that they might tear Moses to pieces. Rugio's angels were met with great resistance by holy angels under Sangius, who held them at bay, keeping them from diving into the mass of people gathering around Moses.

Rugio brought his sword down hard across the chest of Sangius, who was buffeted, but held his place.

"Give way, traitor!" said Rugio.

"The Lord resists you, rebel," said Sangius, who recovered his balance and swung hard with his own sword, just missing Rugio. Beside them one of Rugio's demons yelped in pain and disappeared as an angel's weapon found its mark.

"They cannot get through," said Kara. "They are being resisted by the Host!"

"Something greater than the Host is here," said Lucifer. "We were able only a short time ago to penetrate these lines with ease. Now even Rugio cannot get through! I suggest we move back to Rameses."

"Agreed," said Kara, looking about nervously.

"Brothers! Do not be afraid!"

The wind made it difficult for Moses to speak. Sand was being kicked up in great clouds over the camp. He squinted through the dusty air at the sea of faces looking to him for some word of hope, some sort of consolation.

"Stand with me! I promise you that these Egyptians who harass today will never harass us again. They will be no more after today!"

"How are we to fight Pharaoh's army?" said a man. "Our wives and children are here with us and we have no weapons!"

"Listen to me," said Moses. "The Lord Himself shall fight for you!"

Rugio and his warriors had tried everything they could to penetrate the line of holy angels, but they were unable to break the ranks. This was indeed something extraordinary. But no matter—General On had given the order to sound the trumpet. Lucifer and Kara joined Rugio above the Egyptians.

"Bit of trouble getting through the enemy?" Lucifer asked Rugio.

"Yes, lord," admitted Rugio. "They fought with a force that was not their own."

"The Lord fights for them," said Lucifer grimly. "Even as Moses has said!"

"He had better begin then," said Kara. "For there goes Rameses' guard!"

The angels turned to see Rameses' crack shock troops—his personal guard, charging the Hebrew lines. The sound of chariots and horses caused the Hebrews to race toward the beach in a panic. Moses stood firm on the rock, encouraging the people to have faith in their Lord.

"Looks like Moses will stand between Rameses and the people," said Kara.

"He won't need to," said Lucifer, looking at a great, billowing cloud rising up behind the Israelites.

The holy angels bowed their heads low as the cloud of God's presence moved over the Hebrews and stationed itself between the people and the Egyptians. The horses reared and revolted, stopping their charge. The charioteers tried to regain control of their ranks.

The cloud, resembling a gigantic, twisting column, planted itself like a tree firmly rooted in the sand of Egypt, daring any trespassers to engage it. Rameses was beside himself, enraged that once more Moses had trumped his efforts. He called for Maret-men to assemble the gods on behalf of Egypt to best this desert god once and for all. Maret-men conferred with Jannes and Jambres, and the three of them began to call upon the great gods of Egypt to avenge the honor of Pharaoh.

General On, dumbfounded, called back his troops. One charioteer, enraged by the death of his son and tired of the tricks of Moses, charged the cloud in a violent dash. Rameses and the other Egyptians watched as he entered the cloud and vanished with a brilliant flash of light—man, horse, and chariot—never to be seen again.

"Hold, you fools!" called out General On. "We shall not pass through that sorcery until it lifts! Tie down these chariots and mind your horses! The wind is rising!"

"I believe more than the wind is rising, general," said Rameses.

Chronicles of the Host

Red Sea Crossing

Indeed something greater than the wind was rising. For as the Lord commanded, Moses raised his staff over the water and the sea divided itself! All through the night the winds blew, so that the Hebrews were able to cross the sea on dry land! Among the Host such rejoicing occurred as had not been heard since the announcement of the Creation itself!

Seething like a caged animal behind the cloudy curtain, and hindered by the blowing sand that was cutting into him like little knives, Rameses could only listen in increasing frustration to reports that Moses and his people were slipping away. Our fallen brothers were at a loss as to what they should do, but urged on by Kara, they continued to fan the flames of anger among Egypt so that chase might be given when the opportunity came.

Never one to be without coordination, Lucifer was already thinking in terms of the other side of the sea, the Sinai, and what new strategies might be employed there against a new people in a new land. Egypt was lost to him; Moses had succeeded in getting his people out. But getting them into a hostile land would be something else entirely...

Lucifer stood on the beach on the other side of the Yam Suph, the place of the crossing. He watched as the Hebrews crossed, terrified that at any moment thousands of tons of water might come crashing down upon them. The children seemed satisfied enough, watching the figures of great sea creatures swimming in the murky waters on either side of them, as the just-rising sun shot its rays through the tidal walls. The adults, however, were in a hurry to make it to higher ground.

Moses emerged from the crossing, Michael at his side, and stood upon a large, reddish boulder on the rocky shoreline so the people could see him and be encouraged. On and on they came—a sea of people with a promise. Aaron had already begun giving thanks for the Lord's deliverance and many were joining him in hymns to the Most High, even though most of the people were still in the midst of the pathway.

"Welcome to Sinai, archangel!"

Lucifer stood with Pellecus and Rugio. Next to them were Berenius and a number of aides. Among them was Drachon, whom Lucifer had appointed as prince over Sinai in the coordination of a very new war against Israel.

"I see you waste no time, Lucifer," said Michael, whose own angels were beginning to gather as the number of Hebrews emerging from the divided sea path grew steadily. "Another day, another battle, hmm?"

"Just so, Michael," replied Lucifer. "But if I know Kara, this battle isn't over yet!"

"Great one, the cloud is lifting!"

Rameses watched as the cloud that had separated them from their quarry did indeed dissipate. He looked at General On, who nodded his head.

"Maret-men!"

"Yes, my pharaoh," responded Maret-men. He looked up from the shrine he had innovated in his attempt to conjure up the gods of Egypt. Jannes and Jambres, exhausted from the night's intercession, looked up as well.

"The gods of Egypt have heard you," said Rameses. "The cloud has been destroyed. Now, take your place with the men and take the gods with you!"

Maret-men bowed and reluctantly took his helmet once more. He had hoped that his success in garnering the support of the gods would buy him a place on the Egyptian side of the sea—for in his heart he knew he would never see Egypt again.

"Farewell, great one," he said. "May the gods always smile upon you!"

"General On, sound the pursuit!" said Rameses. "I shall enjoy the spectacle from the sacred soil of Egypt. It is not fitting that a pharaoh should engage in the hunting down of criminals and sorcerers!"

"Yes, my lord," said General On. "But are we to pursue them…through there?"

He pointed to the gaping pathway in the water that divided the seas.

"Where else?" asked Rameses. "Our gods are with us now. Go while they are still fighting for us!"

"As you command, great one," said General On. "Sound the alarm. Divisions prepare. May the gods of Egypt smile upon us!"

A great cheer went up among the division commanders.

"And may the God of Moses have mercy upon us," added Maret-men under his breath.

Kara stood beside Rameses in his chariot, encouraging him while he watched his troops move onto the dry sea bottom between the great walls of water. The Host had all but abandoned the Egyptian side of the sea and had joined the Hebrews with Moses on the other side. Kara ordered his demons ahead of the Egyptians to throw the remaining Hebrews into panic, so that those already on the other side would know that the wrath of Egypt would yet be satisfied.

Sar, governor of Goshen, was Kara's lead demon. He raced ahead of the chariots with thousands of other demons and was met by a large group of holy angels who were streaming in to throw the Egyptians into confusion.

"Stop them," said Sar, as he grabbed his sword and began to swing it wildly at the Host moving in. Chariots began to topple as holy angels pulled off wheels and frightened horses. General On was barely able to stop a general panic by calling the troops to order. He turned to Maret-men.

"What devil is doing this?" he pleaded.

"The god of Israel is fighting for them," said Maret-men. "We must get out of here before we are all killed!"

"Nobody leaves this place," said General On. "I would rather die than go back to Rameses in shame."

"I am not a soldier!" said Maret-men. "I refuse to die by the hand of a Hebrew's wicked god!" Maret-men threw down his helmet.

"Then you will die by the hand of a pharaoh's general," said On. Maret-men only had time to turn his head before he was run through by General On's short sword. He looked up, surprised for a moment, and crumpled in the chariot. The men around their commander watched in horror as the general casually kicked the dead magician onto the ground. He looked at those around him, held up his bloody sword, and shouted, "Death to anyone who turns back! And death to the Hebrews!"

"Death to the Hebrews," repeated Kara. "How dramatic these humans are!"

"I think we should put some forces on these walls," said Berenius. "Do you suppose that they will remain?"

"Of course they will," said Berenius. "The Lord Creator of the seas will not risk drowning his own people to destroy Rameses' army. They will catch the Hebrews before they get halfway across!"

"Still, I want your legions in support of these waters," said Kara, almost in a panic "See to it!"

Kara noticed that the chariots, which seemed to have recovered from the earlier assault by the Host, were now thundering down the pathway toward the Hebrews.

"I'd say that someone is going to be slaughtered," he said.

As the last of the Hebrews passed through the divided waters and onto the beach, every angel, both good and evil, gathered to watch the conclusion of this remarkable episode. The atmosphere was tense with hostility. The demons hissed and jeered the holy angels, using all manner of foul and abusive language and profaning the Lord's holy name.

Every high-ranking demon under Lucifer stood near the evil leader, who saw pharaoh's chariots finally appear in the distance. He noted the angels, both dark and holy, gathered around the scene.

"Quite reminiscent of Eden, isn't it?" Lucifer called out to Michael and Crispin. "All the angels gathered around for the final decision."

"As I recall, the humans made a poor showing of it that day," added Kara, who had joined his leader. "But it will soon be over."

"Looks to me as if it already is," said Crispin calmly.

Lucifer and Kara looked up, as did the other demons, who began dashing about wildly. The humans too were looking and pointing into the sea, running up from the beaches to higher ground, screaming for their children, dragging their livestock. The sea had begun to collapse on the Egyptians.

"What...?" was all that Lucifer could muster, as he watched the instrument of his vengeance being swept away in the violence of the rushing waves. The people began raising a great cheer, dancing, singing, and expressing their praises to the Most High God.

Michael, Gabriel, and all the other holy angels cheered their Lord as well, enjoying the celebration of the Israelites. Serus looked at Lucifer, returning his glare with a broad grin. Gabriel likewise returned Kara's cold looks with a smile. Pellecus, unable to stand the thought of being confronted by his old enemy Crispin, vanished. Only Crispin seemed aloof from the celebration.

Michael noticed this and turned the guardianship of Moses over to several warriors for a moment. He walked over to Crispin, who was watching the revelry from atop a large, jagged rock. Michael watched the carnival-like atmosphere for a bit. Then he spoke up.

"Looks like most of Lucifer's crowd have cleared out," Michael said. "They never were ones to be good sports."

"They'll be back," said Crispin. "As always."

"What troubles you, teacher?" said Michael. He often used this term with Crispin when something was bothering the wisdom angel. Crispin turned to Michael.

"They are celebrating their freedom from Egypt today," he began. "Tomorrow they begin their freedom in the desert. I have seen these people, Michael. They are quick to turn, hasty to rebel. I only hope that they remember this day, for I believe the time will come when they shall need to."

In the midst of the torrent, Berenius and his legion mustered all their strength to stave off the water, but they could not stop the deluge. It crashed down upon the Egyptians, scattering horse and rider, tearing apart the great weapons of Pharaoh, destroying the greatest army in the world.

The shield that Kara had ordered to hold back the waters gave way as the power and presence of the Almighty overwhelmed it completely, scattering the fallen angels who had created it like so many leaves in a storm. The devils shrieked in anger and fled the scene, abandoning the Egyptians to their ignoble deaths.

General On saw the waters closing in behind him and struck his horses violently, but in the end it was useless. The waters came in on him and smashed him against his chariot, killing him instantly.

All that was left of Rameses' army were the bits and pieces of uniform, weaponry, and bodies of drowned soldiers and horses that washed up on the beach near him. Incredulous, he looked at the small guard who had remained with him and said nothing. He then threw down his sword and screamed to the heavens:

"I submit to You, God of Moses, that the gods of Egypt are weak in Your light. Go now, take Your people, and leave me alone. For I have done battle with You...and I will fight with You no more."

He looked down at one helmet with an insignia of special rank upon it, the waves lolling it against the rocks. It was the helmet of General On. Rameses walked over and picked it up, noting the deep gash in its side.

"General On," Rameses said, speaking to the helmet almost tenderly. "We have both been fools. You have paid with your life...and I have paid with my kingdom."

He looked at hundreds of helmets and other military objects now blanketing the beach and ordered his men to pick up everything. All that he had was now lost. He would forever keep this helmet and the other remains as a perpetual memorial to the folly of contesting the true and living God.

CHAPTER 20

"It won't be long before they turn on Moses."

Chronicles of the Host
New Life, New Hope

What a glorious day it was when the waters shut forever the door on Egypt, and the children of covenant began a new life in a new land. From the morning of the first day in Sinai, the Host recognized that, apart from the Most High's grace and provision, the humans stood little chance of surviving in the desert. We also kept a wary eye for the enemy, although for the time being, they seemed to have vanished just as the Egyptians.

The people quickly fell into a routine of moving within the power and presence of the Most High, either following His great column of smoke by day, or resting under His fiery Presence at night. But the question on everybody's mind was: Where is Moses taking us?

Ever vigilant, Michael stationed his greatest warriors about the camp, always cautious, always watching for any movement or intrusion by the enemy. But it was quiet...too quiet.

We knew that the enemy was only regrouping for a future strike. All we could do was wait patiently. As for Lucifer, wherever he was, the Host realized that he was spoiling for revenge following the exodus from captivity...

"Four hundred years of captivity thrown away,"

Lucifer stared coldly at his war council. It was the first convening of this level of leadership since Moses' victory in the desert at the Red Sea. Attending were Rugio, Pellecus, Kara, Berenius, and the seven leaders of the seven world regions. All of them were curious as to their next move, but none of them dared ask Lucifer outright— especially Kara, who had fallen out of favor since the disaster in Egypt.

"Four hundred years we kept the vile Seed contained," Lucifer continued. "We had them broken and hopeless." He began manifesting a bluish aura as his anger welled up. "How foolish of us not to have killed Moses as a child!" He looked at Kara. "And you, Kara, I hold responsible."

Every eye shifted to Kara, who squirmed a bit. Pellecus couldn't help but smile at Kara's discomfort. Rugio also smiled. Kara looked back defiantly.

"My lord, I understand my responsibility in this," Kara began. "But may I remind you all that four hundred years were prophesied before the people should be delivered? How could I combat the words of the Most High?"

"You fool!" snapped Pellecus. "Everything we are combating is prophetic. And it all has to do with the bloody Seed. The Seed is the supreme prophecy with which we must contend. If we cannot prevent these smaller events from occurring, we shall never stop the Seed and its destructive intent!"

"Well said, Pellecus," said Lucifer, beginning to calm down now. "All of these smaller 'events,' as you put it, are a part of the larger plan of the Most High. Indeed the four hundred years were spent and the people were freed just as God had promised. And so the Seed continues down its damning path."

He looked over the group, which was meeting on the Dead Sea plain. The area was littered with pieces of salt and dead branches, still giving evidence of the massive destruction that had occurred here in Abraham's time. Lucifer picked up a large salt-encrusted stone.

"You see how the salt has encased this rock?" he asked, showing it to all the other demons. "The Seed of the Most High—that which He nourishes and cherishes—is like the stone inside this salt. Our task is to penetrate the outer shell and get to the heart of the matter!"

Lucifer violently flung the stone against a much larger rock, shattering the salty casing and exposing the rock. He then picked up the rock and held it in front of the others.

"We must get through the influence and impact of the Most High's Presence," he continued. "We must expose the Seed and destroy it. But in order to do that, we must evade the presence of God. Even now He accompanies them day and night." He sighed. "How pathetic that so great a God is reduced to the task of a caretaker to this rebellious lot, who would turn on Him without hesitation!"

The others laughed a nervous laugh—the first such liberty they had felt comfortable enough to take since the meeting began.

"And so the attack must come, my brothers. We must compromise these people and put an end to the Seed's threat. But we have learned that it shall not be through an external offense. We've seen that brutal force is only contested by the Host. We must somehow penetrate the hearts of Moses' people and create disturbances from within."

Pellecus looked around to see if anyone else was going to speak, then began talking. "The humans have shown a marvelous capacity for self destruction. I suggest, my prince, that, left alone, they will find their own way to compromise the Lord's working in their pitiful lives."

"I quite agree, Pellecus, but we cannot take that risk," chided Lucifer. "We must remain proactive and on the attack—relentless and unyielding—but subtle and, as I said, from within. We must divide the nation from its heart; then its head will follow. We must work around Moses and not through him!"

"As long as Moses has their confidence, they will follow him," said Rugio, who rarely spoke up at the conferences. He then muttered, "I would enjoy tearing him in half."

For a fleeting moment every mind envisioned such a thing with great satisfaction.

"Unfortunately, Moses enjoys the protection of the Most High and the most powerful angels in the heavenlies," said Pellecus. "It will be about as easy to get to him now as it was to get to him when he was a baby in the Nile."

"They key is not Moses," said Lucifer. "The key is, as always, the human propensity to wander. That is the legacy we left them at Eden. Our mistake in Egypt was that we directly assaulted the Lord's honor. We have learned a great lesson here. Let me explain further."

Lucifer picked up a handful of sand and salt, and slowly sifted it out of his fingers. "We must not forget that these people are now in the wilderness of an alien and hostile land. No longer do they enjoy the bounty and security of Egypt. I tell you—give them some time in the blistering sun, with little water; give them a few more weeks of pitching camp and tearing it down on a moment's notice; let them experience hostile raiders and scorpion bites and endless horizons!"

Lucifer smiled. "It won't be long before these people turn on Moses and establish their own nation apart from God! It is in their nature to rebel. And I believe that, with some encouragement, they will not only overthrow Moses and his simple brother, Aaron, but will turn on the Most High as well!"

As Lucifer spoke a demon appeared and, discreetly making his way over to Kara, whispered something to him. The others watched and waited. Kara smiled and nodded his head. He seemed delighted with what he heard and looked at the others with a knowing, confident expression. Most of the demons present nodded back in response. A few ignored him altogether.

For all the faults that the others saw in Kara; in spite of his foolish inclination to boast and then be bested; even though he was currently out of favor with Lucifer, Kara maintained an enormous advantage over the others: he maintained the greatest network of agents and information gatherers on earth. This fact made him quite dangerous in the hostile world of territorialism that was part of Lucifer's government. Every devil knew that Kara could use his information to damage a rival as easily as to further the war against the Most High.

"Well?" asked Lucifer finally.

"My lord, you have often said yourself that the Lord Most High has a propensity for leaving open a door," he began.

"Yes, yes, well?" said Lucifer.

"It seems that at a place called Marah, Moses threw a stick into a pool of bitter water and made it sweet for the people to drink. It was the Lord, of course, and Moses was merely following instructions..."

"What is your point?" demanded Pellecus. "You, of all of us, should understand the Lord's power over water!"

A few snickers escaped the group.

"The point, my learned brother, is that Moses had to do this in order to satisfy the complaints of the people." He looked at all the angels as if he had stumbled upon a wonderful revelation. "Moses commands a nation of grumbling, petty Hebrews!"

"We have known that since they came to Egypt," said Tinius, who had recently begun attending the Council of War. "They always complained."

"Ah, but that was under the taskmaster's whip," continued Kara. "That was when they were in bondage. Now they are delivered...and still they murmur and grumble."

Kara waited for his words to be absorbed by the council. Lucifer looked intently at Kara, then nodded slowly in understanding. Pellecus too seemed to understand, albeit grudgingly, since the words came from Kara. The others seemed lost as to the significance of Kara's words.

"Don't you see?" Kara went on. "You were just saying, and rightly so, that an assault on Moses directly would never be successful. The way to get at Moses is through these rotten, childish people..."

"Who murmur at every turn," continued Lucifer, picking up Kara's reasoning. "How true that these people are some of the most ungrateful people in the world. And how ironic! They are in covenant with the Creator of the universe, yet they grumble at the first bit of thirst—and in a desert!"

"Exactly, my prince," said Kara. "And a grumbling, ungrateful people are not going to be prayerful or faith-filled."

"Which means we can have greater access to them," mused Pellecus. "Interesting. So what are you proposing, Kara?"

"Just this," said Kara. "We take full advantage of this opportunity to discourage, distract, and embitter this rabble against Moses and the Lord God. We turn the people, his family, even Aaron and Miriam, against him. We scour the nation and find the leaders among them whom we can encourage to oppose Moses outright. Once Moses is overthrown, we will then have the rebel leaders escort the people back to Egypt."

"Brilliant!" said Lucifer. "We will make the hardships of the desert, and consequently of freedom, so harsh, that they will beg to return to the comfort of Egypt."

"You really think these people will return to the bondage of Egypt?" asked Pellecus. "They clamored for four hundred years to be released."

"If there is one thing I have learned about humans, dear Pellecus," said Lucifer, "it is that when they are pressed, they will trade their freedom for a sense of control—even if it means returning to bondage. We learned that in Eden—and we are seeing it now!"

He turned to Kara.

"Unleash your agents," Lucifer said. "Uncover every element of discontent among the Hebrews. Anything we can exploit I want a full report upon. We'll have Moses begging to get back to Egypt himself!"

Once more the immense camp of Israelites was on the move, the cloud of smoke having indicated that the journey must continue. The trumpet had sounded and the cry had gone forth, "Let God arise! Let His enemies be scattered!"

Crispin and Michael surveyed the scene: uncooperative animals; cranky children; wives and mothers hastily organizing the household goods; fathers and sons herding the animals or grabbing their weapons for the next leg of the journey.

"It's a marvelous thing to watch these humans push themselves along," said Crispin, looking at a mother chasing down her young child. "On they go."

"But when will the Lord bring them into the land He swore to them?" asked Michael. "These people have such a limited ability to endure, it seems."

"Indeed," agreed Crispin. "I have been teaching the Host on the ways of men. I am astonished every day by some new ability to choose recklessly. And yet..."

As he spoke an ancient man walked by, singing praises to the Most High God for the deliverance He had brought them. Crispin continued, "And yet they have a capacity for touching the Lord's heart."

"There's Gabriel," said Michael, hailing the powerful archangel arriving from the North.

"Hello, my brothers!" Gabriel called back.

"Well, Gabriel," said Crispin. "You are certainly a welcome sight. I thought you were meeting with the Elders."

"I just returned from them, good teacher," Gabriel answered. "The people are on the move again, I see."

"Yes, the cloud broke this morning," said Michael.

"What news from the Elders, Gabriel?" asked Crispin.

"The same, I'm afraid," said Gabriel grimly. "The enemy is planning a new assault on the people."

"Naturally," said Crispin. "And we shall defend them as always."

"Perhaps," said Gabriel. "But their faith grows weak. The Elders reaffirmed the Lord's command that, apart from a sovereign move on His part, we cannot interfere or help in situations—unless a prayer of faith is being offered up."

"But Gabriel, there are many righteous in this nation," responded Michael.

"I agree. There are some individuals of remarkable faith. But these people must learn to act in faith as one. And so often they disintegrate into individuals who are discontent and seem on the verge of rebellion."

"They have a great teacher in rebellion," mused Crispin.

"And it is rebellion that is Lucifer's latest ploy," said Gabriel. He then recounted to Michael and Crispin the briefing he had received from the Elders. Apparently they had received the information from one of the more gossipy demons. It seemed that Lucifer was seeking to divide the nation from within.

"He certainly has the right people for it," said Crispin. "These people are bent on complaining."

"He'll exploit it if he can," agreed Michael. "And we are to simply allow the enemy access to the camp?"

Just as Michael finished, a fight broke out between two men. One of the men, from the tribe of Gad, was accusing the other, a Levite, of having taken some of his animals. Behind each man stood a grinning devil. The demons chattered with each other, enjoying the fruit of their interference. They looked in the direction of Michael and Crispin, nodded their heads in mock salutation, then returned to watching the scuffle.

"No, Michael," said Crispin. "We don't need to allow the enemy access to the camp. The humans have already given it to them!"

As Crispin finished speaking, he and the archangels could see groups of two and three of the enemy drifting in and alighting in various parts of the camp. Some were in dialogue, as if planning their movements; others seemed focused on particular individuals and headed straight for them. Crispin noticed that as the devils came in they sidled up to their particular charges to observe them.

"This is exactly what I have been teaching my students about this war," Crispin observed. "Notice how they learn about the humans to whom they are assigned and then begin making suggestions to incite their base passions."

"I only wish we could deal with them immediately," said Michael, a bit frustrated.

"True, Michael," agreed Gabriel, looking about him as if sensing something in the air. "There is certainly not a great deal of prayer being offered up these days."

"These humans!" snorted Crispin. "Like many of my students. They believe that only things which come easily are the sweetest attainments. The Lord God releases them from four hundred years of bondage; He humbles the Egyptian gods; He brings them out with great wonders—and what do they do? They find occasion to murmur, just days into their new freedom. And with Lucifer's angels fanning the poison that is already within them, I'm afraid we are going to have quite a difficulty ahead!"

"Why are they so susceptible to suggestion by Lucifer's angels?" asked Michael. "Can't they tell the difference between what is pure and what is profane?"

"Of course they can, Michael," said Crispin. "They are spiritual creatures by nature and as such are very aware of spiritual suggestion. There are times when these people demonstrate remarkable ability to hear from the Lord and communicate with Him. Take Moses, for example. Or Abraham. Flawed as he was, Abraham had a heart for God that allowed the Lord to speak to him. The problem is not in hearing a voice—the problem is in making a choice."

"And humans seem bent on choosing wrongly," said Gabriel.

"So it seems," said Crispin. "Ever since the corruption in Eden they have had a tendency to stray. Remember Eve's desire to know good and evil? Well, humans now know good and evil—and they seem to opt for the evil."

"Which our friends exploit with great success," said Michael, looking at a group of demons sitting among some men who were resting from their labors. They were speaking angry thoughts into the minds of the men—thoughts directed at Moses.

"Yes, Michael," agreed Crispin. "But as always, I must point out that all that Lucifer can do is suggest. It is human responsibility to discard what he says or allow it to take root." Crispin stood and surveyed the vast sea of people around them. "If the Hebrews are to be the harbingers of the Seed they had better learn that with this great honor comes the great responsibility of choosing wisely. And they'd better learn quickly with the enemy closing in like this."

"Moses! Moses!"

Moses sat across from Aaron in his tent. The two men looked haggard and careworn. The crowd outside the tent was becoming more and more bold in their demands that Moses provide for them food and water and a definite destination and...

"Moses, what are we to do?" asked Aaron. "The people are not going to let up until we provide an answer for them."

"Moses, my children are hungry!" came the desperate and angry voice of a woman. Others joined in support of her.

Moses looked up at Aaron. He smiled a weak smile.

"Aaron, you of all people should know that you or I can provide no answer for these people," Moses answered. "The Lord God knows what is happening. He will direct us. I have prayed to God; He has answered and will provide."

"When will you tell them?" Aaron said, wincing at the sound of a small rock bouncing off the tent. Moses watched as the rock glided down the roof above him dropping to the sandy surface with a dull thud.

"This evening," said Moses. "This evening I will address the people."

"Well done, Kara," said Lucifer. "The people are certainly agitated."

"Thank you, my prince," said Kara, glad to be back in good stead with Lucifer. "These people are given to agitation. It is only a matter of appealing to the carnal passions that drive them."

"As always," added Pellecus. "The human propensity for degradation will always be our advantage. I think sometimes that the less we interfere the better the war goes for us."

"Quite right," said Lucifer, surveying the camp from the top of a hillside where he stood with the others. He looked at the pillar of fire, which had manifested as the sun was setting. "But as long as they are guided by so present a God, we will always have to remain vigilant."

"And as for Moses?" asked Pellecus. "Who is going to be assigned to him?"

"I have decided to assign Rugio to Moses," said Lucifer. "Quite an appropriate counter to Michael's obvious interest in him. The bitterness that Rugio holds for the archangel will be a great motivator for him."

"Moses is not our only obstacle," said Berenius.

"You mean Joshua?" asked Lucifer.

"Yes, my lord," said Berenius, a bit surprised at Lucifer's acumen.

"Joshua does indeed present a bit of a problem," said Lucifer. "Moses is obviously grooming him to take over when his day comes. I understand that Serus has been assigned to him. I have just decided, Berenius, that you shall be over Joshua. I want you to use whatever means you can to discourage and dissuade him from being a part of this disastrous journey into the desert."

"Disastrous?" asked Pellecus. "For whom. The Hebrews—or us?"

"Hear me. This will be our message to all of the principle humans involved. Moses has led these people by sorcery into a desert from which there can be no escape except to return to the servitude of Egypt—where at least they were well fed and allowed to live in relative peace."

"Interesting strategy," said Pellecus. "Then what we need from among these creatures is a leader. One who is respected and whose opinion carries weight with the people."

"Excellent summation, Pellecus," said Kara. "I believe I have found a prime candidate for our little Sinai adventure." He spoke as one who has a bit of information that he cannot wait to divulge. He looked at the others.

"Well?" said Lucifer.

"I have found among the Levites a man of great influence. I believe in due time we shall be able to set him up against Moses and many will follow him."

"And who is this man?" asked Lucifer, becoming impatient with Kara's need for drama.

"Korah, the son of Izhar," said Kara. "The perfect subject. He is well acquainted with the leading families; he worships at Moses' side and has his full confidence. He outwardly supports Moses but secretly covets his authority. He is an absolute fool who sits under the very authority he desires to usurp! He reminds me very much of..."

Kara stopped before concluding his statement. Pellecus smirked at Kara's discomfort. Lucifer ignored the obvious comparison.

"Very well, Kara," said Lucifer. "Cultivate this Levite and when the time is right, turn him against Moses."

"He shall be a viper in the midst of the reeds, my lord," said Kara.

CHAPTER 21

"We are here to watch the demise of Moses."

Moses stood before the congregation of Israelites in what was becoming an all-too-familiar situation—explaining to the increasingly hostile crowd their predicament. Kara's agents were in the crowd, working up the anger that was brewing and trying with all their might to disrupt the proceedings. They wanted to demonstrate a lack of control on Moses' part and to illustrate a deficiency in his leadership.

Aaron, Joshua, and the leaders of the various tribes attempted to quell the unrest among the people so that Moses could speak to them. Beside Moses, Michael kept a vigilant, wary eye on Lucifer's demons, making sure that not one even came close to Moses. In reality, not many demons dared approach Moses with the archangel nearby. Kara and Rugio, of course, were the exception.

"Ah, Michael, still guarding the prophet from his own people, I see," said Kara, as he and Rugio crossed over toward Michael.

"I believe he is very well protected," said Michael. "From humans and demons."

"Come now, Michael, do you really believe we would stoop to assaulting Moses personally when his own people are apt to tear into him at any moment?" Kara purred.

"Moses can handle these people," said Michael. "And they certainly are not grateful at times." He looked at Kara and Rugio intently. "But then both of you understand what true ingratitude is."

"Hold, archangel," demanded Rugio. "We are not here to discuss the liberated angels. We are here to watch the demise of Moses. And mark me! Lucifer shall have him one day as a trophy."

Before Michael could answer Rugio, Moses began to speak to the people. Kara listened with great interest, keeping an eye on certain faces in the crowd. He particularly watched Korah and Dathan, reading their reactions to Moses' every word.

"Hear the word of the Lord!" shouted Moses. The people finally were silent enough that Moses might be able to speak to them. Even Lucifer was impressed with the authority Moses carried when he spoke under the Lord's anointing.

"Every day since leaving the hardship of Egypt you have grumbled at me and Aaron. Many of you have called us traitors or charlatans. Others have said it would be better to return to Egypt—and some in fact have. But I must warn you that it is neither Aaron or me against whom you grumble. You grumble against the Lord God Almighty!" At these words, a column of fire—the glory of the living God—burst in magnificent brilliance within the cloud over the desert. Many people fell on their knees. Others began to pray aloud, begging the Lord to forgive their murmuring.

Chronicles of the Host

Provision and Law

Moses explained to the people that from that day forward the Lord would provide for all families a daily portion of bread from Heaven—something called "manna," which in the Hebrew tongue means "what is this?" Crispin told us that the only possibility of survival for these rather coarse people was their dependence upon the Most High. The manna was a lesson in God's grace of provision, if not in humility. Every family was allowed just what was needed for one day's provision. However, on the sixth day, which the Lord had blessed, the people were allowed to take a double portion—so they would not violate the sanctity of the seventh day, which God had made holy and a day of rest. What a marvelous significance this would eventually take on—but more on that subject later in the Chronicles.

Indeed the grace of God poured forth upon the people every day, as the manna from Heaven sustained them in their desert sojourn. But the people continued to wonder where Moses was taking them, and we angels also were curious as to when they would finally enter the land given to them through Abraham.

Mt. Sinai

When the people arrived at Mt. Sinai, Moses announced that God wanted to meet with him on the mountain—to give Moses further instructions as to the nation's destiny. Leaving the people under Aaron's charge, Moses went up to meet the Lord, whose glory had descended upon the mountain.

And so it was that at Sinai the Most High introduced His people to His law—chiefly in the Ten Great Commandments, which He gave to Moses on stone tablets. The law would set the people apart from every other nation, and would distinguish forever the God of Abraham from all gods everywhere.

For the Host, the introduction of the law provided a measure of hope that perhaps now the people of God might begin to respond to the Lord in a proper manner. It also meant that the prophecy given to Abraham—that all the world should be blessed through his seed—was advancing rapidly, for now the people were distinguished from all peoples by the holy law of God!

For our enemy, the law represented another opportunity to reveal the corrupt nature of mankind—a means of tripping up the plan of God by encouraging a shortfall of the law's provisions. And indeed, given mankind's poor record thus far as seen in the bloody history of the earth, it was no wonder that the enemy was encouraged by a code of conduct, which they believed man would never be able to live up to.

None of us could have known, however, that the law of the Most High was never intended to lead man, but to point him to something else...something far greater than law...

"Why is it that the Most High must always create these magnificent effects?" asked Berenius, as the cloud continued to emanate the glory of God from the top of Mount Sinai. He stood with Lucifer, Pellecus, and several other of Lucifer's highest-ranking angels just outside the camp, watching the towering and fiery billow.

"Because humans love the spectacular, Berenius," said Pellecus, uncomfortable with being so near God's Presence. "Haven't you noticed how often Moses refers to the wonders the Lord performed in Egypt? With these hard-hearted people, unless the Most High performs something spectacular, and then reminds the people of what He has done, they will forget Him. Quite pathetic, to be sure."

"Or brilliant," said Lucifer, entranced by the cloud of glory. "The Lord knows that by reminding the people of what He has done for them he is establishing a record of trust—something on which they may hang their faith."

"Well, Moses is certainly taking his time with the Lord," said Rugio, a little bored by it all. "Perhaps he is not even up there. Perhaps he is doing all of this simply to strengthen his position among the people."

"That's ridiculous, Rugio," said Kara. "Of course Moses is meeting the Lord."

"And how would you know this?" fumed Rugio. "Your demons couldn't get through to Moses on Sinai any more than my warriors. I was going to finish him as he climbed but was unable to get near even the base of that place."

Kara gave Rugio a cold stare.

"Enough!" said Lucifer. "Rugio makes a good point. Of course Moses has only been gone for a few weeks. But to these humans he seems to have delayed on the mountain for an interminable period of time."

"What are you thinking, my prince?" asked Rugio, eager to make a move against Moses at long last.

"Just this, my warrior," said Lucifer, looking at his most dedicated demon, then at them all. "Delay, to a human mind, often leads to impatience. It causes a break in trust, foolish decisions, and idiotic choosing. Perhaps delay even leads to searching for the divine in more earthly places."

He stood up, his silhouette painting a dark figure in the blazing mountain display behind him. For a moment he turned and looked toward the mountain, but could not bear the light long. He then turned and faced the others.

"So...what are you saying, my lord?" asked Pellecus, who found it difficult to look in Lucifer's direction with the brilliance of the Lord blazing behind him.

"I believe, Pellecus, that these people are due for a foolish decision!"

"My lord?" asked Pellecus.

"Don't you see?" Lucifer asked. "These people are on the brink. It won't be long until they fall of their own accord. All they need is a little stimulus...something to drive them...to catch their imagination...to take the place of the leader and God who have abandoned them...another god...an idol to lead them back to Egypt!"

"And what sort of idol do you suggest?" asked Pellecus, a bit doubtful of the whole idea.

"These are humans, Pellecus," said Lucifer, smiling. "All we have to do is create the occasion—they will create the idol!"

"I don't like this, Michael," said Serus.

The mood in the camp had taken a definitely negative turn. Everywhere, it seemed, were mutterings about this or that, mainly against Moses' leadership and suspicions of what he was really doing all this time on Sinai. Michael was disgusted at the display of disloyalty after so short a time. As Serus and Michael walked through the center of the camp, they listened to bits of conversations going on around them:

"How do we know he's even meeting with the Lord?"

"I heard that he is meeting with Rameses to negotiate our return to Egypt!"

"I don't trust him!"

"We never really knew him until he just appeared out of the desert in Goshen."

"I'm getting tired of the manna."

"Even Joshua has abandoned us to die out here!"

"The enemy has certainly been doing his work here," remarked Serus.

"The demons are in great number these days," agreed Michael.

It seemed to the pair that the enemy angels were becoming bolder in their appearances at the camp. Spirits that encouraged everything from anger and gossip, to perversion and idolatry, had begun to work on the minds and hearts of the people as part of Lucifer's plan to take advantage of Moses' absence from the camp.

As Michael and Serus walked through the various tribal camps, many unholy angels spewed ugly curses at them, cajoling and boasting how they were going to bring these people down to defeat. Some walked right up to Michael, dared him to strike at them, and then laughed when he ignored them.

From the north side of the camp a trumpet sounded and people began streaming towards a newly erected edifice made of stone and decorated with all sorts of garlands of desert flowers. Above it was a great number of shrieking, howling devils, so dense that they created a dark cloud that was invisible to the humans, but which shrouded the scene like a dark and foreboding canopy.

A great shout went up, followed by a silence. Michael and Serus looked, appalled at the unfolding scene: groups of men were carrying baskets full of jewelry, rings, coins—the plunder of Egypt—and emptying them on a blanket spread in front of Aaron. Surrounding the shimmering pile of gold were a number of men who looked to Aaron excitedly, nodding at the great spoil that was coming in.

"Aaron looks a bit out of sorts, doesn't he, Michael?" came a voice.

Michael turned to see Lucifer standing behind him. Next to him was Rugio, grinning a smirking grimace that bore into Michael. Nearby Kara was directing the demons to maintain order within their own ranks but to continue inflaming the people. In some cases the devils were chasing about as recklessly as the people, and Lucifer had ordered that strict discipline be maintained.

Michael didn't answer Lucifer. Serus thought for a moment of answering Lucifer, but then decided that he had better keep a lookout for Joshua, should he return, to make sure that the young man was protected from these increasingly berserk people. More of the Host were arriving, including Sangius and Crispin, who had been at the Academy when word reached Heaven of what was happening. Crispin was amazed at the scene.

"I only just arrived, Michael," said Crispin, who then noticed Lucifer and Rugio. "Take heart. Even though there is a dark influence here, prayers are being lifted up by a good number of the people. That is what has brought us here."

"Ah, prayer," said Lucifer. "Such a powerful weapon. Unfortunately it is used neither well nor often!"

"Sometimes it only takes one person praying, you rebel spirit!" said Michael. "One prayer can send you reeling, Lucifer!"

"Agreed, Michael," said Lucifer. "But fortunately the humans are sectioning off the dissenters in this matter. Some of the Levites who are related to Moses and don't want to be a part of this great adventure, are being...held for their own safety."

As they spoke, Michael could see armed guards roughly escorting groups of people to a tent at the end of the camp.

"How did you manage *that*?" asked Michael.

"I must say that I cannot take credit for that idea," said Lucifer. "The humans grew tired of Joshua's incessant preaching and defending of Moses before he disappeared to find the missing prophet. They decided, of their own accord, to arrest the others. Humans can be quite inspired at times!"

"True indeed, Lucifer," remarked Crispin. "Poor choices have inspired many unfortunate outcomes—both on earth and in Heaven."

"Spare me your lecture, teacher," said Lucifer. "Actually, in terms of inspiration, I must credit you, Crispin, with what goes on. You see, it was you and your unenlightened teachings at the Academy that drove those who seek truth to vacate Heaven in the first place."

"You say it as if the choice to leave was yours," Crispin said. "I would say that you were vacated, and not the other way around."

Lucifer smiled a half-smile and continued. "Be that as it may, whether it is deemed rebellion or liberation, this is the fruit of choice! You are indeed watching the birth of a new nation! But not one led by a trickster from the desert who has abandoned his people. No,

Crispin, this is a new nation with a new god who will lead the people back to bondage where they belong—and where they will disappear in human history and the dust of Egypt!"

"I would have thought that your adventure in Egypt would have taught you something about playing at god," said Crispin. "There is only one God in Heaven!"

"You forget, dear teacher. This is not Heaven."

"Bring to Aaron all of your jewelry—any gold that you have!"

"Someone break into the treasure tent and bring some of the Egyptian plunder!"

Korah and Dathan watched as the people continued bringing gold in various forms to Aaron and laying it at his feet. When they were finally finished, Aaron sifted through the treasure with a bemused look on his face.

"Well Aaron, what shall it be?" asked Korah. "You are our high priest! Fashion for us the god who has delivered us out of bondage, that we might carry him ahead of us!"

A cheer went up from the crowd as people anticipated the image of the god of Israel. Aaron looked vacantly at the gold and then back at Korah.

"I have no idea what the God of Israel looks like," he said. "I never saw Him."

Unseen by the humans Kara stood by Korah and spoke into his mind:

"Surely Moses saw Him on the mountain before returning to Goshen..."

"How did Moses describe Him? Moses met with Him, didn't he?" said Korah.

"Yes, but he never saw Him," said Aaron. "No human has ever seen Him."

"And yet Moses said he spoke with Him face to face. Did Moses deceive us?..."

"So how do we know that Moses even spoke with Him?" asked Korah, as several men in the crowd affirmed his question. Aaron looked up angrily.

"I have no idea," he said. "Moses told me that the Lord appeared to him in the form of a consuming fire."

"Ah yes," said Korah. "The bush that would not burn."

"Perhaps fire is the emblem of this god. Let the fire decide..."

"If the God that delivered us has chosen fire as His image, then fire it should be!" said Korah, who lifted a chain of gold over his head and held it up for all the people to see. "Let Aaron fashion us a god out of the fire!"

A loud cheer went up, and the people suddenly began dancing, singing, and reveling in the presence of their new god, who would be born from Aaron's flames. Aaron ordered a very hot fire built within a stone platform. He tossed the gold into a large bronze disc set over the flames. As the gold melted, the people officially proclaimed Aaron high priest of the God of Israel—the god of the golden fire.

Kara ordered his demons skilled in design into the flames. Taking the melted gold, they fashioned it into an image of a golden calf, which, to the people, seemed to miraculously take shape of its own power. The people were astonished. Even Aaron was amazed and wondered if perhaps the God of Israel was indeed present.

Kara laughed in delight. More and more devils arrived, and the celebration began taking on a sensual and unbridled feeling.

"The people are casting off restraint," commented Lucifer, who had come over to Kara. "Just as the angels in Heaven did."

"These simple people actually believe that the gold formed itself into the image of a calf," said Kara. "Humans are so dreadfully stupid."

"I told you Korah was worth pursuing," said Kara. "Even Pellecus had to admit that I was right. Korah will serve us well in the new order of things."

"If it were not in his heart to rebel, you would not have been able to exploit him," cautioned Lucifer. "All we can do is suggest through the human spirit and mind. But I am grateful that they are so prone to failure."

"It will be interesting to watch Moses' reaction when he discovers that the god he has been worshiping is the image of a calf!" remarked Kara.

"Yes. And Aaron, Moses' brother, as their priest," said Lucifer. He looked at the face of the calf. "It looks as if the Most High God has taken on new features after all!"

CHAPTER 22

"A Seething Core of Wolves."

Chronicles of the Host

A Noise of War

The Host waited anxiously for Moses' return. We knew that something marvelous and far-reaching was happening between creature and Creator on Sinai! But we also saw that the hearts of the people had deteriorated into horrible and base confusion, spurred on by Korah's rebellious actions and encouraged by Aaron's reluctant participation.

As for Moses, upon receiving from the Lord the law that would forever change the direction of Israel, the prophet made his way down the mountain, now to enforce the law upon a people who had become lawless. In the 40 days and nights that Moses had been gone, the people had moved from a nation that feared the Most High to a nation that forgot Him.

They had the impudence not only to disgrace the holy name of the Lord Most High, but also to profane the first two holy commandments that the Lord had delivered to Moses—that of having no other gods before Him, and of not making a graven image to the Lord. By declaring the Most High to be an earthly god, borne in an image of gold, the people had broken both of those laws before Moses had even gotten off Sinai...

The holy angels held back bitter and angry emotions as they watched the people slip from rebellion to debauchery. Men and women, in unrestrained expression, danced, drank, caroused, and feasted—all in the name of the calf of gold. "This is the god who brought us out of Egypt!" they proclaimed, and Aaron was named the high priest of the new order.

Above them, swirling about like a dark whirlpool, were thousands of the enemy, dark spirits of licentious character, calling upon the people to further degrade themselves and calling to the holy angels in lewd and derisive comments. The people, unaware that they were opening themselves up to such suggestion, whipped themselves up into a frenzied and frantic pace. Some were convulsing on the ground, claiming that they were possessed by the god of the calf, and prophesied in his name, proclaiming a great destiny for the future Israel.

Lucifer was delighted with the disintegration that had occurred in so short a time. He stood with Pellecus, who, keenly observing the fray, made mental notes for future instruction at the new academy he was creating to teach the rebel angels Lucifer's order of things. All seemed quite well.

"This is certainly a satisfying day," said Lucifer. "These people are completely out of control."

"Most of them," said Pellecus. "A few remain faithful to Moses and committed to the Lord. They have not stopped praying since Moses and Joshua left."

"Let them pray, Pellecus," said Lucifer. "It will demonstrate that in face of the overwhelming will of a people, even the Most High is powerless!"

Suddenly, the noise of the camp began to diminish, until there was almost complete silence. High on a rock overlooking the scene stood Moses and Joshua. They could only make out the silhouette of the prophet, with the burning mountain behind him. Next to him stood Michael and Serus.

"Michael certainly looks a bit upset," remarked Lucifer.

The devils immediately began howling, hissing, and cursing Michael. They dived in and out of the people to agitate them and foment murderous thoughts toward Moses for disturbing their celebration.

Moses looked at the wreckage of his people and wept angry tears. He held the two stone tablets that the Lord had given him, on which were the Ten Great Commandments. Moses was ashamed for the Most High, that the Lord would even consider being in covenant with so wild and careless a people. He walked in closer, ignoring some of the catcalls.

As he came near a man who was convulsing and prophesying under his breath, Moses said, "Be gone from my sight!" Unseen by Moses or any other human, a spirit of religion and seduction shrieked, cursed, and disappeared into the heavenlies. The man slowly got up and staggered away, frightened at the prophet's wrath.

"Why are you disturbing our feast?" came a voice from the crowd.

It was Korah.

"You have been gone from us, Moses," he continued. "We thought you had abandoned us. So Aaron has fashioned us the god that you sought on the mountain."

Behind Korah were several devils, including Kara, who had been seeding within Korah's mind an increasing opposition to Moses. Kara was happy that the venom of rebellion he had planted had rooted so deeply.

Moses, however, ignored Korah and looked beyond him to Aaron. Aaron immediately dropped the emblems of worship he had crafted and fell to his knees. Many of the crowd did likewise, though others continued to revile Moses for interrupting the festival to the new god.

"What did these people do to make you lead them into this great sin?" Moses asked his brother. "How could you have done this?"

"My brother, these people are bewitched!" began Aaron. Korah and some of the other leaders grumbled. "They begged me to make a god to go before us. They said you would never return. And so I had them bring me their jewelry and some of the plunder of Egypt. I threw the things in the fire and this calf emerged, fully shaped as you see it!"

"It is the work of devils!" screamed Moses, tearing at the image with an axe. Michael ordered some angels to help Moses, and man and angels destroyed the image. Moses ground the bits of it into powder. He mixed the powder with water and made the people drink it.

"You want a god that you can see and feel," he yelled for the whole camp to hear. "How about one you can taste? Drink this, you rebellious lot! Let it mix in with your sour bellies and your empty hearts!"

Then Moses called for those who were loyal to the Lord to come forward. Almost instantly the tribe of Levi proclaimed their allegiance to the living God, and Moses ordered them to kill the profaners in the camp. Brother fought brother as the Levites killed some three thousand people that day.

A pitched battle took place in the heavenlies as well, as war broke out over the camp between Lucifer's angels and Michael's legions. Michael's angels scattered the vile and venomous devils who had held sway over the camp for 40 days. He ordered the camp cleansed of every filthy spirit upon the fresh authority that Moses had brought. As for the testaments of stone, Moses dashed those into pieces. He felt that so unruly a nation was undeserving of so gracious a God.

Chronicles of the Host

New Beginning

The carnage was horrible, and Lucifer's angels thoroughly enjoyed the fruit of their work. Though they did not succeed in completely capturing the nation of Israel, they had proven how corruptible the heart of Israel truly was. They took the events that had happened at Sinai as boding well for their future efforts against the people of the Seed.

As the anger of the Lord subsided, He restored to Moses the tablets, and Israel became a people under law—the only nation on earth to be given the precepts of the Lord Most High! Israel was to bind the words to its heart and make them known to all generations. For a brief time Israel was a nation at peace both with itself and with its God.

The Lord Most High instructed the people on every detail of their lives, in order to distinguish them from every other people on earth. They were to be a people of the law—and their lives were to reflect this. The Lord also ordered the construction of a Tent of Meeting, an earthly place where the Presence of God would meet with the high priest of the land. Some of the angels commented on such a poor house for so great a God. But the wisest among us realized that it was the glory of God that made a place holy, and not a structure—be that in Heaven or on earth.

The day that the tabernacle was completed, the glory of God filled the tent so that nobody could even stand to enter it. Thus did the Most High lead Israel from site to site, ever inching toward the final destination in Canaan. This was a time of great learning, as God was teaching them His law. He was preparing them for the life of faith of a people through whom would come the one to right all things.

Thus did Israel live at peace with their God...but only for a brief time.

"Moses!"

Moses looked up from the scroll on which he was recording the history and laws of the people of God, recognizing the Voice that had become so well known to him.

"Yes, Lord?" he responded.

"For two years I have borne the offenses of these people. They have murmured against Me; they have complained when I provided food and water. Your own family, Aaron and Miriam, turned against you. Fire has come down and consumed many. You have interceded for these stiff-necked people, and I have heard your prayers."

"Yes, Lord," said Moses, bowing low. "As the record here shows in this testament that I am writing, You have been more than gracious. I have recorded how You created the earth; how You planted a garden and turned it over to a man and a woman whom You made in Your own image; how this man rebelled against You and was cast out of Eden; how You promised that one day through the seed of the woman You would reconcile the broken fellowship.

"I have written how You caused the earth to be flooded and preserved the Seed in the family of Noah; and how You made a promise to our father Abraham that all the nations on earth should be blessed through him. I told of Your wonders in Egypt and how You delivered your people from the mighty hand of the pharaoh. And now, O lord, I am recording how You have given us Your instructions on worship and how we may approach You; Your directions on how to construct a tabernacle of meeting; Your design for an ark in which to store the testament; and how You consecrated Aaron and the Levites as a priesthood unto You. You are truly a glorious God!"

"It is time to go forward into the land to which I have called you. Go now and send forth some men to spy out the land, for Israel shall soon enter into the land."

Moses found Aaron and told him exactly what the Lord had spoken. They welcomed the instruction, for it meant that they would soon leave the Desert of Paran and be in the land that had been promised to their fathers. Moses summoned the tribal leaders, the heads of all the families except Levi's. Then he selected the spies who were to leave the Desert of Paran and explore the land that would soon be theirs.

As the men gathered for the instructions, many people milled about outside Moses' tent. People listened with interest and excitement as Moses spoke, for they too were ready to move on and claim the land that was theirs. Moses told the handpicked men that they were to explore the land and report on everything they saw—cities, commerce, agriculture—everything that they could discover.

"Make note of the sort of fruit that grows. Record the number of cities you encounter. Tell us whether they are walled or open. Find out all about the people who inhabit the land. Give us a report on the soil. In fact, bring back samples of the land's produce. I want you to discover everything you can about the land God has given to us."

As the men set out, fully provisioned for the journey, an unseen figure loomed nearby.

If humans could have seen him, they might have made out the reddish bead in his eyes. He watched the men pass by without incident.

"Have no fear, Moses," said the figure. "I believe they will discover much more than you realize!"

He then vanished to report to Kara on this newest development.

"Spies in the land?" repeated Lucifer. He looked at the council with a feigned concern and then said, "It sounds as if the Lord has taken a page from Kara's strategy book!"

The council burst out laughing.

"Yes, we know about the spies, Tinius," Lucifer continued. "Kara has already briefed us on all that."

"And what shall we do?" Tinius asked. "Word is already getting all over Canaan that the Hebrews are approaching. The Canaanites know what happened in Egypt, and they are beginning to panic. I'll not have the gods of Canaan cast down as the gods of Egypt were. I have worked too hard to create the Baals and the others and I'll not give them up."

Lucifer was amused at Tinius's uncharacteristically bold outburst.

"Steady, Tinius," said Lucifer. "They are merely looking around at this point. They have not yet crossed over as a people."

"But what is to stop them, my lord?" asked Lenaes, echoing Tinius's comment. "If Rameses could not stop them; if the sea opened up for them—what is to stop them from coming into Canaan?"

Lucifer surveyed room, scanning the faces of the angels who sat on his council.

"Nothing."

"You said...?" asked Tinius.

"I said nothing will prevent the Israelites from entering the land that God has given to them. Ultimately they shall enter."

"Then what hope have we to wage war?" asked Tinius, whose exasperated question was affirmed by many in the room. "If they return to the land of promise, the Seed is sure to emerge and then we are all finished!"

"If I may speak," said Pellecus, rising from the table in the abandoned Hittite palace. "I have gone over this with Lucifer, and we have come to the conclusion that the introduction of the Hebrews into the land they are promised by the Most High does not necessarily mean that we are 'finished,' as you have put it, Tinius."

Tinius sat down, still frustrated.

"Rather, we have seen in these people the uncanny and predictable pattern of self-destruction. Instead of worrying about their entry into the land, I suggest that we focus on the continued demoralization of their leadership."

"How so, good teacher?" asked Kara. "I have been developing a seething core of wolves among those naive sheep for some time now. But they have no impetus to strike—no cause—nothing to bite into, so to speak."

"We shall give them a cause," said Pellecus, looking to Lucifer, who now stood to address the group.

"What Pellecus is saying," continued Lucifer, "is that we shall introduce a...'cause'...as you so eloquently put it, Kara, to the people."

"I have no doubt about that," said Kara, a bit disturbed that he was not included in this apparently previously discussed issue. "What cause shall we introduce that hasn't already been tried?"

"You're correct, Kara. We have been cultivating many attitudes among the people," said Lucifer. "Dormant and seething attitudes, which I believe will eventually bear us much fruit. We have seen how delay caused the people to lose heart when Moses took so long on the mountain. We have seen how their appetites have caused them to murmur against the Lord when their rotten bellies were not full. We have seen how quickly they proclaimed another god when they felt abandoned by the Most High."

"Yes, of course," snapped Kara. "But what are you thinking of introducing now?"

"Fear."

"Fear, my lord?" repeated Kara, a bit skeptically.

"Yes. Fear. It has been our experience that the fundamental human flaw—the greatest hindrance to their ability to hear from and follow the Most High—is fear. The fear of the unknown. Fear that robs them of reason and takes away their ability to trust in the Lord's provision. The sort of fear that caused Abraham and Sarah to give birth to Ishmael, or that drove Jacob to rob his brother of his birthright.

"Fear is a great motivator, when used strategically. Therefore, I believe that the fear of the unknown in Canaan will strike terror in the heart of every man and woman." He looked at the group, and smiled a knowing smile at Pellecus. "Such is the power of a terrifying report about the land."

"A bad report about the land?" said Kara. He laughed a bit. "What shall they report about that shall frighten these people? What is there in Canaan to be afraid of that they did not face in Egypt...or in the desert, for that matter?"

"It isn't what they have faced that matters, Kara," said Lucifer. "What matters is what they have not faced—that which is housed in the minds of faithless men."

Lucifer cocked his head back as if visualizing the scene in his mind. "When the spies return with news of giants, and walled cities; when they see some of Tinius's Baal-like gods appearing to them in the night; when they hear of great warriors with whom they will have to fight—they will give a report so frightening that the people will surely rebel against Moses and the Lord will be finished with them once and for all!"

Joshua sat next to Caleb outside the tent that they shared. They were enjoying the final warmth of a dying fire. The other members of the exploration team had gone to sleep, and Joshua and Caleb remained awake for the night watch.

The excursion into Canaan was now in its twentieth day. They had just come through Hebron and were now headed toward the Valley of Eshcol, whose fruit was reportedly wonderful. Impressed by what they had seen already, Joshua and Caleb were encouraged by the land's richness.

The angels listened as Joshua and Caleb discussed the sights thus far: the beautiful land; the cities and houses that would become Israel's; the bountiful produce; and of course, the fierce people whom they would someday fight.

Caleb looked up at his friend. Joshua, called Hoshea by Moses, was of the tribe of Ephraim. The Ephraimites were very closely allied with his own tribe of Judah. He had seen how these tribes had taken a leading role in the affairs of Israel, and even now, on this trip, they seemed to be the ones encouraging and leading the other spies, who had grown less than enthusiastic about the mission.

"Joshua."

Joshua looked at Caleb.

"I am hearing some talk from the others."

"Yes, I have heard too," said Joshua, stirring the little fire with a stick. "They are just weary and want to see their families."

Caleb looked around to make sure that they were quite alone.

"I think it is more than that," he said in a low voice.

Serus and several other angels sat near the two men, watching them silently. For Serus, this had been an enjoyable assignment. He had grown fond of Joshua, who along with Caleb, seemed to be the exhorter on this trip, ever since the spies had set out from the Desert of Zin. Joshua was extremely courageous, and according to Michael, he was also being considered for the position of Moses' successor.

Several of Pellecus's demons—former wisdom angels who had a talent for entering into the minds of men as they slept and bringing horrifying dreams—skulked about the camp, going from tent to tent. At one point, one of them looked at Serus and grinned a bizarre smile that made him look more simian than spirit.

"There they go, spreading their poison," said Archais, who had accompanied Serus on this particular assignment.

"Nothing we can do about them, I'm afraid," said Serus.

"I'd like to do something," said one of Serus's companions, who had stood up when the demon had grinned at them.

"I understand, my friend," said Serus. "But they are going into the hearts and minds of men who have already succumbed to fear. These men have already made up their minds to oppose the Lord's plan; therefore, they have opened themselves up to such incursions by the enemy."

A scream broke the night air. A man rushed out from one of the tents, muttering that he had seen a demon spirit who warned him that the land was going to devour them. The other men rallied around him and listened to his story. Some confirmed that they, too, had had such a dream.

The devils stood around snickering at their work, quite satisfied that they were a success. Serus and his crew, keeping a careful eye on both men and devils, watched as Joshua and Caleb went to the others. The man who had had the dream, a Danite named Ammiel, became angry when he saw them.

"I told you that we were going to die here," he screamed. "It's obvious that we are unwelcome by the gods and people of this land."

The others wore silent scowls that betrayed their agreement with Ammiel's assessment. Joshua looked back.

"A nightmare. A walled city. A warrior..." Joshua began with a hint of disgust in his voice.

"No! No, Joshua," said Ammiel, who was drinking a bit of wine that someone had brought him. He wiped his mouth with his robe. "Not a nightmare. A demon creature! Not simply a walled city...a fortress. And not just a warrior...a giant!"

"Anak's own descendants!" piped in Palti, the Benjamite.

"Listen to me," pleaded Joshua. "The Lord has promised us this land. He will give it to us if we are willing to fight for it!"

Shammua stood to speak. He had been quiet all along. As a member of the tribe of Reuben, the firstborn of Israel, his opinion carried a great deal of weight with the group. He looked over the faces of the men, glowing from the dying embers of the fire.

"I say this," he began. "We are to finish this mission and make a report to Moses. But as far as I am concerned, I have seen enough to tell me that we are bringing our families into a hornet's nest. I for one will not see my wife and children destroyed in this land of demons and giants!"

The group agreed heartily with Shammua's assessment. Joshua and Caleb were disappointed by the lack of courage among these leading men of Israel. Caleb stormed off into the night and Joshua looked at Shammua.

"You would discourage the plan of Almighty God for our people, because you are afraid?" he asked.

"No Joshua," said Shammua. "I would discourage the plan of Moses, because it is foolishness!"

Had Joshua been able, he would have seen just off Shammua's shoulder the reddish eyes and ape-like face of a demon grinning wildly at him.

CHAPTER 23

"Moses, what were you thinking?"

The people were filled with curiosity at the size of the cluster of grapes, which had to be hauled in by two men. They gasped at the pomegranates, dates, olives, and other wonderful foods they had been without for so long. From time to time a child, too young to remember such delights, plucked a grape and tossed it into his mouth, to the amusement of the adults.

Inside Moses' tent, the leaders of the expedition reported exactly what they had found in Canaan. Before they were allowed to fully give their reports, though, Moses told them to appear before the people who were clamoring for news about their future homeland.

One by one the men addressed the crowd, extolling the wonderful nature of the land and its produce. They spoke of green valleys and plenty of water, great herds of livestock and lush grazing fields. It was truly a wonderful place. But as they spoke, the spirits of fear that had accompanied the explorers in Canaan began arriving and covering the spies' eyes with their hands. Into unsuspecting but open minds the devils spoke the fearful thoughts that they had cultivated on the journey. Caleb and Joshua, ignored by the offending devils, merely hung their heads in shame as one by one the men reported:

"The people who live there are mighty!"

"The cities are fortified with great walls and well-defended!"

"Great giants, Anak's very descendants, live there!"

The Israelites recoiled in horror as the men painted a bleak and frightening picture of life in Canaan. Though a place of great beauty and wealth, in spite of its reputation for flowing with milk and honey—all in all, Canaan was to be avoided by any people who wanted to survive. Shammua assessed the situation for all the men with his simple statement: "We were like grasshoppers in our own eyes!"

Lucifer had arrived for the final summation by Shammua. He applauded Pellecus's subtle intrusion into the minds of the explorers. Pellecus acknowledged Lucifer's gratitude and began speaking, when suddenly Caleb blurted out:

"We should go and take this land!" he implored. "We can most certainly do it!"

"Silence him!" ordered Lucifer. The devils immediately began moving in and out of the people's minds. An already tense attitude instantly turned hostile, and the people shouted Caleb down.

"That's how you deal with dissenters," said Lucifer. "Human mobs always come together when they are afraid of something."

Off to the side and keeping careful watch on Joshua, Caleb, Moses, and others who merited special attention from the Most High, Michael and Serus looked at the pitiful display in amazement.

"I shall never understand humans," said Serus. "The Lord is indeed a longsuffering God to put up with such nonsense."

"Longsuffering, yes," agreed Crispin, who had arrived with a group of student angels to demonstrate to them the fickleness of the human heart. "But my feeling is that there is a limit to His patience."

"But where does one cross the line?" asked Michael. "I for one am ready to move on from these people!"

Crispin laughed. "I'm sure, Michael, that were it up to you or me, these people might have ceased to be long ago. But the Lord is true to His promises. And that is the difference between a creature and a Creator."

Chronicles of the Host

Fearful Night

The evening passed slowly as the people of God became people of fear. On the very edge of realizing a great promise, the Israelites tossed it away on the strength of the bad report.

Many meetings occurred throughout the camp that night, as groups of men discussed the future of the nation. The question that passed every lip was: Can we actually move into this land or not?

There would be a fearful reckoning before the issue was decided...but it was not to be decided by the faithless spies, or faithful men, or even angels, good or bad. It would be decided by the Lord of Hosts...and would affect Israel for the next 40 years...

"This should prove a very interesting meeting," said Kara, as Moses emerged from his tent with Aaron.

Joshua and Caleb took their places with the two elderly leaders in front of the assembly of Hebrews. The air was filled with a tense feeling of unrest. The men waited until the appropriate time, and then Shammua, encouraged by Korah, stood to speak.

"My demons have been hard at work," remarked Pellecus. "All night long."

"I'm sure they have done remarkably well," said Kara. "Almost as well as my demons might have done, given the chance."

Pellecus smiled at Kara's obvious jealousy for having been passed over in this action. "Lucifer calls upon you when an issue requires gathering information," Pellecus said casually. "But when a subtle approach to the mind is needed, he defers to me."

"Well," said Kara. "Let us see how well your demons did. The fool Shammua is about to present the people's case before Moses."

Shammua walked over and greeted Moses with great respect. Moses received him coldly and asked him to proceed. All eyes were upon Shammua as he recounted, once more, the excursion into the land. He walked about, stressing his desire "as much as any son of Israel" to claim the land that had been promised them. His tone began to get more and more hostile as he spoke, and in the end he was accusing Moses and decrying the whole idea of entering into Canaan.

As Shammua talked, Pellecus gave a signal. Hundreds of demons began hovering over the assembly, pouring in from every direction and creating a dark covering over the entire scene. Only around Moses and Joshua and a few elders who stood with them, where Michael had set up a parameter of very powerful, hulking warrior angels, was there a break in the darkness.

"Moses, what were you thinking?" Shammua demanded. "We would have been better off never to have left Egypt! In fact we were better off dead there—or in this desert. Here at least we will not have to witness the plunder of our possessions and the murder of our families, which we will surely witness if we proceed with this idea of moving into Canaan.

"I was there, Moses. I saw it. You did not. Only these two who are blindly loyal to you offer up any opposition to the will of the people." He held up a small child for everyone to see. "Do you want to watch this little one perish at the hands of Anak or on the altar of Molech?"

He set the child down and looked over in the direction of Korah.

"I say it is time to forget this nonsense, select a new leader, and return to Egypt, where at least we know we will survive with our families!"

A cheer went up from the crowd. Devils were buzzing all over the camp, jabbering excitedly and moving in to further agitate the crowd against Moses and his loyalists. Kara was impressed with the scene.

"Your angels are doing a marvelous job, I must admit," said Kara. "Who is that who is influencing Shammua so well?"

Pellecus indicated the small, black, shadowy creature that had attached itself to Shammua and seemed to be resting its head on Shammua's shoulder.

"That is Kreelor."

"Ah yes," said Kara. "Formerly the Temple steward. He is still bitter at having been talked into throwing in with us." He laughed at remembering Kreelor's pleading ignorance when confronted for his complicity with Lucifer during the attempted rebellion. "He hasn't spoken to me since we vacated Heaven!"

"He is quite useful now," said Pellecus. "And as you can see, he is doing quite well handling Shammua."

"I'll mention to Lucifer about having him permanently assigned," said Kara, who was having thoughts about recruiting Kreelor away from Pellecus.

"I already have," said Pellecus, with a sly look on his face. "And he already is."

After Shammua's address to the assembly, Moses and Aaron didn't say a word, but simply fell to their faces on the ground in shame of what the people were asking.

Joshua angrily tore his clothes and began addressing the people. Serus, ever watchful, stayed right with him as he spoke.

"Israelites! Brothers! Do not do this dreadful thing," Joshua began. "It is the Lord God of Abraham who brought you out of Egypt to bring you into this land of which we speak. Yes, there will be some challenges. But do not be afraid! The Lord God will go before us into the land and will sweep the enemy before us!"

"*I say we stone them here and now,*" came a voice.

It was one of Pellecus's demons. Everyone looked about to see who said it, but it didn't really matter. People began to pick up on the theme and call for stoning the men on the spot. A few actually picked up stones as people began pulling away from the four men.

Michael stood by, sword drawn, as did his angels, ready to protect and even kill any person who made an attempt on Moses' life. Serus moved close to Joshua. He did not have the same authority to kill if necessary, but he could more than handle any human that might attempt something. Besides, it really wasn't humans who concerned him. He was watching the increasing number of both Kara's and Pellecus's demons closing in on the group.

Suddenly the devils shrieked and scattered like leaves in a maelstrom, disappearing in every direction. Kara and Pellecus were thrown to the ground in a great shudder as the glory of God burst forth over the tabernacle of meeting. Even the humans saw the brilliant display, so intense that they had to turn their heads from it. Most of them dropped to their faces in fear, humbling themselves before God's mighty presence. Moses and Aaron stood, helped to their feet by Joshua and Caleb.

Moses entered the tent, with Aaron, Joshua, and Caleb waiting outside. The people remained uncomfortably quiet, fearful of what the verdict would be when Moses returned. Korah managed to slip away to his tent to await the news there. Shammua remained behind with the other spies, trying to encourage them that perhaps this was another of Moses' tricks.

Michael and Serus waited with everyone else. Gabriel, Crispin, Sangius, and many other leading angels among the loyal Host had arrived as well to hear what judgment the Lord had rendered.

"I fear, Michael, that this time they have gone too far," said Serus.

Michael remained silent and motioned Serus to do the same. The other holy angels shuddered in reverence at God's mighty presence and what it portended. Even the normally conversant Crispin remained silent.

Kara had recovered himself by this time and, though he remained on the ground, he managed to skulk away, complaining bitterly of the Lord's undue interference and questioning the justice of it all. Pellecus, who could hear Kara's nonsense somewhere behind him, could only shake his head at the foolishness of such a highly placed demon.

When Moses finally emerged from the tent, his face was very grim indeed. All eyes were upon him. Even the children seemed to sense the importance of the occasion and remained quiet. He waited until Aaron stood next to him and then began to speak.

"The Lord your God is slow to anger, abounding in love, and forgiving of sin and rebellion," he began. "The Lord God has forgiven your insolence and your rebellion in not going up into the land..."

A huge relief moved through the camp as people began to feel a bit more at ease with Moses' words. Korah, listening from his tent, hung on every word. The 12 spies who were indirectly implicated in the charge were stone-faced and silent, averting their eyes from anyone in particular.

"The Lord God reminded me that you have tested Him ten times now, since He delivered you from bondage in Egypt. You shall therefore not enter the land that He promised you. The Lord declares that since you desire to remain in the wilderness, in the wilderness you shall remain. All of this evil generation from the age of 20 and up shall die here in the desert. You shall not see the land the Lord promised you. Rather your bones shall rot here. Only Joshua and Caleb and their families shall the Lord your God bring into the land. For you have tempted the Lord, and He has spoken against you!"

Moses returned to his own tent. The sounds of anger and bitter complaining gave way to weeping and wailing by the people, who now would remain in the desert until their deaths. Joshua wept as well at the sight of his people, who, because they did not have the faith to endure Canaan, must now have the will to endure the wilderness.

"Such a dark time for the people of God," commented Crispin finally.

"And a dreary time for angels as well, good teacher," mused Michael.

In his tent, Korah brooded about the developments. Dathan and a few others were with him. Now Moses had not only arrested his movement toward returning to Egypt, but had relegated the people to hardship in the wilderness for the next 40 years—and under the law that he had composed on the mountain! The more he thought about it, the angrier he got. It was clearly a case of vengeance on the part of Moses to punish the people for not agreeing to his personal dreams of conquest in Canaan.

Evidently Moses had never recovered from losing prestige in Egypt when he went from a ruler to a runaway. And since the people were unwilling to crown him king in Canaan, he now was content to remain a prisoner of Zin.

"Who does he think he is?" came a voice in Korah's mind.

"Yes. Who does Moses think he is?" thought Korah.

"Are you going to stand by and allow Moses and his family to dictate to millions of people what their destiny is?"

"I cannot simply stand by and allow Moses to rob me of my destiny as a ruler in this nation," Korah said aloud.

"But what shall we do?" asked Dathan. "Moses has decreed it so."

"Perhaps it is time to confront him and expose him."

"We shall expose him for the fraud that he is," said Korah. "And that sorcerer brother of his as well. We will expose them and then stone them according to the law! They are conjurers and experts in witchcraft and all manner of evil arts that Moses learned in Pharaoh's house."

"And then what?" asked Dathan.

"And then I will lead the people back to Egypt and away from this accursed desert. I am of the house of Levi, am I not? Who is Moses to be prince over all of us? If indeed one Levite holds the authority to rule and take us *out* of Egypt, where at least we were well-fed, then who is to say that another of the tribe of Levi cannot take us *back* to Egypt? I shall lead the people to the true promised land!"

They exited the tent, agreeing to take the plan up with other key leaders in Israel. Inside the tent, Pellecus said, "Well done, Kara. You certainly know this man's heart!"

"Of course I know it," said Kara smugly. "I helped create it!"

Lucifer stood on a hillside, surveying the camp at dusk. He was amazed at how the camp had so quickly settled into the routine and the realization that the desert would be their home for a good many years. Glancing at the tabernacle, where God resided periodically and dramatically, Lucifer sneered with contempt.

"Well, Most High God," he said. "It seems that You can never shake Yourself from rebels. It seems that all of Your creatures are bent on escaping Your Presence. Even these pitiful creatures made in Your very image have a rebel nature within their hearts that drives them always away from Your face.

"Law? For these lawless hearts? You truly believe that these sordid and sensual people will be able to abide Your law? They broke it before it was even born on Sinai. And now You desire to build a nation—a kingdom of priests—to carry Your law forward, when they cannot even keep it themselves? I have known You to be a God of the downtrodden and a friend to widows and orphans, Most High. When did You become the God of rebels and outlaws?"

He pointed down at the camp.

"These are Your people, Lord? These who would cast You off in an instant if given the opportunity? The only way You hold them is by terrifying them with great billowy smoke and fire and bloody Niles and blotting the sun! What sort of allegiance is measured by intimidation?

"I suggest that You have failed, O Lord. These people shall never bring forth the Seed that I have so long dreaded. I am more confident than ever that in the end, the base and carnal instincts of humans will always win out over Your clever compelling—even when done with great thunder and lightning!

"In the final outcome, O Lord, You will vacate this miserable world and leave it to fester in the sin that You Yourself created by giving these miserable creatures the ability to turn on You. And I shall be here ready to lead them in a new and glorious season on earth. Stay in the heavens, O Lord, for that is where You belong. But leave earth to me!"

Chronicles of the Host

Korah's Reckoning

True to Lucifer's brash boasting before the Lord, the people were stirred up once more. Korah, a distant relative of Moses, had rallied some 250 other leaders in Israel, determined to end Moses' leadership and take the people back to Egypt. Once more Moses met a delegation of leading Israelites who questioned his ability and right to rule over them. And once more Moses responded with great authority as given Him by the Most High God...

"I put it to you, Moses, that your leadership over us is presumption and not legitimate authority!"

CHAPTER 24

"Korah has set quite a nice trap."

Korah was building his case against Moses brick by brick, and his audience of 250 men spurred him on heartily. Moses, in a situation far too familiar, stood in front of the Tent of Meeting, listening to the complaint against him.

"It is not you alone with whom we have a grievance," Korah continued. "Your brother, Aaron, has usurped the position of high priest, and together the two of you have conspired to lead this nation to a place of desolation and wilderness. How petty! I put it before this nation that you are a man obsessed with power. And because power was taken away from you when you murdered an innocent man in Egypt, you returned years later to grab whatever measure of power that you could.

"My question is a simple one, Moses. Why? Why have you set yourself above us? Are you any better than the rest of us? Am I not a Levite? Have I not duties to our Lord as well? Do you truly believe that only you and Aaron are holy?" He shouted loudly for all to hear, "This entire nation is holy to the Lord! Every man here! And all of them are separated to the Lord and the Lord is with them!"

A great cheer went up from the people as Korah moved over to allow Moses to speak. Dathan patted Korah on the back and spoke laudatory words in his ear. The rowdy crowd finally settled down as Moses waited for silence.

Like spectators in an arena, the Host of Heaven and the fallen angels watched the confrontation with great interest. Since the assembly was taking place in front of the holy Tent of Meeting, the devils stayed clear of the area and watched instead from more heavenly perches.

Crispin observed the hesitancy on the part of Lucifer's angels, and called to them, inviting them to come in for a closer viewing. They responded with profanities that caused Michael to look at Crispin with a "Why did you do that?" sort of look. Crispin smiled.

"It is amazing how Lucifer dismisses the Lord with one hand, but calls his angels back from His Presence with the other," Crispin said to Sangius. Sangius, who had once been close to Lucifer, agreed.

"Lucifer shall never attain to such a Presence," said Sangius. "He hates the presence of God because he shall never have it."

"Yet these poor, simple humans are making accusation of the Lord's chosen right under the shadow of the tent of His Presence. At least the devils have the sense to respect the Lord's Person. Korah has no idea what he is courting."

Moses walked up and down the rows of men who stood to accuse him. Some stared back at him with intense vigor; others avoided his eyes altogether. He then stood upon a small platform brought for the occasion and addressed the crowd for what he hoped would be the last time on this issue.

"You have tested the Lord once more, and now the Lord will test you," Moses began. "I am weary of your accusations. You don't accuse me in this...you accuse the Lord! Therefore the Lord will prove who shall stand before Him..."

Watching from his vantage, Lucifer suddenly said to himself, "Watch out now..."

"My lord," asked Pellecus.

"There is something sly going on here," said Lucifer.

"Don't worry, my prince," said Kara. "Korah has set quite a nice trap."

"A trap has certainly been set," said Lucifer. "But for whom?"

"Tomorrow," continued Moses, "you and your followers are to bring censers and incense before the Lord. Whomever the Lord chooses will be holy."

He then looked at one group in particular—Korah's group.

"As for you Levites, you who were chosen by God to enter into His service in the Tabernacle...isn't it enough that you have been so honored? You who rushed to the Lord's side when the golden calf was destroyed—do you now covet the priesthood as well by attacking Aaron?"

He then turned to Dathan and Abiram, who had been with Korah.

"And you two—you also accuse me?" said Moses.

Dathan, unaccustomed to being thrust into the light, suddenly found his voice and began hurling offenses at Moses.

"You Moses! You said you were taking us to a land flowing with milk and honey. Instead, you brought us out of such a land to die in the desert. Yes, I accuse you—of deceiving your own people and betraying their trust."

"Tomorrow, Korah, the Lord will judge between us," Moses said. "I pray He will have mercy upon you!"

"And I pray that the people will have mercy upon you, Moses," said Korah, dismissing the assembly. Dathan followed him, giving Moses a proud look as he left.

That evening Kara met with Berenius and instructed him about the upcoming contest. Because Moses had picked censers as the weapon of choice, Lucifer had ordered that Korah's censers must light. Berenius was given the task of manipulating the censers and creating a flame to demonstrate for the people their fitness to lead. And so he organized his lead demons into pairs—each assigned to a censer. The demons assured Berenius that at the proper moment the censers would burn brilliantly and prove that Korah was indeed chosen by God.

"Has it really come to trickery?" asked Rugio. "I mean all these censers and smoke and nonsense. How low must we sink to prove our power?"

Pellecus, Rugio, and Kara, who made up Lucifer's inner circle of leadership, were meeting in summary of the latest events. On the whole, Lucifer was satisfied with the way things had been going. The people's blatant opposition to Moses, and therefore to the Most High, was a gratifying development. If the war must be fought by grinding everything to a creeping or halting progress, then so be it—anything to delay the Seed.

"Trickery?" asked Lucifer. "You believe that trickery and deceit are not viable weapons for us?"

"Yes, of course," said the warrior. "But at some point we must exercise our power to destroy these people outright. I am weary of their existence!" Rugio's aura began manifesting as his anger grew. "I hate Israel," he snarled.

"Don't we all?" said Lucifer.

Pellecus and Kara smiled at Lucifer's disarming statement.

"I am simply saying that I am tired of rule by deception. I crave force!"

Lucifer stood from the rock on which he was seated, overlooking the camp of Israel. He indicated the many fires below and said:

"Do you see all of those flames of light?"

All of the angels looked down at the camp, dotted with thousands of small fires in and around the many tents.

"Each of those flames represents something that might destroy us. What began as one man and woman has become a nation that threatens our very existence. You talk of deception as if it is not a weapon. I maintain that it is our greatest weapon. What we cannot take by force we can influence through the minds of men. We shall never be able to confront the Most High directly—we saw that! But we can destroy His plan through His people. Thus, whether it's smoking censers or idols that speak or familiar spirits of dead relatives makes no difference to us. It is the hearts of men that must be destroyed. And it is only through deception that this will happen!" He looked intently at Rugio. "You'll have your opportunity to strike at Michael. I know that you are storing a great amount of hate for him. That is good. Hate is a great motivator. But in due course, my warrior. In due course."

"Besides," said Kara pointedly, "the last confrontation by force that you had with Michael saw you and your greatest angels bested. I would not be in such a hurry to..."

Rugio screamed an angry curse at Kara and drew his sword. Kara backed down in terror, shielding himself with his arms and calling upon Lucifer to put a stop to it. Pellecus remained impassive, wondering how they were ever to win a war with such leaders.

"Rugio! Put your sword away at once!" ordered Lucifer. "Save your anger for the field of battle! And you, Kara. Make certain that the censers light up on cue. Do not fail me in this."

He began walking away.

"I must visit the other four members of this council in their domains. I shall return when the contest begins."

He looked over the camp, still blazing with fires.

"By tomorrow these lights will have moved on...towards Egypt. And Moses and Aaron will be buried under a pile of bloody stones!"

The men of Korah stood before the Tent of Meeting, each holding a censer filled with incense. Some of the men were nervous; others were exhilarated. All of them were curious as to the outcome of it all. Next to each man, unseen by them of course, was one of Berenius's devils—each prepared to create the fiery climax that would prove Korah's leadership. They were grim-faced, ugly demons, who were very nervous because of their proximity to the tabernacle of the Lord's Presence.

Korah walked among them, instructing them on how to hold the censers and how to pray and all. Dathan and Abiram stood with him. It would be a great day for Israel, they boasted with confidence. Next to the men was a curious pile of stones that had appeared overnight. Shammua, the chief agitator among the spies who had gone into the land, guarded the pile. He held one stone ominously.

Moses finally emerged from the tent with Aaron. He looked over the scene and felt the same disgust for these rebellious people that he had felt for some time. He was ready to be done with them. Michael, as always, accompanied him, and received the usual "unwelcome" from the many devils in the area.

A great shaking in the heavenlies suddenly erupted as the shekinah—the glory of the Lord—appeared over the Tabernacle. A few of the demons scattered, but those standing with Korah's men stood firm—albeit frightened.

From his place on the hillside, Lucifer watched the proceedings with the Council of Seven who had assembled to watch the final chapter of Moses' prophetic and bothersome career. Kara took great satisfaction in watching the discipline of Berenius's angels, who did not flinch when the Lord's Presence manifested. They had been trained—as well as warned—not to do so.

The men of Israel became silent in the face of God's Presence, and all eyes were upon Korah as he walked up to Moses.

"I have assembled the men as you requested," he began.

"Not as I requested," corrected Moses. "As the Lord requested."

"Ah yes, as the Lord requested," said Korah. "Be that as it may, we are ready for whatever it is that you have planned for this day."

Moses suddenly convulsed, as if in great torment, and fell to the ground upon his face. He began weeping bitterly. Korah was wondering what sort of display this might be. He figured he could use this as another example of Moses' sorcery and demonic ties. The people could hear the muffled pleadings of Moses—he seemed to be interceding for them.

"My Lord," he cried out. "Will You condemn the whole assembly for the sins of one man?"

Korah was now getting angry at this display. What trickery was this?

"Moses, your drama no longer works here!" he said. "The people no longer believe your..."

"People of Israel, hear me!" Moses spoke loudly. "These men have asked to be chosen of God—and so they have been! Hear, O Israel, and act! Move away from the house and tents of these three—Korah, Dathan, and Abiram! The Lord shall meet them there!"

The men with Korah suddenly felt a panicked rush and began running to their tents to protect their homes and belongings. Korah was rapidly losing control of the situation and ran to his tent, in case Moses was preparing to attack with some of the Levites who had remained loyal. Dathan and Abiram also rallied their families at their tents. In a few minutes the three men—Korah, Dathan, and Abiram—stood with their families outside their tents, prepared to defend them.

"What is this?!" Lucifer screamed. "Kara, light those censers at once!"

Kara gave the order and the devils next to the men with the censers caused the censers to begin bursting into flame. Some of the men dropped their censers in fear, but quickly recovered them. Others took comfort in the fact that, whatever happened to Korah, at least they had been accepted.

"Keep an eye on Moses!" Kara screamed to nobody in particular.

"Don't worry about Moses," said Lucifer, who was watching Shammua's men gather stones from the pile and infiltrate the men with the censers.

Moses had moved down to the tents of Korah, Dathan, and Abiram. Many of the devils who had lit the censers were now moving over these same tents. Michael remained with Moses, sword drawn. Rugio also moved in, sword drawn, keeping an eye on Michael and hoping for the chance to get in a blow.

The people had pulled back from the three men's tents, isolating them. Korah remained smug, though a bit unnerved by what was happening.

"Is that the smell of incense?" he said sarcastically. "I believe, Moses, that you said my men should bring censers to prove who was with the Lord."

A few of the crowd agreed with him. Moses ignored them. With the men were their wives and little ones. Moses felt compassion for these innocents, and yet he understood the reach of sin—that one man's behavior affected many more than himself. And so he addressed the crowd:

"Men of Israel—these men have accused me and Aaron of betraying your trust. They have asked for a share in this leadership. I say to you that the Lord will now prove who is His own."

He pointed to the men who stood before their tents. As he did, one of Dathan's daughters ran to him. He picked her up and looked at his wife with fear for the first time. Korah remained confident that this was simply another of Moses' tricks and that the lit censers had already made their case.

"If these men die a natural death, then the Lord is with them," he continued. "But should they die an unnatural death...something completely out of the ordinary...If the earth should open and swallow them up—they and their families and all that they own alive into their graves—then you shall know that these men have offended the Lord your God!"

Korah nervously began to reply a contemptuous remark, when suddenly the earth beneath his feet convulsed violently. He looked at Moses with sheer fright in his eyes as Moses stepped backwards from him. The devils all around were jeering and laughing hysterically, for the death of any human was to them gratifying. Michael watched with a mixture of pride in his Lord and compassion for the little children who were about to follow their fathers' sins to their graves.

It was all over in a few seconds—the earth beneath the tents and feet of Korah, Dathan, and Abiram opened like great jaws. Every one of them and all their possessions disappeared in a screaming, roaring terror. The sounds of the children tore at the heart of Moses, but it was out of his hands. Then the earth shut upon them and all was quiet once more.

Suddenly great rays of light began shooting from the cloud of glory above the Tabernacle into the 250 men who were holding the censers. Men and devils shrieked as the judgment of God poured forth upon that body of men. Shammua only managed to take one step before he was cut down, still clutching a rock with which he had intended to open Moses' skull. All of the 250 men died within seconds. The people of Israel panicked, believing that God would kill them all.

As for Korah, Dathan, and Abiram, they perished and were gone from the community of Israel forever. Moses ordered that the censers be taken and hammered into sheets to overlay the altar—for the censers were holy to the Lord. This was done to remind the people that only those who had been ordained by God—Aaron and his descendants—could rightfully bring incense before the Lord.

Chronicles of the Host

Desert Sojourn

Following the defeat of Korah and his rebels, the Host presumed that perhaps the men of Israel would finally begin to recognize the Lord's authority through Moses. But in true human fashion, and with encouragement from Lucifer's unrelenting angels, a group opposed Moses the very next day! This time the Lord wasted no time and sent a plague among the people that was only stopped through the intercession of Moses and Aaron.

On many other occasions did these rebellious people offend the Lord; and many other times did He deal with them harshly. Even Moses fell into sin, and because of his offense at Meribah in disobeying the Lord, he himself was barred from entering the Promised Land! But eventually this evil generation died in the desert, as did Aaron, Miriam, and others, as had been foretold by Moses.

A series of victories over local Canaanite rulers encouraged the people as they continued on their trek toward Canaan. At Mount Hor, because Edom refused to allow the Israelites to travel though their territory, Moses gave the order that they would have to go the long way around. This caused the people to balk and complain, for which the Lord sent venomous snakes to bite their heels.

Forty years after the spies had been sent into the land, the people of God, emboldened with a new generation, were prepared once more to enter the land of promise. They seemed unstoppable, as one by one the pagan kings fell before them: Arad; Sihon, king of the Amorites; Og, king of Bashan. And then they reached the borders of Balak, king of Moab, who had a different strategy in mind for dealing with the invading people of Israel...

"My king! Are you well?"

Balak, king of Moab, was lying on his bed, drenched in the sweat of another nightmare. His steward brought him some wine and the king sat up. He looked at the steward and took the cup, drinking it greedily. The king rose from his bed and looked over the city. All seemed quiet enough...for now. But the dreams he had been having and the news from the other kingdoms in his region indicated that his very throne was in jeopardy.

His own advisors also were feeling the dread, as were the people. All of Moab, it seemed, was terrified of the coming threat from the south. Only last week, delegations from the people pled with the elders to do something before it was too late. Balak had considered a military solution, but upon hearing of the deaths of Og and Sihon, and the destruction of their kingdoms, he had decided upon another course.

"Bring me writing material and our fastest courier," he demanded. "I will send a message tonight!"

As the steward exited the room, Balak's chief minister, Zora, came in. The king greeted him and explained that he was sending for help and was willing to pay any price for it.

"And to whom are you sending, majesty?" asked Zora.

"Balaam of Pethor," said Balak. "He is a great seer, a man known to every country in the world; a man whose knowledge of the divine will bring this invasion to its knees!"

"I'm sure the elders will approve," agreed Zora, watching the king write. "I shall personally escort them to Pethor with the message."

"Excellent," said Balak.

"I shall, of course, need to draw upon the treasury. Balaam is gifted—and he charges a handsome fee for his services."

"Yes, yes, pay him whatever he asks," said Balak. "Here, how does this sound?"

He handed the letter to Zora, who read:

To Balaam, son of Beor,

A great people have come out of Egypt; they cover the face of the land and they have settled next to my kingdom. Come, and put a curse on these people, because they are too powerful for me. For I know that you are blessed with a special gift, and those whom you bless are blessed, and those whom you curse are cursed!

Zora thought the letter perfect. The king gave the dispatch to his courier and told him to assemble the elders immediately. Balak looked at Zora, comforted that he had taken such a measure.

"Perhaps now your majesty will be able to sleep," said Zora.

"Perhaps," said the king. "But I shall not sleep well until Balaam arrives and curses Israel for their incursions. He will call upon his god and humble the desert god of Israel!"

Chapter 25

"These people cannot possibly keep the law."

Rugio and Kara watched as Balak drifted off to sleep. They had decided to allow him a good night's rest. Thrown together by the circumstances into an uneasy alliance, Rugio, whose regional authority included Moab, and Kara, whose tactics for subtle deception were needed, stood together in the king's bedchamber. Next to Rugio were his two main aides, Nathan and Vel.

"Balaam's reputation among the Hebrews will certainly work to our advantage," said Kara. "He claims to worship the Most High as they do."

"It certainly had an effect on Balak," agreed Rugio. "I must admit that the dreams you have been introducing into his mind drove him right into our plans."

"My plans, you mean," Kara snorted.

"At any rate, as principal ruler over this region, I applaud your efforts on behalf of Moab and the gods that reign here in our name. Despite our conflicts of the past, I must say that I am grateful." Rugio added, "Should the time come when you need my assistance, I hope that you will call upon me."

"Have no fear, Rugio," said Kara as he vanished. "I shall. In the meantime I must be off to Pethor. Balaam is about to be visited from the great divine..."

The elders of Moab arrived and were admitted into Balaam's luxurious home in Pethor. They could not believe how richly fitted the house was. Balaam's art of divination certainly had paid off! Balaam took the message and then invited the elders to have some wine while he read the message.

When he had read the note and considered it, he went into the room where the elders were relaxing.

"I am gratified that your king thinks so highly of my gift as to send for it," he began. Balaam was dressed in a purple robe that had gold thread woven in strange lettering and magical symbols along its sleeves. His belt was crimson, and he also had a huge emerald, which, he explained, was a gift from a "grateful king from the east for whom I performed some little service."

"As you know, I am familiar with the God of the Hebrews. I have studied Him and He speaks to me, although I don't know Him as His people do. Nevertheless I respect Him and shall see what He instructs in the matter. Spend this night as my guests, and I shall give you an answer in the morning."

As Balaam sought the answer from the Lord as to what he should do, Kara entered his room. He intended to appear to Balaam as an Angel of Light, and order him to Moab at once. But before he had an opportunity to manifest before Balaam, the Presence of God filled the room. Kara immediately fled.

"Lord?" asked Balaam, sensing His Presence.

"You must not curse these people, for I have blessed them."

"As You command, O Lord!"

The next morning, Balaam told the elders from Moab that the Lord had appeared to him and that he was unable to curse the Hebrews. Zora tried to reason with Balaam, but it was no use. The elders left, feeling that perhaps Balaam had indeed heard from the Lord. Zora, however, suspected something else.

"It is my opinion that it was not the Lord who spoke to his heart but the size of the offering we brought him," concluded Zora.

He was speaking to the king and his chief elders. Behind them, watching the proceedings, were Rugio, whose administration of this territory was being tested, and Kara, still Rugio's sometime ally.

"You mean to say that our offering insulted him?" asked one of the elders. "I thought it extremely generous."

"Perhaps to an average seer it was generous," said Zora. "But Balaam is renowned throughout the world. He is called upon by kings and generals; his lifestyle bespeaks expensive taste."

He looked at Balak, who sat drinking from his cup and listening to the discussion.

"I suspect, majesty, that were we to increase the sum of his payment, we might secure his services—appeal to his vanity, so to speak."

"Very well," said Balak. "I authorize you to draw upon the treasury whatever you deem necessary. I further order the most exalted princes of this land to accompany you and speak once more to Balaam at Pethor. We need him...so get him."

As the men excused themselves from the king's presence, Balak walked to the window and peered out over the city. Kara and Rugio looked at each other. Rugio was puzzled.

"If he would not accept the money the first time, why should he now?" asked Rugio. "The Lord already spoke to him on this."

"Balaam is a diviner, Rugio," said Kara. "He is capable of hearing many voices." He smiled at Rugio and picked up a gold medallion. "We shall speak to what truly drives his heart."

He tossed the coin into the king's cup, splashing some of the wine onto the table. Balak turned at the sound, and upon seeing the cup gave a puzzled look. As he reached for the wine, Rugio knocked it off the table. Balak left the room screaming that his chamber was haunted. Kara and Rugio laughed and vanished.

Zora handed the letter from Balak to Balaam. Once more Balaam received the delegation from Moab, this time consisting of some of the greatest men in the land. He bid them relax in his courtyard while he read Balak's second letter to him:

This is what Balak, son of Zippor, king of Moab says:
Do not let anything keep you from coming to me and I will reward you quite handsomely and do whatever you say. But come and put a curse upon these people.

As before, Balaam told the delegation that he would have an answer for them in the morning. But before he even arrived at his bedroom he was hindered by a figure in his hallway—a figure of a man...or was it a god? The being was brilliant, as if made of light, and emanated a peaceful, almost intoxicating, sense of love.

"*Balaam, son of Beor, hear me.*"

"Is it You, O Lord?"

"*Because you obeyed me when I was testing you, I have granted you the great wealth that these men bring to you—for I know it is in your heart to receive their gift.*"

"Yes, Lord, it is indeed a great sum. I had decided to go with them this time."

"*Well done. Take the gift and do what is in your heart to do. For I have opened the door for you.*"

As quickly as the apparition had appeared it vanished. Balaam rubbed his eyes to make sure he had truly witnessed this spectacle, and then retired to his bedroom. Had he been able, he would have heard the laughter of Kara and Rugio in the hallway.

"The Lord has graciously given permission for me to come with you," reported Balaam to the delegation the next morning. "However He requires certain provisions."

"Such as...?" asked Zora suspiciously.

"I can only do what He tells me to do—no more."

"Agreed. What else?"

"Well, in the matter of the fee," Balaam began in a distressed tone. "The Lord requires that an honorarium be given in His holy name as well."

"I see," said Zora. "And to whom are we to give the honorarium in his name?"

"Why to me, of course," said Balaam in an astonished manner. "I am to deposit it at His temple outside of Babylon on my next journey there."

"Yes, of course," said Zora. "After you have performed your services you will be paid in full. In fact, until you have served our king we shall hold the fee in honor of the Lord at the treasury in Moab."

Balaam thought about it for a minute. He was ready to let it all go but the fabulous amount offered, plus the honorarium he had just wheedled out of them was too much to pass up.

"Very well," Balaam said. "I shall depart for Moab in the morning."

"We shall ride on ahead of you to announce your arrival," said Zora, bowing his head. The others bowed their heads as well. "Balak will be most grateful."

"Grateful kings are what I live for," said Balaam, smiling at the delegation as they left the room.

Gabriel was waiting on the road to Moab. He was speaking with a new assignee named Jerub, who had most recently been attached to the Temple warden in Heaven. Jerub longed for a place on earth serving with one of the archangels and was promoted as a commander in training. Gabriel was to let him observe his interaction with humans.

"Are you certain that he will approach on this road?" asked Jerub.

"Of course," said Gabriel. "First rule of an assignment, Jerub. Always scout out the intelligence so you know what to expect. The enemy is cunning, but humans, though unpredictable at times, usually are creatures of habit. As this is the quickest road to Moab, I can assure you that Balaam shall be on it."

Jerub nodded his head in acknowledgment.

"Besides, I received a report before your arrival that he was on this very road."

Jerub smiled. He liked being assigned to Gabriel. Had he been with Michael he might have been thrust into something a bit more daring, but with Gabriel he was assured good fellowship and something interesting.

"Gabriel, might I ask you something?"

"Yes Jerub, that is why you are here."

"Why were you assigned to this particular duty? I mean, it seems that any angel might be capable of…"

"Rule number two, Jerub. Don't question your orders."

Jerub nodded, but in a frowning sort of way, because he wasn't quite satisfied with the answer.

"However," Gabriel continued, "Because I am the chief messenger of the Lord and an archangel, the Lord Most High ordered that I appear here in advance of the Lord's angel and clear out any unclean spirits. They are innumerable in this carnal land."

"The Angel of the Lord? Here?" asked Jerub.

Gabriel smiled.

"Yes, Jerub, the Angel of the Lord."

"But who is he?" asked Jerub. "We have of course studied him at the Academy and have heard of his appearance to Hagar, but…is it true that it is the Lord Himself?"

Before Gabriel had a chance to answer he stood and suddenly ordered Jerub to the side. The two of them stood off the pathway as a figure of a man on a donkey appeared in the distance.

"Is that…?"

"Quiet," said Gabriel.

As they watched, an angel appeared before them on the pathway—the Angel of the Lord. It was the very angel who had appeared to Hagar; and also one of the three angels who had appeared to Abraham at Mamre.

Balaam was accompanied by his two servants, who were responsible for carrying the different ceremonial tools of his trade: robes, scrolls, incense, and other mystical objects. As he approached the place where the angels were, the donkey suddenly stopped. Balaam wondered what was happening and goaded the donkey forward, but instead the animal veered off into the field.

"You stupid beast!" screamed Balaam, who began beating the donkey with a stick, driving it back on the path. The donkey looked back at Balaam, and then, turning its head back to the road, continued on.

"I'll get rid of you if you do that again," Balaam said aloud.

His servants continued following behind.

The donkey proceeded cautiously, for she had seen something that Balaam had not seen: the Angel of the Lord, sword drawn, ready to strike at the donkey's master!

Gabriel motioned to Jerub.

"Come on, we're moving," he said.

Balaam approached a narrowing in the path between two large grapevines. A wall was built on either side of the road, making the passage very narrow. It was here that the Angel of the Lord once more straddled the path. Gabriel and Jerub sat on the wall a bit farther down the road so they could observe the encounter.

When the donkey saw the Angel of the Lord in her path again, she moved to one side to avoid him. In doing do she scraped up against the wall, dragging Balaam's foot against it. Balaam screamed in pain and began beating the donkey once more. Gabriel felt sorry for the animal. Her eyes were seeing more clearly than her master's, even though he who made his living "divining" the unseen.

"Where to now?" asked Jerub, wondering why the Angel of the Lord let Balaam pass on by. "He got through twice already."

"No," Gabriel responded. "He will speak to him this time."

"The Angel of the Lord will speak to that false prophet?" asked a puzzled Jerub.

"Watch," Gabriel said as they vanished to meet Balaam farther down the road.

The Angel of the Lord had moved to a point farther down the path, where it was so narrow there was no room to turn to the right or the left. When the poor donkey saw the figure again, she gave up and lay down on the path. Balaam was furious and began to beat her for a third time.

"Now watch," said Gabriel.

The donkey turned her head toward Balaam, who was still beating her. The Lord opened the donkey's mouth and she began to speak:

"What have I done to you that you have beaten me these three times?"

Balaam could not believe his ears. He stopped beating her and looked back to see if his servants had heard anything. He then looked back at the donkey. As a seer, he had experienced many bizarre things, but this was the first time an animal had spoken to him.

"I don't know how you can speak," Balaam said in a low voice so his servants would not hear him speaking to the animal. "But you made me look like a fool. If I had a sword right now I would kill you."

"I have been your donkey for a long time," the donkey said. "Have I ever acted like this, or thrown you, or run you under a tree limb?"

"Well, no," said Balaam.

Suddenly the Lord opened the eyes of Balaam. Standing before him was the Angel of the Lord, sword drawn as if to use it against him. At first Balaam shrank back in fear, and then he pulled off the donkey and fell to the ground, face down.

The Angel of the Lord then spoke to him:

"Why is it that you have beaten this poor animal these three times? Don't you know that I am here to oppose you because the path you have chosen is a reckless one? I permitted you to go with these men under the condition that you obey Me. Instead, because of the greed in your heart you seek only more personal gain. You plan to do what is in your heart—and what these men ask of you."

"My Lord," said Balaam, "I go in Your service."

"You go to curse My people, but I told you to do otherwise," said the Lord. *"Had this animal not had more sense than you, and moved away from Me, I would have surely killed you and spared the donkey. Your pride has set you against Me!"*

Balaam swallowed hard and then said, "I did not know You were in the road to oppose me, Lord. I have sinned and will go back if You are displeased."

"No, you shall go ahead," said the Angel of the Lord. *"You shall go with these men, but you will only be able to say what I tell you to say. I shall humble this king of Moab with the words I give you to speak."*

Balaam agreed to do everything the Lord ordered, and the Angel moved out of his way. He and his companions continued on down the path unopposed. The Angel of the Lord vanished, leaving Gabriel and Jerub on the path.

"I hope Balaam has the sense of a man who has just been rebuked by the Lord," said Jerub.

"I would be pleased if he had the sense of a donkey!" said Gabriel with a sly grin on his face.

Chronicles of the Host

Balaam's Blessing, Moses' death

True to the Lord's words, Balaam was unable to curse the people of the Lord. Three times did Balak, king of Moab, hire Balaam to curse the people. And all three times, as Balaam began to speak, he would deliver an oracle of the Lord that blessed the enemy of Balak rather than curse him.

Furious that he had been so treated, Balak refused to pay Balaam any of his fees. He sent the would-be prophet back to Pethor, but not before Balaam uttered these magnificent words from the heart of the Most High:

> *A star will come out of Jacob;*
> *A scepter will rise out of Israel.*

The Lord had taken the words of a man that Lucifer had hoped would bring curses and confusion upon Israel, and turned them instead into another prophecy concerning the Seed that was one day to be born...

As for Moses, the great prophet and leader of the Hebrews, who had delivered them out of Egypt and led them through the wilderness, he now took them to the edge of Canaan (because of his sin at Meribah, he was not permitted to enter). And so it was that Joshua was chosen by the Lord to succeed Moses as ruler in Israel.

The people had assembled for what they knew was Moses' final address to them as their leader. They knew that Joshua was the appointed successor who would take them into the Promised Land. He had their confidence and their blessing. But for now, all eyes were upon the man who had led them out of captivity in Egypt, and who was about to leave them on the edge of Canaan.

Moses stood before the people, who honored him now as the revered "old man" of Israel. He leaned on a staff to support himself, although he was still strong of body and mind. With Joshua at his side, he spoke to the Israelites for the last time:

"It is time for me to be gathered to my fathers," he began. "I shall not cross over with you because of my sin against the Lord at Meribah. But Joshua, son of Nun, shall take you into the land. Follow him, for he is anointed of the Lord, and the Spirit of God is upon him.

"The Lord has been faithful to His covenant. If you abide in His law, you shall be blessed; if you disobey His decrees, you shall be cursed. Therefore trust in the Lord your God and learn of Him. Establish His word in your hearts and never let it escape.

"Hear, O Israel, the Lord your God is one God! Therefore, love the Lord your God with all your heart, all your soul, and all your strength. Fear the Lord your God and serve Him and be careful to do all that He commands of you! Today the Lord sets before you life and prosperity, or death and destruction. Therefore, choose life!"

"Choose life," sneered Kara. "Not very fitting for a man about to die."

"Kara, you are a fool," said Pellecus. "Moses has no fear of death. In fact, I'm sure he welcomes a reprieve from the burden of this people who devours its leaders."

Lucifer remained silent, listening to the banter of his leaders as they sat near the Dead Sea to discuss the future conduct of the war. Rugio also sat silent, thinking about how the war must take a different direction with the people about to enter the land. A messenger suddenly appeared and spoke with Lucifer. The others waited to see what news had just come to their lord.

"It seems that Moses is about to die," he said. "On Mount Nebo. The Lord, in His sentimental cruelty, will allow the old man to see the land that he labored to bring the nation to, although he still may not enter into it. I sometimes believe that we have more compassion for His people than He does!"

"Moses dead," said Kara. "That will be a relief!"

"I only wish I had been able to tear him to pieces," said Rugio. "Even to degrade his body would give me great satisfaction!"

Upon those words, Lucifer suddenly seemed to be inspired.

"What was that, Rugio?" he asked.

"I said I would like to take Moses' body and desecrate it in front of Israel," he said. "Or tear it to pieces."

"Maybe burn it in front of them," threw in Kara, who was now interested in the conversation. "They always did want to see him destroyed!"

"What are you thinking, my lord?" asked Pellecus.

"I am thinking that Moses will indeed die on Nebo, but will miraculously return to lead the people again. Only this time he will lead them quite differently."

Michael escorted Moses up the mountain that overlooked the land of promise. Moses had said all of his farewells, and was prepared now to die. Joshua had been ordained the new leader in Israel and commissioned by Moses to take the people into Canaan. Moses had done all of the difficult things that God had called him to do. Now he could do a joyous thing by passing from this life into God's Presence forever.

Michael was going to miss the old man. He had grown quite fond of watching over him, from the time he was a baby in the ark until now. But it was the reality of service in God's kingdom that humans came and went, but angels must continue on.

Moses stood to look over the land. He praised the Most High for the beautiful place that Joshua was now going to take the people into. And he was satisfied. He could now die in peace and be buried with his fathers. It was time. Michael watched Moses die a peaceful, painless death—a truly saintly passing. Michael bowed his head for just a moment in honor of this great man.

"Well, well. Loyal to the end I see!"

It was Lucifer.

"What are you doing here?" asked Michael.

"Come now, Michael. Your mission is finished here," retorted Lucifer. "Now be gone and find yourself a new Moses. I'm sure that Joshua will need your help in taking the land."

"My mission is finished here when the Lord releases me," said Michael. "Again I ask you—what are you doing here, Lucifer?"

"I am here to claim what is rightfully mine," said Lucifer.

"Which is...?"

"Moses' body, of course," said Lucifer matter-of-factly.

"You have no claim upon Moses' body," said Michael.

"Ah, but I do," said Lucifer. "Remember that when the fool A'dam turned authority of this world over to me, he also transferred to me the power of death and the grave. So you see, I have a legitimate claim upon this body!"

"You dishonor even death with your appetite for wickedness. The Lord rebuke you, Lucifer," said Michael resolutely.

Upon those words, Lucifer was thrown backwards off Nebo. He came roaring back but stopped short of either Moses or Michael. Then, collecting himself, he said: "Very well. Keep that rotting bit of flesh. But mark me, archangel. One day you shall see that my claim upon death is quite real!" He then disappeared off Nebo.

Michael stayed on guard until the Lord Himself selected a site where Moses was buried. His grave was never found—by men or by angels. Michael's assignment to Moses was completed, and he returned to other duties for the Lord.

Chronicles of the Host

Jordan

So it was that Israel pitched camp at the Jordan, opposite Canaan, and awaited Joshua's command to enter the land. For his part, Joshua ordered a period of mourning following the death of Moses, after which the people would begin their invasion of Canaan.

For the Host, it was the beginning of a new chapter in the life of the nation God had created to bless the entire world. So much was at stake...and so much might finally come to fruition!

As for our enemies, seething and wounded from years of warfare, they found themselves for the first time having to defend the land that was once Abraham's homeland. Like the nations that awaited the coming invaders in fear and confusion, so the enemy awaited the Israelite onslaught. When and where the attack would come was not known. But everyone knew it was only a matter of time...

On the other side of the Jordan, Lucifer sat with the Council of Seven, the key leaders who governed areas stretching across the entire planet. As they looked at Israel on the other side of the river, the mood was not good. They had met to sum up the progress of the war to that time. In the end they concluded that there had been some modest success in delaying the people of God in the wilderness, which meant that they could prepare for the next generation of Israelites while waiting for this one to die off.

"I grow weary of always having to deal with some sort of trouble with the Hebrews," said Prian. "In my domain we simply declare the emperor to be the Son of Heaven and are done with it!"

"Your domain is far removed from the critical aspects of this war," said Kara. "We have been fighting the true war since it began!"

"Don't let your oriental responsibilities lull you into thinking that you are immune from the war's reach," reminded Lucifer. "That is a word to all seven of you. True, the war itself has been contained to the area around the people of covenant. But each of you has a stake in its outcome. Our very survival depends upon our ability to wage a war that will at least force the Lord to compromise His position."

"We don't have the luxury you have, of a people already deceived and steeped in their own deception," lectured Kara. "We must fight an intense effort here and if that means deceiving humans—through trickery as you call it—then that is what must happen."

"Yes, we heard how well you tricked them in Egypt," said Lenaes. "In fact the reports I received were that the major gods of Egypt were humbled one by one!"

"Enough of this," said Lucifer. "The point is that I have come to a realization, as distasteful as it might seem."

They all looked at Lucifer, awaiting his words.

"I have determined that we shall never best the Lord outright. I saw that in the contest in Egypt. The Lord is too powerful for us to defeat..."

"Then the war is lost!" said Belron.

"We cannot defeat the Lord," continued Lucifer. "But we can defeat his people."

"Are they not one and the same?" asked Lenaes.

"Not at all," said Lucifer. "The Lord has created a people and given them a law. Our task is to deceive the people and encourage their constant breaking of that law—something which they seem to do by nature anyway."

"We will defeat the Lord by applying His own law?" asked Kara, who was suddenly interested in the discussion.

"Exactly," said Lucifer. "So long as these people are under the law of Moses, they shall never be in pure covenant with the Lord. Why? Because they cannot possibly keep the law. The very law that God gave them to draw them into covenant, will be the very instrument that we shall use to keep them out of covenant..."

"Consequently, this constant breaking of the law will keep the Seed of the woman from ever becoming an issue that can be used against us," surmised Pellecus.

"Yes," said Lucifer, standing. "I once said that love would cost the Most High everything! I said that one day the Lord would pay a terrible price for His love. And that is what has happened. It was for love that He gave them the law. And it will now be the law that will cost Him their love."

"And Israel?" asked Kara.

Lucifer looked upon the campfires across the Jordan, dotting the blackness like the stars in the heavens. He thought of the prophecy given to Abraham that starry night when the Lord compared his future descendants to the stars in the sky.

"Israel? She shall become a nation of priests and prophets who touched upon greatness...but never achieved it. Who came close to the Lord, but in the end never really knew Him. Who looked to God but never saw Him. And in the end, they shall be a people who, having abandoned their God, will likewise be abandoned by Him. This I swear!"

THE END

Chronicles of the Host series
by D. Brian Shafer

➤ BOOK ONE: CHRONICLES OF THE HOST

Lucifer, the Anointed Cherub, whose ministry in Heaven is devoted to the worship of the Most High God, has become pessimistic about his prospects in Heaven. Ambition inflamed, he looks to the soon-to-be-created Earth as a place where he can see his destiny realized. With a willing crew of equally ambitious angels, Lucifer creates a fifth column of malcontents under the very throne of God. Hot on their heels, however, is a group of loyalists, led by Michael and Gabriel, who are suspicious of Lucifer's true motives. In detective-style fashion, they slowly start to unmask the true nature of Lucifer's sordid plot. *Chronicles of the Host* is a fantastic novel of the beginning of all things. Follow Lucifer's deceptive plans to rule over Earth and his inevitable fall from grace.
ISBN 0-7684-2099-7

➤ BOOK TWO: UNHOLY EMPIRE

The prophetic clock is ticking. Lucifer and his army of "imps" search frantically for the prophetic "Seed of the woman." The memory of God's promise that this seed would rise up and bruise the serpent's head stirs them to shadowy demonic activity. *Unholy Empire* chronicles the duel between God and the fallen angels as both focus their attention on the Seed. The devils watch for any and every sign of the Seed in an all-out effort to stop, delay, compromise, or otherwise destroy this impending prophetic nightmare. If they fail they are all doomed.
ISBN 0-7684-2160-8

➤ BOOK THREE: RISING DARKNESS

The Chronicles saga continues as Israel establishes herself in the land of promise, in spite of the unholy efforts of Lucifer. A satanic shift in strategy occurs as Lucifer forsakes the simple elimination of one family that *might* carry the Seed. Now he is determined to bring down the whole nation. He is obsessed in his efforts to prevent the appearing of this mysterious Seed. Kings, priests, prophets, and pagan nations are deceived into unwittingly becoming cosmic chess pieces in this calculated war between light and darkness. From Jerusalem to Babylon and on to Rome, Lucifer believes he can destroy Israel in a deadly and delicate game of power politics…and he must do so or the nightmare will only intensify: a nightmare that will eventually be realized one starry night in Bethlehem.
ISBN 0-7684-2177-2

Available at your local Christian bookstore.

For more information and sample chapters, visit www.destinyimage.com